# A Man to Call My Own

*Also by Johanna Lindsey*
*in Large Print:*

Angel
Brave the Wild Wind
Captive Bride
Defy Not the Heart
Fires of Winter
A Gentle Feuding
Gentle Rogue
Glorious Angel
Heart of Thunder
A Heart So Wild
Hearts Aflame
Keeper of the Heart
Love Me Forever
Love Only Once
The Magic of You
Man of My Dreams

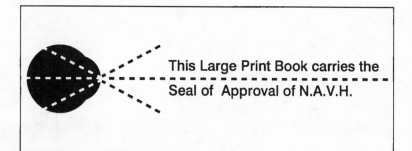

This Large Print Book carries the
Seal of Approval of N.A.V.H.

# JOHANNA LINDSEY

# A Man to Call My Own

Thorndike Press • Waterville, Maine

Published in 2003 by arrangement with Atria Books, an imprint of Simon & Schuster, Inc.

Thorndike Press® Large Print Core.

The tree indicium is a trademark of Thorndike Press.

The text of this Large Print edition is unabridged.
Other aspects of the book may vary from the original edition.

Set in 16 pt. Plantin by Al Chase.

Printed in the United States on permanent paper.

**Library of Congress Cataloging-in-Publication Data**

Lindsey, Johanna.
    A man to call my own : a novel / Johanna Lindsey.
      p. cm.
    ISBN 0-7862-5976-0 (lg. print : hc : alk. paper)
    1. Inheritance and succession — Fiction.   2. Triangles (Interpersonal relations) — Fiction.   3. Women pioneers — Fiction.   4. Ranch life — Fiction.   5. Cowboys — Fiction.   6. Sisters — Fiction.   7. Twins — Fiction.   8. Texas — Fiction.   9. Large type books.   I. Title.
PS3562.I5123M34 2003
  813′.54—dc22
                                                2003059143

# A Man to Call My Own

As the Founder/CEO of NAVH, the only national health agency solely devoted to those who, although not totally blind, have an eye disease which could lead to serious visual impairment, I am pleased to recognize Thorndike Press* as one of the leading publishers in the large print field.

Founded in 1954 in San Francisco to prepare large print textbooks for partially seeing children, NAVH became the pioneer and standard setting agency in the preparation of large type.

Today, those publishers who meet our standards carry the prestigious "Seal of Approval" indicating high quality large print. We are delighted that Thorndike Press is one of the publishers whose titles meet these standards. We are also pleased to recognize the significant contribution Thorndike Press is making in this important and growing field.

Lorraine H. Marchi, L.H.D.
Founder/CEO
NAVH

* Thorndike Press encompasses the following imprints: Thorndike, Wheeler, Walker and Large Print Press.

# Chapter 1

Mortimer Laton was buried that morning in Haverhill, Massachusetts, the town where he had been born and lived his whole life. Actually, the town was newly named Haverhill in 1870. It had been known as Pentucket when he was born and raised there.

His wife, Ruth, was buried in one of the older cemeteries that was no longer available, having filled to capacity soon after she was interred there. She wouldn't have minded that her husband didn't rest for all eternity in a grave near her. Actually, she would probably have preferred it that way, since there was no love lost between them.

The large marker that had been ordered for Mortimer was going to read: Here rests Mortimer Laton, beloved father of Amanda and Marian. Amanda Laton had prescribed the short sentiment, and for her it was most fitting. She had adored their father, and he, in return, had been the perfect father to her, providing everything a child needs in order to feel loved and secure. Marian, had she been asked, would have left out the beloved part.

The funeral had been a small gathering, and dismal as most funerals were, despite the fine weather that morning and the spring blooms that filled the grounds. Only Mortimer's servants, a few of his business associates, and his two daughters had attended.

The service had been notably quiet. No hysterics or loud tearful wails that morning, unlike Ruth's funeral seven years ago where Marian had made a spectacle of herself, crying uncontrollably. But then she'd felt that with her mother's passing she had lost the only person who had ever really cared about her.

Something similar should have happened today. Amanda, who had been her father's favorite from the day she was born, should have been crying her heart out. But since the sisters had heard the news that their father had died on the way back from the business trip he'd taken to Chicago last week, somehow falling off the train as he passed between one car and the next, Amanda hadn't shed one tear of grief.

An odd form of shock, the servants whispered, and Marian might have agreed, except her sister wasn't denying that their father was gone. She spoke of his death and discussed it without emotion, as if she were discussing some mundane event of little concern to her. Shock? Maybe, but of a kind Marian had never witnessed before. On the other hand, Amanda was a self-centered person, just like Mortimer. She was probably more concerned with how his death was going to affect her than with his actually being gone.

Mortimer had been capable of loving only one person at a time. This was a realization Marian had come to at a very young age, and, eventually, she'd stopped hoping it could be otherwise. And she'd never seen her father behave in any way that indicated she was wrong.

Her father hadn't loved her mother. Theirs had been an arranged marriage. They were merely two people living together, sharing the same house, sharing some of the same interests. They got along well, but there was no love shared between them. His parents had died before Marian was born, so she'd never seen how he behaved with them. And his only remaining sister had moved away when Marian was still a baby. Mortimer never spoke of her, an indication he could care less what had become of her.

But their father had loved Amanda. There was absolutely no doubt of that in anyone's mind. From the day she was born he'd been charmed and had showered her with attention, spoiled her rotten actually. The sisters could be in the same room yet he'd only see Amanda, as if Marian were invisible.

But he was gone now. Marian could stop agonizing over it. It wasn't as if he hadn't seen to her material needs all these years. In that, the sisters had always been treated equally. It was only Marian's emotional needs that had been neglected.

Her mother had tried to correct that and had succeeded somewhat while she'd been alive. She had seen how much it hurt Marian to be excluded from Mortimer's affections, and while she loved both her daughters, she had spared a little extra affection for Marian. Unfortunately, Amanda had noticed and was so jealous, wanting all her mother's love exclusively, that it caused a breach between the sisters that had long ago gone beyond fixing. There was no tactful way to put it. They really and truly hated each other.

It wasn't just the jealousy issues. Those might have been overcome. The long list of grievances might even have been forgiven eventually, since most of them had stemmed from their childhood, which was over. But probably owing to the overabundance of spoiling and coddling, both of which fostered her self-centeredness, Amanda was, quite simply, not a nice person.

Whether deliberately or based on a tendency that came naturally to her, Amanda managed with alarming frequency to hurt people's feelings. The alarming part was, she didn't seem to care or notice the damage she caused. And apologies were never tendered.

Marian couldn't count the times, there were so many, that she had personally tried to make excuses for her sister and apologize to the people Amanda hurt. It wasn't as if she felt responsible for her sister's actions. She didn't. Amanda had been nasty and spiteful from as far back as she could remember.

Neither of them had any female friends to speak of. Amanda, because she didn't want any. She had their father to dote on her. He was her best friend. Marian had wanted friends, but she gave up long ago trying to make any because her sister would always drive them away, usually in tears. The result was, other girls didn't want to go anywhere near Marian again if it meant they might run into Amanda.

Gentlemen were a different matter. Since

11

both girls began approaching marriageable age, gentleman callers were in regular attendance at the Laton household. There was a twofold attraction — Mortimer's wealth, reputed to be quite substantial, and the fact that Amanda was very likely one of the most lovely girls in town.

And Amanda actually liked the male attention. She thrived on the flattery. And anytime someone showed up whom she didn't particularly want adoring her, she'd belittle and subtly insult him until he stopped coming around. So she had her favorite group of admirers and she'd had them for nearly a year. But she didn't favor any single one of them to the point of deciding which one she'd like to marry.

More's the pity. Marian wished she would. She prayed each night that her sister would get married and move elsewhere, so she could get on with living a real life herself instead of hiding away, fearful that some man might try to court her and end up one of her sister's targets. The two times she'd shown any interest in a man, she'd learned her lesson well. She wasn't going to be responsible again for seeing them cut to the quick by Amanda's tongue because they'd dared to ignore Amanda in favor of her.

Which was why, even though they were

twins, Marian went to a lot of trouble to disguise that unfortunate fact. Not wanting to draw attention to herself, she chose dresses that were unflattering in color and extremely plain in design. She wore her hair in a severe style better suited to someone's grandmother than a young woman barely eighteen. But her disguise wouldn't really have worked without the spectacles she wore. The frames were large and the lenses so thick, they magnified her eyes to nearly twice their size, giving her an odd, bug-eyed look that was very unattractive.

They sat in their father's study, listening to the reading of his will. Amanda looked beautiful as always, even in mourning black. Her dress was stylish; she'd have it no other way. Adorned with lace and tiny beads in artful designs, it was actually more flattering than some of her fancier gowns. Her coiffure wasn't as frivolous as usual, the golden ringlets more tightly contained for once.

Marian, on the other hand, was as unnoticeable as usual. There were no intricate frills on her black dress to be admired, no stylish bangs to frame her face or detract from the ugly spectacles that dominated her appearance. She was the moth next to the butterfly. While she suspected it was easy to

13

be the butterfly, she knew for sure it was hard work being the moth.

The room was almost unrecognizable, with Mortimer's lawyer sitting behind the desk, rather than Mortimer. They knew Albert Bridges well. He had often been invited to dinner when their father found himself strapped for time and brought his work home with him.

Albert usually called the sisters by their first names. He'd known them long enough to do so. But today he addressed each of them as Miss Laton and he seemed uncomfortable doing his job.

There had been no surprises in the will so far. A few family servants had been left small bequests, but the bulk of Mortimer's estate had been left to his daughters — equally. Once again, it was only his affection he hadn't divided equally, never his wealth. There were interests in a half dozen businesses, income property in town as well as other parts of the state, a bank account larger than either girl could have imagined. But no real surprises — until the end.

"There is one stipulation," Albert told them, pulling at his collar nervously. "Your father wanted to assure that you would be well taken care of, and not be fooled by fortune hunters merely interested in your inheritance. So other than for essentials, none of his estate will be transferred to you until you marry. And until that time, his sister, Mrs. Frank Dunn, will be your guardian."

Amanda said nothing. She was frowning, but she hadn't yet fully grasped the implications. Marian watched her, waiting for the storm to erupt once it sunk in.

Albert Bridges had expected more of a reaction as well, and looking at each girl somewhat warily, asked, "Do you understand what this means?"

Marian nodded, even smiled at him. "I'm assuming that Aunt Kathleen isn't going to change her life to accommodate us just because her brother died, so we will have to travel to her. Is that what you mean?"

He sighed in relief. "Exactly. I know it may seen daunting, having to move so far away from everything and everyone you know, but it can't be helped."

"Actually — I don't mind at all. I have no real attachment to this city —"

The storm arrived. Amanda shot to her feet so fast, she dislodged not one but two blond locks from her coiffure, both on the same side, so she now had a long wave of golden hair curling around and beyond her breast. Her dark blue eyes were flashing like sapphires under a jeweler's light, and her lips had thinned to form a snarl.

"Absolutely out of the question! Do you have any idea where this unknown aunt of ours lives? It's the other side of the world!"

"Just the other side of the country, actually," Marian said calmly.

"That is the same thing!" Amanda yelled. "She lives among savages."

"The savages have been curtailed — mostly."

Amanda glared at her. "Shut up, just . . . just shut up! *You* go live in the wilds of Texas and rot and die for all I care. I'll get married immediately and stay right here, thank you very much."

Albert tried to stop her, to explain further, but Amanda was too furious to listen and stalked out of the room. He gave Marian a long-suffering look.

"She can't just — get married," he told Marian with a weary sigh.

"I didn't think so."

"I mean she can, but then she would forfeit her inheritance. As your guardian, your aunt must give her approval, for either of you to marry."

"Shall I fetch her back?" Marian offered. "She hasn't left the house yet. We would have heard the slamming of the front door if she had."

"I'll go after her." Albert sighed again. "I should have been more clear to begin with."

Albert rose from behind the desk, but it wasn't necessary. Amanda came marching back into the study on her own with Karl Ryan in tow. Karl was one of her hopeful suitors, her least favorite actually, but she tolerated him because he was handsome and considered a fine catch by any standards. As long as a man had other women interested in him, even if only one, Amanda wanted him interested in her instead because she thrived on the envy of other women.

Karl had been on hand that morning to accompany them to the cemetery. Amanda had been too preoccupied to notice that he was the only one of her suitors to come by to offer his condolences. Marian knew that visitors were being turned away at the door with the simple explanation that the girls weren't receiving callers. Someone had decided they should have some undisturbed time for mourning. Marian was grateful because she had no desire to deal with anyone just now. Amanda probably would have objected if she'd known.

Karl had been hard to turn away, though, since he'd come by right after they'd been told the news of Mortimer's death, and he had heard about it from Amanda. He'd been waiting in the parlor since they'd returned from the funeral, prepared to offer as much comfort as he could today. But Amanda didn't appear to need comforting. She needed calming because she still looked furious.

"There, I've settled the matter," Amanda said triumphantly. "I'm now engaged to marry Mr. Ryan. So I'll hear no more talk about leaving home." And then she added snidely, "But I'll be glad to help you pack, Marian."

"Unless Mr. Ryan is willing to travel with you to Texas, to meet your aunt and obtain her approval, marrying him will not release your inheritance to you, Miss Laton," Albert was forced to point out. "Without that approval, you would forfeit everything."

"No! My God, I can't believe Papa did this to me. He knew I despise traveling."

"He didn't die on purpose just to inconvenience you, Amanda," Marian said in annoyance. "I'm sure he thought you'd be settled long before he died."

"I will be most happy to travel with you to Texas," Karl offered.

"Don't be absurd," Amanda snapped at him. "Can't you see this changes everything?"

"No, it doesn't," Karl insisted. "I still want to marry you."

Marian saw what was coming, and tried to spare Karl's feelings. "You should leave for the time being," she suggested quickly. "She's upset —"

"Upset!" Amanda shouted. "I'm beyond upset. But yes, do leave. There's no longer a reason for me to marry you; in fact, I can't think of a single one now."

Marian glanced away, unwilling to see just how crushed Karl was by those few careless words, but not soon enough. She saw it anyway. And he'd looked so happy when he'd come into the room moments ago, his heart's desire unexpectedly achieved. He really did want Amanda for his wife. Heaven knew why, but he did. Somehow, he hadn't seen or had chosen to ignore this vicious side of her — until now.

But hopefully, after he got over the rejection, he would rejoice to have escaped marriage to such a heartless bitch.

# Chapter 2

It was a small ranch by most standards, but even smaller by Texas standards. Nestled in the fertile plains west of the Brazos, with a quarter mile of an offshoot of the river passing through the northeast corner of the spread, the Twisting Barb encompassed some prime land, if not a lot of it. With less than a thousand head of cattle, the ranch had room for more, but its owners had never aspired to be "cattle kings."

There was only one owner now. Red had taken over the running of the ranch after her husband died. She had learned ranching well, could have handled the task with ease, except for one thing — a lack of good cowhands who would listen to her.

At her wits' end, she'd been seriously thinking about selling. All their good cowhands had up and left when her husband died. She'd put out the word in town that she was hiring, but any hand worth his salt sought a job on the Kinkaid spread. The only ones willing to work for her were wet-behind-the-ears teenagers, and young Easterners who'd drifted west for one reason or another but had to be taught every step of the way when it came to ranching.

She was willing to teach. But they weren't willing to learn, at least not from an old gal they viewed as a second mother. Like a passel of youngsters, they'd listen to her, but they didn't *hear*. Her instructions went in one ear and out the other. She'd been on the verge of giving up and selling out when Chad Kinkaid came along.

She had known Chad for many years. He was the son of her neighbor, Stuart Kinkaid, a rancher who *did* aspire to be known as a "cattle king." Stuart owned the biggest ranch in the area and was always looking to expand it. He would have been knocking on her door if he'd known Red was thinking of selling. But she didn't really want to sell, she'd just figured she had no choice, as bad as things had gotten after her husband died. But Chad turned her situation around, and she still gave thanks for the storm that had brought him to the Twisting Barb three months ago.

It had been the last bad storm of the winter season. And the only reason Chad happened to be nearby when it broke was that he'd had a falling-out with his father and was leaving home — for good. Red had put him up for the night. Being an astute

21

man, he'd noticed that something was wrong, and over breakfast the next morning, he'd dragged it out of her, the troubles she'd been having.

She hadn't expected his offer to help. But she should have. Stuart Kinkaid might be an ornery cuss, but he'd raised a real fine son in Chad.

If she were twenty years younger, she'd be in love, she was that grateful to him. But she was old enough, or pert near old enough, to be Chad's mother, and the truth was, though no one else knew it, she was in love with his father. Had been since the day she met him twelve years ago when Stuart rode over to welcome her and her new husband to his neighborhood, and gave them one hundred head of cattle to help them get started on their fledgling ranch.

Stuart had been about the most handsome man she'd ever met, and coupled with his kindness that day, he'd gradually wormed his way into a corner of her heart and stayed there. Her husband never knew. Stuart never knew. No one would ever know if she could help it. And even though Stuart's wife had died long before she'd met him, and her husband had died just recently, she never once thought about doing anything about her feelings for that tall Texan.

Stuart Kinkaid was just too grandiose for her: rich, still handsome, a bigger-than-life personality, a man who could have any woman he wanted if he set his mind to it. While she was a kindhearted redheaded mouse of a woman, who hadn't turned any heads in her youth and certainly didn't now when she was nearing forty.

Chad was like his father in many ways, too handsome for his own good, but she'd never heard of him breaking any hearts along the way, so she didn't think he took advantage of his looks in that regard. He might have been a bit rowdy in his youth, might butt heads with his father quite frequently, but he was dependable. If he said he'd do something, come hell or high water, it would get done. And, of course, he'd been raised to be the best cattleman around. He'd been raised to take over the huge Kinkaid spread.

It didn't take long for Chad to turn the bunch of greenhorns Red was stuck with into a well-oiled outfit. The hands looked up to him, heck, they loved him. He knew how to work men, so even when he had to scold, they didn't feel they were hopeless. They were more than willing to learn from him, and learn they did.

Chad was a cattleman through and

through. The logical choice for him would be to start his own ranch somewhere. But doing that would truly cut the ties with his father, and she didn't really think that was his intention. He was making a point in leaving home. He was giving Stuart time to figure out what that point was and to accept it.

Red was realistic though. Three months was long enough to get one's point across. Chad would be leaving soon, either for another state or to go home and settle things with his father. But he'd be leaving her in good hands, she hoped. He seemed to be putting a lot of effort into training her oldest hand, Lonny, to take over when he was gone. Another month or two and Lonny would make a fine foreman. She had no doubt of that. She just never knew from one day to the next whether Chad would stick around for those couple more needed months.

He probably would. She'd sprained her foot last week, and even though it was feeling better already, she hadn't let on that it was. Chad had been worried about her since the accident, and she was reasonably sure that a worried Chad would stick around.

# Chapter 3

After dinner that evening, Red joined Chad on her front porch to enjoy the setting sun for a while. It was a long, wide porch, but then it was a nice-sized house that stretched behind it. Red's husband hadn't stinted when building their home. Having both come from the East, they were used to fine accommodations.

A second story had been added to the house a few years after they'd arrived in Texas, to accommodate the children they were hopeful of having. Red couldn't say why they'd never been blessed in that regard. It wasn't for lack of trying. It just wasn't meant to be, she supposed.

The soft strains of a guitar drifted around the corner from the bunkhouse. Rufus was right handy with the instrument, and it had become almost a ritual that he'd play a few songs in the evening as the boys wound down from a hard day's work. Red always heard it from a distance. The one place she restricted herself from on the ranch was the bunkhouse.

Chad bunked down with the rest of the

men, but being the son of the richest rancher in the area, no one thought it odd that Red insisted he dine with her in the main house. It was also usually just the two of them who occupied the porch each evening. They didn't always talk. The ranch was running so smoothly that, most evenings, anything that needed to be said got said over dinner, leaving the porch time just for quiet introspection.

Red was going to keep it that way tonight, except Chad's distant look, and the direction in which he was gazing, made her guess he was thinking of his father. She often thought of Stuart, too, but along different lines.

She was amazed that Stuart hadn't found out yet that Chad was staying on the Twisting Barb. Her hands had been warned never to mention Chad's name when they went into town, but with liquor flowing freely on those town visits, there was no guarantee that one of them wouldn't slip and mention it. And they did know that Stuart had hired some of the best trackers around to find Chad.

They had nothing to trace, though, because the storm that had brought him to her had washed away his trail. And no one suspected that he'd gone to roost so close to home, only a few miles away, especially not Stuart. But if Chad was getting homesick, she wouldn't try to stop him from patching things up with his father. The two had always been close, even if they didn't see eye to eye on a lot of things.

"Miss him?" she asked quietly.

"Hell no," he said in a grumbling tone that had her smiling to herself.

"So you're still not ready to go home?"

"What home?" Chad replied with some heavy sarcasm. "It was turned into a circus with Luella and her mama there. Pa arranged that match without even discussing it with me, and just moved them in until the wedding. I still can't believe he did that."

"She's a nice gal though," Red replied in Stuart's defense. "I met her a few years back at one of your pa's barbecues. Pretty, too, as I recall."

"She could be the best-looking thing this side of the Rio Grande, and I'd still run the other way."

"Because Stuart handpicked her for you?"

"That mainly," Chad allowed. "But if that girl has one whit of intelligence in her head, it's there because it got lost."

Red tried to hold back a chuckle, but couldn't manage it. "Guess I didn't talk to her long enough to figure that out," she replied.

"Count yourself fortunate."

Red said no more. She was grateful he wasn't hankering to go home, but sorry, too, because this rift with his father had to be tearing them both up. The truth was, she'd miss him. She might not have loved her husband, but at least he'd been good company, and since his passing, she'd been lonely.

The sky was still blood red when the rider came galloping toward the house at a breakneck speed. "Best step inside, Chad. Looks like the mail runner, and he'd recognize you if he got a good look."

Chad nodded and moved into the house. Red got up to greet the rider. "Evening, Will. Bit late for you to be delivering, ain't it?"

"Yes, ma'am. Dang horse threw a shoe, set me back a few hours today. But figured this might be important, so didn't want to wait till morning." He handed her the letter he'd gone out of his way to deliver, then tipped his hat. "Late for dinner. Have a good evening, now."

Red waved him off, then limped back into the house, stopping next to the nearest hall lamp to read the letter. Chad had retrieved his hat and was about to head to bed.

Her exclamation, "Son'bitch!" stopped him at the front door.

"What?"

"My brother's gone and died."

"I'm sorry. I didn't know you had a brother."

"Wish I never did, so don't be sorry. We never got along. In fact, it'd be pretty accurate to say we hated each other's guts. Which is why this letter doesn't make a lick of sense."

"That you'd be notified?"

"That he left his girls to me. What the hell did he expect me to do with children at my age?"

"Did he have a choice?"

She frowned. "I suppose not. Guess I am their only living relative now that Mortimer's gone. We had another sister, my twin actually, but she died long ago."

"No relatives on their mother's side?"

"No, she was the last of her line aside from her children." Red continued reading, then said, "Well, hell . . . looks like I need to ask yet another favor of you, Chad."

He looked horrified for a moment. "Don't *even* think it. I'm not even married yet. I ain't raising no —"

"Hold on, now," she interrupted, and chuckled over his mistake. "I just need someone to meet the girls in Galveston and escort them here, not adopt them. Apparently, they started on the journey the same time this letter did, different routes, but the mail isn't always faster. They could have arrived already. I'd go, but I'm afraid this sprained foot of mine will hold me up too much."

"That's a long distance to travel, could take up to a week there and back."

"Yes, but at least a good portion of it can be covered by train, and most of the rest by stage. It's just the last leg of the way that you'd have to rough it. But I'll ask someone else. I keep forgetting that you're lying low."

"No, I'll go," Chad said, slapping his hat against his leg. "Pa's finding me at this late date won't matter much. I'll leave first thing in the morning."

# Chapter 4

Amanda and Marian were supposed to have waited in Galveston. It was the final destination of the nice couple that Albert Bridges had found to chaperone them, and they were more than willing to keep the girls with them until Kathleen Dunn arrived to collect them. But Amanda wouldn't hear of it.

She had complained every step of the way so far. Even before they'd left home she'd complained about their rushed departure. But a ship had been leaving the day after the funeral, and Albert had strongly suggested they take it since another wouldn't be available for several weeks. Back on dry land, Amanda should have been somewhat appeased, but no, the crowded port where their ship had docked was her next target for verbal abuse.

Marian had managed to enjoy the sea voyage anyway. It was the first time she'd ever been on a ship, so she found everything about it interesting. The salty air, the damp bedding, the windy and sometimes slippery decks, trying to walk without bumping into things, to get her "sea legs" as one deckhand put it, was all new to her — and the very things that Amanda complained about the most.

It was a wonder that the captain hadn't tossed Amanda overboard. Marian had heard him mumble once to himself about doing just that. And Amanda did have a harrowing moment four days into the journey when she actually did end up dangling from the railing with the sea lapping up the side of the ship. She'd sworn someone had pushed her, which was ridiculous — although, just about everyone on board *had* probably thought about it more than once.

Amanda's behavior had been no more than what Marian expected. When her sister had said she hated to travel, she hadn't exaggerated. And when Amanda was miserable, she wanted everyone else to be miserable as well. Marian managed to avoid that state of mind, but then she'd learned long ago how to simply "not hear" her sister when she got especially annoying. Their escorts had picked up on that as well, and before the end of the voyage, they'd been nodding and mumbling appropriate phrases, but had simply stopped "listening" to Amanda.

This might have been why they didn't try to stop the girls from setting out on their own. It was more likely, though, that they were just glad to be rid of Amanda. And it wasn't as if the two of them weren't old enough to travel alone. They also had their maid, Ella Mae, with them. She was several years older than they, and would be considered a proper chaperone in most circles.

Marian did try to talk her sister into waiting for their aunt to arrive. She pointed out that they might pass her en route and not even know it. But Amanda had insisted that Aunt Kathleen probably hadn't even gotten Albert's letter yet, so their waiting around in Galveston was just a waste of time. Of course Marian had known it was pointless to try to dissuade her sister. No one's opinion mattered to Amanda except her own, and she was never wrong. That she was frequently not right was beside the point.

Several days later they found themselves stranded in a small town nowhere near their intended destination. A number of mishaps and unexpected incidents contributed to that sorry state, but in the end, the fault was still wholly Amanda's. Did she accept the blame? Certainly not. In her mind, everyone else was at fault, never her.

While it was taken for granted in the East that the quickest way to travel was by train, that particular convenience hadn't spread across Texas yet, which is why they had traveled there by ship instead. There was one railroad line in the south of Texas that ran from the coast northwest toward the middle of the state, and a few short branches off of that, but the line ended far short of their final destination. Although they had intended to ride the train to the end of its line, a group of thieves altered that plan.

Marian viewed the train robbery as something she'd tell her grandkids about, if she ever had any. Exciting after the fact, it had been terrifying while it was happening. The train had come to a screeching stop, and before anyone recovered from that, four men had burst into the passenger car shouting and waving their guns. They'd seemed nervous, but maybe that was normal under the circumstances.

Two of the men had passed down the aisle demanding that valuables be handed over, while the other two guarded the exits. Marian kept most of her traveling money locked away in her trunks, and carried only small amounts in her purse, so she didn't hesitate to hand it over. Amanda, however, carried all of hers in her purse, so when it was yanked from her side, she screamed angrily and tried to retrieve it.

A shot was fired. Marian couldn't honestly say if the man had missed his mark deliberately, or missed because of nervousness, but the bullet did fire over Amanda's head — just barely. Her scalp probably felt the heat from it because her face was left streaked with gunpowder, it had happened at such close range. But since it briefly put Amanda in shock, which caused her to sit down and shut up, he didn't shoot again and moved on down the aisle to finish his robbing.

The result of that robbery, aside from their depleted funds, was that Amanda flatly refused to travel any farther by train. Not that the train would have taken them much farther, but they disembarked at the next town and took a stage from there instead. The stage, of course, didn't follow the same route as the train. It headed east, though it would resume a northwesterly direction after the next stop.

But it never reached its next stop. The driver, after being harangued by Amanda every few minutes about the bumpy ride, started drinking from a flask of liquor he kept under his seat, got thoroughly drunk, and got himself and his passengers thoroughly lost. For two days he tried without luck to find the road back to his scheduled route.

It was incredible that the coach didn't break down, without a decent road to travel on. It was incredible, too, that the driver didn't just take off without them, he was so furious with himself and Amanda, for driving him to drink. It was the scent of fried chicken that finally led them to a homestead where they got directions to the nearest town.

And that was where they were currently stranded, because the driver did abandon them at that point, and his coach as well, since he figured he was going to lose his job anyway. He simply unhitched one of the six horses and rode off on it without a single word. Actually, he'd said two words, mumbled them rather while Amanda was shouting at him for an explanation as he prepared to depart. She wouldn't have heard him say, "good riddance," but Marian did.

Unfortunately, it wasn't just a small town he left them in, but a town that was barely populated. Of the fourteen original buildings, only three were still occupied and doing business. It was a case of misguided speculation. The founder of the town had thought the railroad would be passing that way and had hoped to make a small fortune when it did. But the railroad bypassed them, the founder moved on to speculate elsewhere, and the people who had set up businesses there slowly sold them or abandoned them.

The three buildings still open for business were the saloon, which doubled as a general store since the owner happened to be good friends with a supplier so still got a shipment of goods every so often, a bakery that managed to get some grain from a farmer in the area, and a boardinghouse that called itself a hotel and was run by the baker.

It wasn't really surprising that of the few occupants, not one knew how to drive a stagecoach or was willing to try to figure it out. The stage was left parked where it had been abandoned, in front of the hotel. Someone had been kind enough to unhitch the rest of the horses from it, but since there was no food for them in the abandoned stable, they were set loose to feed in a field of overgrown grass behind the town — and wander off if they were so inclined.

That was after Amanda insisted that she could drive the stagecoach to get them out of there. Having had a look at the room in the hotel where they were going to have to stay, and finding it to be the worst lodgings they had encountered yet, Amanda had been absolutely determined to get out of that town immediately, or at least, before they had to sleep in that horrid room.

Marian didn't care for their lodgings either. The sheets on the single bed had holes in them and might have been white once, but were a moldy gray now. There was a round hole in one wall as if someone had sent his fist through it. The rug on the floor was a breeding nest for fleas since an old dog had been living in the room. You could stand there and watch the fleas bouncing around on the rug, waiting for their host to come take his daily nap. And there was no telling what the splotches on the floor had come from.

But no matter how much they hated the idea of staying there, Amanda's alternate plan wasn't worth considering even if she could have gotten the stage to move. She couldn't. She did frustrate herself trying though.

Marian and Ella Mae simply stood on the porch of the hotel and watched. They weren't about to get in that coach with Miss Know-It-All driving it. The few townsfolk had a good laugh watching, too, before they went back into their respective buildings. And Marian and Ella Mae spent the rest of the afternoon cleaning their room so it would be at least somewhat tolerable to sleep in.

They were stranded indeed, and had no idea for how long. No telegraph available there, no stage line, no extra saddles to be had in case they considered riding out on the extra horses, no carriage to rent that they could have handled, and no guide to lead them back toward the railroad anyway.

Amanda, of course, complained about their new circumstances from morning till night. Mentioning that it was exactly such complaining that had gotten them stranded in the first place was pointless. And although Amanda made it sound as if they were never going to see civilization again, Marian was more optimistic, especially after the baker remarked that stagecoaches were too valuable simply to abandon, and someone would come looking for the vehicle to get it back in service.

Marian didn't doubt that their aunt would be looking for them, too, or have someone looking for them. She was probably going to be furious with them for setting out on their own and causing her extra difficulties in finding them. Not a good way to start out with this relative neither of them knew, who was now their guardian.

# Chapter 5

Four days had come and gone in that dismal, soon-to-be ghost town. With only a few old-timers about, or at least, no men that Amanda could possibly get jealous over if they happened to pay Marian any attention, Marian became lax in keeping her spectacles shoved up the bridge of her nose. It was a luxury being able to see clearly all of the time, rather than only when she peered over the rims of the spectacles, or removed them.

She had been wearing spectacles she didn't need for about three years. The idea had come to her when she'd found a pair and curiously tried them on. She'd caught her reflection, and the change in her appearance was so dramatic, she'd gone home that day to complain of vision problems and headaches and as a result had been told absently by her father to take care of it. She did, and had her own pair of spectacles a month later, as well as a few spare pairs.

She'd been very proud of that idea. She'd already been trying to change her appearance from her sister's, so they would no longer resemble each other even a little. She wore her hair in a completely different style. Amanda had already started using some makeup back then. Marian still didn't use any. Amanda preferred clothes in the height of style, yet still somewhat flashy. Marian went with stylish, but toned-down clothes in less becoming colors.

That still hadn't been enough, though, to make her "unnoticeable," which was the goal she'd been shooting for. Until her next bright idea. The result was a pair of spectacles that when in proper position magnified the size of her eyes, giving her an owlish, unbecoming look. Of course she couldn't see a thing through them, everything being a blur, which caused her to seem quite accident-prone. And people naturally tended to stay clear of people who bumped into things on a regular basis.

Now, the three dogs in town gave warning that someone was approaching. The barking was far off in the distance though, and since those dogs seemed to bark at nothing and each other on a regular basis, Marian didn't really pay attention. She was reading an old newspaper she'd found on the porch of the hotel, only because it was a blistering hot day and there was a slight breeze coming down the main, or rather, only street.

She did take notice, however, when each of the townsfolk came out of their respective buildings and started staring toward the entrance of the town. They apparently could tell the difference in the sound of the barking, to know that the animals weren't just making noise because they could, but had found something of real interest.

Amanda was napping in the stagecoach in the middle of the street. She'd actually worn herself out with her complaining, though the exceptional heat of the last few days had probably helped. And she'd gotten so badly bitten by the fleas in their room that she'd taken to sleeping in the coach each night and napping there in the hottest part of each day.

The barking didn't awaken Amanda, but the first words spoken nearby did. The baker wasn't baking today and had come out on the hotel porch to stand next to Marian. Both of them were shading their eyes to get a better look at the stranger riding down the street.

He rode a very fine-looking animal, the kind rich men back home would sell for horse racing. Golden in color, with a pure white mane and tail, he was a large, sleek stallion, a good-sized horse for a man on the tall side. As for the man himself, his wide-brimmed Western hat shaded too much of his face for anyone to tell what he looked like yet, other than that he had a wide chest and shoulders under a faded blue shirt, black pants and vest, and a dark blue neck-erchief or bandana as they were called in these parts, an item that seemed to serve all kinds of purposes on the range.

"Just a cowboy," the baker, Ed Harding remarked next to Marian. "Doesn't have the look of a gunfighter."

"He's wearing guns," Marian pointed out, her eyes still on the stranger.

"Everyone wears guns out here, Missy."

"You don't."

"I'm not everyone."

These old-timers tended to say a lot of strange things like that, Marian observed. They were a wealth of interesting informa-tion though, about the West, and she en-joyed talking with them when they weren't busy.

The dogs continued to bark and follow the stranger into town. They bothered the horse not at all. The man glanced at them occasionally, but otherwise seemed to ignore them, too. He stopped when he reached the stagecoach, still parked in the middle of the street. He tipped his hat toward Marian, a mere matter of courtesy, before he set it back on his head and stared at Ed Harding.

"I'm looking for the Laton girls. And this looks to be the stage they were last known to be traveling on."

"You got that right, Mister," Ed replied. "You from the stage line?"

"No, from their aunt, here to fetch them to her."

"And about damn time," Amanda was heard from, and in one of her more disagreeable tones as she pushed open the door to the coach and climbed down to the street.

The man lowered his hat to tip it in Amanda's direction, then with one finger pushed it back behind his forehead again. "Have the girls been a nuisance, ma'am?" he asked her in reference to her remark.

She stared at him as if he were daft. Marian was too busy staring agape at him as well, but not over what he'd said. That hadn't even registered yet. No, from the moment he'd raised his hat so his face became fully visible, she'd been arrested by a set of very handsome features.

Lean, smooth-shaven cheeks, square jaw, a straight nose over a mustache kept neatly trimmed. He had the same two-toned shade of skin on his forehead that most of these Westerners seemed to have as a result of

44

working under the hot sun with their hats on. His tan line was barely discernible actually, though he was nicely bronzed, suggesting he didn't always wear the hat — or kept it pushed back a lot, like he had it now.

His hair was darkest black, though speckled with trail dust at the moment. Not too long, his hair fell just an inch or so below his nape. Marian guessed he might usually wear it slicked back as many men did, but presently it was parted, a curly lock leaning toward each temple. Thick black brows arched over pure gray eyes the shade of summer rain clouds, with no tinge of blue in them.

It was a good thing that her overall appearance was so very unremarkable, because for once, Marian completely forgot to shove her spectacles back up her nose. But the man hadn't spared her more than a fleeting glance before speaking to Mr. Harding, and now, his gaze, typically, remained on Amanda.

Even wilted by the heat, with sweat running down her temples, soaked into the cloth beneath her armpits, and some of her flyaway bangs matted from it, Amanda was still flamboyantly lovely. It wasn't surprising he was still staring at her, even if she hadn't answered his question yet, and he could simply be waiting on that answer.

When Marian realized that *she* was staring, she did three things in quick order. Got her spectacles back in their camouflaging position, made sure her hair was still severely drawn back, and started fanning herself with the old newspaper she had in hand.

She was going to wait for Amanda to recover and do the talking, another thing she was used to doing, to keep attention off herself. But Amanda, having just woken from her nap, was still slightly disoriented and giving no indication that she would.

The continued silence, aside from the yapping dogs, was getting ridiculous, so Marian finally said, albeit hesitantly, "I have the feeling you were expecting younger — children perhaps?"

He was quick, he didn't ask what she meant, just said, "Well, hell," as he glanced her way, then back toward Amanda again.

For the first time, Marian actually felt annoyed, to be so totally ignored. Which was crazy. She strived so hard to achieve that very result. And it would serve absolutely no good purpose to gain his attention. In fact, doing so would be detrimental to this man's peace of mind as well as hers.

So it was a good thing, at least to Marian's

way of thinking, that Amanda finally collected her scattered thoughts, and asked, "Who are you?"

"Chad Kinkaid. For the time being, I work for your aunt."

There was no quicker way to get dismissed from Amanda's mind as a male worthy of her attention than to mention you were a mere employee — of any sort. Amanda didn't waste her time on anyone who wasn't richer than she was.

Without giving him another look, she crossed the narrow strip of dirt road between the stage and the hotel to reach the shade on the porch. Chad Kinkaid was in the process of dismounting. Amanda's belligerent employer-to-employee tone of voice stopped him.

"There are a total of seven trunks that need to be reloaded on the stage. Do get started, so we can depart this sorry excuse for a town immediately."

He sat back in the saddle, glanced at the stagecoach again. "You expect to travel in that?"

"I repeat, seven *large* trunks, Mr. Kinkaid, and not a single vehicle in this town able to transport them other than this stage."

"Then they get left behind."

A gasp. "Absolutely not!"

He and Amanda stared, or rather, glared at each other for a moment, a brief battle of wills. He ended up sighing, probably figuring it wasn't worth the effort to argue the point.

Marian thought it prudent to ask, "You do know how to drive this stage, don't you?"

"No, ma'am, but I reckon I can figure it out. Where are the horses? The stable looked boarded up and empty as I passed it."

"Indeed, like many other buildings here, it was abandoned long ago," she informed him. "So the animals were set loose in the field behind town."

A moment later, the gunshot startled them all, well, all of them except Chad Kinkaid, who fired it. The dogs that had followed him in had still been barking around his horse's feet. The shot hit the dirt near them and sent them hightailing it elsewhere.

Amanda had squealed in surprise, one hand had flown to her chest and was still there. "Was that really necessary?" she asked derisively.

Chad Kinkaid pulled his hat back down over his forehead, gathered his reins in preparation of riding off, and with a lazy smile, said, "No, ma'am. It was a pleasure though."

# Chapter 6

"Insufferable lout," Amanda mumbled before she went inside to repack the few things she had unpacked.

Chad Kinkaid had ridden off, but, apparently, Amanda didn't think that he would abandon them there as their driver had done. That would never occur to someone as self-centered as Amanda.

Marian wasn't nearly as positive of that and quickly walked around the hotel to the back of it to make sure he was just going to collect the stage horses. She gave a sigh of relief a few moments later when he rode out from between two of the buildings farther down the street and into the field where the horses were grazing. All five of them were still there, too, though widely scattered.

She watched for a few minutes as he started to gather them together. One gave him trouble, didn't want to be put back to work. He removed a looped length of rope hooked to the back of his saddle, started twirling it in the air above his head, then let it fly toward the horse. The loop at the end landed perfectly over the horse's head and tightened with a yank before he could shake it off.

Marian had heard about lassoing, but she'd never had an opportunity to witness it before. The baker had apparently called it right. Chad Kinkaid was a man who knew how to work with cattle and horses. A cowboy, and the first one she'd actually met since arriving in Texas. He undoubtedly knew the area and would be a perfect escort. If only he weren't so handsome as well . . .

Like most handsome men, he'd probably try to woo Amanda. They all did. If they thought they had the least chance with her, they made the effort. She was just too pretty for them not to try. A few of those she had kept dangling over the years, whom she actually encouraged, didn't even know what a shrew she was. If she wanted them to keep coming around, she showed them only her best side. She was very good at deceiving men.

Chad Kinkaid wouldn't stand a chance though. He just didn't fall into the handsome *and* rich category that was mandatory for Amanda. Marian hoped that after her sister calmed down some, she wouldn't decide that Chad would make an amusing diversion. If she turned on the charm for him, he was bound to fall in love with her, and that would be really too bad for him.

It wasn't likely, though, that Amanda would calm down, at least not until she was on her way home to Haverhill. She was going to be her nasty self until then, and everyone around her was going to feel the sting of her displeasure because she simply couldn't stand for anyone not to be miserable when she was miserable herself.

Amanda really did hate this trip and the reason for it. Having to live with their new guardian and abide by her dictates already had her hating their aunt, and she didn't even know her yet.

Neither of them had anything but a vague memory of her, Kathleen had left home when they were so young. What Amanda hated most was that she couldn't marry whom she wanted to, that she'd have to have Kathleen's permission first. Their father would have let her have her choice, no matter whom she chose, because he'd always given her anything she wanted.

Their aunt wasn't likely to be that generous, would take her duty seriously just because it was a new and unexpected duty. At least, Marian would look at it that way, so she took it for granted that Kathleen would, too.

But hopefully Chad would see Amanda

for what she was and not be intrigued by what he might think were merely the rantings of a spoiled brat. Still, Marian would have to take her usual precautions and discourage him as well. Because much much worse could happen if for some strange reason he turned his interest in her direction instead.

She went back into the hotel to pack. She found Ed Harding before going upstairs and asked him to let Mr. Kinkaid know that there were only five horses to collect, so he wouldn't waste his time looking for the sixth. She'd thought briefly about telling him herself, but decided the less contact she had with him the better.

She didn't have much to pack, none of them did. There had been no bureau or closet anyway, so they'd been mostly just living out of their trunks. Two were Marian's, one was Ella Mae's, the other four were Amanda's. She had been loath to leave any of her personal valuables and trinkets behind, even though their home in Haverhill hadn't been closed down, but left with a caretaker to guard against theft.

They were finished and waiting on the porch again before the five horses were hitched to the stage. At least she and Ella Mae were. It was actually a good opportunity to get Chad Kinkaid annoyed enough with her to dismiss her completely from his mind.

He was fiddling with the harness on the lead horse when she approached him, and asked, "Do you have proof that our aunt sent you to escort us?"

He glanced sideways at her, but then put his attention back on the horse. "I mentioned your aunt, you didn't," he pointed out, his tone indifferent.

"Well, yes, you did, but everyone in this town knows that we recently lost our father and are traveling to live with our aunt."

That got his eyes on her again with a narrowed frown. "I've never set foot in this town before."

"So you say, but —"

"Are you accusing me of sneaking into town in the last day or so, hearing your tale that 'everyone' knows about, and cooking up a plan to abscond with you and your sister?"

Put that way, it sounded really horrible. He'd have to be the worst sort of person to cook up such a plan. She winced mentally. She should nod in agreement. She couldn't bring herself to do it. She didn't need to. He was already furious with her.

He reached inside his vest to pull out a letter he had stuffed in a pocket there. He literally shoved the letter in Marian's face.

"This is how I knew where to find you, Miss Laton, and having *not* found you where you were supposed to be, I've spent every day since tracking you down."

There was definitely some censure in those words, and even worse in the tone. He was put out, extremely, that he'd had to go to a lot more trouble to fetch them than he should have had to. Marian found herself blushing even though it wasn't her fault that they hadn't been in Galveston as they should have been. But he was even more put out over her accusation. Well, that had been the whole point, hadn't it? To have him dislike her and, thus, ignore her henceforth.

The letter was the one that Albert Bridges had sent to their aunt. Of course, Marian hadn't doubted he was who he said he was. She hadn't needed proof.

But she pretended to be satisfied with the proof he offered and with a sniff and a shove of her spectacles more tightly to the top of her nose, she said primly, "Very good. I'm glad we are in capable hands," and she walked away.

It was probably his annoyance that made him say to her back, "Capable? No, just my hands." At least, she hoped it was just his annoyance.

# Chapter 7

Chad didn't have to make that run so fast. There'd been six hours of daylight left and the next town with a stage depot in it could have been reached before dark at a normal pace. But the horses were fresh, and he was still angry, so they arrived an hour before nightfall. He took the rest of his anger out on the depot employee who tried to get out of supplying them with a regular driver at no extra cost, and even wanted to keep the coach they already had in their possession. Not likely. The way Chad saw it, the sisters were owed a free ride all the way to Trenton as compensation for the ordeal the last driver had put them through.

The ladies were put up in a hotel for the night — a decent one. At least he heard no complaints from them. Which hadn't been the case for most of the day. The ride he'd given them had produced a heck of a lot of screaming from inside the coach, which he'd ignored. Probably all from that schoolmarmish spinster with the overactive imagination.

Three whiskeys later in the nearest

saloon, and he finally stopped grinding his teeth. He still wasn't happy. He was stuck with women, not girls, and three of them. He should have asked for clarification from Red before he set out. He shouldn't have just taken her remark about "girls" to be an accurate description of her nieces. He should have said, "hell no," to doing her this favor, but unfortunately, it was too late for shoulds and shouldn'ts.

It had been bad enough when he'd thought he'd be traveling with children all the way back to the ranch, but most of the children he knew were well behaved, and he'd expected no trouble from them. Women, on the other hand, could be nothing but trouble, and from what he'd seen of these sisters so far, the "could be" was a definite "would be."

Still he should have figured out sooner that the Laton girls were women, especially after he'd had to track them down. But having it set in his mind that they were too young to be a bother kept him from wondering over the remarks he'd heard about them along the way, and not once were they actually called "women" to his recollection. "Those *gals* were in a terrible hurry," and "The *girls* wouldn't listen to reason," and "Those *little ladies* left the train faster'n harlots leaving a church," didn't exactly point out that they were females who might draw his prurient interest.

*Might?* Hell! That Amanda was as pretty as a picture. Blond hair in a light golden shade and done up to frame her oval face with fashionable curls and ringlets that suited her perfectly. A pert little nose, rose-colored cheeks, a soft chin, and the most luscious lips he'd seen in a long time. And dark blue eyes that sparkled like polished gems, surrounded by thick black lashes a bit smudged from the heat, indicating they probably weren't naturally black, but still, the kind of eyes a man could get happily lost in.

If that wasn't enough, she also had an eye-catching figure a man could drool over. Plump breasts, a trim waist, gently rounded hips, and she wasn't too tall, not much more than a half foot shorter than he, which was rather ideal to his way of thinking.

Her snappishness upon meeting him was understandable. She'd been abandoned in a near ghost town, had suffered through a train robbery before that, and Lord knew what else. For a gently reared lady, the West could be a harsh place, and she'd already experienced more than a fair share of the harsher side. The least he could do was get her to the Twisting Barb without further incident.

As for her sister, the schoolmarmish spinster — with those horrid spectacles she wore, he really couldn't think of her any other way. That wasn't kind, but after the insult she'd dealt him, he had no kind thoughts for her.

They were as different as night and day, so much so that if you didn't know it, you'd never guess they were sisters. Both blond, yes, both blue-eyed and nicely shaped, but the resemblance stopped there.

Marian was obviously the older of the two, and probably made bitter over her spinsterish state. She was probably jealous of Amanda because her younger sister had gotten all the good looks in the family. She wore her hair in an ugly bun and pulled back so severely it was probably as painful as it looked. She held herself stiffly, stomped about like a man, and had been dressed in dull dun gray.

She might be able to pretty herself up some if she tried, but then again, with those spectacles that gave her a bug-eyed look, she probably figured there wasn't much point in trying. She was the kind of gal that if she set her sights on a man, he'd be running in the opposite direction real quick.

The less he thought of her, the better.

The next morning just after dawn they rode out. The ladies weren't too happy about leaving at such an early hour, but it was necessary to reach the next depot before nightfall. At least they were back on the regular stage route, so there should be extra depots along the way between towns for changing the horses and feeding the passengers, and if not, at least there would be designated areas for rest stops.

The driver didn't seem worried about it, though he admitted he'd never driven the route toward Trenton. Will Candles was a crusty individual in his late forties, hair gone to gray early, long handlebar mustache he was right proud of. He'd been driving stagecoaches for about ten years, and mule trains before that, so he knew his job well.

Two days later, Chad had another unpleasant run-in with the spinster. They stopped around midday at one of the better-run depots. It had a stable, a restaurant, offered a wide variety of trade goods, and even had lodgings in case of inclement weather.

The weather had remained good, and was growing a little cooler the farther they traveled northwest. The team was changed while they had lunch. There was a slight delay in leaving though because one of the fresh horses lost a shoe as it was led out to be hitched up. Since the depot only serviced one route, it only kept six horses on hand, so the shoe needed to be refitted if they wanted the fresh horse.

Chad had tried to keep his distance from the ladies as much as possible, if for no other reason than he *was* attracted to Amanda Laton and traveling, with its attendant discomforts, wasn't a good time for romantic notions. When she was at her new home and settled in, he would decide whether to act on that attraction. So he took his meals with Will, rather than with the ladies, and rode half of each day up on the coach with him, and the other half on his horse, but never inside the stage.

Amanda and the maid, Ella Mae, had already boarded the coach when the horse lost his shoe, and elected to wait inside it. Marian had been purchasing something in the general store and, unaware of the delay, probably thinking she was holding up their departure, came running out to the coach and ran right into Chad's back.

He thought nothing of it. She was a very clumsy woman, always bumping into things — and people. He simply moved out of her way. But she seemed all flustered by the accident and even seemed about to apologize, but then must have changed her mind. How the hell she could end up blaming him for it he couldn't guess, but she did.

"You tried to trip me, didn't you? And it's not the first time. Is it something you developed as a child? Picking on other children with weaknesses? A very mean thing to do. Outgrow it!"

Chad wasn't just surprised at her accusation. He was so incredulous at being blamed by her for something that she *knew* was her fault, he was rendered speechless. And having insulted him thoroughly for the second time, she then yanked her skirt back away from him, as if it were in danger of getting contaminated, and flounced off.

He almost yanked her back. He even started to reach for her. A good shaking might be just what she needed. But he stopped himself. The ridiculous ideas that got into her head weren't worth wasting his time over. The trouble was, his time was wasted anyway, in mulling over just how infuriating that female was.

The stage robbers who stopped the coach a couple hours down the road couldn't have known it wasn't a good time to hold him up. There were two of them, each gripping pistols in both hands. One actually looked like a girl behind the mask, or a very young boy, short and skinny as all heck. The other, their spokesman, was a big brute of a man.

The call was given to lay down arms and throw out all valuables. Chad, riding up on the driver's seat with Will at the time, didn't oblige. Will did, and quickly. He'd been through countless robberies on his job and had a firm personal policy that he wasn't paid enough to risk his life trying to protect what was in other people's pockets. Chad might have felt the same way, if the spinster hadn't got on his bad side again that day.

Rifle already in hand, since it had been cradled in his lap, he said, "I'm not in a good mood. If you have a lick of sense, that should tell you that you really don't want to mess with me today. If I have to shoot, I'll be shooting to kill. So why don't you think about that for a moment, then get the hell out of here."

It was probably a little more than even odds that bullets could have started flying right then. Robbers were known to take such chances, and these two already had their weapons at the ready, while only Chad was now armed to oppose them. But they weren't likely to know that there were only women in the coach, so they had to consider that more weapons might be brought into the equation.

However, with Will laying down his weapon as ordered, at that precise moment they only had Chad to deal with. One rifle was all it would take, though, with good aim. The question was then, did they think they might be better and faster? Only they knew how good they were.

There was a brief spat of whispered conversation between the two, then some swearing. Chad patiently waited it out. He'd almost been hoping they wouldn't back down. But while he wouldn't hesitate to put a bullet through the big fellow, he drew the line at shooting teenagers or female desperadoes, whichever the kid was. So he was somewhat relieved when the short one kicked the dirt, then hightailed it into the brush where their horses were staked. The big guy backed away more slowly, but in another moment, he was gone from sight as well. Chad still waited, alert, and didn't relax until he heard their horses galloping away.

"That was real stupid," Will grumbled as he retrieved his gun from the floorboard and shoved it back in his holster. "There's usually a few more hiding on the sides, ready for any opposition."

"Usually didn't apply here, now did it?" Chad replied with a shrug.

"No, but you sure as hell didn't know that. Just pure luck that it was only them two. Why I've seen so many bullets flying at a coach once, the dang wheel was shot off. And *that* time, only two of the robbers made themselves visible as well, but it turned out there were six in all."

"Maybe you need to find a new job."

"Maybe I do," Will agreed with a snort. "But in the meantime, why'n't you get yourself in a better mood so you don't go getting me killed."

Chad figured that was just nervous tension shooting its mouth off, so he didn't take offense. But when the same nervous tension came at him from a different direction, he sure as hell did.

She shot out of the coach, her face red with fury, and started shouting at him, "Don't you *ever* put us in jeopardy like that again. You — we could've been killed! A few trunks of clothes and money aren't worth human lives!"

He plays the hero and gets his head chewed off. It was the last straw. He jumped down from the coach, grabbed the spinster by her arm, and dragged her a good twenty yards away before he stopped, and snarled, "I've a hankering to shake you until you rattle. Say one more word, and I just might.

That was a controlled situation, Missy. If I didn't already have my hands on my rifle, it might've gone differently. And if you hadn't already riled me with your silly accusations, it might have gone differently as well. So maybe you should consider keeping your mouth shut from now on, and you might just arrive at the Twisting Barb in one piece."

He left her there to go check on Amanda. She was probably still frightened, might need comforting. He opened the coach door to find Ella Mae's calm eyes on him — nothing seemed to ruffle the Latons' maid, and Amanda fast asleep. The little beauty had slept through the whole thing.

# Chapter 8

Marian was in the very pits of the doldrums. She wasn't used to making such a complete fool of herself, *and* doing it deliberately. Granted she would usually start out with any new acquaintance, at least any that might have a chance of becoming a friend or a suitor, by giving them a bad first impression of herself, just enough for them to mark her down as not worth knowing.

This was her safety tactic, to make sure right from the start that her sister wouldn't get jealous. And she'd been doing it for so long that it was automatic on her part.

She'd made that effort with Chad Kinkaid the day he'd found them. Accusing him of nefarious deeds, when she'd had no doubt he was there to rescue them, should have been enough. He'd been obviously insulted and avoided her ever since, wouldn't talk to her, wouldn't even look in her general direction. The perfect results. She just hadn't counted on the effect he would have on her.

There was no getting around it, she liked him — too much. The initial attraction she'd felt toward him didn't diminish with his cold shoulders as it should have. She found herself thinking about him constantly, listening for the sound of his voice, trying to catch glimpses of him when he rode beside the coach, everything she shouldn't have been doing, but she just couldn't seem to help herself.

Amanda hadn't noticed her interest in Chad yet because she was consumed with her own discomfort. But if she thought for even a second that Marian liked him, she'd put herself out to win him for herself, not to keep him, of course, but just to spite Marian.

So it wasn't that Marian needed to reinforce Chad's dislike of her. He already disliked her just fine. It was that she needed to burn her own bridges more thoroughly, to make sure that there was absolutely no possibility, ever, that he could be hers. Because even if she lost her last bit of sense and let him know that she liked him, she knew she couldn't compete with her sister over him.

Amanda would use every trick in the book to get what she wanted. If what she wanted was a man, she'd even sleep with him, even if only once, just to get him thoroughly devoted to her. She'd done it before, and made sure that Marian knew about it, if it happened to be a man Marian had shown some interest in. So until Amanda was married and had moved somewhere far away from her, she couldn't begin to think of getting married herself.

So she'd made a fool of herself, again, and now she was miserable with embarrassment because of it. And it wasn't even intentional this time. Bumping into Chad that afternoon had been no more than an accident. But finding herself about to apologize for it had set off alarm bells in her head. She didn't want him to think she was just clumsy. That wasn't a bad enough trait to prompt extreme dislike. Another unwarranted accusation was, though.

But she could have at least been a little more inventive. Charging him with being mean to children was beyond ridiculous. It just showed how utterly flustered she'd been, finding herself in such close proximity to him that she couldn't even think straight.

She would have thought she couldn't get more embarrassed. But lo and behold, he faces a little danger during that aborted stage robbery, and she loses all common sense. She wasn't even sure what was worse, experiencing fear for him or behaving like an idiot because of it.

Definite doldrums. Then to find herself eating dinner with him that night of all nights, when high color was rising up her cheeks every few minutes, when she couldn't stop thinking about her silly behavior. But there was no help for it, at least not that night. The town was small, there was only the one eating establishment in the single hotel, and only one table left empty in it, and the dining room was closing — the cook already gone home — so she couldn't make some excuse, then come back to eat later, and neither could he.

At least they weren't served a round of the usual long-winded complaints from Amanda with the meal. She'd slept through the entire robbery that day, so hadn't had to experience any worry over it, had only been told about it afterward, when they were halfway to the next town, and was actually in a somewhat good mood because of it. And Amanda in a good mood meant flirtation with every man within her sights.

Marian found the food tasteless, could barely swallow it. She had so many mixed feelings stirred up that her head began to ache. It was one thing to know what could happen and quite another to sit there and watch Amanda gain Chad's rapt attention. Even poor Will Candles got utterly flustered by Amanda's smiles. It made Marian sick to her stomach.

The headache was a good excuse to leave, and she took it. So what if she went to sleep hungry. She'd be lucky if she could sleep at all.

No one but Ella Mae really heard her make the excuse or noticed her leaving, she did such a good job of making herself ignorable. She found her way to the room she'd be sharing with her sister and their maid, even though the light had burned out in the hall. She was too miserable to light the lamp in the room, either. She just released her hair from the tight bun, tossed her spectacles on the nearest table, dropped her dress to the floor, and crawled under the covers on the bed to nurse her misery.

Such an abundance of diverse feelings actually had one benefit, they exhausted her more than she realized, and, thankfully, she fell right to sleep. She hadn't expected to. And she had no idea for how long, she just knew she had been deeply asleep and was startled abruptly awake by the surprised voice that shouted "What the . . . ?"

Since their trip had begun back in Haverhill, she had gotten used to being awakened by Amanda, who wasn't the least bit considerate of others when she came to bed. But it wasn't Amanda standing there next to the bed. Marian recognized that deep voice and was surprised enough herself to screech, "Get the hell out of my room!"

He'd had time to recover, and said calmly now, even a bit dryly, "This is my room."

"Oh." Mortified again. That was a bad habit she was developing. "Then I must apologize."

"Don't bother," Chad said.

"Then I won't," she bit out, then added stiffly, "Good night."

She'd realized two things during that brief conversation. Chad had yanked down the covers before he'd realized someone was already in the bed, and the room was still dark. Like her, he hadn't lit the lamp just to get into bed. That meant she could get out of there without letting him get a good look at her and hope she didn't trip on the way out.

It was a good plan, which she implemented immediately. But she didn't count on him flicking one of the matches that were kept next to the oil lamp at about the same time that she started moving. She hoped he was glancing toward the lamp to light it, and not at her. She didn't pause to find out, dashing quickly off the bed and out the door, and ran smack into Will Candles on his way in.

She knocked him over, mumbled a quick,

"Sorry, so sorry," but didn't stop. Could her cheeks get any hotter? Probably not. Nor did they cool off once she was safely behind the right door a few more steps down the hall. The only thing she could be grateful for at that point was that the room was still empty, so she didn't have to explain to her sister or maid what she was doing running around the hotel in her underwear.

# Chapter 9

Will sauntered into the room a moment later, dusting off his clothes, his scruffy wide-brimmed hat on crooked. "Was that who I thought it was, you lucky son'bitch?"

Chad, sitting on the edge of the bed he would be sharing with the stage driver, was wearing a thoughtful frown. "And just who did you think it was?"

"Who else? A good-looking young fella like you wouldn't bother with the quiet one —"

"Now hold on, that's not what was going on. She mistook the room for hers. That's why she went tearing out of it in such an all-fired hurry when I showed up. Did you actually get a good look at her?"

"Sure — well, I reckon not. But that was a mighty fine figure in that skimpy cam-i-sole and ruffle-assed bloomers," Will said with a chuckle. "And only one of them's got such a nice shape."

Chad stood up, picked up the spectacles lying on the table, and twirled them about once in front of Will. "She left these behind."

Will blushed slightly, said, "Well, hell, all women look mostly alike under their wrappings, I guess. Never figured so much long hair could be bound up in such a tiny bun though. I didn't imagine that, did I? That was some really long golden hair that went flying past me."

Chad didn't know what to think, other than that his eyes might have been playing tricks on him. He'd seen her profile as she shot out of the bed, at least a partial view, what with her long hair covering a good portion of it. And he could have sworn, for a second there, that his ears had deceived him in leading him to believe it was Marian's voice he was hearing, when it was actually Amanda dashing out of the room.

He'd turned to watch her exit as well, and his confusion had continued. From behind, with those long blond curls bouncing around her hips as she ran, and only wearing the ruffled bloomers that fit snugly down to her knees and the thin white camisole that clung like a second skin from her breasts to waist, that female body was just too shapely to belong to the spinster. It had to be Amanda's.

Once she was out of sight, he'd finished lighting the lamp and spotted the spectacles on the table, as well as the puddle of a brown dress on the floor, the same one Marian had worn that day. Confusion was back.

It had been the spinster, but she sure as hell hadn't looked like a spinster just then. The profile had so closely resembled her sister's, he'd been positive for a moment that it was the sister. Yet to look at the two of them in the bright light of day there was absolutely no resemblance between them — well, maybe there was. Maybe he just hadn't noticed it before because it was hard to notice anything about Marian other than those spectacles that made her eyes look deformed.

He held those spectacles up in front of his face, brought them closer to his eyes, winced and dropped them back on the table. He saw nothing but a solid blur when he looked through them. He felt a moment's pity for the girl. She had to be nearly blind to need such thick spectacles. The pity was incredibly brief, though. She was still a mean-tempered, ornery, insulting female that any man in his right mind would stay the hell away from.

He'd been managing that just fine for the most part and would continue to keep his distance — after he returned her spectacles to her in the morning. He was actually looking forward to that, just to clear away the last of his confusion, to get a good look at her without the spectacles detracting from the rest of her features.

When he found Marian the next morning, she was just coming out of her room, and damned if she wasn't already wearing another pair of spectacles. Try as he might, he simply couldn't see beyond the oversize eyes and tightly compressed lips. The nose was the same, if stuck up in the air, the cheeks just as sharply defined, the forehead might be the same, the brows weren't, and the chin he wasn't sure of.

Nor did she give him much chance for an extended observation. Red-cheeked over what had happened last night, she snatched the folded dress and spectacles from him, grudgingly mumbled her thanks, and hurried on past him for a quick breakfast before they departed.

He'd been tempted, really tempted, to snatch away the spectacles riding so high on her nose. He didn't quite have the temerity. Well, he did, he just didn't want to have to deal with the immediate tongue-lashing he'd no doubt get for it, or the harangue and insults that were sure to follow nonstop until he could dump her in Red's lap and be done with her.

And besides, Amanda had finally paid him some attention last night over dinner. He'd been beginning to wonder if she wasn't the least bit interested in him. She gave no typical clues to indicate that she might be, ignored him for the most part. Quite a unique experience for him. But after last night, it was definitely worth considering, getting to know her better — after he got her home.

Just two more days should see them riding into Trenton, then another long day out to the ranch. He could wait that long to see which way the wind blew where Amanda was concerned. And as for her sister, he wished a strong wind would just blow her away.

# Chapter 10

When they were a day away from Trenton, Chad began wondering whether he was ready to have it out with his father again. A confrontation was sure to take place if he rode into Trenton. Which was why he debated long and hard with himself whether or not to send the ladies into town with just Will, or to accompany them.

If he didn't go in with them, then he'd have to explain to them why, and the thought of that pretty much decided him in the end. Besides, three months away from home was long enough, more than enough time for Stuart to have cooled off. They should be able to discuss the matter of marriage calmly now, rationally, without each of them blowing off the handle . . . Well, he could hope.

One more day and Stuart would know he was back in the county. And he'd find out if his father could be reasonable about his grandiose dreams of founding the biggest cattle empire around — at Chad's expense.

The ladies were settled into yet another hotel and would be dining soon. Chad left to find a saloon since he wasn't hungry yet. The sun had set, or at least the last tints of red would be gone from the sky in a matter of minutes. A storm was in the area, but would hopefully be gone by morning. He really didn't want any delays at this point.

He almost didn't see Marian standing in the shadows on the porch, staring at the storm clouds moving in from the west. She turned to see who was behind her, then turned back, ignoring him. He bristled only for a second over the cold shoulder, then gave a mental sigh of relief, since he didn't really want to talk to her.

"Is my aunt a — nice person?"

He stopped at the top of the porch steps, tilted his hat back. There was nervousness in that question. If it had been as abrasive as her usual remarks to him, he would have pretended not to hear her and kept going. It still struck him odd, what she was asking, considering Red was her relative, not his.

"What kind of question is that?"

"Well, my father had many faults, and she is his sister," she replied.

"Your father wasn't a nice person?"

"That's a matter of opinion — and whom you ask. Amanda would say he was the nicest person in the world."

She turned slightly now, not to face him,

but so she could look at him sideways. Primed to ignore him again was how he saw it.

"But you wouldn't?"

"He wasn't mean or anything like that. Yes, I suppose I can say he was nice in a general sense. But the question was about my aunt," she reminded him.

"You haven't communicated with her at all since she moved west?"

She shook her head. "No, and I barely remember her from before she left."

"Well, she's a sweetheart. I can't think of a single person who knows her who doesn't like her."

"Really?"

She sounded like a scared little girl begging for some reassurance. Despite how much he disliked her, and that was a lot, he still found himself smiling and telling her what she needed to hear.

"Yes, really. She's kindhearted, generous to a fault. She'd probably give you the shirt off her back if she thought you needed it. And I wouldn't be surprised if she's as nervous about meeting you as you are about meeting her. She never had any kids of her own. Not that you can be considered a child . . ."

An image of that luscious womanly body

running out of his room the other night flashed into his mind. No, definitely not a child.

"What about her husband?" Marian asked. "I do remember Father mentioning once that she moved west immediately after she married."

Chad felt a moment's discomfort, not liking having to be the bearer of bad news. And he couldn't help being amazed at the lack of communication in their family, that she hadn't already heard this particular news.

Red and her brother should have at least kept in touch over the years. Of course, for as long as he'd known Red, she'd never mentioned having family elsewhere. Not that that was odd, when a lot of folks came west just to forget what they were leaving behind.

To get the subject over with for his own sake, he was probably a little more blunt than called for. "Your uncle died last year. Your aunt has been running their ranch on her own ever since."

"Goodness, I had no idea."

She didn't seem sorrowful over the matter, so he guessed, "You didn't know him?"

"No, I don't recall ever meeting him.

There was a mention once —" She paused, frowning as she sifted through her memories. "I think it was my mother who said it, that Kathleen married Frank Dunn just so she could leave Haverhill. I remember thinking at the time that that must have been a powerful desire she had, to see more of the world."

Or a powerful desire to get away from her small corner of it, Chad was thinking.

There could likely have been a rift between brother and sister. That would explain why neither had kept in touch with the other. Yet they were still family, and the only family each had left, thus Red got guardianship of his daughters.

"Well, you'll have lots of time to ask her all about it," Chad pointed out. "We'll be in Trenton tomorrow night, and at the ranch by late the next day."

When it occurred to him that he was standing there having a normal conversation with the spinster, a slight bit of color rode up his cheeks. But then full dark had arrived, and although he could still see her, because his eyes had adjusted to the darkness, he couldn't see her clearly, so it was easy to forget that she was the ornery sister with the wild imagination.

The rain arrived a moment later, a full

downpour, with mist from it floating up onto the porch and urging the two occupants back inside. Well, hell, so much for finding a friendly saloon tonight, Chad thought.

In the small, well-lit lobby, he had just enough time to see Marian shove her spectacles up her nose and flounce off without another word. So much for normal. Her rudeness prevailed. She didn't even bid him so much as good night.

# Chapter 11

Riding into Trenton late the next afternoon, Chad tried to view the town through a stranger's eyes, as Amanda would see it. It was a good-sized town, bigger than most of the ones the ladies had passed through getting there. It had grown considerably from when his father had settled in the area.

The original main street was much longer now. Two blocks had been added to the right, three blocks were squared off on the left, with two more beyond that. And the town was still growing, despite there being no indication that the railroad would ever reach it. But it had a stage line, with connecting routes to Waco up north and Houston down south, and passengers passing through had been known to like what they saw in Trenton and elect to settle there instead of continuing on.

The Kinkaid ranch was partly responsible for the growth, even though it was situated some ten miles west of town. Stuart could have built his own store on the ranch to see to the needs of his large force of employees, but he preferred to support the town instead. There was also a wide selection of farmers settled east of town, and a sawmill up north only a day away.

Straight lines, wide streets, shade trees planted long ago a decent size now, there wasn't much the town didn't offer. Three hotels, four boardinghouses, two more restaurants in addition to the three dining rooms in the hotels that were open to the public, a general store as well as many shops dedicated to specific items like shoes, guns, saddles, furniture, jewelry, even several clothing stores. Three doctors had set up shop, two lawyers, a dentist, two carpenters, and other folk with assorted occupations. For entertainment there were four saloons, two of them considered dance halls, a theater, and several brothels on the outskirts of town.

It was mostly a quiet town. Stuart frowned on excessive rowdiness in his men, as did the saloon owners, and while the cowhands would and did raise hell on the weekends, it was more good-natured, rather than destructive, and a good many of them would show up in one of the town's two churches come Sunday morning.

Occasionally there'd be a gunfight in the streets, but more often than not the sheriff would intervene and try to talk the combatants out of it, usually with success. It was too bad he was retiring next month. He'd kept the peace in Trenton for many years, had been reelected four times.

Chad had expected to cause somewhat of a commotion, riding into town that day. The rift with his father and his taking off would have made the gossip rounds in town. Red's cowboys had brought back the news that Stuart had hired not one but three trackers to find him, and of course, not one of them had discovered where he'd gone into hiding.

So he was surprised, even a little perturbed, when the Concord Stage, much bigger than the smaller stage that usually passed through town, drew more notice than he did. In fact, that stage drew so much notice that they were pulling up in front of the Albany Hotel before anyone actually recognized him riding beside it.

But then the expected greetings and remarks came at him from all sides as a crowd started gathering and growing there on the steps of the hotel.

"That you, Chad?"

"Where you been?"

"Your father know you're back, boy?"

"Where you been keeping yerself?"

"That filly cried for all of a week, I heard,

when you ran off on her."

"This mean you're getting hitched now?"

"We getting invited to the shindig?"

"Where you been?"

Chad answered none of the questions, hitched his horse to the rail in front of the hotel, and moved to open the coach door. Amanda stepped out first, and that pretty much silenced the crowd. He'd figured it would. Trenton didn't see many women as pretty as Amanda Laton. There was almost a collective gasp before the silence.

Amanda usually delivered a complaint or two each day as their journey ended. He couldn't really blame her. A delicate woman like her would get easily worn-out with so much traveling. But she held her tongue with such a large audience on hand, even smiled at such a welcome. A good many of the men staring at her probably fell in love in those few moments that she moved gracefully into the hotel.

Chad stayed with her, but only to avoid a new round of questions that were sure to start up as soon as Amanda was out of sight. At least he told himself that was why he took her arm and led her inside, that it had nothing to do with subtly showing that he'd staked his claim. But then he *had* noticed that even Spencer Evans had stepped out on the porch of his saloon to observe the commotion. Chad hoped he'd stay there. He had enough on his mind without having a confrontation with his old nemesis.

He and Spencer went way back. Born the same year, they'd known each other all their lives. For a brief time, half of one summer anyway, they'd even got along — but they were too young then to have figured out yet that they didn't really like each other.

Competition got in the way of what might have become friendship. Chad supposed that was natural enough, their being the same age and near the same weight and height. Soon enough they were competing over anything and everything. Schoolwork, fishing, hunting, shooting, racing, didn't matter what, they each had to be the better at it. But Spencer turned out to be a sore loser and had started many of those first fights.

It wasn't long before they didn't need much of an excuse to fight, since the fighting turned out to be just another form of competition between them. They'd busted up the schoolroom so often in those days, the town officials elected to abandon the small, one-room schoolhouse in favor of the church, in hopes it would have a more calming influence on the boys. It didn't, but at least they took their fights out into the churchyard thereafter.

They might have outgrown these tendencies, might still have become friends someday and laughed over the antics of their youth. Anything was possible. But then they got old enough to start noticing females . . .

Wilma Jones was the first they both took a liking to. Six fights later and after Spencer had carved "I love you, Wilma" on every single plank of her house late one night, the Joneses moved back East, taking Wilma with them.

Agatha Winston was the second girl they both noticed, again at the same time. They were sixteen by then, and their fights were getting a little more bloody. Aggie happened to get in the middle of one of them and got her nose broken. Chad guiltily suspected it was his fist that had done it, but he'd never been quite sure. She'd refused to talk to either of them after that and still didn't, even though she was married with three kids now.

The kicker, though, was Clare Johnson. She'd bloomed late, or they just hadn't paid attention since she was a couple of years younger than they were. But she was a real nice girl, always helping out the younger children in school. She aspired to be a teacher herself someday.

Chad became infatuated with her soon after his seventeenth birthday, his first — and last — serious interest in a girl. He took her on a picnic, invited her to keep him company while he fished, danced every dance with her at the shindig following the Wilkses' barn-raising, and was sure he was the first to steal a kiss from her because she'd blushed so bright red afterward. He never would have thought to do more than that. She was a nice girl, the kind you courted slowly, then married.

He tried to keep his interest a secret this time. He didn't take her out to places where Spencer would notice — Spencer was too uppity to go to barn-raisings, so Chad was sure he hadn't heard about the dancing. But Spencer was doing his own secret courting of Clare that Chad didn't know about — until it was too late. And Spencer didn't abide by the rules, he didn't stop with a kiss.

He actually seduced Clare, then the son of a bitch bragged about it, so Chad would know he'd lost. Spencer didn't consider that his bragging would effectively ruin Clare — or he didn't care. It was more important to him to win.

The fights escalated after that. Chad and

Spencer couldn't be in the same room without trying to kill each other. And that sorry state of affairs continued until Spencer's father, Tom Evans, finally got fed up with paying his share of the damages his boy had caused and shipped him off to finish his schooling with relatives back East. The town breathed a collective sigh of relief — until months later the peace and quiet actually got a bit boring and some folks were bemoaning the loss of their weekly entertainment in watching Chad and Spencer go after each other wherever they happened to meet.

When Spencer Evans finally returned to town after his father's death to take over the Not Here Saloon, the townsfolk were filled with both dread and expectancy. But enough time had passed, both boys were men now, and fortunately, the town now had two saloons, so Chad actually made an effort to avoid Spencer. He didn't always succeed, and there were still the occasional fights between them, but nothing like what had gone on during their youth.

Clare was still in Trenton. She'd helped in her father's tin shop until he died, then she sold it. She worked in Spencer's saloon now, handled the entertainment, onstage and otherwise. And every time Chad thought of her these days, he despised Spencer even more.

But Amanda wouldn't be staying in town more than one night, and Red's ranch was a good day's ride from town, so he didn't expect Spencer to come sniffing around. Besides, Red wouldn't allow a seducer of innocents to court her very innocent niece.

# Chapter 12

"You dismissed the coach? That was our personal coach!"

Chad tipped his hat back, looked up at the morning sky, counted to ten. It looked like Amanda was going to require all of his patience today. Good thing he had a lot.

He glanced back at the ladies standing at the top of the steps in front of the hotel. Only Amanda was glaring at him incredulously. Marian was examining her nails in a somewhat suspect display of indifference. Their maid looked bored as usual.

He'd brought them three mounts to ride. He'd spent a good thirty minutes in discussion over those horses to make sure they were suitable for ladies before he left the stable. He supposed he *should* have warned them that they'd be traveling the rest of the way on horseback. But he simply hadn't thought it was necessary. Everyone and their mother got around by horseback out here.

Patience well in hand again, he told Amanda, "It wasn't your personal — anything. The only reason you got to use it as long as you did was because I browbeat the depot employee into allowing you to use it, since it was one of their drivers that abandoned you and the coach. I had to threaten to break his neck if he didn't agree. But that coach is too big for the narrow road out to the ranch. Besides, Will took off with it at the crack of dawn, so it's long gone already."

Amanda took on a mulish look. "I am *not* riding a horse. You'll just have to rent us a carriage then."

Well hell, when she got ornery, she really got ornery. It was a good thing she was so pretty that a man could overlook a few annoying traits.

He sighed. "Horses you can rent. Wagons to haul supplies you can rent. But if there's even one carriage in this town, I'd be mighty surprised. Trenton isn't big enough to need them. Folks around here walk where they want to get to. And lastly, the narrow track out to the ranch winds a good distance out of the way to keep to flat land, takes an extra half day using it, which means sleeping outdoors for the night. With horses you can cut a straight path and get there before dark tonight."

"Then you'll just have to rent us a wagon, won't you?" Amanda replied.

His explanation had been reasonable. Did she really want to rough it on the side of the road? Or was she just being stubborn? Some women, when they took a stand, refused to back down from it for any reason, even when proven wrong without a doubt.

"I've already done that for your trunks. The driver will be here at any moment to pick them up and get them delivered by tomorrow."

"Then what is the problem? I'll simply ride with the wagon."

"You're missing the point," Chad replied. "That means an extra day —"

"No, *you* are missing the point," she cut in. "I am not riding on the back of a horse, not today, not tomorrow, not ever! So if some other means of transport cannot be arranged, I'll be staying right here."

"You won't win this battle, Mr. Kinkaid," Marian inserted. There was a distinct note of humor in her tone, but whether it was at his expense or her sister's was anyone's guess. "She's afraid of horses."

"I am not!" Amanda swung around to face her sister. "I just refuse to subject myself to the extreme aches associated with sitting on a horse for any length of time."

"You won't like riding on a wagon," Chad pointed out. "It's not designed for comfort either. Nor is sleeping on the ground for that matter."

"On the ground? Don't be absurd. I would sleep in the wagon, of course."

"The wagon would be loaded with —"

"It will just have to be unloaded," Amanda interrupted him again, and in a tone that defied argument.

"It won't fit all three of you."

"And your point is?"

He stared at her incredulously. He didn't miss the implication. A wagon just for her own individual use was what she was saying, yet where he came from, what was good for one sibling was good for the rest. Was he going to have to go through this whole argument again with the spinster if he agreed to this nonsense? Get another wagon just for them all to sleep in?

Marian actually laughed — at him. His expression over Amanda's remark right then would probably have made a bull snicker. With less patience, he might have exploded at that point. But for some odd reason, he didn't mind her humor. It was the first time he'd heard her laugh, and the sound was actually pleasant, even somewhat contagious. He didn't laugh as well, but the urge to do so did take a few notches off of his annoyance.

She must have read his mind, too, because she said, "Guess it's a good thing I don't mind sleeping on the ground — or riding a horse for that matter."

"You've never been on a horse before either," Amanda said petulantly.

"Yes, but unlike you, I'm willing to try new things. And how difficult can it be, plodding along at a walk beside a *wagon*."

Marian was rubbing it in, that they were going to be delayed just to accommodate Amanda's stubbornness. It didn't work though. Not even a slight blush was forthcoming from the lovely blond.

And then the wagon in question pulled into view, coming around the corner just down the block. Marian started laughing again.

"Oh my God, mules," she gasped out between chuckles. "I could probably get to Aunt Kathleen's quicker if I walked."

This time Amanda did blush. She was also furious, observing the mode of transportation she had insisted she would ride on. And she turned that fury on Chad.

"Is this your idea of a joke? You expect me to ride behind mules?"

"Riding behind them was your idea, not mine. I brought you a perfectly good horse —"

"Which you can exchange for those mules. And I don't care how long it takes. If I can't have a carriage, I at *least* have to have a wagon pulled by horses."

Chad started counting to ten again. While he was at it, Spencer showed up. He was all dandified, wearing his Sunday best though he wasn't a churchgoer, which meant he'd hoped to catch the ladies before they left town and impress them with the debonair ways he'd learned during those few years he'd been shipped back East to finish off his schooling.

"Good morning, ladies." Spencer tipped his hat. "I couldn't help overhearing that you may need my assistance — if a carriage is what you require."

He might have said ladies, but his eyes were all over Amanda. And she was impressed, to go by the smile she offered him. Women did seem to get all silly when they were around Spencer Evans, finding his boyish looks exceptionally handsome. Dark brown hair, emerald green eyes, and the confidence that came with being a successful man of business.

"Indeed, sir. And you are?"

"Spencer Evans, at your service."

"We were *told* there were no carriages to be had in this town."

"Some people are too ignorant to know any better," Spencer said.

"But you *do* have a carriage for hire then?" Amanda confirmed.

"Brand spanking new, delivered just last month," he was pleased to say. "But I'll hear no talk of hiring. You're most welcome to use it, however."

Chad turned away, began counting to one hundred this time. He hadn't missed the digs from both of them. The last thing he wanted to do was fight in front of Amanda, but if he said even two words to Spencer, that's probably what would happen. Her barbs he could ignore, Spencer's he couldn't.

But they weren't waiting for his reaction. They were still ironing out the details. And it was easy to see where this was leading, not just a generous offer on Spencer's part to ingratiate himself with Amanda, but an opportunity to see more of her.

Spencer was saying, "I'll come by to fetch it tomorrow afternoon —"

"Don't bother," Chad cut in, unable to keep quiet any longer. "Someone will bring it back."

"No bother at all. I'm already looking forward to one of Red's home-cooked dinners."

Spencer had done his homework. He knew who the Laton sisters were and where they were going, had probably found Will Candles last night and grilled him. Chad had actually expected him to show up in the hotel dining room last night to meet them. He might have and been too late. The ladies hadn't tarried over dinner, had retired early to bed, so if Spencer had wasted time slicking himself up before coming over, he would have missed them.

It took an extra hour to finally get going. Chad had to buy some blankets for the night, food for dinner. And there had been a teeth-grinding moment when Spencer pulled up with his *brand spanking* new carriage and Amanda admitted she didn't know how to drive one. After making all that fuss, she couldn't even drive the thing?

That news even surprised Spencer, long enough to keep him from offering that service as well. The maid spoke up and said she was capable of driving it. Spencer *would* have offered if he hadn't been rendered momentarily speechless. And Chad would probably have broken his nose for it. He was plumb out of patience. But that was usually the case after a run-in with Spencer Evans.

# Chapter 13

They camped next to a water hole. It wasn't the best-tasting water around, but Chad had brought a supply, so they didn't need to drink it. He did the cooking himself. Marian actually offered to, but if she cooked the way Red did, and they both hailed from the same place, he'd rather eat roots, so he declined. Besides, he didn't trust Marian not to burn the camp down, she was so clumsy. The farther she stayed from the campfire, the better.

He'd managed to cool off, his temper, that is, as the day got hotter. A pure waste of time, riding alongside a carriage, but what the hell, it was only one more day. Amanda even magnanimously elected to sleep in the carriage, since it was a two-seater and she was short enough to fit on one of the padded seats, if she curled her legs that is. The padding was what swayed her, but at least he didn't have to unload the wagon for her — after it finally caught up to them.

Chad half expected Spencer to show up that night with some flimsy excuse about making sure the ladies were all right. It was something Chad might have done if he wanted to see more of a woman who had caught his interest. But then he was forgetting that Spencer was town raised. His particular town might be in the middle of Texas, but there was still a big difference in being raised in the comforts of town and roughing it out on the plains, which anyone raised on a ranch was used to.

And Spencer had already used up his quota of flimsy excuses. Looking forward to Red's cooking — Chad gave a mental snort. The bastard didn't even know that if Red had ever cooked a meal in her life, it had probably burned, that she employed cooks for herself as well as the bunkhouse for just that reason, which she wasn't ashamed to admit.

The maid Ella Mae offered to clean up after dinner, which was nice of her. She was a quiet one. Brown hair kept in a soft bun not nearly as severe as Marian's, green eyes, a few years older than the sisters, she went about her duties without drawing much attention to herself. She was a plain-looking woman, except for the hint of humor always in her eyes. Marian spoke to her as if she were a friend. Amanda spoke to her with more respect than he'd heard her use with anyone else. Neither treated her as a menial servant. They didn't tell her to do things, they asked. He supposed she'd been with them long enough that she was more like family.

Of course, as families went, the sisters didn't exactly behave like they were related. They didn't talk much to each other, but when they did, they rarely had a nice word to say. He figured they'd had an argument somewhere along their journey and just hadn't made up yet. That might explain some of Amanda's testiness as well — and the spinster's rudeness.

Amanda had left the campfire to prepare for bed. Chad watched her surreptitiously for a bit as she fussed with the blankets he'd bought to find one for her use. Ella Mae had brought her a bucket of water. She used it to wash the dust from the day off her face and neck, but then took it with her behind the wagon for a bit more privacy.

He was finding her more and more lovely with each passing day. He hoped he wasn't getting smitten — not yet anyway. With no encouragement coming from her other than a few smiles, and those had been passed out to others as well, not just him, he still didn't know whether he stood a chance in hell of gaining her affections.

Usually there were clues, lots of them, small subtle ways a woman let a man know she was interested in him. He'd never been in doubt about a woman's interest, well, certainly not for this long. Of course, he hadn't been obvious about his interest in her either. He had decided to wait before making any move on her, so maybe she was keeping her own feelings firmly under wraps until he started dropping some clues of his own.

With Amanda gone from sight, he glanced back toward the campfire and was surprised to find himself alone with the spinster. The fire was reflected in both lenses of her spectacles, two miniature campfires in exact detail. It looked most odd, but then she *always* looked odd with those spectacles shoved so far up the bridge of her nose.

She seemed tired tonight, even though she had chosen not to ride a horse today after all, since the carriage had more than enough room for both sisters. He still grudgingly admired her gumption over that, to be willing to ride a horse, when apparently neither sister had ever sat on one before. He had briefly thought about teaching her how, once they were at the ranch, but then gave himself a mental kick for even vaguely considering it. The more distance he kept from her, the better for him.

He'd made a pot of coffee — a habit from those long late-night watches over a herd being taken to market. He figured only he'd be drinking it, so he hadn't made much. But she'd poured herself a cup when he wasn't looking and had set it near the fire to keep it warm.

He glanced away, not wanting to encourage conversation with her if he could help it. But out of the corner of his eye he saw her reach for her cup, and almost stick her hand into the fire instead.

He shook his head, stared right at her, and said, "You need to find yourself a new eye doctor. Trenton just happens to have one."

Her eyes moved to him, then back to the cup she'd managed to get hold of. "There's nothing wrong with my vision," she replied indignantly.

"You're as blind as a bat."

"What an unkind thing to say," she said with a humph.

"You get top honors on unkind remarks, Missy. I'm just stating the obvious."

"Which isn't the least bit true."

"Isn't it? How many fingers am I holding up?" When she said nothing, he added, "Uh-huh, I rest my case."

She lowered her head a bit, conceding, he

thought, until she replied triumphantly, "Three."

He mumbled under his breath. "You were guessing."

"And you have trouble admitting when you're wrong, don't you?"

"When's the last time you had your eyes checked?" he countered. "To go by those antiquated spectacles you wear, it was probably when you were a child. What can it hurt to have a new exam?"

He thought he was being helpful, but even in the dim light of the campfire he could see her blush. And her hiss was further indication that he'd hit a sore spot.

"My eyesight isn't a concern of yours. And you have *got* to stop talking to me before she notices and —"

She stopped, looked immensely flustered, as if she'd said something she shouldn't have. Chad leaned back on his bedroll, resting on one elbow. He was only mildly curious. Well, that wasn't exactly true, but he hoped he was giving her that impression.

"She? She who?"

"Never mind."

"Then let's get back to your eyes."

"You don't listen very well, do you?"

"Sure I do. I heard something about not talking to you anymore, but since you don't care to elaborate, then it can't be very important."

"Trust me, Mr. Kinkaid, this is one can of beans you don't want to open."

He raised a brow. Did she have a real concern — or was she setting him up for another outlandish insult?

He laid on his Texas drawl a bit thick, "Well now, darlin', you've managed to prick my interest —"

"Too bad."

It was a gift she had, how easily she could annoy a man. He sat up stiffly. He jammed a stick into the fire to stir it up, added a few more thick branches so it would last through the night.

"Thank you," he thought he heard her say, though he couldn't imagine why.

She got around to telling him when he pointed out, "You could have just walked away."

"I happen to be chilled, have been for the last hour. I'm not sure why. The night isn't that cold. But I was trying to get warm by the fire before I went to bed. *You* could have walked away though, or at least stop making it so obvious that we're having a conversation."

"I'm not dumb. My bed is here next to the fire, and I'm already in it and staying in it.

So why don't you just cut to the meat and tell me what the problem is?"

"You wouldn't understand."

"I probably would, but since you're too embarrassed to explain —"

"I'm not embarrassed," she cut in. "I was merely trying to save you some —"

When she didn't continue, he suggested, "Confusion? Aggravation? Good job, lady, you've really managed to save me a lot of both."

Since his sarcasm couldn't have gotten much heavier, it wasn't surprising that she was back to blushing enough to burn a barn down. But he'd managed to annoy her, too, enough to get her to spill the beans.

"Very well, our 'talking' is likely to give Amanda the wrong impression. If she thought, for even a minute, that I liked you — which I don't, mind you," she was quick to add. "But if she thought it, she'd turn her charm on you to win you for herself. She'd do it not because she likes you — and I have no idea if she does or doesn't — she'd do it just to spite me."

She'd managed to amaze him. He'd never heard of anything so silly, but then he should have suspected that something absurd like that would come out of her, considering how wild her imagination was.

"Gotcha. So all it takes to gain her interest is to pretend an interest in you. Sounds pretty easy. I'll keep it in mind."

She stared at him hard for a moment before she said, "You know, I think I'd rather freeze than continue this conversation. You've been warned. Proceed at your own risk."

He smiled. "I always do, darlin'."

# Chapter 14

"You gonna come along quiet-like, so I don' have to bash your head none?"

The question was a gruff whisper. Marian was surprised she even heard it since it was muttered quite a distance away and not to her. But she'd been unable to sleep after that aggravating conversation with Chad after dinner.

It had infuriated her, really, how pleased he'd looked upon hearing her explanation, as if he were already thinking of using that ploy to gain Amanda's attention. She'd felt like kicking him. She certainly hadn't felt like talking to him anymore.

She was still castigating herself for revealing the truth about Amanda, which she'd never done before, and for thinking Chad was smart enough to have figured out by now that Amanda was better avoided than pursued.

Now, awake, and sharing a blanket with Ella Mae on the hard ground under the wagon, every little sound was gaining her notice, especially that ominous whisper . . .

Except she hadn't heard the stranger

enter their camp. He'd gotten all the way to the campfire where Chad was sleeping, was leaning over him, had spoken to him, and had gotten there without making a single sound.

She could see him clearly from where she was lying under the wagon. He was really big, wide as well as tall, could easily weigh three hundred pounds. He looked wild, at least, very uncivilized, clothes filthy, a thick bearskin coat, long gray-brown hair so matted, he probably hadn't seen a comb in the last ten years. And she could smell the stink. He'd brought the odor with him.

Chad had to be awake by now, though he hadn't moved and wasn't giving any indication that he'd heard the question. The giant mountain man got impatient for a response, thumped him hard on the chest with the butt of his pistol.

"You hear me, boy?"

"If I didn't," Chad replied dryly, "I could sure smell you — boy."

A chuckle. "You know me. I've worked for your pa before. You know I don' want to hurt you none if I don' have to. But you will be coming with me. Means five hundred to me. Means I'll be spending a nice warm winter this year, and I do favor warm winters at my age."

"I'll match that price if you take your stink elsewhere."

"Now that won't rightly do 'cause I gave your pa my word that I'd have you home 'fore morning. Have to keep my word, boy, you understand. It's a matter of trust — and more jobs when I need 'em."

"And pretty pointless. He knows where to find me now. He can come to me."

"I reckon he don' want to," the giant replied. "Matter of pride, you know. After all, you're the one that hightailed it, not him."

"You don't know anything about it, Leroy," Chad said with a degree of disgust.

"I don' need to know, don' get paid to know. Now are you coming — ?"

A sigh. "I'd oblige you, if I didn't have women here that can't be left alone. And no, you're not dragging them another ten miles out of the way when they're only a few more hours from home. You can tell my pa I'll come by to see him sometime next week."

Leroy shook his head. "That ain't getting me my five hundred, boy."

"It will keep you from getting a hole in your chest, *boy*," Chad countered.

The gun was cocked, the sound incredibly loud in the still of the night as Chad got to his feet. The big man chuckled again, not seeming the least bit intimidated by the thought of being shot.

He even said in his congenial tone, "Your pa didn't say I had to bring you home in one piece, just to bring you home. You don' really want to take me on. Six shots, if you got that many, ain't gonna stop me. I've taken worse and lived to crow about it. So why'n't you come along nice-like, and save us both a passel of pain."

Marian was moving stealthily toward the two men who were discussing violence so casually. They were talking loud enough that they didn't hear her, and she stopped each time when they weren't. She'd picked up a big branch, a small log actually, thick and heavy enough to do some serious damage. Whether she could actually swing it at the man called Leroy was the question.

Fights with her sister were one thing, and while they might get vicious, they never started out with that intent. But this was entirely different, attacking someone she didn't know with the intention of hurting him enough to alleviate the menace. She wasn't sure she could do it. But it didn't sound like she had much choice.

Another step should have her close enough. Her hands began to sweat nervously. She raised her impromptu club with its branchy spikes over her right shoulder, positioning it for a full momentum swing, and took that last step.

And broke a twig under her bare foot.

Both men turned immediately in her direction. Both pointed guns at her. She froze completely, eyes wide with fright.

Leroy started laughing first. Very well, so there hadn't been any time to think of dressing. So she was standing there in her ruffled underwear with a log raised over one shoulder and her loose hair tumbling down the other. It wasn't *that* funny, at least not enough to cause Leroy to laugh so hard he got tears in his eyes.

"What the hell you gonna do with that, gal?" he asked her. "I clean my teeth with toothpicks that size."

# Chapter 15

She shouldn't have been standing there. The kind of trouble the mountain man had brought into their camp had nothing to do with her, and everything to do with Chad. He could have handled the situation without her help. But Marian hadn't known that when she'd decided to "save" him.

Now her brave effort was being laughed at. It was the gross exaggeration, though, that made her highly indignant. Leroy had probably never cleaned his teeth once in his whole life, let alone used small logs to do it. He had said that merely to point out that she was no threat to him. So she swung her club straight at his head. But he caught it easily and, with no effort whatsoever, tugged it out of her hands and tossed it toward the fire.

She would have huffed some at that point. Some help she had been. But Chad had taken advantage of the distraction she'd provided. Leroy's chuckles were cut short as he crashed to the ground, Chad's pistol butt cracked over the back of his head. It put him out completely — for the moment.

And Chad wasted no time in tieing him up, just in case he regained consciousness sooner than he wanted.

Trussed up, gagged, weapons confiscated — an entire arsenal had come out of that humongous bearskin coat — Leroy no longer presented much of a danger. And Marian had remained to watch longer than she should have. She wanted to ask Chad what that had been about, but it wasn't really any of her business, and she was suddenly very mindful that she was still standing there in her underwear.

She turned to leave, hopefully without drawing Chad's notice. But he noticed, said, "Hold up, Amanda."

She froze for the second time, realizing that she wasn't wearing her spectacles. She had forgotten to grab them before coming to his rescue, which was really stupid of her. And now he thought she was Amanda.

He'd reached her back, grasped her shoulders. "That was a brave, if foolish thing you tried to do."

He was too close. She was starting to feel things other than foolish after watching him. She'd stayed too long, should have left him immediately. He was half-dressed himself, wearing only his pants, his hair mussed from sleeping. And he'd worked up a sweat while dealing with Leroy. Chad Kinkaid bare-chested was too sexy by half, his skin glistening in the firelight.

But he thought she was Amanda . . .

She should correct him — no, that would be even more foolish. It wouldn't hurt for him to think she was Amanda for a few more moments. It would be much better than his finding out she and her sister were twins — if he hadn't already figured that out. He'd been around them enough to have guessed by now. But most people who knew they were twins quickly forgot about it because Marian wore her disguise so well.

But at the moment he really did think she was Amanda — and at the moment, she really didn't want to push him away.

He turned her around, tipped her face up to his. "But thank you. That could have gotten messy if you hadn't distracted him."

She was embarrassed by his gratitude and looked down as she asked, "Who was he?"

"A buffalo hunter, bounty hunter, Indian scalper, trapper, you name it, he's probably done it. But the West is getting too tame for him — or he's gotten too old to live the way he used to in the wilds. He hires himself out now for odd jobs that pay well."

"And you knew him?"

"Not really, just in passing. He stops by

my father's ranch every so often just to see if there's work to be had other than normal ranch work."

"And got lucky this time? Your father has to pay someone to get you to visit?"

Chad smiled. She wished he hadn't. He was far, far too close, and that smile of his . . .

"It's more complicated than that," he said softly, too softly.

He was going to kiss her. She knew it was coming, should run like hell in the other direction, because he wouldn't be kissing her, he'd be kissing Amanda. But she couldn't get her feet to move. And deep down, she wanted that kiss, no matter that it wouldn't really be hers.

Opportunities like this just didn't come her way. Her own doing, but still, she'd put her own life on hold until Amanda got settled, yet it seemed now like that would never happen. She was old enough to marry, wanted to marry, wanted a man she could call her own. But until Amanda married and moved on, she didn't dare pursue her own desires.

Although it was deceitful to let Chad continue thinking she was someone else, the temptation was too great to say nothing, to take his kiss and ignore that he thought he was giving it to Amanda. And the time for agonizing over it ran out.

It was worth it. That thought floated through her mind as his mouth moved over hers and enthralled her senses. Oh, yes, definitely worth it. Such a heady feeling raging through her, blood racing, heart pumping, too much excitement. And when he gathered her close, she was afraid she was going to faint, pressed against him, feeling all of him, tasting him, it was too much all at once.

She had no idea how long he held her like that. She was so lost in her own sensations that time didn't matter. He could have kissed her all night, and she probably wouldn't have known the difference. It could have been only mere moments though, and when he did lean back finally, he didn't seem anywhere near as affected as she was.

She could barely think straight. He merely smiled, caressed her cheek, and said, "You should get some sleep. We'll discuss this in the morning."

That got her eyes open wide and alarm bells clanging. "No — no, there'll be no discussion of this. It didn't happen, well, it shouldn't have, so do *not* mention it to me — ever."

He grinned at her, didn't seem the least bit disturbed by what appeared a sudden attack of propriety on her part. "If you say so, darlin'. Long as we know otherwise."

He turned back toward the fire and his bed next to it. While he wasn't watching her, she rushed back to the wagon and her own bed underneath it. Ella Mae had been wakened at some point herself by all the commotion and had witnessed that kiss. She was lying on her side, leaning on one elbow. She rolled her eyes a bit when Marian plopped back down next to her.

"You know what you're doing?" Ella Mae asked.

"No."

"That was bad of you."

"I know."

"You should tell him the truth — and show him. That's if you want him for yourself."

Ella Mae never pulled any punches, but then she didn't come from the lower social rung. Her family had been working-class, but not poor. They'd disowned her though when she got pregnant without a husband to show for it. She'd miscarried the child, which she still mourned in quiet moments. She'd been on her own ever since.

She did her job, she did it extremely well,

but she didn't care if she kept it or not because she knew she could find another job easily. Which was why she was treated more as an equal than as a servant, and why both sisters valued her. Marian also considered her a friend. Even Amanda, who had driven away five other maids, never once turned a harsh word on her. Ella Mae wouldn't tolerate it, would up and leave, and Amanda knew that. She wasn't about to risk losing someone who did her hair up perfectly and kept her wardrobe in excellent condition.

Ella Mae was sometimes *too* frank, though, and this was one of those times. Marian didn't want to talk about her feelings for Chad, which were hopeless in her mind, so best left unshared even with a friend.

But Ella Mae persisted. "Do you want him for yourself?"

She could have denied it, but there wasn't much point. She might have kept Amanda from noticing the direction of her yearning looks, but Ella Mae was more often with her than with Amanda, and she'd raised a questioning brow at Marian more than once about it.

"I think I do," she admitted.

"Then tell him."

"I can't. You know how jealous she'll get.

And it's her he wants."

"He doesn't know her. He doesn't know you either. You should let him get to know you."

"Stop it. You know what happens when a man shows any interest in me. Amanda then reels him in and keeps him dangling indefinitely — and rubs it in my face."

"Those were boys she did that with. You've been making yourself as ugly as you can for several years now. You've never given a man a chance. They can't all be so gullible to fall for her ploys."

"Maybe not," Marian replied. "But I'm not going to be responsible for even one more man getting hurt like that. I can bide my time."

"Biding time is easy — and gets you nowhere," Ella Mae pointed out.

"I'm in no hurry."

"Aren't you? You want to lose this one that you really want?"

Marian sighed. "I don't have him to lose. He's already made his preference plain."

"So has she. She's shown no interest in him. She's barely civil to him."

Marian grinned at that point. "Which is why I can bide my time. He's different from the others. He hasn't made a fool of himself over her yet. I think he may be waiting to see if she's worth the effort."

"Or waiting until he doesn't have to worry about keeping us alive."

Marian made a face of disgust. "Oh, sure, shoot my conclusion down. Some encouragement you are."

Ella Mae chuckled with a shake of her head. "Mari, you make life too complicated. And he's made his move. He kissed her — or thinks he did. Consider that while you try to get to sleep."

# Chapter 16

Her guilt was incredible. Marian woke up with it, wallowed in it, couldn't shake it. The disguise she fostered was deceitful enough, but she did it for a good reason: to save other people from Amanda's spiteful manipulations. But actually to pretend to be Amanda . . .

Her sister had done that often when they were children, just to get people mad at Marian. She thought it was a wonderful joke, though she was the only one who found it funny. Marian had tried it only once before, with their father, because she so craved the attention he gave only to Amanda. But he hadn't been fooled. He'd known immediately that she wasn't his favorite, and the scolding she got was so embarrassing she'd never tried it again.

It wasn't pleasant, sharing the same face with someone you detested. It wasn't fun either, always worrying about other people's feelings to the complete exclusion of your own. It was simply hell having a sister like Amanda.

Marian avoided the campfire that

morning, where Chad was handing out a quick breakfast before they started on the last leg of their journey. She preferred going hungry to being near him just then, she was so afraid he was going to see through her disguise.

She did accept a cup of coffee though from the wagon driver who, the night before, had set up his own fire on the other side of the wagon. When asked why two had been necessary, he'd mentioned something about deceiving would-be robbers, and he'd added that even when he was alone on the road, he always lit two fires, then never slept near either.

The mountain man had been moved into the wagon sometime before anyone else had awoken. He must have regained consciousness and cooperated because there was simply no way Chad, even with help from the driver, could have hoisted a man that size. And it had been done so quietly, the women sleeping under the wagon hadn't been disturbed.

Marian just happened to notice his bound feet near the back of the wagon when she circled round it. Chad obviously didn't want to leave Leroy behind, but didn't want the others aware of his presence either. To spare him a lot of questions, she supposed.

She still kept an eye on Chad, dreading the moment when he came face-to-face with Amanda. She didn't trust him not to mention the kiss, even though she'd warned him not to. And Amanda wouldn't pretend ignorance. If something caught her curiosity, she'd demand an explanation.

Amanda was the last to make an appearance. It was too much to hope that she wouldn't feel like eating that morning. She went right to the campfire, took the offered plate of food without a thank-you, and proceeded to ignore Chad completely as usual.

Last night Marian had actually been sorry to learn that Chad's father owned a ranch. That meant he might not be completely without means as both sisters had first thought, and Amanda's interest in Chad might perk up. But then Amanda had missed hearing about his father's ranch, once again having slept through all the danger and excitement. With luck, this time, though, she wouldn't find out about it after the fact.

Ella Mae was still at the campfire, too. Amanda started talking to her. Marian didn't have to be present to know her sister was now complaining about the discomforts of sleeping outdoors — now that she had an interested ear. Not that Ella Mae was the

126

least bit interested. Like Marian, Ella Mae had learned long ago how to tune Amanda out.

Chad was listening, however, and after a few minutes, he was frowning. Marian would give anything to know what the frown was for.

It could simply be that Amanda had just thoughtlessly insulted his cooking efforts. It could be that it was the first time he was being treated to one of her diatribes — he usually only caught the tail end of them when she was almost out of steam and not nearly so derogatory. But it was more likely because she was treating him as if he weren't present while he was sitting only a couple feet from her.

He'd probably assumed that things would be different now between him and her. A natural conclusion after a kiss that hadn't been rejected. He'd stated his interest very clearly with that kiss. She'd done the same by accepting it. The cold shoulder he was getting from the woman whom he'd thought he'd kissed probably felt like a slap in the face — which is what Marian *should* have done last night, rather than let temptation get the better of her good sense.

Finished eating, Amanda carelessly tossed her plate toward the fire and started to head back toward the carriage to finish preparations for leaving. His frown more intense, Chad started to follow her. Marian sucked in her breath, watching them, waiting for him to grab Amanda and turn her around, to demand an explanation for her — what? Her lack of interest, when she had no interest in him to begin with?

Marian's guilt mounted. She should stop him, take him aside and make her confession. He was going to despise her for it. But she'd already gone to great lengths to make him despise her anyway, so that shouldn't matter to her.

She took a step toward him, but he stopped. She stopped. He spent all of five seconds staring at Amanda's retreating back then swung around with what seemed almost a shrug. A shrug? Surely not. Or was a kiss stolen in the middle of the night not important to him? Maybe he kissed all the pretty women he came across if given the opportunity.

Marian could breathe again, but now *she* was frowning.

# Chapter 17

Amanda was almost too confusing to bother with. That was the conclusion Chad reached that morning, well, almost. But Amanda definitely did seem like two different women, soft and yielding at night, a veritable termagant during the day.

Rudeness must run in their family, he figured. No, that wasn't true. There wasn't a rude bone in Red's body, and she was the Laton sisters' blood relative.

The confusion he was beset with now was his own fault. He should have stuck to his guns and waited until the trip was over before finding out which way the wind blew with Amanda Laton.

He knew from experience that tempers could flare easily when you were doing something you didn't want to do, and he'd overheard enough comments to know that she hadn't wanted to come to Texas in the first place and was hating everything about the trip there. So her flare-ups of rudeness were actually somewhat understandable, or at least, there was a pretty good reason for them. Once the trip was over, she'd probably be completely different.

But she was so damn beautiful last night, there was just no way he could have restrained himself from kissing her. And she'd tried to rescue him. He was touched by that, never would have expected it from her. She was always so aloof, so indifferent — to him anyway.

But the previous night, she'd melted in his arms. He'd been surprised, delighted, had felt his desire rising, then, strangely — it just didn't feel right. And for a moment, he'd actually wondered why he'd kissed her.

It had nothing to do with the kiss, that had been sweet. It had nothing to do with how easily she'd yielded. It had everything to do with her. She just didn't add up, was too confusing by half, cold as ice one moment, hot the next, as if she were two . . . different . . . women. No way. Campfire light wasn't very bright, but they'd have to be twins for him to make that kind of mistake — well, hell.

He shouldn't feel poleaxed. He'd seen it coming, just hadn't acknowledged it. Siblings could resemble each other closely, but what were the odds on having so many identical features unless they were twins. Of course they were twins. It was just that one was blind as a bat and ornery as sin. And there was no way he would have kissed that one.

So they were twins. That changed nothing, and still didn't explain his confusion over Amanda. Or maybe it was just him. Maybe he wasn't as interested as he'd thought.

Actually, that was probably the whole problem. He *should* be interested, but was he? Really? Or did Amanda remind him too much of Luella, a gorgeous outer shell with nothing he liked very much underneath? Which was another reason he'd been waiting for the trip to end before pursuing her, to give her time to relax, or recover — depending on how she looked at it — to settle in and be her normal self again.

He expected a big difference in her attitude in the next few days. She'd have nothing more to complain about. Red's home was Western in flavor, but very comfortable. And she had one of the best cooks in the county working in her kitchen. Once her aches and pains were gone and she was surrounded by comfort and family, he'd find out what Amanda was *really* like.

He'd seen her worst side — at least he hoped that was as bad as she got, because he'd never seen much worse. He sure was looking forward to seeing her better side.

★ ★ ★

The carriage rolled up to the Twisting Barb a little before noon, the wagon with the luggage, and Leroy, probably thirty minutes behind them. Chad would have to explain about Leroy. They'd been too far out in the middle of nowhere just to leave him behind. No homesteads close enough for him to walk to if they took his horse to delay him. And the road was not well enough traveled for someone to find him if they left him there still tied up.

But he didn't really expect any more trouble from Leroy, now that they were at the ranch. Someone could take him back to find his horse — Chad hadn't bothered to look very hard for it. And he'd emptied Leroy's guns of ammunition, so he could have those back.

His father must be getting senile, or desperate, to send someone like Leroy after him. Especially when he would have been told that Chad was heading to the Twisting Barb. He couldn't figure out the point of it — unless it was to make a point. Stuart could have easily ridden over to Red's ranch himself, would probably have beat them there — and maybe that's what he'd done. And perhaps not finding Chad there before nightfall last night, as he'd thought he would, he'd sent Leroy to find out why.

But that meant Leroy would have been part of his father's entourage, and Chad couldn't see Stuart wanting that foul-odored old coot riding anywhere near him. Stuart never went anywhere these days without a minimum of four gunmen escorting him, men able to handle any kind of trouble that showed up. But they were all clean and well-mannered, and they worshiped Stuart because he paid them so much.

Red came out on the porch to greet them. She looked nervous as hell. Because she hadn't seen her nieces since they were tykes? Or because Stuart had showed up and had been giving her a hard time over his son's working for her?

Chad hadn't expected to see his father quite so soon, wasn't braced for it, but he had expected to see him in the next day or so, now that Stuart knew he was in the county. He'd allowed him to find out that he was back when he had decided to ride into town, knowing full well that someone would hightail it out to the Kinkaid spread with the news.

A couple of the hands had run up to see to the carriage and help the sisters and their maid down. The spinster was the first up on the porch.

Chad was just dismounting when he heard Red ask, "Which one are you?"

"Marian."

Red seemed to relax somewhat, since Marian also looked nervous, and offered her niece a big hug, "Welcome, Mari. I used to call you that, you know. Do you remember?"

"No, but my mother called me Mari, too," Marian said with a hesitant smile.

"I'm sorry about your father."

"Yes, that was an unfortunate accident."

"But I want you to know I'm very glad to offer you a home here for as long as you want."

"Thank —"

"Is this it?" Amanda cut in, as she mounted the steps. "A ranch house, and a small one at that? I'm expected to live *here?*"

Red's blush was immediate. Chad winced for her. She was nervous enough, but to be met with such derision was beyond rude on Amanda's part.

Red said defensively, "I know it's nothing so grand as your home in Haverhill, but you won't find too many places out here nicer. My husband put a lot of work into —"

"Not nearly enough," Amanda cut in again. "But I don't know why I expected better, when every town we've passed through out here has been horribly primitive."

Chad had heard enough. Incensed for Red's sake, he was about to burn his bridges by telling Amanda to shut the hell up, but Marian beat him to it.

"Can you refrain from being rude for five seconds, sister dear?" she said with a tight little smile, "Or is that beyond your capabilities?"

Amanda gasped and immediately raised her hand to slap Marian for the insult, well deserved or not. Chad jumped forward to stop her, but he wasn't close enough. It wasn't necessary. Marian had expected retaliation, apparently, and was prepared for it. With a slight shove, she sent Amanda tumbling down the steps and into the dirt.

# Chapter 18

There was a lot of screeching. Chad was too well-bred not to help Amanda to her feet. She didn't thank him. He was getting used to that. She did continue to hurl invectives at her sister while she whacked dust and dirt off her skirt.

Marian wasn't paying the least bit of attention to the diatribe. Red stared at Amanda, looking all worried, but the spinster put an arm through hers and gently urged her inside. Chad decided that's where he'd rather be as well, and joined them.

Stepping through the door, though, he barely recognized the place. Red had broken out of storage, or managed to find, all kinds of delicate knickknacks and figurines, had changed the serviceable curtains to fancy drapes, put new rugs on the floor. The antlers above the mantel in the main gathering room were gone, replaced by a framed mirror. New paintings were on the walls. One he recognized from Doc Wilton's office. He wondered how much she'd had to pay him for it.

Red had tried to give her home a more

Eastern flavor, something the girls were more used to. He liked it better the way it had been, where a man didn't have to worry about knocking over the clutter. Just showed how nervous she really was about meeting these nieces of hers.

While he was examining all the new finery, he didn't miss the man sitting on one of the sofas, his arms spread out on the back of it like he owned the place. No, it was impossible to miss that big black-haired, blue-eyed Texan. Chad just chose to do so.

Red had good manners though, and led Marian over for a formal introduction. "This is a neighbor of mine, Stuart Kinkaid. He owns the biggest ranch in the county, possibly the whole state."

"I'm working on it," Stuart chuckled as he stood up and grasped Marian's hand for a good shake. "Nice to meet you, Miss Laton."

"You as well, Mr. Kinkaid."

"Your aunt's told me all about you, as well as some of the difficulties you've had getting here."

"Oh?"

"Chad sent a few telegrams," Red explained.

"I'll have to throw a barbecue sometime next week," Stuart continued. "To give you gals a proper welcome."

"How — country," Amanda said dryly, coming in the door with a hard shove, to make sure it slammed back against the wall. "I'd like a bath, Aunt Kathleen. A hot one. You *do* have plumbing here? And *hot* water?"

Red was blushing again. "If you'll excuse us, Stuart, I'll show the girls to their rooms and get them settled in. You're welcome to stay for dinner again."

There was an uncomfortable silence as Red directed the women toward the stairs. Father and son eyed each other, but said not a word yet.

Chad had missed the old man, though he wouldn't say so. But damn, it was good to see him again. Chad was tall, but his father had a few inches on him. Fifty-two, and his hair just as coal black as if he were Chad's age, Stuart sported a mustache as well, but that's where the similarities ended. He had wider shoulders, longer legs, was gruff in his manner, opinionated . . . well, hell, they were probably more alike than Chad would like to admit.

Enough time had passed that he was hopeful they could reconcile. Hopeful — but not sure. Both of them were stubborn, and their tempers could easily flare up again.

Kinkaids didn't squabble in public — if they could help it, though the public sure heard about their squabbles soon enough. Usually because they got loud. But with the women vacating the room quick enough, both men remained patient. The very second they were alone, Stuart started out with an accusatory tone.

"So this is where you've been hiding out?"

Chad raised a brow. "Hiding? Red needed some help, or I'd have moved on. I hope you didn't grumble at her for letting me stay here without telling you."

"Course not," Stuart said defensively. "I like Red. That gal's got gumption, trying to hold on to this place after Frank up and died on her."

Stuart cleared his throat before saying any more, realizing he'd started off on the wrong foot. In a much milder, if gruff tone, he said, "From what I heard last night, she still needs help. I can send over one of my foremen."

"You implying I can't handle it?"

"Don't look for something to bite into. We both know there's nothing you can't handle."

Chad nodded curtly, moved over to the cold fireplace, stared into the new mirror there, not at himself but at his father. This reunion was going better than he'd expected. 'Course, they hadn't touched on the meat of their differences yet.

"You misplaced one of your men," Chad remarked.

"I did?"

"He'll be along shortly with the baggage. He'll need to be untied."

Stuart laughed. "Sorry. I got a little impatient last night."

"So I gathered. What the hell you doing riding with Leroy in tow? That ain't your style."

Stuart shrugged. "He's been hanging around all week looking for work — and making some of the men nervous. I figured I was sending him on a wild-goose chase, that you'd show up here before he'd find you, then he'd move on. Didn't figure you'd weigh yourself down with vehicles and take another day to get here."

"I didn't figure on that either, but then one of the ladies refused to travel by normal means."

"The noisy one?"

Chad made a face. Of course Stuart would have heard all the screeching that had gone on outside. They could have heard it out back in the bunkhouse, Amanda was so loud.

Chad found himself explaining, though he wasn't sure why, "She's had a bee in her bonnet from day one. She didn't want to come here, hates traveling. But her attitude should improve now that the traveling part is over."

"Don't kid yourself, boy. That's a born and bred nag if I've ever seen one. Probably spoiled rotten, too. Pretty little thing, though. I suppose she caught your interest?"

"Some," Chad admitted.

"Seriously?"

"Not yet."

"Good." Stuart grunted. "Nags don't usually grow out of being nags."

Chad rolled his eyes. "I told you why she was being difficult. Not that it's any of your concern — and when did you get to be such an expert on nags?"

"Since I spent two months with Luella's mother," Stuart mumbled.

Chad burst out laughing. He couldn't help it. Luella's vacant looks had been indicative of her mind, but her mother had been a nonstop chatterer the few times he'd been in her presence. That chattering must have got a lot worse after he left.

Stuart even grinned after a moment, but only for a moment. With nothing settled yet between them, he wouldn't unbend enough to relax. In fact, he finally broached the subject they were both waiting for.

"You ready to come home, boy?"

"You ready to admit who I marry is none of your damn business?"

"Can we at least talk about it?"

"We did that. I talked. You didn't listen," Chad reminded him.

"You didn't give Luella a chance, either," Stuart was quick to point out.

"It didn't take but five minutes to know I wanted nothing to do with her."

"But she's beautiful!" Stuart complained.

"Then you marry her."

"Hell, no."

"Why not? She's *beautiful*," Chad said, throwing that reasoning back at him.

"She's too young for me," Stuart grumbled.

"And she's too dumb for me. So can we agree that neither of us wants her in the family and drop the subject already? Or is she still at the ranch?" Chad asked with a frown. "If you tell me she's still at the ranch —"

"She ain't," Stuart cut in to assure him. "Went home last month. She would've waited around indefinitely for you, really liked the idea of marrying you, but her pa got insulted by your absence and came to fetch his womenfolk home. And not a minute too soon. Her mother was driving me nuts."

Chad grinned. "Then I guess it's safe for me to come home soon as I wrap things up here."

"Told you, I'll send over —"

"I'll finish what I started," Chad interrupted.

Stuart frowned now. "I hope you don't want to stay here longer to court the nag."

Chad resented his father's description of Amanda, when he'd barely met her. "Let's get at least one thing clear. Your approval of who I marry would be nice, but it's not the least bit necessary."

"You want to bring a bride home to live under my roof," Stuart growled belligerently, "then I reckon I should have a little say in it."

"Who says we'd live under your roof?" Chad shot back. "We could, but I could just as easily build my bride her own house so you don't have to deal with her."

Stuart mulled that over for a second, then chuckled. "That would work. That would work just fine. All right, boy, if you're not going to double my empire, at least give me a lot of grandkids who might."

"When I get around to it. But no more pushing, and no more rounding up fiancées for me. We got us a deal?"

Stuart slapped him on the back with a big smile. "Damn, it's good to have you home."

Chad was aware he hadn't got an answer. His father liked to leave himself escape routes. But that was all right. It was good to be home — and on good terms with his father again.

# Chapter 19

Red was on her way back downstairs to see to her other guests when the noise started. She turned around, headed back to her nieces' room, and found their maid just leaving it.

She saw Red and shook her head. "Be best not to interfere, ma'am," Ella Mae warned. "This is long overdue. They'll be easier to live with afterward."

Red bit her lip. It wasn't hard to decipher the maid's meaning. The noise was very obvious, which made it hard for her not to want to interfere.

"But won't they — hurt each other?"

"No more'n two cats in an alley. They don't really know how to fight. A few scratches, maybe a bruise, a lot of rolling around. It's not the first time, ma'am."

"I see."

It was all Red could think to say, but she didn't see at all. Those weren't children on the other side of that door brawling, but grown women. And although it had been apparent from what had happened outside, that her nieces, or at least one of them, was going to be a problem, she hadn't guessed how much of a problem until now.

This was entirely her brother's fault. She had known Mortimer wouldn't make a good father any more than he had made a good brother. The kind of favoritism he'd practiced since they were children wasn't normal. He'd picked her twin sister to be his constant companion, and Red might as well not have existed for all the attention those two paid her — except when they wanted to rub in the fact that she would always be excluded from their little circle. She'd grown up with it, had hated him for it, and had seen it happening again when his daughters were born.

It was the major reason she'd wanted to leave Haverhill, and why she'd married Frank Dunn, who'd had plans to start a ranch out West. She hadn't loved him. He'd been a means to an end. She'd figured that moving out West would place her far enough away from her brother to afford her a measure of peace and happiness. And it had. She'd had no further communication with Mortimer and his family. She'd wanted none.

She'd used Frank. There was no nicer way to put it. But she'd repaid him by being a good wife. He'd had no complaints and didn't blame her for not giving him any children. Well, he wouldn't, because a doctor had implied the fault was his, not hers. He'd felt somewhat guilty after that for not giving her any children, but, such was life, and they'd had a good one together until he died.

Well, actually, not so much *good,* as comfortable. And if another man was capable of making her heart race, no one knew it but her.

Her heart had done a lot of racing last night when Stuart had showed up and pretty much invited himself to dinner. She'd gotten through the evening without making a fool of herself though, at least, not too much of a fool.

She'd giggled a few times, which she rarely did. She'd been tongue-tied a bunch more. And she'd blushed more than she had since she was a girl. But then she'd never been *alone* with Stuart before. Anytime she'd ever seen him, other people had been around.

She hadn't expected it to be any different last night either when she'd invited him and his men to dinner while they waited for Chad to arrive. But she didn't know his men never ate with him, and only he'd been sitting there in her dining room when she showed up for dinner — and started acting like a schoolgirl.

But Stuart had probably figured it was guilt making her behave so oddly, because she'd housed his son for the last three months without letting him know about it, when the whole county knew he was looking for Chad. At least he hadn't remarked on it to her. And he hadn't expressed any disappointment in her either, when she explained why Chad was staying with her. In fact, he'd scolded her a bit for not coming to him for help when she'd needed it.

She'd put Stuart up for the night when it became obvious that Chad wasn't going to make an appearance last night. His men were put up in the bunkhouse, but there was no question about putting the biggest rancher in the county there. She'd gotten no sleep, of course, with him just down the hall from her. And she'd made herself deliberately scarce at breakfast time. She hadn't seen him again until the maid had come to tell her the girls were arriving.

And what a surprise they were.

They were twins, but most folks probably wouldn't notice that right off. She remembered they had been identical when they were children, and it had been difficult to tell them apart. But not anymore.

Poor Marian had had to introduce herself. Red had taken her for a servant at first glance. But she'd realized her mistake quick enough on closer examination. Such an odd look the girl had, with those spectacles, and such a shame she had to wear them.

Amanda, now, was as pretty as expected. Even as children, it had been obvious the girls would be beauties, and Amanda had certainly turned out to be just that. Her behavior, too, had been somewhat expected. The result of being spoiled beyond redemption. She was so much like Red's sister had been, it was uncanny. And exactly why Red had left home. She had refused to watch her brother's favoritism divide his daughters, as it had his sisters.

She hadn't been there to see it, but obviously, it had happened just as she'd figured it would. The little she had seen so far said it all. Amanda had turned out to be a spoiled bitch. Marian had turned out to be a meek little mouse — well, maybe not. The mouse didn't usually fight the cat. . . .

Downstairs, Stuart was laughing his head off. He'd been doing so since the third loud crash above them. The first had been merely startling, the second had been curious, but the third was a definite brawl, and every loud noise thereafter set him off again with another round of laughter.

Chad knew exactly why Stuart was so amused. His father's choice for him might have been lacking in smarts, but she was pretty and quiet. While the one he'd expressed interest in was upstairs breaking furniture and Lord knows what else, and could screech loud enough to raise the rafters.

"I feel sorry for the ugly one," Stuart remarked when he caught his breath.

"Yeah, you look real sorry," Chad replied dryly, and then felt compelled to add, "And Marian isn't ugly, she's just blind as a bat."

"Either way, she won't be able to hold her own for long. The other has a vicious temperament. Saw that with the way she slammed in here."

"Is it just because I might be interested in Amanda that you feel obliged to insult the hell out of her?" Chad asked with a frown.

"Was I doing that?" Stuart shot back innocently.

Chad gave his father a look of disgust, which just garnered another chuckle from him. And although Stuart was possibly just teasing him, the remarks now had him worried about the spinster. He didn't like her, but he didn't want to see her get hurt, either.

Without another thought, he headed

toward the stairs. Stuart called out behind him, "Takes guts to break up a female brawl. I've seen both women turn on a man who tried it before. Damn near scratched his eyes out."

Was that supposed to stop him? Particularly when Stuart was laughing again? Red did, though, coming back down the stairs, blocking his way.

"Don't interfere," she said, seeing his determined look. "I've been told this is *normal* for them."

"Who told you that?"

"Their maid. She's up there guarding their door. Seems to think they'll both be in a better mood after letting off steam that way."

Red looked dazed still. Chad put a sympathetic arm around her. She had to be taking this hard. This had to be a far cry from what she'd been expecting.

He tried to put it in perspective for her. "The maid's probably right. It was a hell of a trip for them, train robbers, stage robbers, a mountain man showing up in the middle of the night intent on dragging me home at the point of a gun. One thing after another since their ship docked, when they come from a quiet little town back East where nothing much ever happened. Could make anyone blow her top."

She gave him a curious look. "You don't have to make excuses for them."

"I know. Just trying to make it sound better for myself," he replied.

She tsked at him in annoyance, which brought on a slight blush. He was supposed to be making *her* feel better, not himself.

They both noticed at about the same time that the noise had quieted down behind them. Not completely. The girls were talking to each other, nothing distinguishable, but at least that meant neither of them was dead.

In all seriousness, Chad told his friend, "Do yourself a favor, Red. Get them married soon and off your hands. That's my advice."

"Are you looking to help me out there?" she grinned up at him.

"If all she needed was to blow off a little steam, and if she starts acting like the lady she's supposed to be, I just might."

"She? Never mind, I can guess." She gave him a sad look and a sigh. "Let's hope you're right."

He wondered why Red suddenly looked sad, but decided he'd rather not know. It was probably no more than her overall reaction to this reunion with her nieces. And who could blame her for being so disappointed?

# Chapter 20

At home, Marian had never given much thought to the noise she and Amanda made when they went after each other. They were careful to keep that kind of fighting private. And since no one ever remarked on it, she just assumed that no one ever knew.

There had been no avoiding that fight today. It had nearly taken place in public, right there on the porch. But Amanda had come to her senses and waited until they were alone.

They'd been given separate rooms, thank God. Amanda hadn't stayed in hers, though, had followed along when their aunt showed Marian to hers. Marian knew then what was coming, was braced for it. Ella Mae knew, too, and tried to prevent it by not leaving when Kathleen did. Amanda actually told her to get out. And no sooner did the door close than she threw herself at Marian.

It was one of their more vicious fights. They both came away with clumps of hair in their hands, skin under their nails, teeth marks, and bruises aplenty. Amazingly, not a single mark marred their faces afterward. But then it was almost an unwritten rule between them that their faces were out of bounds. All other bruises could be hidden, but facial marks would be evidence of their undignified scuffles. And then, too, scratching one face was like scratching the other, when both faces were identical.

There was no winner. There rarely was. Their fights would end when they both got tired, and since they were pretty much in the same shape, they usually got tired at about the same time. This one was no different and soon enough wound down to verbal insults, as most of them did.

"You could have at least waited until our aunt got to know you a little better before showing her what a shrew you can be," Marian said as she pulled herself up onto her bed.

Amanda had gone straight to the nearest mirror to examine her face. "Why?" she shot back. "I don't intend to be here long enough to get to know her at all."

"And where will you be?"

"On my way back home, of course."

"With husband in tow? You really think you can find someone to marry you here that quick?"

"Don't be an ass," Amanda swung

around to snort. "There's no one out here worthy of me."

"So you're going to give up your inheritance?" Marian concluded.

"You can be really dense sometimes, Mari. No, I didn't come all this way to give up anything. Aunt Kathleen will be more than happy to send me home, and with advance approval of any man I want to marry."

"You plan to make yourself *that* much of a headache?"

"If I have to," Amanda purred.

Marian shook her head. She shouldn't be surprised. Amanda rarely did anything without a motive in mind.

"As much as I'd love to see you on your way, you're probably deceiving yourself. Some people actually take their duty seriously, Mandy."

"Don't call me that. Amanda is much more sophisticated than that childish nickname."

"But the shoe fits, sister dear."

"Like your childish effort to disguise that you're my twin? That kind of shoe?"

Marian smiled when Amanda's lips twisted with anger. It had taken many years for her to develop the cast-iron skin she needed to be able to shrug off her sister's insults. To give an appearance of indifference. And to give back as good as she got. As long as no one else was involved, as long as it was just the two of them, she couldn't be cowed anymore. It was only when someone else was in danger of drawing Amanda's vicious interest that Marian would back down.

"Do you want competition again?" Marian replied with a false look of surprise. "You can't stand being the center of attention anymore? Well, then, why didn't you say . . ."

"Oh, shut up."

Marian should have felt a little better, for winning the verbal round, at any rate. Amanda flounced off angry. Marian lay down to await the promised bath. And all she could think about was whether Amanda had overheard the introduction to Stuart Kinkaid.

If she did hear it, then she'd take Chad off the "employee" list and move him to the "due to inherit something big" list. And she would set out to charm him, lure him in, and tie up his emotions in a tight little knot that she'd never release. Not because she wanted him, but simply because she could. Because it thrilled her to no end to manipulate men like that. It was the one thing she did very well.

If that wasn't enough for Marian to worry about, she found out almost immediately when she went downstairs later that the altercation with her sister hadn't gone unnoticed, or rather, unheard. Her aunt was the first to ask her if she was all right. She might have thought she was referring to her overall condition after the trip, except she seemed too concerned. And then Chad discreetly asked the same thing, and looked just as worried.

By then she was so embarrassed, she was ready to bolt back upstairs and never come down again. But then Chad's father came in from outside, looked her over from top to bottom, and said, "Well, I'll be damned. So you won? Good for you, gal."

He was making an assumption based on no visible bruises, she realized to her mortification. She'd never know where she got the nerve to reply, "No one won."

"Well that's too bad," he grumbled, then added gruffly. "Next time win. Makes the bruises feel worth it."

She laughed. Half-hysterically, but still, she laughed. And felt her embarrassment melt away with it.

# Chapter 21

Marian was beginning to realize that the people in Texas might look at things differently than they did back East. The main reason for her earlier embarrassment was because back home even the servants would have scorned such unladylike behavior from two supposedly well-bred ladies. Their contemporaries would have been scandalized. Their father would have scolded her severely and coddled Amanda until she felt better. All of which kept both girls from airing their differences in public, which, sometimes, was a test of patience to the extreme.

But it was so different out here. In two of the towns they'd passed through, she'd seen men brawling in the streets. In one, a gunfight had just finished. But with so many thieves abounding in the area, it was no wonder decent folks succumbed to base instincts. If you had differences, you settled them with fists or guns. Well, men did anyway. But apparently women could, too, without raising too many brows.

Marian gathered all of this as she listened to Chad and his father "catching up" —

they hadn't seen each other for several months. And Kathleen joined in their discussion of cattle rustlers, a small bank robbery that occurred only forty miles away, a gunfight between two of Stuart's cowhands — both survived it, but got themselves fired for it — a horse thief who got himself posse-hanged before he could make it to trial.

She was fascinated that her aunt wasn't the least bit shocked by such occurrences. But then Kathleen was a surprise in many ways.

She wasn't as old as Marian had expected. At least, she didn't look it. Her hair was as bright a red as it had ever been. She wore it in a simple, single braid. Her white blouse and plain brown skirt were without a single adornment. No jewelry, not even her old wedding ring to mark her a widow. But she had a wonderful smile. Who needed fancy lace and ruffles with a smile like that?

With her tanned skin and plain garb, she wasn't the least bit fashionable, but she was a handsome woman just the same. Shapely, too, and in good health. Funny, frank, and relaxed because Amanda hadn't made an appearance yet to stir up tensions, Kathleen was a pleasure to be around. Marian was relieved to find she liked her immensely already.

Surprisingly, tensions rose again without Amanda's help when Spencer Evans arrived as promised to retrieve his borrowed carriage, and so late in the day that Kathleen was obliged to invite him for dinner as well as put him up for the night. She was fresh out of extra rooms, though, what with Stuart staying over one more night, and the girls and their maid staying in separate rooms.

"The bunkhouse will do me just fine, Red," Spencer said, as he made himself comfortable on one of the sofas.

Marian took offense at his calling her aunt Red. Even when she heard Chad do the same thing later and realized it was Kathleen's nickname, it made no difference. She disliked the debonair Spencer right off because it was so obvious that Chad didn't like him.

Kathleen was a gracious hostess though, even if she didn't know Spencer that well. Stuart treated him like an old friend, but then she was to find that Stuart treated everyone that way unless they gave him cause not to. Chad barely said a word to him and vice versa, which was probably a good thing. The tension between those two was palpable.

And while it usually pleased Marian to be

ignored, as Spencer was doing to her, she found it rather insulting to be so *completely* ignored, as if he really didn't see her there at all. Most men looked at her, even if their eyes never lingered, but Spencer made a point of avoiding looking in her direction even once.

Fortunately, Kathleen hadn't tried to introduce them, after Spencer said right off that he'd met her niece yesterday. Niece, not nieces. But Kathleen would have assumed he was referring to the one who was present. While it was obvious to Marian that he'd meant the one he was anxiously waiting on to make an appearance.

Amanda was quite late in showing up, so late that Kathleen could postpone dinner no longer — the cook had sent her daughter Rita in three times with odd eye and head signals pointing toward the dining room. Flustered by then — she wasn't used to having so much company, nor keeping them waiting when such appetizing aromas were floating through the house — Kathleen herded everyone into the dining room.

As expected, or at least, Marian knew to expect it, Amanda arrived as soon as everyone was seated. Grand appearances were her forte, after all, and she loved making people wait on her. In her mind, she felt she was worth the wait. Most men thought so, too, unfortunately, and those present were no exception.

It couldn't be denied, though, that Amanda looked exceptionally beautiful. Her hair had been washed and artfully styled. There'd been plenty of time for Ella Mae to press one of her prettier dresses. And she'd slept most of the afternoon.

At any rate, she was all smiles when she announced, "I'm sorry to have kept you waiting, gentlemen. But you'll understand that after such a harrowing journey, I required a little extra rest."

Spencer and Chad both shot to their feet, stupid looks of bedazzlement on their faces. Even Stuart's mouth dropped open a bit as he stared at the vision before him. Only Marian noticed how their aunt had been deliberately excluded from the greeting — well, Kathleen probably noticed, too.

Amanda then proceeded to hold court there in the dining room. She was at her charming best, which meant she had decided to enthrall every man present, including Chad's father. She probably thought it would be amusing to have both father and son fighting over her.

She was in for a surprise though. Stuart might have been momentarily amazed by her beauty, but it didn't take long to see that he was more interested in the food than he was in a chit young enough to be his daughter.

Marian was close enough to hear him whisper to Kathleen, "Would you be mad at me, Red, if I bribed your cook over to my house?"

"Damned right I would."

He frowned, though it was obviously feigned. "Last night I figured I got lucky. But tonight, well, can't deny it now, this is some of the best grub I've ever eaten. You sure you'd get mad?"

"You can't go stealing a gal's cook, especially when that gal can't cook."

He laughed at her admonishment. "Then I'll just have to mosey on over this way more often, I guess. Hope you won't mind the company."

"Not at all. You're welcome anytime."

Marian noticed the blush about the time she realized her aunt was taken with Stuart. She couldn't tell if he was aware of it or not. The signs were subtle, but they were there: her aunt's blushes when nothing was said to warrant a blush, the covert looks when she thought no one would notice.

God, Marian hoped she wasn't as obvious where Chad was concerned. She probably was, but because no one ever paid attention to her, no one other than Ella Mae was likely to find out. And she was blushing a lot herself, for absolutely no reason other than she'd found herself sitting next to Chad at the table.

Their knees bumped. Their elbows collided. Marian whispered apologies each time, even for those that weren't her fault. He didn't seem to hear though, as he was too busy listening to every word out of Amanda's mouth. She stepped on his foot deliberately. Hard. He even missed that.

Dessert was being served when Chad said in an aside to her, "If I didn't already know how lacking in coordination you are, I'd think I was under attack. Now what the hell are you blushing for? I was only teasing."

Men didn't *tease* her. She just wasn't the sort anyone would feel comfortable teasing. And besides, she *had* been attacking him, because it was so obvious that he was going to make a fool of himself over Amanda.

She was saved from answering him because Amanda noticed his attention had strayed for a moment and typically addressed her next remark to him to get it back. Much to Spencer's annoyance, since he'd been trying to hold her attention solely to himself. Amanda definitely had a conquest in him.

Spencer had been telling her about his saloon. Marian found the name of it odd enough to mention it to Kathleen, who was seated to her left.

"Did I hear him correctly? His business is actually called the Not Here Saloon?"

"Yes."

"You don't find that an odd name?"

"No more than some others. The more outlandish the better seems to be the thinking when it comes to naming things out here."

"Now that you mention it," Marian allowed, "I suppose I have seen a few signs that were even more odd on the journey here, so odd, I couldn't imagine what sorts of businesses they actually were."

Kathleen nodded. "In this case, it used to be the No Tea Here Saloon. Descriptive, though unusual in itself. I think old Evans just wanted to make sure his customers wouldn't get confused about what sort of establishment they were in. But a letter or two wore off the sign over the years, the 'E' and the 'A' of Tea to be exact, and when a painter passed through town and was hired to do up a new sign, the fellow had one too many drinks himself before he got to painting, then left town before Mr. Evans got a look at the finished product. But he decided to go ahead and hang the new sign anyway, at least until he could find another painter."

"Which he never did," Marian concluded.

"Oh, more painters passed through town, one even set up shop and is still there. But by then, folks were used to Not Here. And as it happens, there's even a tombstone in the cemetery that reads 'Andy died Not Here, but over there, or was it yonder? Who knows, except anyone who was also Not Here to notice.' Be a shame to change the name after that was the general consensus."

Marian smiled, "Yes, that would immortalize the name, wouldn't it."

"Not that anyone knew who Andy was," Chad remarked from her other side. "He was just a sod buster passing through who died in the saloon right after the new sign went up. At the time, old Evans was getting a lot of ribbing over the sign, and our local tombstone carver thought he'd join in the fun with the cryptic inscription."

Marian was back to blushing. He'd actually been listening to her conversation rather than Amanda's? Actually, it wasn't *that* surprising once she thought about it.

Amanda might hold a man's rapt attention; but she did it with her beauty, not with a sparkling personality or interesting conversation. Her conversation tended to get boring quickly since it usually centered on herself.

# Chapter 22

Marian greeted the new day with a nice feeling of optimism. The sun was brightly shining. The smell of fresh-baked biscuits had floated upstairs. She liked the house she'd be living in and the room she'd been given. It was fairly large, with a lot of windows offering soft breezes. A corner room, with one side overlooking the bunkhouse, the stable, and the garden behind the house, the other offering a clear, unobstructed view as far as the eye could see.

She just might take up painting again, if she could find the supplies for it in Trenton. There was certainly room for an easel, and there was lots of light. She'd given up that enjoyable pastime several years ago, after she'd wanted to hang her best painting in the parlor at home, and her father had laughed at the idea, then proceeded to join Amanda in belittling her talent. She hadn't picked up a brush since.

But only her sister was around to scoff at her efforts now, and, she hoped, not for too much longer. Whether Amanda got what she desired and was allowed to return home with Kathleen's blessings to marry whomever she wanted, or whether she accepted the first offer of marriage she got here and dragged a new husband back home with her, Marian suspected it would be soon, since Amanda never dallied once she decided on a course of action. Which accounted for a good chunk of Marian's optimism.

Marian knew that the time for her to stop altering her natural appearance and start living a normal life was at hand. It was cause for excitement. She was so tired of pretending and tired, too, of having to insult men just so they'd avoid her. She'd burned all her bridges at home and had every eligible male there despising her. But she could have a fresh start here, if Amanda would just leave sooner rather than later.

There was only one man here who despised her so far, and she hoped she could keep it at that. That he happened to be the only man who had ever set her pulse to racing was too bad. But the rest of her optimism had to do with him. He might understand if given a full explanation. They might be able to start anew, with no further pretenses in the way — as long as Amanda didn't decide to use him as a means to get home.

That he was currently fascinated by

Amanda wasn't the monumental stumbling block it seemed to be. Most young men were fascinated by her until she revealed her true nature. Chad didn't seem to be completely under Amanda's spell yet, not if he could twice turn his attention toward her last night at dinner. He'd even *teased* her, or so he'd said. So maybe she hadn't done such a good job of making him despise her after all.

All wishful thinking on Marian's part as she dressed to go downstairs. But still, her optimism was riding high. In fact, she couldn't even remember the last time she'd been in such a good mood.

She'd probably been more worried about her reception here than she'd realized. After all, Kathleen was Mortimer's sister. She *could* have been just like him. But she wasn't. Not at all. And all Marian's fears had been put to rest with the warm welcome she'd received.

The large dining room was empty when she reached it. She found the kitchen, but only Consuela the cook was there. A big, hefty woman in her middle years who obviously enjoyed eating what she cooked, Consuela was of Mexican descent, but had been born and raised in Texas, so she spoke in the same lazy drawl Marian had been

170

hearing ever since she arrived.

Consuela shoved a heaping plate of food in Marian's hands without comment, more food than she could possibly eat at one sitting. Still she sat down at the worktable there and tried to make a dent in it.

"Am I late?"

The cook shrugged. "Depends what you have in mind to do. If you want to eat with Red, you'll have to get up at the crack of dawn. Work starts early around here, and this is a working ranch. But we have no formal mealtimes. I feed Red when she gets up, again when she comes in around midday — if she comes in. She doesn't always. And again just after dusk. Food is available anytime, though, so just come help yourself when you get hungry."

The woman looked a little embarrassed after saying all that. Marian guessed she wasn't used to talking so much, or of having anyone other than Kathleen or her daughter Rita invade her kitchen.

Marian smiled. "Thank you. I'll try to get up earlier, so I can eat with my aunt. I think I'd enjoy that."

The woman smiled back. Marian had a feeling she'd said the right thing and had just been accepted by a member of the household.

Amanda was still sleeping, of course. Twelve hours a day in bed was normal for her, whether she was asleep for all twelve of them or not. Beauty rest, she called it. Marian figured that Stuart had left for home earlier and that Spencer had either left or was a late sleeper owing to the hours he kept as the owner of a saloon. Chad, apparently, was back doing whatever it was he did for Kathleen, so she didn't expect to see him today.

She wandered outside after breakfast. The day was already getting hot, but it was a dry warmth, and there was a nice breeze swirling about the ranch to keep it from getting too uncomfortable — yet.

A dust cloud on the horizon indicated someone was riding toward the ranch. She hoped it was Kathleen, but as the horse got closer, she saw it was one of the cowhands. She waited by the stable, but he didn't ride that way. Instead he rode directly toward the bunkhouse nearby. He did notice her and tip his hat, even offered a friendly smile in passing.

The smile encouraged her to approach him and introduce herself before he disappeared inside the bunkhouse. She wasn't usually so bold, but she was going to be living here and didn't want to seclude herself from the other people who lived on the ranch.

"Good morning," she called out as the cowhand was dismounting. "I'm Marian Laton."

He glanced her way again, waited for her to reach him. "Lonny Judson, ma'am. I'm Red's foreman — or soon will be. Chad's been teaching me the job."

He was a nice-looking young man in his midtwenties with blond hair and green eyes. He sported a short, full beard a few shades darker than his hair. He probably thought it made him look older and thus more likely to succeed in the job he was being groomed for. It didn't, but then the few cowhands she'd seen yesterday when they arrived were much younger, more her age, so it probably didn't matter.

"A pleasure to meet you, Lonny. Will my aunt be coming home for lunch, do you know?"

"Doubtful, ma'am. A few head of cattle went missing during the night. She's been out scouring the range for them all morning."

Marian was disappointed. She'd been hoping to have a nice long talk with her aunt, to get to know her better.

"Is that a normal occurrence, for cattle to just wander off?"

"Yes, ma'am, though they usually don't go too far — unless they get helped."

"Helped?"

"Rustled."

"Rustled?"

He chuckled. "I'm sorry. I don't meet too many Easterners who might not understand some of the words we use out here. Rustling refers to the theft of cattle, especially when brands are changed to try to hide the fact. Men have been known to start ranches with rustled cattle, though most of the rustling these days is done for quick profit, with the cattle being herded south and sold across the border in Mexico."

Marian frowned. "Do my aunt's cattle get stolen often?"

"No, her herd isn't big enough to be the target of that kind of operation, not like Kinkaid's spread. She notices when just a single cow is missing, and goes looking for it. Big ranches like the one Chad's father owns have too many cattle for anyone to notice a hundred missing here and there, so rustlers tend to concentrate their efforts on those."

"It is illegal, right?"

He grinned at her. "Yes, ma'am, just not as harshly dealt with as horse stealing. It all depends on the rancher. Red ignores the loss, if she thinks a cow has been stolen to feed some hungry family. But if she catches any real rustlers whittling away at her herd, she escorts them to the sheriff pronto. It's not a killing offense, but it can earn a man a good chunk of time in prison, so most cattle rustlers are either desperate for food or hardened outlaws."

"Well, thank you for the information, Mr. Judson, I do appreciate it."

"Just Lonny, please. We're not formal out here."

"Lonny, then. I do worry about my aunt missing lunch, though. Do you think —"

"We have our own cook out on the range," he cut in. "She'll come by for some grub before the day is out. No need to worry about her, but if you'd like to come out to the range to find her, I can saddle you a horse."

"No, I — well, I'd like to, yes, but I haven't learned to ride yet."

"Carl's already headed out with the chuck wagon, or you could have ridden with him. You could ride double with me, I reckon. The herd isn't that far off today."

Marian smiled brilliantly. "I'd love to, thank you."

He blushed at her smile. "Just give me a few minutes to change clothes. I'm still damp after taking a spill in the river, when I thought to check the other side of it for tracks of the missing cattle. Been feeling the sniffles coming on, or I would have just let the sun continue to dry me off." He looked up at the cloudless, big blue sky. "And you won't have to stay out on the range all day. You'll be able to ride back with Carl. He don't stay out long after he serves up lunch."

"That will do nicely."

He nodded. "Better fetch a wide-brimmed hat, then, and some long sleeves. I don't want to be responsible for you getting sunburned."

"Sleeves I can manage, but I don't think my bonnets have the kind of brim you're talking about. Will a parasol do?"

He started to chuckle. "Well, it probably would, but it's also likely to get the boys laughing so hard, they won't get any more work done. We just don't see ladies riding on horses with parasols around here. One of the women in the house should have a hat you can borrow. I'll pick you up out front the house in five minutes."

Marian agreed and rushed off to get protection from the sun. Consuela did have a hat she could borrow. She'd seen it on a peg by the back door in the kitchen earlier. It was a few sizes too big for her, but it would do for today.

She was looking forward to the outing, was even feeling a little excited as she hurriedly changed her blouse, thinking she might run into Chad out on the range. It would be a nice distraction, since she had nothing else to occupy her time until she figured out what she could do to keep busy on a working ranch. She wanted to talk to her aunt about that, too.

# Chapter 23

The herd was grazing nearby, so the ride really wasn't that long, less than a mile. Tomorrow it might be much farther away. Lonny explained to Marian that the herd got moved around a lot, from water hole to water hole, to the river and back. It was fortunate that the herd was close by because Marian ended up having to sit sideways on the back of Lonny's horse, and the position was precarious, even nerve-wracking.

She hadn't considered the trouble her long skirt would cause when she'd accepted Lonny's invitation to ride out. He hadn't either. But she was loath to beg off because of that, would have been really disappointed if she'd had to, so she made do.

When the herd came into view, Marian was surprised. She'd heard more than once that Kathleen's herd was small in comparison to others, yet spread out as it was grazing, it looked like a tremendous number of cattle to her.

There was one odd animal in the midst that caught her eye. "What is that?" she asked.

Lonny didn't know what she was talking about, so she pointed. He chuckled then. "That's Sally. We don't see too many buffalo down this way, ain't too many herds of them left. But this one wandered in one winter, probably lost, and decided to stay. The cattle tolerate her because she doesn't cause any trouble. She's been here so long, the old girl probably thinks she's one of them."

Marian continued to stare. The buffalo was nearly twice the size of the other cows. And ugly. There was no better word to describe it. Well, it was ugly in a majestic sort of way. It was like nothing she'd ever seen before, and . . .

It happened too quickly. One minute she was riding along nicely, and the next she was being dragged through the dust. She shouldn't have taken her hand off of Lonny's back to point at the buffalo. She should have been paying attention and seen that they were about to cross a small ditch.

It wasn't that wide a ditch, but the horse must have figured it was and decided to leap across it — and unseat Marian in the process. At least she was able to grab Lonny's arm on the way down, not that that could have stopped her from landing in the dirt. But he was quick enough to clasp her forearm and hang on to it, so although she was completely off the horse, she didn't exactly land on the ground. She was pulled along a few feet while he fought to stop the horse, which turned about in circles with her weight and Lonny's, who was leaning over to keep his hold on her, dragging it to the side.

She was facing backward, her legs stretched out, so when he finally got the horse to stop, it was easier just to lower her the rest of the way to the ground. Easier for him, but sitting on the ground at a horse's feet didn't give her the feeling that she was safe yet. Not that she leapt to her feet. She was too dazed. Her arm felt like it had been pulled out of its socket. The oversize hat she wore had slipped forward, dislodging her spectacles, so they were sitting crookedly, halfway off her nose. And she was coughing from the dust she'd stirred up dragging her boots across the ground.

"Damn, that was close," Lonny said as he dismounted, acting as if he'd saved the day.

He had kept her from landing hard in the dirt, but she'd still fallen off and gotten the wits scared out of her, so she wasn't feeling especially thankful yet. "Maybe you should shoot that horse," she just about growled. "He's dumped two of us off his back today.

He's probably thinking it's a fun thing to do now."

The burst of laughter came from her other side, and unfortunately, she recognized it and felt her cheeks explode with hot color. "I was going to ask if you're all right," Chad said as he reached for her hand to help her up. "But if you can say something like that, I guess you are."

Marian didn't take his hand, not immediately. He'd come out of nowhere — well, she had vaguely heard another horse charging toward them. But that meant he'd witnessed her tumble, so her embarrassment was complete. He already thought she was as clumsy as you could get. She didn't have to reinforce that impression.

She took a moment to adjust her spectacles and put the hat back on straight before she accepted his hand. And got yanked to her feet. It was a good thing she'd given him her left hand because her right arm still smarted and she would have screamed if it had been pulled that hard. As it was, her borrowed hat got dislodged again, slipping backward this time. But it got caught on her bun and dislodged that, too, not completely, but enough that her hair was no longer tightly contained.

She was about ready to scream at that

point, and, finally looking at Chad and seeing how amused he still was, it was all she could do to restrain herself.

"I was admiring your buffalo a little too long," she said tightly by way of excuse.

He tipped his own hat back. "She ain't my buffalo. She's Red's buffalo. Your aunt allowed Sally to stay. Had I been here at the time, I would have just brought her home for dinner."

Lonny started snickering at Chad's double entendre. Marian would have missed it otherwise. "It's too ugly to eat," she pointed out.

That caused both men to laugh again. Lonny explained, "It don't have to be pretty to eat. But cattlemen prefer cattle. Buffalo is too tough. And Chad was just kidding. He's as protective of Sally as Red is. Figures the old gal has survived this long, she deserves to live out her days in peace."

Marian found that sentiment rather admirable, but she wasn't going to say so. She was still annoyed with Chad for laughing at her.

Chad finally got around to asking Lonny, "What's she doing out here?"

"She came out to see Red. She back yet?"

"No, but you know how she is. She won't give up until she finds those cows. Weren't you helping her?"

Lonny blushed at the stare he was getting from Chad. "I needed a change of clothes after my horse got spooked by a floating branch in the river and dumped me. I'll make another round now."

Marian suddenly found herself alone with Chad. There were cowhands nearby, some working with the cattle, some sitting around a campfire, but none of them close enough to keep her from feeling alone with him.

She was flustered, and not just from her fall now. "What are they doing?" she asked, trying to get Chad to take his eyes off of her.

He looked in the direction she nodded. "Branding some of the new calves."

"May I go watch?"

"If you can stand the stink."

She wrinkled her nose. She hadn't immediately associated branding with the burning of cow hair and flesh.

"Never mind. I probably should get back to the ranch, since my aunt isn't here. Will the cook with the wagon be here soon? Lonny mentioned I could ride back on the wagon."

"Carl's already left. He came by early, made us up a pot of chili, and took off to haggle for some fresh cheese from one of the farmers in the area."

She frowned, glancing behind her in the

direction of the ranch. "I suppose I could walk back. The house isn't that far away."

He lifted a black brow at her. "You'd rather walk a mile than ask me to take you back?"

The answer was absolutely yes, but she wasn't going to embarrass them both by saying it. At least she had an excuse to avoid such close contact with him, which she really didn't think she could handle. Being this close to him was bad enough because it was reminding her about that kiss the other night . . .

"I'd rather not get back on a horse just yet," she admitted.

He grinned, appeased. "Riding double when you can straddle the horse is one thing, but trying it sitting sideways, and behind the rider who's holding the reins is just asking for a fall — as you found out. The best way to learn that a horse isn't as dangerous as you're probably thinking it is now, is to get right back on one. I'll put you up front. There's no way you'll fall out of my arms."

He didn't wait for her to decline again. He mounted his horse, moved it closer to her, and held out his hand. She stared at it, chewing on her lip some. She knew she had the gumption to get back on the horse. That wasn't the problem. What scared her were her own desires. But what made her take his hand and mount the horse was her picturing herself walking across that open range, past cactus and scrub brush with him following along behind her on his horse, laughing at her supposed cowardice.

He did squeeze her in between the horn on the saddle — and him. It was a tight squeeze. She felt way too much of him, his leg, which both of hers were forced to rest over, his chest, and his arms closing her in.

"Relax," he said, amused by her stiffness. "I don't bite. And this won't take long."

He took off at a gallop. It was actually a fluid movement that didn't bounce her much at all. But all she could think about was him. Her heart was racing, and not because of the ride. She knew very well she wouldn't fall again.

His arms had her boxed in on both sides, one supporting her back, the other across her front. He held her tightly, probably to give her a feeling of security. At one point he flicked the reins and his arm brushed across her breasts. She nearly gasped out loud and hoped he didn't realize what he'd done, or what he was doing to her newfound desires.

"How do you like it here, now that you've settled in?" he asked her.

She was grateful for the distraction. "I love it, actually," she admitted. "But then there isn't much about this part of the country that I don't like."

"Really?"

She heard amazement in his tone, which wasn't surprising. He'd overheard a lot of Amanda's complaints and had probably thought she felt the same way, but just wasn't as vocal about it.

"Yes, really," she replied. "The people are so friendly — well, aside from the un-lawful element. And the scenery is magnificent. The vast openness is so different from back East, and the sunsets are so pretty they take my breath away."

"Okay, I believe you," he said with a chuckle. "I take it you're getting along with Red?"

"How could I not? She's as wonderful as you said she was. She's made me feel right at home, as if I'd always lived with her."

Chad had managed to distract her enough that they arrived at the ranch before she knew it. Instead of dismounting though, his arm wrapped tightly across her middle so he could just lower her off the horse. Even though he leaned over as he did so, his arm still ended up sliding up her chest and over her breasts before her feet touched solid ground again. She sucked in her breath, and her pulse leapt again, as her thoughts scattered and a swirling sensation started in her belly . . .

Suddenly she was on solid ground again, next to the porch, and Chad was saying, "You look silly as all hell in that hat."

That was just what she needed to hear to get her mind, and senses, back on an even footing. "Thank you for pointing that out," she said indignantly. "I would have used a parasol, but Lonny said I'd look silly as hell in that as well. Actually, those weren't his words. He said it more kindly."

"I was teasing," Chad said.

"Sure you were," she replied, yanking the hat down as far as it would go.

She tried to ignore his laughter as she marched stiffly into the house. Worse, she almost ran into Spencer and Amanda, who were just leaving the dining room.

Marian ran up the stairs so she would miss them, but not before she heard Amanda pout, "Must you go so soon?"

"I've already dallied longer than I should have, darlin'. But I couldn't leave without seeing you again."

Marian paused at the top of the stairs to watch them walk arm and arm to the front door. Their behavior seemed much too familiar for such a short acquaintance, but then Amanda occasionally dismissed formalities when she favored someone. And Spencer was an ideal candidate for her sister's favors. He was handsome, debonair, and a property owner. The mention that he had relatives back East would also make him suitable in Amanda's mind to marry and take home, if her first plan failed, and she couldn't sufficiently exasperate their aunt into sending her home to Haverhill with her inheritance in hand.

After watching his behavior last night, Marian had no doubt that Spencer was interested in her sister. And today he'd stuck around just for the chance to see Amanda once more. Now he was going to have to ride hard to get back to town before dark, and he'd have to leave the carriage behind. So much for his excuse for coming out to the ranch. But the main thing was that Amanda obviously liked him. Now if she would just think along the lines of matrimony where he was concerned . . .

# Chapter 24

Marian was sitting in one of several rocking chairs on the wide porch, gazing in amazement at one of the most extraordinary sunsets she'd ever seen. She'd witnessed some nice ones on the trip there, but nothing to compare with today's spectacular display. What had started pink and turned to orange had turned nearly blood red, and it completely covered the horizon. Even the size of the sun, before it sank completely, had been bigger than anything she'd ever seen before.

She knew that her aunt was home and she should go in the house to find her, but she was loath to miss even a moment of that sunset. So she was glad when the door opened and she turned to see that her aunt had found her instead.

"There you are," Kathleen said, and sat down in the rocking chair next to her.

"Is it okay if I call you Aunt Kathleen?" Marian asked hesitantly. "I know your friends call you Red, but Aunt Red just seems — odd."

"Sweetie, you can call me anything you like. We aren't formal out here."

"I've noticed that. I rather like it, actually. I'm not late for dinner, am I?"

"No, not at all. If anything, dinner will probably be late tonight," Kathleen said with a sigh.

She had been frowning when she opened the door, and looked very weary. She had shaken that off momentarily when she saw Marian there and had smiled in greeting, but she was back to looking weary again.

Marian was almost afraid to ask, knowing what her sister had been up to that day. "Is something wrong?"

"No," Kathleen started to deny, but then sighed again. "Well, yes. I just got my ear chewed off by Consuela. She's taken a dislike to your sister, I'm afraid. And my maid refuses to clean her room, refuses to go anywhere near her for that matter. It just took me thirty minutes to get her calmed down, and nearly that long to convince Consuela to send a plate up to Amanda as she requested, since she apparently doesn't want to eat with us tonight. That's why dinner will be late."

Marian leaned back in her chair, sighed a little herself. "I don't usually offer explanations, but you're family, as well as our guardian, so you have a right to know certain things about us. First off, Amanda and

I don't like each other. We never have, never will. You may have gathered that from overhearing that fight yesterday. She's made my life miserable from as far back as I can remember."

"Because she was Mortimer's favorite."

"Yes, and has rubbed that in my face continuously for most of my life. How did you — ?" Marian started to ask, then amended, "Never mind. Of course, you were there when we were young and probably saw it firsthand."

"Sweetie, that's the main reason I got the hell out of there as soon as I could. I didn't want to watch you two grow up with the same bitter feelings my sister and I shared."

"You have a sister?" Marian asked in surprise.

"Had," Kathleen corrected. "She died when we were fourteen. She was my twin — and Mortimer's favorite. He was only two years older than us. All three of us should have been close. But neither of them seemed to be able to share their feelings with more than one person at a time. They bonded early, were inseparable, did everything together, and excluded me from all of it. And like you, my face got rubbed in it. Neither of them was very nice."

"I'm sorry."

"No, *I'm* sorry, because I was afraid you'd experience the exact same thing with Mortimer, except in a father-daughter relationship, and it looks like you did. It certainly wasn't your fault. I hope you never thought that it was."

"No — well, maybe for a year or two when I was young," Marian admitted. "My mother helped me to get past that. She was always there for me, until she died. I remember she told me once, about big hearts and small hearts, and that not everyone could be blessed with a big one that had room to care for a lot of people. She promised me that mine was big, and that I was the lucky one for it."

Kathleen smiled. "I liked your mother. She was a good woman. I pitied her, too, for marrying a man who didn't love her."

"Why did he marry her then?"

Kathleen shrugged. "I never asked. Probably for the same reason most men of means marry, to have children so they can ensure they have someone to leave their wealth to. She was only a little disappointed that he didn't turn out to be an ideal husband, and she got along well enough with him, from what I could tell. I don't think she was raised to expect a grand love. Many women think a good provider is more important, and he was that at least."

"Were you raised to expect a grand love?"

Kathleen chuckled. "Sweetie, I wasn't raised to expect *anything*. My father was all business. It was a rare day that he spent any time with his family. He left the raising of his children completely in his wife's hands, and to be frank, those weren't capable hands. If anyone is to blame for the way Mortimer turned out, it was our mother. She taught him that he needed no one but himself to be successful, and maybe one other to share his triumphs with. I think she hoped to be that 'one other.' She really adored him. But he disappointed her in that."

"But isn't that what most boys are taught? That they can be successful at anything if they work at it hard enough?"

"Indeed," Kathleen agreed. "And if that was all she'd stressed, then he might have turned out much differently. But she also coddled him, she babied him, she made him believe that he could do no wrong."

"Like he did with my sister."

"And mine." Kathleen nodded.

"I'm still a bit amazed that I never heard about her. Not one mention in all these years."

"Actually, that doesn't surprise me at all.

Once she died, Mortimer put her out of his mind. I thought he and I might grow close after that. But no, once excluded from his affections, always excluded."

"I think Amanda did something like that when our father died. I thought she might be in shock, but it was more like she'd removed all memories of him, so it simply didn't bother her that he was gone."

"Don't let that sadden you."

Marian blinked. "Did I look sad?"

"For a moment. But don't be. The person Mortimer loved most was himself. People like that don't get mourned. It may have seemed like he loved my sister, and yours, but after many years of reflection, I've come to doubt that he really did. They were more like pets to him, things that needed to be nurtured so they'd be there to amuse him. Of course, I could be completely wrong." She ended in another shrug.

"You never noticed a similarity?" Marian asked curiously.

"In what?"

"Both sets of twins. You and your sister. Me and mine. Maybe he just didn't want to divide his affection between two people who looked exactly alike?"

"I hate to break this to you, sweetie, but you don't exactly look like your sister."

Marian stared at her aunt, watching Kathleen wince for having been so unflatteringly frank, then started to chuckle.

Kathleen sighed in relief. "I'm glad *you* find that funny. I'm sorry. Let me just pull this foot out of my mouth."

"It's all right, really." Marian grinned. "I was going to tell you anyway, before we got sidetracked on the subject of my father. You see, I don't need to wear these," she said, shoving the spectacles up her nose by habit.

Kathleen frowned. "You don't? Then why do you?"

"To make my life at least somewhat bearable. You see, Amanda is very jealous. She won't tolerate competition of any sort, especially not where men are concerned. So I've found it necessary to hide the fact that we look alike."

"But that's silly. So she'd lose a few suitors to you. She can't expect to have every man y'all cross paths with eating from her hand. Her hand just isn't big enough."

Marian chuckled again, amazing herself that she could find anything amusing about this. But then her aunt's perspective *was* refreshing. And it was nice to be able to talk about her problem with someone other than Ella Mae.

"Well, that's just the thing. She does —"

"Dang," Chad cut in, coming around the corner and seeing them there on the porch. "Don't tell me I missed dinner."

Kathleen stood up. "No, not at all. Goodness, I didn't realize it was getting so late. I was having a nice chat with my niece and let the time escape me. Come on in, children. Consuela isn't in a mood today to have her food getting cold."

Marian didn't follow her aunt inside immediately. She needed a moment to compose herself, since all of her senses had leapt with excitement — and alarm — at the first sound of Chad's voice. Had he heard what they were discussing before he came around the corner?

Surely not. They had been talking quietly. And although he was standing there at the door waiting for her to go inside before him, his expression was normal. Then it wasn't . . .

He grinned and said, "Where's the hat?"

# Chapter 25

Dinner was very nice that evening, even though the food was nearly cold. Kathleen was embarrassed a bit about that, since her cook was renowned for serving her creations at the perfect temperature, no matter how long people were delayed in coming to the table. That it wasn't that way tonight was Consuela's way of letting the household know that she wasn't happy.

Of course the reason for her displeasure wasn't there to notice it. But Marian figured the odds were pretty good that the food sent up to Amanda had been much colder. It had been really stupid of her sister to insult the only cook in the house. But then her sister's options had been limited, since Kathleen only employed the two household servants.

Cold though it was, the food was still tasty, Consuela being such a marvelous cook. And the conversation was relaxed with just the three of them present. Kathleen was chatty and explained a bit about what she did during the day. It certainly wasn't a routine one would expect a woman to be doing — deciding which cows to breed and which to take to market, nursing motherless calves, chasing down strays.

"I'd like to help," Marian offered. "That is, if you think I might be useful. I don't mind hard work."

Kathleen looked a bit skeptical. "There isn't really much that's suitable for a lady to do around here. Don't you have a pastime you enjoy? Reading, embroidery, something like that?"

"I used to paint," Marian said a bit shyly, not very confident of her talent after her family's derision. "I was thinking I might check in Trenton, to see if there are any supplies I can buy there to start." Kathleen was smiling, so she added a bit defensively, "Not a good choice?"

"On the contrary, I see we have even more in common than I thought. I used to paint as well. In fact, my old supplies are around here somewhere. I never find the time for it anymore, but you're more'n welcome to dig all that stuff out and make use of it."

"I'd like that. Thank you. I'd also like to learn to ride. I'd love to join you occasionally, when you ride out to check on your stock."

"You've never ridden at all?"

"Prior to today, no, and today wasn't very

— successful — as I'm sure you've heard. Father kept two coaches, and a carriage for the summer, but no horses just for riding, so Amanda and I never had an opportunity to learn."

"Well, we'll definitely have to take care of that," Kathleen said, and looked at Chad. "Would you mind teaching her?"

He put his fork down, but didn't answer for a moment. Then with a glance toward Marian and a smile, he said, "Sure, be glad to. Long as I don't get blamed if you take a few spills while getting the hang of it."

Marian stared at him. Kathleen chuckled. "He's joking. It takes a lot of effort to fall off a horse when you're in control of it, and you don't need to put that much effort into it."

When Chad laughed, too, Marian realized that Kathleen was teasing her. She grinned to show she didn't mind. But she wasn't the least bit used to being teased. It was something she'd like to get used to, though.

She was still embarrassed, not because of the teasing, but because of Chad's pause before he'd answered. He didn't really want to teach her to ride. That was obvious, and she couldn't blame him. She'd done a good job of making him want to avoid her.

But, apparently, he found it difficult to

say no to Kathleen. Marian could understand that. She would probably find it just as difficult. Kathleen was simply too nice, the kind of person you didn't want to disappoint.

Marian didn't want Chad teaching her to ride either, but for a different reason. She was finding it harder and harder to be in his presence and pretend indifference to him.

She wasn't going to insult him in front of Kathleen, however, by refusing his offer. She could do that when they were alone, no doubt to his great relief.

They were about halfway through the main meal when Chad glanced around and asked somewhat in surprise, "Amanda isn't joining us?"

Marian almost laughed. She had the feeling that he'd only just noticed Amanda's absence. If so, that was a firm indication that he wasn't deeply enamored with her yet.

Kathleen merely said, "She spent most of the day in her room resting, and wanted to take her meals there as well. Poor dear must be really exhausted after the trip, to need so much rest."

Marian almost choked. Poor dear? She wondered how long it would take Kathleen to realize there was nothing "poor" or "dear" about Amanda. She wished she'd been able to finish explaining about her sister. Kathleen deserved some type of warning before Amanda got nasty in her campaign to get shipped home with permission to do as she pleased.

Marian hoped Chad would leave right after dinner so she could spend a little more time alone with her aunt before she retired for the night. It was still early. They could finish their talk. But as it happened, Kathleen had no sooner escorted them back to the porch and waited until they were seated there, then she yawned and announced that she was turning in early.

Marian should have done the same, but that would have been yet another insult to Chad. It would have smacked of cowardice as well, and she'd rather not add to all the other bad impressions she'd made on him.

Still, she felt immensely uncomfortable as the door closed and Kathleen's footsteps faded away. She hoped he didn't expect conversation. No, he wouldn't. They didn't like each other, so why should they talk? For that matter, why should they stay in each other's company when they didn't like each other? Why didn't *he* leave?

There wasn't much light on the porch. No lamp had been lit out there since the lamps in the main gathering room hadn't been turned off yet, and some of their light spilled out through the two windows that faced the porch.

She tried not to look in Chad's direction. It was hard. The one time she did, she found him staring at her, at her lips in particular. He was probably just lost in thought and didn't realize he was staring. But still, it gave her gooseflesh, having his eyes on her.

"What is Chad short for?" she found herself asking out of pure nervousness.

"Short for?"

"It's a nickname, isn't it?"

"No, darlin', it doesn't get any longer."

She heard the humor in his tone, which annoyed her. It had been a natural mistake. The name didn't usually stand on its own. And she should take him to task over that "darlin'," except she'd heard for herself how common the use of that word was out here, no different than the old-timers calling her "missy," or the train attendant calling her "ma'am." It meant nothing. There wasn't a speck of endearment in it.

"Thank you for clearing that up for me," she said a bit stiffly.

"My pleasure."

She had a feeling he would have tipped his hat if he'd been wearing it just then rather than holding it in his hand. She'd like to tip his rocker over. He could be so damn irritating — no, it probably wasn't even him, it was her reaction to him, her nervousness, her — wanting him when she knew she couldn't have him.

"By the way," she said. "You don't need to teach me to ride. I'll manage —"

"I said I would," he interrupted.

She was letting him off the hook. Couldn't he see that?

"Yes, but my aunt shouldn't have put you on the spot like that."

"It's no big deal," he replied, though impatience crept into his tone.

"You've already done quite enough," she pointed out, her own tone getting sharper over his stubbornness. "And I'm sure you have much more important things to do than to waste your time on me."

"I said I'll teach you," he said, his voice getting much louder.

"You don't have to," she gritted out.

"I'll teach you, dammit!"

"Fine, you do that!"

She stood up to leave in a huff and wasn't about to bid him good night or anything else. Stubborn, exasperating, contrary man. But he shot to his feet at the same time, probably with the same intention.

They collided instead, there in front of

the door. His hands gripped her shoulders to keep her from falling, and started to set her away at arm's reach. His eyes were drawn to her lips again though, stayed there for a long moment, and suddenly he was yanking her back toward him.

He was kissing her. *Her.* There was no mistake this time. Her spectacles were firmly in place, her hair as tightly drawn back as ever, and she was wearing one of her dull, it-had-seen-better-days dresses.

It was so unexpected she just stood there, shocked, and let his mouth move heatedly over hers. But not for long. There was just too much passion in the kiss for her not to respond, especially when her emotions had already been stirred up with anger. It was exchanging one passion for another and it was a smooth exchange. . . .

He set her away from him, quite abruptly. "It was you that night Leroy found us," he said in an accusing tone, "pretending to be your sister."

Marian stiffened. He knew they were twins? But she wore her disguise so well!

"Who told you we're twins?"

"No one had to tell me, darlin'. I'm not the one who wears spectacles, you are."

So that's why he'd kissed her? Just to make a comparison with that other kiss, because he hadn't been sure it was her that night, but now he thought he was? That wasn't very flattering, but then she was the sister who never got flattered. She should have known, though, that he wouldn't kiss her just because he wanted to.

Disappointed more than she wanted to admit, she said, "I never deliberately pretend to be my sister. Amanda enjoys little tricks like that, I don't."

Suddenly he looked very embarrassed, if you could go by his darkened complexion. Apparently he was tongue-tied, too. "I — that —" he began, then closed his mouth before he stuck his foot in it.

She realized he was confused because she hadn't admitted anything. She'd merely stated a fact. Just as well. She didn't want him to guess her feelings for him when he still had designs on Amanda.

"There's no need to explain," Marian said. "I understand that was a mistake." She opened the door to leave before her throat closed up on her, and added curtly, "Just don't let it happen again."

She heard a thud against the closed door. It was some consolation to think he'd thrown his hat at it. She hoped it was dented out of shape. Serve him right for trampling on her emotions like that.

# Chapter 26

Marian was awakened an hour before dawn by a slamming door and shouts in the hall. Her sister was on the rampage about something.

At home, Marian would have turned over and put a pillow over her ears to try to get back to sleep. This home was new, though. The people in it weren't used to Amanda's tactics yet. So she crawled out of bed with a disgusted sigh and tried to find her robe in the dark.

"I need another room!" Amanda was shouting in the hall. "The one you gave me is intolerable. It's bad enough this house is as rustic as an old log cabin, but it's also as hot as a furnace."

Kathleen had apparently arrived to find out what the noise was all about, because her voice, while not loud, was still clear, "There are no other rooms."

"Find one! Unless you want me sleeping on the porch where all your neighbors will notice."

"Aside from the fact that my husband and I used to do that during a hot spell or two, we have no neighbors anywhere near enough to notice."

"So you're going to force me to sleep on a porch? This is how you intend to conduct your guardianship?" Amanda demanded.

Having finally found her robe in the dark, Marian arrived in the narrow hall outside the bedrooms in time to see Kathleen's vivid blush. Kathleen had brought a lamp with her. Amanda was standing there in her thin underwear with her hands on her hips, putting on a good act of being furious.

"I will be happy to give you my room, but it won't make much difference," Kathleen said, still trying to keep her voice calm. "You haven't adjusted to this warmer climate yet. And I do remember what it was like, my first months here. We arrived in the spring and were still building the ranch that first summer. It was horrible. But by the following summer the heat wasn't so bad. We had adjusted to it."

"Why are you telling me this?" Amanda demanded. "I hope you know I could care less?"

Marian sighed in exasperation. She should be immune by now to feeling disgust over something she'd experienced so many times before, but she wasn't, at least not when other people were involved.

She crossed her arms over her chest, and asked her sister dryly, "Did you force yourself to stay up all night, Amanda, just so you could wake the household before dawn? Of course you slept for most of the day yesterday, so I suppose it wasn't all that hard."

"I can't sleep in this miserable heat!"

"Of course you can. I managed to with no problem. It wasn't even that hot last night."

"And just how would you know?" Amanda shouted. "You were *sleeping!*"

Having done what she'd intended, which was to wake Kathleen and put her into an amends-making frame of mind, Amanda slammed back into her bedroom. Kathleen's shoulders slumped, either with relief or dejection, it was hard to tell which. Marian put her arm around her aunt and urged her to follow her downstairs.

"It will be dawn soon," she said. "No point in trying to get back to sleep. Let's make some coffee and finish that talk we started last night."

Kathleen nodded, but admitted, "I'm not very good at making it."

"I don't know how either, but I watched Chad make it one morning. Between us, we should come up with something that's at least drinkable."

It wasn't, and they both laughed over the

result, which eased some of the tension for Kathleen at least. Marian knew Consuela would be arriving soon, so she immediately broached the subject at hand.

"What you witnessed upstairs was mostly, if not entirely, contrived," she began.

"She was drenched with sweat," Kathleen replied. "And I do remember how miserable I was with the unusual heat my first months here."

"She was drenched with water," Marian corrected her. "On her temples, forehead, neck, and chest. If you had looked closely, you wouldn't have found her drenched at any of the normal places where sweat first gathers. Not that it really matters. It was still a performance for your benefit."

"Why?"

"So you'll send her home with your blessing to marry whomever she wants."

Kathleen frowned. "I can't do that. I didn't ask for the responsibility, but I was given it, to make sure you girls aren't taken advantage of by fortune hunters or other men of questionable motives."

"I know, but you see, that doesn't matter to Amanda. She's very self-centered."

"Like my brother was?"

"Yes. But unlike your brother, she can, and will, get very nasty if she doesn't get her way. She didn't want to come here. She wants to go home. And she really resents that now she must get permission to marry, when she always expected our father to let her marry whomever she chose."

"Would he have?"

"Probably," Marian said. "Well, it would have been easy for him to, since all her suitors at home were quite acceptable to him. She's also furious that her inheritance is out of her reach until she does marry. She would have married immediately just for that if it didn't require your blessing. She just can't stand being denied anything."

"So the problem is that my approval is required, as was stipulated in your father's will? It's too bad some of her suitors didn't elect to follow her here so I could meet them. I have a feeling that what my brother would have found acceptable isn't necessarily what I would deem acceptable."

"That's quite possible. Personal wealth was the only criteria he ever considered important in a suitor. The same goes for my sister, actually; at least, she won't even look at a man unless he's well-to-do. And some of those suitors *would* have followed her, to the ends of the earth if it meant they could win her. She's very good at keeping men dangling — and from finding out what she's really like."

"Is one of them coming then?" Kathleen asked. "That might be a solution."

"No. The one who offered to come, she cut him to the quick. And we departed so soon after the funeral, the others didn't even know she was leaving town."

"Well, we have good men here for her to choose from, a few who are even quite rich," Kathleen replied. "I can think of at least four offhand that I could easily approve of. She already knows one of them."

"Chad?"

"Yes, he's probably considered the best catch around these parts."

It wasn't going to be easy for her to talk about Chad and Amanda as a pair. She tried to be unbiased in doing so, without revealing her own feelings in the matter.

"She hasn't exactly been nice to him, since she had the impression that he was just an employee of yours, and that put him beneath her notice. Which doesn't mean he's not already smitten with her. Most men who meet her usually are. And now that she knows he's more than that, she might even consider him as a last resort."

Kathleen chuckled. "Chad would probably be highly insulted, to hear himself called a 'last resort.'"

Marian felt the blush starting. "Please don't repeat that to him. It's certainly not my opinion. It's just that Amanda isn't going to want any man from this part of the country when she has her mind set on forcing you to send her home so she can do as she pleases. But if she doesn't get her way in that, then yes, she'll probably pick a man here just to get it over with."

"Just to get it over with?" Kathleen repeated.

"If she does marry someone here, she'll badger him and make his life miserable until he agrees to take her home to Haverhill because she won't stay here any longer than she has to."

"I hate to say it, sweetie, but it would be a rare man indeed who would uproot himself for his wife's convenience. I turned down a half dozen proposals back home waiting for a man who didn't want to stay in Haverhill; I knew all those others would never consider leaving. A wife doesn't exactly have a choice in the matter."

"I know that, and you know that, but Amanda views things only from her own perspective, and that doesn't include being told she can't have what she wants."

"Yes, but she's gotten away with that because my brother let her. A husband isn't likely to tolerate that sort of nonsense."

"I hope you're right, Aunt Kathleen. I'd still pity the man if she has to marry one here. Actually, I'd pity any man she marries, no matter where. It's unfortunate, but I really don't think she will make a good wife. She doesn't have it in her to make someone else happy. She's too self-centered."

"Now that's too bad. Sounds like I'd be doing a man a disservice to allow him to marry her."

Marian groaned to herself. She hadn't wanted to give *that* impression. She wanted Amanda to get married just as much as Amanda now did.

"Not if he knows what to expect and wants her anyway," Marian offered.

"I suppose," Kathleen agreed reluctantly.

Marian sighed. "I didn't tell you all this to make your job seem impossible, merely to warn you about what to expect so you aren't manipulated into doing something against your better judgment."

"I understand that, sweetie, and I do appreciate it." And then Kathleen chuckled. "If I didn't know better, I'd think that giving me guardianship of Amanda was Mortimer's way of getting even for my taking myself out of his sphere of influence. He didn't like me, but he did like rubbing

213

my nose in how useless he thought I was."

"I'm sure he didn't die before Amanda was settled in marriage just to spite you."

Kathleen grinned. "I know."

Marian smiled back, understanding now that her aunt had just been trying to lighten the mood some. She still had to caution her, "If you'll keep in mind that what you've seen so far is nothing compared to how bad it can get, you'll have an easier time dealing with it."

"What about yourself? It doesn't bother you that you have to wait on your inheritance until you marry?"

"I haven't given it much thought, actually, but then it's not something I expected this soon anyway. I guess I don't see marriage as a form of independence the way Amanda does."

"You aren't hankering to go home like she is?"

"No, I could care less if I ever see Haverhill again. Besides, I kind of like it here in Texas. I probably would have made a good pioneer."

Kathleen chuckled. "I know what you mean. I loved Texas from the moment I stepped off the boat. I'm glad those few mishaps you had on the way here didn't affect your opinion adversely."

Marian grinned. "I wouldn't exactly call train and stage robberies mishaps, but in reflection, they were probably more exciting than frightening, at least, certainly something I never would have had the chance to witness at home."

"It's too bad your sister didn't view them that way." Kathleen shook her head. "It's amazing that you two turned out so different."

"Not really. She's a result of our father's indulgence. I'm a result of his indifference."

"I'm sorry — no, actually, I'd say you were the lucky one. It probably didn't seem like it while you were growing up, but I'm sure you've realized it by now."

Lucky? Not yet. But soon — unless she had to stand back and watch Amanda marry Chad as a last resort. For her aunt's sake, though, she nodded. She'd given Kathleen enough to think about. The warning had been necessary. Discussing her own pathetic situation wasn't.

# Chapter 27

Marian wandered out to the stable later that morning. Her intention was to ask the first cowhand she came across if he wouldn't mind teaching her to ride. When Chad got around to setting up a time for his coerced lesson, she really hoped to be able to tell him no thanks, that she'd already been taught.

She was looking forward to being able to ride, even feeling somewhat impatient about it. Being so isolated out on the ranch had a lot to do with it. Spencer's carriage might still be taking up space in the stable, since he'd left too late to take it back to town with him, but it wasn't there for her use even if she knew how to hitch it up and drive it. Walking anywhere was out of the question, too, not that there was anything nearby worth reaching.

But unlike her sister, Marian already had it pretty much set in her mind that Texas was going to be her home permanently, and by choice. There wasn't a single thing that she missed about Haverhill. There was really nothing there for her but bad memories, so she had no desire at all ever to return there, or anywhere else back East, for that matter. And she rather liked this part of the country, despite the heat.

The openness, the raw, untamed nature of the place, traveling for days without seeing any form of settlement, the friendliness of the people — well, discounting the lawless element. It could be frightening, but it was also exhilarating. You simply never knew what was going to happen next. People didn't just live here, they adapted, they did without, they helped each other. They survived.

Yes, she would stay here. And whether she ended up living in a town or a good day's ride away from one like Kathleen did, she wanted to learn the things that everyone else seemed to take for granted out here. Riding a horse was at the top of that list.

She'd even borrowed one of her aunt's odd-looking riding skirts, or rather, breeches for the task. Made out of rawhide leather, the garment was so loose and wide, it looked like a skirt if she were just standing about in it, but once mounted on a Western-style saddle, they were more obviously very baggy breeches.

She was disappointed to find the stable

completely empty, at least of people. There were four horses in stalls there, two of them Spencer's, and several more in the corral next to the stable. She decided to get acquainted with the horses, as long as she was there, and tried coaxing one to her for petting. It just swished its tail and ignored her. She tried another, but got ignored again.

She was hesitant to get any closer, with the stalls so narrow and the memory clear in her mind of seeing a horse gone wild on the street when she was a child. With its bucking, kicking, and biting, that horse had injured five men who tried to get it under control before its enraged owner finally shot it. She'd heard someone say how stupid the fellow was, that it was his own ill treatment of the animal that had caused it to rebel. None of these animals looked mistreated, but still, a memory like that was hard to shake off.

"Bring a sweet with you next time if you want to get his attention."

Marian turned toward the front of the stable. With the verbal coaxing she'd been doing, she hadn't heard anyone approach. And with such bright daylight directly behind him, he was just a dark silhouette there in the doorway to the stable, sitting quietly on his horse, his hat tipped down low. But she knew that voice, knew it very well. Her heart was already beginning to pick up speed.

"I was just introducing myself," she explained.

He chuckled, rode farther in until the glare from outside was no longer obscuring his features from her. "That's fine, except, without an offering, they could care less — which you've probably noticed."

She grinned. "Yes, they've been trying to make me think I'm not really here."

"A treat or two, and they'll remember the sound of your voice and perk up whenever they hear it, which is why it's not a good idea to favor them all unless you want to fill your pockets with sweets. Just concentrate on the one you'll be riding for now."

"Which is?"

"None of these. There's a mare out in the corral, docile, perfect for a new rider. You ready to do this?"

It was rather obvious that she was, considering where he found her. And she wasn't going to get into another "you don't have to" argument with him about it.

So she replied, "If you aren't busy."

He nodded, dismounted. "I think Red has an old saddle still around, smaller than the standard ones kept for the hands, which should do you fine."

He disappeared into the tack room, came out loaded down with horse trappings. "Follow me," was all he said as he headed toward a side door that opened directly into the corral.

It was a two-tiered door, and the top half had already been open. She stood out of the way as he tossed a rope around the neck of one of the horses and led it inside to a stall. The other two horses both tried to follow. He let one do so, but closed the lower half of the door again on the mare. She gathered her lesson was going to take place out in the corral.

The mare she was to get acquainted with wasn't a very pretty horse. A splotchy gray, with tail and mane that might have been white at some point, but were stained a yellowish gray now. She wasn't as big as the other two horses had been, though, which made her ideal for the purpose — less distance to fall from.

Chad returned after a few moments and started picking up the gear he'd dumped on the ground. "Pay attention," he said without glancing at her. "In case you ever need to do this yourself. It's not likely you ever will, since there's usually at least one hand on the property who tends to the horses and stable."

"Where is he?"

"Sick today, or at least he was this morning when we rode out. Which is why I'm back."

Well, she should have known he hadn't come back for her. Actually, he'd probably been quite disappointed to see her there in the stable when he rode in, might even have thought she was waiting on him. How embarrassing. But he'd given no indication that he was being put to a bother, and he began explaining everything he was doing as he did it.

When he finished, he fell silent and surprised her by removing all the gear he'd just dressed the horse in and piling it back on the ground. "Now you try it."

A test. She hadn't expected that. And she hadn't been paying complete attention to what he'd done either, which was his fault, for making her stand so close to him to watch. It certainly didn't seem to bother him, being that close to her, but it had definitely bothered her.

She had managed to put that kiss he'd given her last night out of her mind. She would never have been able to get to sleep if she hadn't. And she'd had other things to think of this morning, thanks to her sister. But now, standing next to him, so close she could even smell him, she could think of nothing else.

He had drunk some wine with dinner last night. Not very much, but still, some people got more daring — or stupid — after imbibing. She avoided all forms of alcohol herself. It made her act silly. Amanda did, too, since she couldn't abide not being in complete control of all her faculties. But so many times she'd watched Amanda's beaus get overloud, obnoxious, even excessively amorous, to the point of trying to steal kisses in front of others, and simply because they had a low tolerance for alcohol.

She didn't think Chad had such a low tolerance, but the wine probably did account for his audacity in wanting to compare kisses last night. She really wished he hadn't been so bold though. He'd just been conducting a test, didn't even consider that he might be getting her hopes up — then dashing them so thoroughly.

He'd seen through her disguise! No one had ever done that before. Of course, he didn't know it was just a disguise. He thought she really needed the spectacles. But still, he'd seen beyond them and figured out that she and Amanda were twins. With that knowledge, it wasn't odd at all that he might begin to wonder which one of them he'd kissed that night by the campfire, especially when Amanda had so completely ignored him the next morning.

He could have just asked Marian to clear up his confusion. He should have asked, rather than tried to figure it out on his own by comparing kisses. She might even have owned up to it. There wouldn't have been any reason not to since he knew they were twins. He'd been right, but what if he'd been wrong? Did he even once consider that and what it would do to her? And to accuse her of pretending to be Amanda, as if she'd done it deliberately!

He probably didn't know what to think now, or maybe he was just relieved that he hadn't made a mistake and kissed the wrong sister to begin with. But thankfully, they'd both elected not to embarrass themselves any further by mentioning that kiss again. In fact, his behavior thus far today was as if it hadn't happened.

Which was fine with her, except, it did happen, and it had been so nice, so incredibly thrilling, her first real kiss, at least, the first one meant for her and not because she'd been mistaken for her sister. A comparison, yes, for the wrong reason, yes, but still hers. Both times had been wonderful, but last night there had been much more passion.

It was that passion she was remembering now. Coupled with the heady emotions he always stirred in her when he was near, it was no wonder she couldn't concentrate on the task at hand. She'd found herself staring at *his* lips, at the hands that had pulled her to him, at the way his hair curled around his neck, the way his shirt stretched over taut muscles as he moved about, things she shouldn't be looking at. But she couldn't seem to help it.

The test. What was first? The blanket. She picked it up, shook it out, twice, spread it over the mare's back, took longer than necessary smoothing out the wrinkles, straightening it, all the while trying to steady her breathing, which was getting quite erratic.

"She's not going to her first shindig," she heard him say with distinct impatience behind her. "It doesn't have to be perfect."

She nodded, kept her blush averted, reached for the saddle. It was heavier than it looked, though with a little straining, she lifted it off the ground. She was doubtful she could get it up on the mare's back though.

He must have guessed her thoughts because he said, "You'll probably have to swing it a bit first, get some momentum going to help."

She tried that, and ended up tossing it right over the mare's back. That got a chuckle out of Chad. He even moved around the docile mare to retrieve the saddle, brought it back to her in one hand.

"At least you know you can lift it now," he commented, some humor still in his tone. "Try not to let go of it this time so you can stop it from sliding over. And don't hit her with it. Horses don't like saddles to begin with, but they really don't like having one thrown at them."

Was he teasing? Probably not. And he was going to make her do it again, when he'd already conceded that it was something she'd probably never have to do on her own. This part of the lesson was a "just in case" part. Or was it his way of getting even for having to teach her? Now *that* she could believe, and it made her stiffen her spine, determined to get the mare saddled if it killed her.

It took two more tries. When the saddle finally landed where it was supposed to, Marian's smile of accomplishment was brilliant. His was genuine, which made her castigate herself for attributing to him petty motives he didn't have.

Her breathing was even more labored by then. She'd worked up a sweat with her exertions. But that had nothing to do with why she started trembling when he touched her to turn her back toward the saddle, which still needed to be strapped on.

He must have felt her quivering flesh. He couldn't help but hear the heavy breathing, might even be able to hear her heartbeat, it was so loud.

He drew in his own breath, released her like a hot brand, said sharply, "Don't do that."

Like I can help it, she wanted to growl. But she moved away from him, took several deep breaths. It didn't help. Something had been stirred up inside her that wouldn't be quelled.

And then she heard in an angry undertone, "Damn, you couldn't get more explicit with an invitation if you tried. Do I look like I'm made of stone?" just before he dragged her back into the stable.

# Chapter 28

The lesson wasn't over as Marian had at first thought. It was just beginning. It just no longer had anything to do with horses. But she didn't know that when Chad pulled her back into the much cooler stable.

She couldn't see anything for a moment, the quick transition from such bright sunshine outside to the shadowed interior made the stable seem darker than it was. But by the time her eyes adjusted to the dim light, she found herself lying on a pile of hay in one of the empty stalls, Chad's body half-covering hers, his mouth preventing any protests, not that she thought to make any.

She was too dazed. It had happened too quickly. And she wasn't even sure why. What he'd muttered about invitations and stone didn't make much sense to her. That he was kissing her again didn't either. They had agreed the kiss last night was a mistake, at least, she'd assumed they had. And he hadn't been drinking this time. So she was running out of reasons to explain why he'd *want* to kiss her.

He was doing more than that. She didn't realize it at first, his kiss was so consuming. But when his hand covered her breast, the abnormal heat from it was the first clue that there was no longer a cloth barrier between them. Her shirt was unbuttoned, her camisole pulled down.

Panic was her immediate reaction, that she was half-naked somewhere other than in the privacy of her bedroom. She managed to break the kiss off for a moment, and gasped out, "What if someone comes in here?"

"Do you care? I don't."

She had to think about that. How could she think when he was still caressing her breast? Actually, if he stopped right now, she'd probably cry. And no one was likely to intrude at this time of the day. No, she didn't care either. If someone did show up, she would worry about it then.

She let him find her mouth again. She wrapped her arms around his neck, her silent answer. His kiss got more ravenous, his tongue exploring deeply. She was losing all thought again, caught up in a tide of turbulent sensations far beyond her meager experience.

His caresses became more bold, slightly rough, his breathing as ragged as hers. She had a feeling he was caught up in his own passion. She hoped he had more control of it than she did.

His mouth moved lower, sucked on her neck. It tickled, it fired her blood, made her want to curl around him. Lower still and his lips surrounded her breast. She knew his mouth wasn't that hot, yet she felt scorched there, was afraid he was trying to fit the entire mound in his mouth. Impossible, her breasts weren't that small, yet it didn't seem as if he was going to give up trying.

The sensations were getting deeper. Vaguely, she felt him fighting with her skirt, realized he wanted it off. He was having no luck, so he tried a different route.

"There should be a law against women wearing breeches," he growled, when his hand couldn't get very far up from the bottom of the loose riding skirt.

She felt like laughing. She surprised herself by giving in to the urge, then teased in a prim tone, "Did you really want to get naked in a stable, on a pile of hay?"

"Use your imagination. I *know* you've got a good one. Imagine you're lying on silk."

"Was that a yes?"

He laughed now, a great burst of laughter. He rolled over, pulled her with him, positioned her so she was sitting across his waist, her knees bent at his sides, just about all of her within reach of his hands. He made quick work of getting rid of her shirt, spread it out on the hay next to them. Her camisole was pulled over her head. That, too, became part of the blanket he was fashioning on top of the hay.

The lifting of the camisole dislodged her spectacles, though, which she fixed automatically from habit. But he reached for those, too. Her reaction to that was also automatic. She leaned back, avoiding his reach.

"Take them off," he said simply.

"No."

He started to frown, but her breasts distracted him. His hands covered them both now, kneading them. Her head dropped back with a moan she couldn't contain. With her legs straddling him, she was feeling a new heat now, deep in her core.

"Stand up, where you are," he said, his voice more husky than usual.

She didn't want to lose the touch of his hands, but she could find no reason to deny him this time. She wasn't sure she *could* stand up, though, because she was trembling. She managed it, but looking down at him as he began to slowly unbutton his shirt, her knees nearly buckled.

"Let your hair down," he ordered next.

She complied immediately, pulled out a

few pins, shook her head, and the whole golden mass came tumbling down her back, over her shoulders, curled about her waist.

"I knew it would be that long — and beautiful. No more buns for you. If I see you wearing another bun, I'll personally steal all your hairpins."

She grinned at the thought of him sneaking into her bedroom to steal hairpins. Actually, if she happened to be in it at the time . . .

"Unfasten that contraption you're wearing so I can get rid of it."

She sucked in her breath again since he happened to be unfastening his pants as he said it. It took a really long moment for her to think clearly enough to realize the "contraption" he meant was her skirt. She fumbled with it, her fingers trembling even more. And he did yank the skirt down the second he saw it loosen.

He sat up then, tore out of his shirt, barely sparing a moment to add it to the improvised blanket. He pressed his cheek against her lower belly and put his arms around her. His hands slid up her back, then slowly down, over her hips, then lower, taking her bloomers with them.

Though the air wasn't stirring in the confines of the closed stall, she felt a slight chill, standing there like that, but only for a moment. His breath was hot on her belly, his chest warm against her thighs. He was gently lifting one of her legs to unlock them from her remaining clothes. Her hands went to his head, her fingers sliding through his hair. Baby-fine soft it was, the touch giving her such pleasure, she realized she'd wanted to do that ever since she'd met him.

When he lifted her other leg, she lost her balance and slid down him until her knees touched the ground on either side of him again. The hand he'd placed behind her head pulled her lips back to his. And while kissing her, he somehow managed to get her boots off as well.

The next thing she knew, she was being laid down on the improvised blanket, and he was grinning down at her as he asked, "It's silk, right?"

She would have said absolutely, would have agreed with anything at the moment, for that matter, but she couldn't find her voice. He looked so boyish with that grin, so handsome, she felt a swirling sensation in her belly that made her feel faint. And he must have sensed what she was feeling because his expression turned so sensual she caught her breath.

His mouth was back on her, and his

hands, infinitely gentle as they caressed her bare skin, exploring what couldn't be reached before. She questioned nothing he did, just accepted the pleasure of his touch and tried to concentrate on each moment, each new sensation so that she would always remember it. But it was happening so quickly, and she was so caught up in the passions he stirred in her, if she remembered anything at all it would be the heat, the craving, and her amazement that it was even happening.

He stopped kissing her so that he could watch her as his hand trailed down her body. His look was filled with awe, or was it her imagination? But he did seem overly taken with the sight of her bared limbs, or maybe just surprised, since the clothes she tended to wear gave no clue that she was as shapely as she was. Either way, she was amazed she wasn't embarrassed, to have him looking at her like that. Well — maybe just a little.

His hand continued to move down her thigh, then slid up the inner side of it, and stopped at the junction. She gasped, which brought his mouth back to hers. But it wasn't that gasp he tried to catch, it was the ones he knew would follow when his fingers delved into her. Her nerves leapt in pleasant shock, arching her body toward him, spasms she had no control of. His body moved closer to absorb them, was suddenly settled completely over her, and before she guessed why, he was entering her.

The pain was sharp, but gone so quickly, she'd have no clear memory of it. Feeling him fill her, though, and so deeply, made up for it, bringing her a pleasure she never could have imagined. He did no more than that for the longest moment, was giving her time to adjust, time she didn't really need. When he began to move in her finally, she was more than ready. He was still trying to soothe her though. While he rested one arm behind her neck, he slid his other hand up her cheek, over her ear, into her hair — catching on her spectacles and taking them off her.

She was sure he'd done it deliberately, though maybe not. His look of surprise could have been due to his having the spectacles in his fingers. But he was staring at her face, both of them completely still. He knew she was Amanda's twin, he'd admitted that, and yet she felt more naked without the spectacles than she did without her clothes.

"Can you see me at all without these?" he asked her.

"Yes."

"Good, because I want you to see how much I'm enjoying this."

The tone was husky, but the words affected her amazingly, removing all her shyness and reminding her that he was still deep inside her. She wrapped her arms around his neck, and said just as huskily, "Then what are you waiting for?"

He caught his breath, but then frowned for a moment in confusion, "Amanda?"

Marian didn't answer, was too distracted at that point to think. He was thrusting deeply into her, again and again, and within moments, it carried her right over the edge into the most sublime ecstasy of her experience, a pleasure that continued to flow through her until he received his own several moments later.

They were both still again, breathing slowly returning to normal. Marian held off her thoughts as long as she could, trying to savor what would undoubtedly be a unique experience, never to happen again — with him. Marian felt anger welling up in her and sensed Chad might be feeling the same way. He seemed in no hurry to address it either. Yet simmering there between them was the notion that he thought she was Amanda. And he'd made love to her anyway.

He leaned back. He stared down at her for

the longest moment. Now, without realizing it, she was glaring up at him. But before either of them could say anything, they heard a voice near the front of the stable.

"You here yet, Chad? Horses need feeding — well, hell, looks like I'll have to . . ."

The mumbling stopped. It was the sick cowhand, worried about the animals. Chad swore beneath his breath when the cowhand added, "Oh, didn't see you there, Lonny."

Chad whispered as he grabbed his clothes and donned them quicker than he'd removed them, "Get dressed while I get rid of them. We'll talk about this later."

Later? If she saw him later, she just might shoot him — well, after she got some lessons on shooting.

# Chapter 29

Chad didn't need to ask Lonny if he'd heard anything in the stable. The grin Lonny was wearing was easy enough to decipher. He sent the cowhand back to bed and urged Lonny outside. They stopped halfway between the stable and the bunkhouse.

"What are you doing back here?" Chad asked.

"The same thing you are — well, maybe not."

Lonny's grin turned into a chuckle that really grated.

"Whatever you heard, keep it to yourself."

"Of course," Lonny replied. "But I've got to say, you are one lucky son of a bitch. Don't think I've ever seen a gal as pretty as that Amanda is."

"Wait a minute. Not that it's any of your business, but I was with Marian."

"No way. Marian's too prim and — and —"

"Spinsterish?"

"Well, yes, now that you mention it. Besides, I heard you call her Amanda."

Chad sighed. "That was a mistake. Just for a brief moment I had some doubt, but I didn't mean to voice it aloud."

"You're saying you couldn't tell them apart? It wasn't that dark in there, and those two are nothing alike."

"In behavior, no, they aren't, which is what confused me for a moment. But in looks, they're identical, Lonny. Twins."

"Yeah, right," Lonny scoffed.

Marian took that moment to rush out of the stable, without noticing them off to the side. Her long blond hair was floating about her, the cuffs on her sleeves unbuttoned, her short boots held one in each hand. There was something distinctly sexy about her looking so disheveled — and mad. She definitely looked mad. But then he hadn't missed that glower she'd given him. She obviously hadn't missed him calling her Amanda.

Damn! He'd have to explain later, and apologize. Her boldness had simply thrown him off. And her impatience. He hadn't expected either from her. Of course, he never would have expected such passion from her either.

"I rest my case," Lonny was saying. "That was Amanda."

Chad rolled his eyes and asked dryly,

"Did you miss the part where I said they're twins?"

"Did you miss the part where I said 'no way'?"

Chad couldn't help grinning at that point. "Okay, I understand your doubt. Took me a while to notice it myself. Those ridiculous spectacles that distort her eyes are too much of a distraction, and anyone with any decency won't stare at her long enough to notice that the rest of her features are exquisite — and identical to Amanda's. The problem is, sometimes you can't help wondering which one you're dealing with."

Last night when he'd kissed her, he'd been sure he was kissing the same woman he'd kissed by the campfire that night. But Marian had denied it, had even got huffy about it. Yet he'd been so sure, had even been relieved to have his confusion finally put to rest, only to end up confused again with her denial.

He simply had no trouble accepting that Marian had tried to rescue him from Leroy that night, and that she'd done so quickly and spontaneously that she'd forgotten to put her spectacles on first — and had been able to see perfectly without them. Which would mean that there was nothing really wrong with her eyes. In fact, she probably couldn't see a damn thing through those silly spectacles, which would account for her abnormal clumsiness.

Believing that it had been Amanda that night had never really sat quite right with him. It had looked like her, yes. He'd had no reason then to think otherwise. But attributing such a selfless act to her had just seemed — strange. And in fact, it was the only nice thing he could attribute to her. But he had no trouble attributing a selfless act to Marian. Yes, she'd gone out of her way to insult him more than once, but he had to wonder about that with what he had learned since. He suspected her rudeness might have been deliberate, part of that jealousy thing with her sister that she'd only half told him about.

He understood the jealousy part now, or at least most of it, which Marian had tried to explain to him without giving him any details. It hadn't made much sense at the time, when she made herself as ugly as she possibly could. It simply wasn't conceivable that Amanda could be jealous of her. But they were twins. One hid her beauty, the other let it shine.

But there were ways to tell them apart, thankfully. Amanda's hands were always moving, to draw attention to her face, her breasts. When she smiled, it never seemed real. If she had a sense of humor, she'd lost it in her displeasure over the trip. If she had anything good to say about anything, he'd yet to hear it. Her mannerisms were different, as were her temperament, her tolerance, her patience. And she was a complainer. Actually, she was probably exactly what his father had called her, a born-and-bred nag. Her beauty had blinded him to all of that, but he saw it clearly in comparison to Marian.

He still didn't understand the reason for the deception though. It made no sense at all for a woman as beautiful as Marian to want to hide her beauty. But she couldn't hide what she'd felt today, a powerful desire for him that he'd reacted to in the most primitive way.

His reaction still surprised him. He usually had much more control over his baser instincts. Actually, he had never before lost control quite so thoroughly. Or maybe he just hadn't wanted to stop what was happening between them. That was more likely the case. It was like the kiss last night, something he'd been unable to resist taking. And every time he'd kissed her, she'd yielded, telling him without words that she wanted him, too.

# Chapter 30

Marian took a leaf from her sister's book and spent the rest of the day in her room. To keep from driving herself mad with her own thoughts, she asked Rita to help her find Kathleen's painting supplies. And once that had been easily accomplished, she carried them all to her room.

When Chad showed up for the promised talk with "Amanda," he'd have no luck. Amanda's tactic of hiding in her room was an old one, since she actually felt she was punishing everyone else by denying them her presence.

Marian was hiding for a much different reason. She didn't want to be around to see Chad waiting around for her sister to make an appearance, or to be asked to talk Amanda into coming down. She wouldn't be surprised if he asked. But he wasn't going to find out, at least today, just how much he'd blundered in his conclusions.

She still couldn't believe he'd done that. God, she'd been so elated that he could actually want her, *her*, not Amanda. But she should have known better. He'd wanted

Amanda from the start, and that wasn't going to change. Just because she was Amanda's twin.

He probably thought all along today that she was Amanda, and the worst part was, it was her own fault. What she'd told him last night — that Amanda liked to play tricks on people by pretending to be her — would have been fresh in his mind.

She probably should warn Amanda that Chad was under the mistaken impression that he'd made love to her. But then she'd have to listen to her sister gloat about her fallen virtue, despite the fact that her own had fallen long ago. Marian just couldn't stomach that on top of everything else that had happened today. Besides, it was no more than Chad deserved, to have both sisters refusing any intimacy with him. Maybe in the future he'd pay closer attention to just whom he was making love to, the dense man.

A few hours after she started painting, she finally began to relax enough to take note of *what* she was painting. She was surprised. She didn't paint from sketches because while she was rather good at sketching, she didn't enjoy it as much as painting. But then she painted just as well from memory, so didn't need to do both.

Actually, she shouldn't really be surprised at what had taken form on the canvas. Though she'd been trying to put him out of her mind, he was still lurking there. So finding the basics of Chad's face staring back at her from the easel merely had her shaking her head in disgust at herself.

It was a good resemblance, though. She hadn't lost her talent through lack of use. The eyes needed work, not the shape, but the color. The chin needed more definition so it would look stronger. The skin tone would have to be darker to reflect his deep tan. And she should probably add his hat, tipped low as he usually wore it. . . .

What was she thinking? She wasn't going to finish a portrait of *him*. She removed the canvas, set it behind the easel so she wouldn't have to look at it, and replaced it with a fresh one. She'd have to be more careful, at least until she could restock Kathleen's supplies.

There had only been four large canvases to work with, two medium-sized ones, and one miniature, but Marian wasn't a slow painter. She could finish a portrait in one sitting if she put her mind to it and was careful, so the supplies wouldn't last her very long.

She decided on a different sort of portrait,

while the memory was still somewhat fresh, one that actually amused her to paint. It wouldn't amuse Amanda, if she ever got a look at it.

She painted her memory of the train robbery, in particular, Amanda's sitting down with her look of shock and gunpowder all over her face just after she'd been shot at. The passengers around them were a blur, had been a blur at the time, so she left them that way. The two robbers who had marched down the aisle were in the picture, the one who'd shot at Amanda more clearly defined. Though she could only depict half of his face, since the other half had been covered with his bandana, his eyes were rather distinct, more golden in color than brown, and very round in shape.

She started smiling before she was even half done, her mood greatly lightened. Though there hadn't been anything amusing about that robbery as it was happening, Amanda with her face blackened from gun smoke and shocked into silence, was priceless. Maybe she'd let Amanda have a look at it when it was finished, after all.

She grinned at the thought, but knew she wouldn't. Amanda would destroy it, just like she'd destroyed the last picture Marian had done of her that didn't show her at her best.

She was surprised when the light faded and she realized that it was almost evening. But then she always seemed to lose track of time when she painted. The knock came at the door shortly thereafter.

"Dinner in fifteen minutes," she heard Rita call out.

She wasn't planning on going downstairs, not tonight anyway, but she did want to catch her aunt to let her know that, before Kathleen went down. She retrieved her spectacles. While she was painting was the only time she refused to wear them. Of course, she always painted in private, where she wouldn't be interrupted, so it didn't really matter.

The second knock at the door came before she reached it. She assumed it was Rita again, making sure she'd heard her, but Kathleen was standing there when she opened it.

"I was told you started painting this afternoon," her aunt said. "May I see your progress? Or do you prefer to wait until you've finished each piece before anyone views what you're working on?"

"I don't mind," Marian replied with a shy smile, and opened the door a bit wider.

"Oh, my." Kathleen's surprise was genuine as she approached the easel. "Did she really get that close to gunfire?"

"She was shot at when she wouldn't give up her purse without a fight."

"That was — rather brave of her."

Marian grinned at her aunt's pause. "No, it was about as stupid as she can get, when there were four of them, all with drawn guns, and we had no reasonable way to prevent the robbery. She's lucky he only tried to scare her."

"Or he missed."

"That, too."

Kathleen had to cover her mouth to hide her own amusement over the depiction of Amanda's surprise. "You're very good. It looks just like her, despite the gunpowder."

"It's all right to laugh, now that the danger is over. Her expression *was* quite funny."

Kathleen released her humor with a chuckle. "Still is. I'm impressed, sweetie. Staring at this makes me almost feel as if I were there and — oh, my."

"What?"

"I just noticed, the robber, I think I know him. Goodness, he looks just like John Bilks who used to work at the general store in town. He got fired when it was discovered that some money was missing from the cash box. The owner wanted him arrested, but there was no proof that he actually took the money. He moved on soon after — and has apparently progressed to train robbing. I'll bet the sheriff would like to see this painting."

"I'm pretty sure Amanda would object to that," Marian replied with a grin.

Kathleen, squinting her eyes at the painting, said, "You think so?" and they both chuckled. But then she suggested, "Maybe a miniature then, of just John Bilks? We can give it to the sheriff when we go to town on Saturday — and get you more canvases while we're there. You're obviously a much faster painter than I ever was. Were there at least enough in my old supplies to hold you over till then?"

"Yes, I —"

Marian didn't finish. Kathleen had moved to the side to look over the material that had been dug out of storage — and caught sight of the half-finished portrait of Chad still leaning against the back of the easel.

"Oh, my," Kathleen exclaimed before turning to look at her. "Your talent is simply amazing. And you do this from memory, don't you? Yes, you must. Incredible — and

I'm glad you like him. Now, there's no need to blush about it. Any young girl your age would."

Marian looked down. "It's not that, it's — no one has ever complimented me on my painting before. My father insisted I had no talent, that I was only wasting my time —"

Kathleen cut in angrily, "Mortimer was a bastard, I'm sorry to say. If he could say something like that, I have no doubt it was because his 'favorite' had no talent in that area. She doesn't, does she?"

"No."

"As I thought. It probably infuriated him that you outshone her in this. And you should have known better. Just look at this painting. You've already captured the heart and breath of him, and it's not even finished."

"He does have an interesting face."

Kathleen burst out laughing. "Interesting, huh? I suppose you could put it that way. Now come on, dinner's waiting. Let's get downstairs before Consuela sends out the posse."

Marian didn't move. They'd been talking too long for her to claim she had a headache as she'd planned to do. But she wasn't about to sit down to dinner with Chad, not tonight, not until she lost the urge to shoot him on sight for the conclusion he'd drawn.

"You go ahead, Aunt Kathleen. I think I'm going to turn in early —"

"Oh, come on, you still have to eat. And it's just the two of us tonight. Chad's already begged off. He ended up hanging around my kitchen for quite a while this afternoon for some reason, and Consuela stuffed him to the brim. She can't stand to have a man underfoot without feeding him."

"Well, I suppose I could eat a few bites."

# Chapter 31

Chad showed up for dinner anyway. They were about halfway done when he walked in, sat down, and asked what was for dessert. Kathleen teased him a bit about his horse's objecting to the amount of food he was putting away. They bantered back and forth, both laughing, moods light, until he introduced a new topic.

"Is Amanda ill?"

"No, she'd just rather not join the rest of us," Kathleen replied.

"Don't tell me she *still* needs resting up from the trip?" he asked.

"Possibly. She hasn't taken to the heat very well. You're used to it, so you barely notice it, but —"

"I notice it. It just hasn't been that hot lately, at least not enough to wilt the lady. So she's still pouting over being here?"

Kathleen coughed. Marian stared. To hear him call it on the mark, well, it didn't quite make sense to her, since he'd never spoken derisively about Amanda before. But then she was forgetting that he was probably still angry with her sister because he thought she'd played one of her tricks on him that morning.

She was amazing herself by how calm she'd remained ever since he walked in. Bantering with Kathleen, laughing, he'd behaved as if nothing out of the ordinary had happened that morning — until he mentioned Amanda. Then his tone had changed abruptly.

Her own anger was still simmering beneath the surface. Not that she still didn't want to shoot him. Of course, she knew she was being unfair. She'd known from the start that he'd wanted Amanda.

"I'm glad y'all didn't wait on me," Amanda said in the doorway, using a thick, if poor imitation of a Texas drawl. "And no, I haven't been pouting, darlin'," she added, staring at Chad as she fanned herself vigorously. "Goodness, you aren't still annoyed that our little tryst in the stable got interrupted this morning, are you?"

Marian sucked in her breath. How on earth had Amanda found out about that? And why was she deliberately reinforcing Chad's conclusion that it had been her that he'd made love to?

Chad was blushing profusely, with Kathleen now staring at him wide-eyed. This was just the sort of scene Amanda loved to create, but for once it probably wasn't completely deliberate, or planned. She'd obviously overheard his less-than-flattering remarks about her and was now getting even with him. She wouldn't have come right in, because it would have taken her a few minutes to get her rage under control.

Marian was doing some blushing of her own. God, this meant Amanda had overheard a lot more than the table conversation just now. She had to have been in the stable this morning. There was no other way she could know about what had happened there.

But she had no reason to be in the stable. She didn't like horses, and she didn't know how to drive a carriage even if it had occurred to her to escape with the one still on the premises. There was simply nothing to draw her there — except Chad. She'd either seen him return to the ranch and decided to amuse herself with him for a while, to relieve her boredom. Or — actually, it was more likely that she'd simply been watching from her room when they were in the corral, saw Chad drag Marian back inside the stable, and was curious enough to come down to investigate why — and found them making love, *and* overheard what he'd said.

She must have thought it hilarious, that he'd drawn the wrong conclusion. She'd probably been laughing over it all day and plotting how to make the best use of what she knew in order to hurt Marian. This little scene wasn't for Chad's benefit. Amanda could care less what he thought. He was merely a tool to use, and a perfect one, since Amanda now knew that Marian wanted him for herself.

This was so typical of Amanda. She was getting to rub Marian's nose in the fact that men always preferred her. She was also getting to scandalize Kathleen, which was part of her current agenda. And she would let Chad know how little he mattered in the scheme of things. She wasn't done showing him the consequences of straying from the path of worshiping her. No, Marian didn't doubt that at all.

She felt sick to her stomach. She might have wanted to shoot Chad herself, but she wouldn't have wished Amanda's vindictiveness on him. And it was pointless for her to speak up with the truth. Amanda would call her a liar, so would Chad for that matter, since he'd been so sure which woman he'd made love to.

Amanda was only half-dressed. Marian hadn't noticed right off that her sister was making yet another visual statement about the heat. She was without her camisole and probably her bloomers, too, to go by the slimness of her skirt. And her blouse was unbuttoned down the front beyond decency. It was thin enough to show the shadow of her nipples beneath it, not that the deep V of her blouse wasn't close to showing them off even more. She'd probably come downstairs to shock them with her attire, but with Chad there, she'd found better ammo to use.

Marian hoped Kathleen would realize this was just another performance for her benefit, but a glance at her aunt showed she was only just recovering from her initial shock and was blushing again because of Amanda's state of undress.

"We'll discuss your — activities, after you get dressed," Kathleen said sternly.

Amanda raised a golden brow at her and leaned back lazily against the doorframe. "I am dressed, as much as I can tolerate in this heat. Besides, a marriage blessing is all that's required of you, Aunt Kathleen," she added with a tight little smile. "My behavior and the way I dress don't fall under your sphere of influence, so don't think you have anything to say about what I do. I'm only here because there is money involved."

"You're here because your father elected to make me your guardian."

"If you haven't noticed, I'm not a child who *needs* a guardian."

"Then you might want to stop acting like one. Or is this your way of drawing my attention to the fact that you've made your choice about whom you want to marry?"

"Choice? You mean the cowboy here?" Amanda turned her gaze on Chad. "You didn't have marriage in mind this morning, now did you, darlin'?"

Chad was blushing again, probably because Kathleen was frowning at him. "I can explain, Red. It was a riding lesson that got out of hand."

"A riding lesson?" Amanda smirked. "That's a rather crude way of putting it."

Chad ignored the interruption, even though more color in his cheeks said he'd heard it clearly. But it was Kathleen he addressed, assuring her, "I'll take full responsibility for my actions."

Kathleen sighed at that point. "I know you will, never doubted it for a moment. I'm just sorry you have to in this case."

Amanda had been about to decline any further involvement with Chad. Marian was sure of it. She had set up the scene for one of her nasty set-downs, would want to punish

Chad for straying from the path of worshiping only her, and he'd obliged her, had left himself wide open to get his self-esteem demolished. But Kathleen's sympathy for him had her changing her mind — for the moment.

Marian often wished she *didn't* know the way her sister's mind worked, but she did. Amanda had just been given the means to prolong the agony — for all of them. If Kathleen didn't really want Chad to marry Amanda, as her last remark suggested, then Amanda would suddenly find it worth considering, at least temporarily, until a better option presented itself. Plus, she'd have the bonus of knowing it would hurt Marian the most.

Amanda yawned to show her boredom with the subject, even waved her hand for emphasis, and said, "I'll think about it."

"Appears you already did," Kathleen pointed out bluntly.

Amanda merely laughed and strolled toward the stairs. She'd done what she set out to do and would now go gloat over it in private.

The silence that remained at the table was painful. Marian couldn't bear to be a part of it for long, and with a mumbled, "Excuse me," left the room as well.

She got out right before the tears started. So silly of her to let one of Amanda's scenes upset her. She should know better. Actually, this time it wasn't really Amanda's fault. She'd just done what she always did, stir the pot to boiling. What really bothered her was knowing that Chad was a part of it this time, and even further out of her reach than ever.

Being shot would have been a kinder fate for him than ending up with Amanda for a wife.

# Chapter 32

Chad felt like a child caught with his hand in the forbidden cookie jar. His embarrassment was still acute, even though it was now just him and Red left in the dining room. But she was shaking her head at him, wearing a look that said "you disappoint me, boy." And he couldn't blame her. It was her niece he'd trifled with. That was a clear betrayal of trust.

He'd yet to examine the full ramifications of what had just happened and was still somewhat in shock. He was going to have to marry — the wrong woman. How the hell could he have been so wrong?

"You should have gotten to know her better, before you — decided to marry her."

The disappointment was still strong in Red's tone. Chad nodded. "Don't be surprised if I agree with you one hundred percent."

"Then why didn't you wait before doing something so irreversible?"

"I'm not sure I had much choice in the matter. Oh, I could have got the hell out of there, but, I'm beginning to feel set up, as if she planned the whole thing."

"Then it wasn't your idea to make a bed in the hay with her?"

He'd thought he was done with blushing, but his cheeks started to heat up again. "It certainly wasn't the reason I came back here this morning. I found her in the stable, started the riding lesson you asked me to —"

"Wait a minute, I didn't ask you to teach *her* to ride," Kathleen cut in.

"That's just it, it wasn't Amanda, well, it was, obviously, but she'd made herself up to look just like Marian. And she was acting just like Marian. She was even willing to learn to ride, when I know she doesn't like horses — which probably was what convinced me the woman I was dealing with was Marian. So I guess my eyesight as well as my good sense went to hell."

"Well, they are twins. I suppose it would be easy enough for one to masquerade as the other and pull it off," Kathleen conceded.

His lips twisted sourly. "The thing is, I was damn sure it was Marian in the stable this morning. There might have been a brief moment when I had some doubt. Her boldness threw me off, and I asked if she were Amanda."

"I take it she didn't confirm or deny it?"

"No, she got mad about it actually. I thought it was because I called her Amanda, but it was probably because I saw through her ploy for a moment."

Kathleen sighed. "So you did seduce the right sister; at least, you thought you did."

"Red, I don't hide from my own mistakes, but I have to tell you, I didn't do the seducing. She was like a cat in heat, giving off all the signs that she wanted me. Considering what I thought, I didn't try very hard to resist. I'll admit that. And I'm not denying responsibility, either. I could have dredged up enough willpower to get the hell out of there. I didn't. But I didn't start it."

"This makes it much worse, you know."

"You don't know the half of it. I don't even *like* Amanda. I ignored all her bad traits, chalked them up to the trip, was sure once she settled in here that she'd be a lot different. I was attracted to her, yes, very much so. She is damn beautiful, after all. But I was holding off letting her know that until she got here, since her attitude on the trip was entirely too bratty for my tastes. I really thought she'd change though, not get worse."

"I hate to say this, since she is my niece, but from all accounts, what you've seen so far isn't going to improve any. My brother spoiled her beyond redemption."

"But not Marian?"

"No, Amanda was his favorite," Kathleen said. "Marian he ignored completely."

"Is that why she tries to go through life unnoticed? From habit?"

"No, I think it has to do with Amanda's being jealous of her. She started to explain it to me, but we got sidetracked, talking about my brother."

Chad frowned in thought. "Come to think of it, I may have gotten the explanation the night before we got here. I had to drag it out of her, and then I plain out didn't buy it, considering she's about as spinsterish in her looks as she can be."

"You gonna tell me why Marian goes to such lengths to avoid her sister's jealousy?"

He snorted over Kathleen's impatience. "I was getting to it. It was her contention that Amanda could get so jealous, that if she thought Marian fancied a man, she'd turn on the charm and try to steal him away from her, just for spite."

"Just for spite? You mean not to keep?"

Chad went very still, then swore, "Son of a bitch. You think that could be what this morning was all about?"

"Was she a virgin?"

Once again, he blushed. "Yes."

"Then no, I can't see her going to that length just for spite."

"What about her behavior tonight? She didn't exactly give the impression that she wants to marry me. It does kind of fit, Red."

Kathleen shook her head at him. "If she'd already lost her innocence somewhere else, I might agree. But she could have accomplished the objective of redirecting your affections to herself without going to that extreme. And besides, she was pretending to *be* Marian. If she wanted to charm you, she'd do it as herself."

He sighed, conceding, "I suppose, which puts me back to 'not getting it.' I mean, she doesn't even like me."

"You sure about that?"

"Well, aside from her performance this morning of being overwhelmed with desire, yes, I'm reasonably sure."

"Women aren't always obvious about their feelings," Kathleen remarked.

"I know, but when the predominant emotion you usually sense from a woman is disgust, you don't need to be knocked over to get a clue."

"Then I'd go with my first guess."

"Which is?"

"She's decided to use you to get her inheritance," she replied.

"But wouldn't your own contention hold true in that case as well? That she wouldn't go to such lengths, would try to charm me instead?"

"I'd say yes, except I know that her only goal at the moment is to go home, with or without a husband, in the latter case, with my blessing to marry whomever she wants. Now, I'm not about to give her permission to do that, and maybe she's dredged up enough sense to realize that by now. But it's more likely just pure impatience on her part. She knows I'd approve of you to marry her. She can't say the same about any other man she's met out here yet. So marrying you would be her quickest ticket home, and seducing you just guaranteed it."

He scowled. "Marrying me isn't going to get her a trip anywhere."

"Well, I know that," Kathleen assured him. "And you know that, but I've been warned that Amanda doesn't take too kindly to 'no.' If she can't cajole what she wants, she'll more than likely resort to other, less pleasant tactics."

"Like nagging me to death?" Chad mumbled.

Kathleen nodded with a wince. "Or sullying your good name. I wouldn't put that past her, after witnessing her shocking attire tonight."

"There's no way out of this, is there?"

"For a decent man like you? No."

He nodded, stood up to leave. "So when does my sentence in purgatory begin?"

"Your pa's big barbecue is this Saturday. Just got the word about it today. I'll check with the preacher then to see when he can be available, or stop by to see him in town on the way back here on Sunday. You'll want to let your pa know about it, too."

"Oh, God."

"I'm sorry, Chad, I really am."

"Not half as much as I am."

# Chapter 33

Chad couldn't sleep. He wasn't surprised. He wanted a drink badly, but Red didn't keep any hard stuff on the property. He wished she didn't live so far from town. He wished he didn't need a drink. Actually, if he could have a wish granted, it would be to turn back the clock and relive the day.

Someone else couldn't sleep either. He stood by the bunkhouse door and stared up at the main house, wondering whose room still had a light burning in it. And although he watched for a very long time, no one came to the window to give him a clue.

The sick feeling in the pit of his stomach wouldn't go away. Trapped. He'd been used. He knew it, but knowing it wasn't going to dig him out of the pit he was in. Despite the fact that Amanda didn't really want him, despite the fact that he'd thought he'd made love to someone else, the trapdoor was still slamming shut on him. Because she'd been a virgin. Because whether he liked it or not, he'd taken her virginity from her and he wasn't the kind of man who could just ignore it.

Spencer Evans was, that bastard. He'd done it before, would do it again. He had no morals worth mentioning, could care less if anyone got hurt in his pursuit of pleasure. It's too bad Amanda hadn't set the trap for him instead — not that it would have gotten her married.

Chad gave up the notion of getting any sleep that night, and, just past midnight, he jotted off a quick note for Lonny with instructions for the next couple days, then rode out to get that drink he was hankering for. He had to pay a visit to his father anyway, to give him the bad news — another reason why he'd like to get thoroughly drunk first.

The moon obliged him. A big one was out that lit up the countryside in a soft gray. Not that it mattered, since he was still pretty much riding blind, his thoughts — and regrets — too distracting to keep his mind on the trail for the most part. He had a smart horse, though, which got him into town around four in the morning.

Not Here didn't stay open all night, but O'Mally's Saloon never closed its doors, whether it did any business or not. Not that Chad would consider frequenting Spencer's place even if it was the only place open.

The last two customers were just staggering out of O'Mally's when he arrived. Archie the bartender went back to reading a dime novel after he shoved a bottle and glass in Chad's direction.

Harry Sue was the only saloon gal up for the night shift, so nicknamed because of the abundance of dark hair that grew on her legs and couldn't be hidden by the knee-high saloon outfit she was forced to work in. Not that a man wouldn't admire her shapely legs. A pretty girl despite that, she was quick to offer him any service he might require, but left him alone when he declined.

He should have been thoroughly sloshed by dawn, had certainly worked at it, but it was taking longer than usual — or Archie had passed him a watered-down bottle. Harry Sue had lingered nearby, just in case he changed his mind about getting a better look at her room upstairs, but she was sleeping at one of the tables now since he hadn't offered conversation or anything else to keep her awake.

Her replacement would probably be showing up soon, and some of the townsfolk soon after, since O'Mally's actually served coffee from dawn till noon, though at the same price as the cheapest rotgut. Chad would really rather not be found there by anyone he knew, but he wasn't leaving until the drink did its work and he could stop thinking.

But as if his luck hadn't turned rotten enough, Spencer Evans pushed through the swinging doors along with the sunrise. To find out what Chad was doing there, no doubt. He knew he should have stabled his horse instead of just removing the saddle and leaving him tied up out front where it might be recognized, but he really hadn't thought he'd still be there come daylight.

Archie perked up at the sight of Spencer. He looked worried, but held his tongue. Most business owners in town tried to get the two rivals to leave their premises before the fists started flying, but Archie didn't own O'Mally's, so he wasn't that concerned about a brawl there.

It was still a ridiculously early hour for Spencer to be up and about, night owl that he was. Chad wouldn't be surprised if Spencer hadn't promised half the town a buck or two to let him know whenever Chad showed up. He *did* seem to make an appearance far too often, no matter which establishment Chad entered.

But Spencer made no pretense of just happening to pass by this time. He leaned against the bar next to Chad, tipped his hat back, and asked straight out, "What are you doing here?"

Chad didn't answer, didn't even glance his way. Spencer mumbled something under his breath.

Louder, Spencer said, "I'd as soon not be having this conversation either, but I'm not going to pretend indifference where this particular lady is concerned. Are you finally out of there? On your way home? Can I stop worrying about you trying to court her while I'm not around?"

"Go away, Spencer."

"This is a public place."

"So go get *public* in some other part of it."

"You always were amusing after a few drinks. You got turned down, didn't you? I knew she wouldn't find you to her taste," Spencer smirked. "Drowning a broken heart then, are you?"

Chad finally glanced at his nemesis. It was too ironic by half, that he'd finally beaten Spencer to the prize, only for it to be one he didn't want. And Spencer had never been this obvious before either, that he wanted the same woman. He always tried to hide his interest. Sneaking about to win was his style, for the shock effect — hell, they were very alike, Spencer and Amanda. He couldn't think of two people who deserved each other more. It was too bad she hadn't figured that out before she plotted to ruin his life instead.

Ordinarily, Chad would have thrown it in Spencer's face, that he'd won. Not that he usually won when it came to women they were both competing over. Spencer was better at making promises that he had no intention of keeping. But Chad would have liked to throw it in his face for once. Tit for tat, it was exactly what Spencer would have done.

But considering what he'd won, he didn't feel like a winner at all. He and Spencer were both going to lose this time around, and he didn't feel like discussing why, when his only reason for being there was to drink enough so he could wipe it from his mind.

So he said only, "I repeat, Spence, go away."

"Give me a straight answer and I will. She's still available, right?"

"Marian is."

"Who the hell is Marian?"

Chad rolled his eyes, though he wasn't surprised at all that Spencer didn't recognize the name. He'd had eyes only for Amanda since he'd first seen her. He might not even know she had a sister, might have missed that entirely, he'd been so centered on Amanda when introductions were made. But if he'd noticed Marian at all, he would have likely gotten to the same first impression that Chad had.

So he merely replied, "The spinster."

Spencer snorted. "Like I'd give a hoot about her. Now are you deliberately trying to provoke me in not telling me what I need to know, or do you just like my company?"

Chad wasn't inclined to tell him, since it was bound to start a fight between them. Not that he wouldn't welcome a fight, but he hadn't counted on one as he hadn't expected to see Spencer during this trip to town. And fighting when he was half-drunk and Spencer wasn't would be rather stupid. But Spencer was going to hear about the wedding in a couple days anyway, when Red had her talk with the preacher. So there really was no reason to keep silent about it.

"I'll tell you what," he offered magnanimously. "Get yourself a bottle of liquor and drink it down to this point." He held up his own bottle to show there was only a quarter bottle of whiskey left in it. "And then I'll consider discussing my woes with you."

"Woes, huh?" Spencer chuckled, visibly relaxed. "I guess that was answer enough for me. I'll leave you to continue drowning your sorrows alone."

Spencer was halfway to the door when he probably heard Chad mumble, "Just as well."

He stopped, frowned, appeared to spend a few moments debating with himself. Then with an angry gesture, he marched back to the bar, growled at Archie, "Give me a bottle of the same swill, and if you ever tell anyone I drank some of O'Mally's inferior rotgut, I'll run your ass out of town so fast, you won't be able to keep up with it."

Chad just watched with partial interest as Spencer proceeded to guzzle down the bottle Archie tossed at him. He stopped to check it once, sighed that it was only half-empty, guzzled down some more, then set it down next to Chad's bottle to measure it, growled that he still had an inch to go, and quickly finished off the inch.

"Now, you son of a bitch, let's hear it," he snarled when he was done.

"I'm impressed," Chad remarked. "And you still have a voice?"

"Do I have to beat it out of you?"

"Seeing as how we both know that wouldn't work, I guess it's your lucky day that I'll hold up my end of the bargain — or not so lucky. You're not going to like what's happened, any more than I do, but the whole town doesn't need to hear about it, so let's take it outside."

Archie sighed, clearly disappointed that he was going to be excluded, but went back to reading his novel as they left O'Mally's. Chad moved out into the middle of the street. He didn't want any eavesdropping in case he ended up saying more than he should due to the liquor.

Spencer grabbed his arm impatiently. "That's far enough. Now tell me."

Chad nodded. "I don't know if you know about the inheritance Amanda can't get her hands on until she marries."

"I believe it was mentioned."

"Well, she wasn't willing to wait for it, at least not long enough to enjoy a normal courtship."

"If you tell me she asked you to marry her, I think I'll kill you."

"No, she didn't ask."

"Damn lucky for you she didn't."

"She tricked me into making love to her, and that pretty much settled the matter in Red's mind."

It was the liquor that delayed Spencer's reaction. For all of five seconds he just stared, which gave Chad enough time to get out of the way of the first swing. But Spencer was too enraged to take a chance that he might miss again and tackled Chad to the ground. In a prone position, the liquor caught up with Chad real quick, and his head began to spin.

"Watch it, before I puke all over you," he managed to get out.

Spencer leapt off him, and snarled, "I'm calling you out. High noon."

"I'll be sleeping at noon, and don't be an ass," Chad said as he carefully got back to his feet. "Would I have been 'drowning my sorrows' as you put it, if I wanted her? I don't. I told you she tricked me."

"Liar! How could you not want her?"

"Maybe because I've been around her a lot more'n you have and have seen her at her worst. She's beautiful, yes, but that doesn't make up for the rest. Cut out her tongue, and she might be bearable."

"That isn't funny."

"Wasn't meant to be," Chad replied. "She's a spoiled brat, Spencer, seriously spoiled. And you're more'n welcome to her, if you can manage to get her to marry you before I get dragged to the altar."

Spencer stopped snarling for a moment, and demanded, "You mean it?"

Chad nodded, then wished he hadn't. The spinning wasn't quite over.

"Red's going to talk to the preacher this weekend, either at my pa's barbecue on Saturday, or before she returns to the ranch the next day," he warned. "So that doesn't give you much time. Yes, I mean it. You'd actually have my eternal gratitude if you can pull it off."

# Chapter 34

Marian awoke groggy-eyed and still fully dressed, right down to her shoes. She supposed she'd gotten some sleep, but probably not much. She hadn't glanced at the clock before she'd shoved her latest painting under the bed, then curled up in a ball on top of the covers.

She'd never painted by lamplight before, but then she'd never painted with tears in her eyes before either. She wasn't happy with the result, Chad, lying on a pile of hay, unbuttoning his shirt, his expression so sensual, there was no doubt what was on his mind — or what he was about to do.

It was an image she would never forget, even if she hadn't put it on canvas. The details were exact, right down to the brown stain on one of his sleeves and the small half-moon scar above his navel. It looked so much like him, she couldn't look at it for long without getting butterflies in her belly. But it wasn't a painting she could ever share with anyone, so it would stay under the bed.

She should destroy it, but she couldn't bring herself to do that. She would have to roll it up after it dried completely and hide it away where Rita and Ella Mae wouldn't find it when they cleaned.

She was still sitting on the bed thinking about it when her door opened without warning. Amanda was the only one who ever barged in on her without knocking, and sure enough, her sister stood there, leaning against the doorframe. She was only half-dressed again, though today with a skirt and just her lacy white camisole. She still carried a fan, though she wasn't using it at the moment.

As expected, she was smiling smugly. Actually, because it contained not only triumph and laughter, but hidden knowledge as well, her smile was much more smug than usual.

"What do you want, Mandy?"

"Oh, nothing in particular," Amanda replied, twirling the fan about by its wrist tie.

"Then close the door on your way out, thank you."

"What? No congratulations? You *are* going to come to the wedding, aren't you?"

Amanda was all but laughing. Marian wondered how her sister managed to restrain herself. Probably because she wanted to lead up to something she'd find even more humorous.

Since Marian was dressed and the bed was made up, with just a wrinkle or two on the cover, Amanda wouldn't guess she'd only just awakened, which would have been proof she'd spent a miserable night. Suspecting that Amanda was out for more blood brought her wide-awake though. She decided to put a dent in her sister's gloating before it went into full steam.

"I wouldn't miss your wedding, Mandy. I've only been waiting several years for you to get around to having one, so I can get about the business of leading a normal life myself — with you out of it."

"You promise not to cry too loudly when I walk down the aisle to meet — him?"

"Well, considering he's all but got a shotgun trained to the back of his head, tears would probably be inappropriate. Not that you can really consider someone to be forced into doing something if he would have gotten around to doing it on his own anyway. Merely a difference in timing. So yes, I think I can restrain myself."

It was the casual tone Marian had managed to muster that brought the twist of annoyance to Amanda's lips. "Don't try to pretend you don't care."

"Now there's another interesting difference in timing. Yesterday morning, I probably would have cared. This morning, no, I'm afraid not."

"Liar! You know you want him. You would never have become a stable trollop otherwise."

Amanda's crudeness managed to draw a blush. "Look who's talking, you of the half dozen or more sordid conquests. But at least you won't have to put any fake blood on the sheets now, since your husband has actually been fooled into thinking he was the first to touch you. Bravo, sister, that was rather brilliant, even for you."

The blush changed sides. "That's not why I did it. As if I'd care what my husband thinks," Amanda scoffed indignantly. "The man I marry will be grateful I marry him, virgin or not."

"A moot point, since the *him* has already been decided," Marian said.

"Yes, it has, hasn't it."

Amanda was back to smirking. This was such a major triumph for her, not acquiring a husband quickly, without having to waste time on courtship, but acquiring the husband that Marian had wanted for herself. This was "getting even" in the grandest way, for every little slight, resentment, and jealousy she held against Marian.

She'd probably even go through with it,

since it *would* get her what she wanted. And if Chad couldn't be cajoled or nagged into taking her home, she'd find a way to get there on her own. He might come after her. Actually, he probably would, since he did want her after all. But after a half dozen or so times of being put to the bother of chasing her down, he'd give up and she'd have exactly what she was ultimately after — her inheritance and no one to answer to.

Marian left the bed, moved over to the door to grasp the handle, an indication that she was going to close it whether Amanda stood in the way or not. Unfortunately, Amanda quickly got out of the way, by stepping inside the room rather than out in the hallway.

"Take your gloating elsewhere, Mandy, I'm really not interested."

Amanda began fanning herself, despite a nice breeze coming in through the open windows, and strolled lazily about the room. "I'm curious," she said, completely ignoring the offer to leave. "Why didn't you speak up last night with the truth? Too noble to force him to the altar yourself?"

"No, because I have a little more respect for myself than you do, to want —"

"I have the utmost respect for myself," Amanda cut in. "It's you who doesn't — or you wouldn't make yourself look like an ugly old maid."

The blush was back, but it was an angry one this time. "You know what, Mandy, you're absolutely right," Marian agreed with her.

She yanked off her spectacles, held them up in front of her with both hands, and snapped them in two, then tossed them aside. She removed the hairpins while she was at it and shook her hair loose.

Amanda hadn't expected her goading to draw such results. She stood there a little in shock for a moment, staring at her own reflection. "You know you won't reveal yourself completely," she said hesitantly, a bit hopefully. "You've worn that disguise too long."

"Too long is right. And thanks for reminding me that I don't need it anymore. You've got your husband lined up. I think it's pretty safe for me to start looking for one now, wouldn't you say?"

"No, I wouldn't," Amanda huffed. "And don't think I don't know what you're up to. You're going to try to win him back, but it won't work, not unless you tell him the truth — and why the hell didn't you?"

"Because he wouldn't have believed me. You heard him there in the stable. He thought it was you all along. He wanted it to be you. And when he's done being annoyed over the 'supposed' deception, he'll be thrilled that he's getting the woman he's wanted from the start."

"Yes, he will, won't he," Amanda purred, letting her conceit surface again. "He won't even mind that I lied. He'll probably be glad that I did — if he ever finds out. It's too bad you wanted him, too."

"Yes, it is, but at least I realized my mistake before it's too late. I can actually thank you for getting me out of that mess. Believe me, I never thought I'd say *that*."

Amanda blinked, frowned, then demanded, "What are you talking about now? What mess?"

"The one created by my mistake. I was foolish enough to think he might like me. I didn't know he was sure it was you he was making love to. If you hadn't lied about it, I would have been stuck with him."

"Dammit, Mari, when did you get the idea that I was stupid? I know what you're doing, but it won't work. You liked him enough to let him have you there in the stable. Don't try to pretend you don't now."

"I liked him, yes, but I wouldn't have let him 'have' me, as you put it, if I hadn't gotten carried away by my first taste of passion. I would have wanted to be sure of his feelings first, and now that I am sure of them, I wouldn't marry him even if for some reason you don't."

"I don't believe you."

"I could care less."

Amanda's lips thinned, a sign that she was no longer sure of her evaluation. Marian tossed in the clincher.

"You know, Mandy, I hate to say it, but in this we're very much alike."

Amanda snorted. "Like hell we are."

"I know, I find it hard to believe, too." Marian grinned. "But what you're overlooking is that I'm not willing to be any man's second choice any more than you are. *Now* will you get out? I have my entire wardrobe to go through, to see if anything is salvageable for the 'new' me. Or maybe you wouldn't mind lending me a few of your dresses until I can find a seamstress in town? You haven't exactly been wearing your clothes lately, so I'm sure you won't miss them!"

# Chapter 35

Amanda slammed the door as she departed. Marian was surprised to find that she felt like smiling. If she'd learned anything from her sister over the years, it was how to put on a good performance, and she'd just given one worthy of a professional. But the question was, had it worked? Not that it would really change anything, other than to save her from more of Amanda's gloating.

Amanda still wanted a husband, the sooner the better in her mind. Marian had only removed one of the reasons for her to accept Chad in that role. The other reasons still applied, that he was willing, that Kathleen approved of him, that the wedding would take place soon. If no one else caught her eye or interest before the date Kathleen set for the wedding, then Amanda would marry him.

Marian picked up her broken spectacles from the floor. She stared at them for a long moment. She could replace them. She did have another pair. But what was the point? It wasn't as if they were back home in Haverhill, where men would be calling on

Amanda every day, and some of them might prefer her instead.

She really did need a new wardrobe though. She'd chosen the drab colors not because she favored them, but because they furthered her "invisibility." But she was done with that charade. And if Amanda felt threatened by having competition again — too bad.

She removed the dress she'd slept in, found a white blouse that was at least neutral in color. As for a skirt — she noticed the riding skirt she'd borrowed from her aunt, the one she'd been wearing yesterday morning . . .

She wasn't going to cry again. She was going to have to stop mourning her loss eventually, and she might as well start now.

She still had to learn how to ride, but she wasn't about to let *him* finish the lesson for her. Besides, she at least knew the basics now of getting a horse ready to ride, which had probably been the hardest part. How difficult could getting on a horse and staying on it be, when just about everyone in this part of the country rode one? She was determined to teach herself the rest.

She donned the riding skirt and headed out of her room. Ella Mae picked that moment to show up, and with only a brief knock first, the maid stuck her head around the door.

"Hell yes!" she said, quickly grasping that the change in Marian's appearance was deliberate. " 'Bout damn time."

Marian managed not to blush. "All my reasons to hide are gone."

"I heard," Ella Mae said, her voice tinged with disgust. "She couldn't stop crowing about it last night when I collected her clothes for washing." And then hesitantly, "Want to talk about it?"

"No."

"Didn't think so. When you feel like it though, you know where to find me. Want me to fix up your hair, or are you just going to wear it wild like that?"

"I feel like wearing it wild, but I suppose that would be going a bit too far in the opposite direction."

"It will take a little cutting on the bangs," Ella Mae warned. "Not much. You'll still be able to pin them back like she does when needed."

Marian nodded. "Just don't give me exactly the style that she prefers. All those ringlets are much too frilly for my tastes."

It didn't take Ella Mae long. She was very good at creating hairstyles that were not necessarily in high fashion, but very becoming to the individual. And she compromised by not pinning Marian's long locks up again but tieing them back with a bright blue ribbon. As for the bangs, she only needed to snip a few, since they were already trained to lean toward the sides. The result was a little fluff, a few curls near her temples, and a whole new look.

"I'd go pay her a visit now to show off," Ella Mae suggested. "But that's just me. You're too nice to play her game."

Marian grinned. The two of them never needed to clarify who *she* was.

"She's not going anywhere, and besides, she already knows I'm done with hiding. Right now, I have an appointment with a horse."

She expected the stable to be empty again. The cowboy who tended to the horses might be back to work, but if he was still sick, he should be spending most of the day resting. But she still hadn't glanced at a clock before heading there, so she wasn't sure what time of the day it was. Somewhere around noon, to go by the position of the sun.

She saw that Kathleen had ridden in for lunch, or for the day. She had put her horse in a stall, an indication she wouldn't be using him again. She was just closing it when she heard Marian approaching and glanced her way.

"Surprised to see you out here," Kathleen remarked, her tone a bit stiff. "But at least you're properly dressed this time."

"I'm Marian."

"Sure you are," Kathleen snorted.

Marian winced. She hadn't expected this. It had been a really long time since she'd had to convince anyone which sister she was.

She'd forgotten how vexing it could be, too, if she couldn't think of something specifically known just to her and the other person that she could offer as proof that she was indeed Marian. She'd been in that frustrating position many times with people angrily insisting that she was Amanda. Fortunately, she'd had several private conversations with her aunt from which she could draw proof.

She mentioned one now. "When you lent me this skirt, you told me to ignore any ribbing from the cowboys about it, that they jokingly called it female chaps. I'm pretty sure we were quite alone when you said it."

Kathleen visibly relaxed. "Yes, and so far on the other side of the room from the door that day, that if anyone had been trying to listen through it, they wouldn't have been able to hear anything. So it *is* you. What an amazing difference!"

"You might want to whisper a word or number to me now, just to make sure you aren't left in doubt again."

"No more spectacles?"

"I never intended to wear them after Amanda got married, and she's just about . . . married."

She hadn't meant to introduce that particular subject. Fortunately, Kathleen merely said, "Yes, she is," and left it at that.

To quickly get her aunt's mind on something else, Marian asked, "How are we going to get to town when we go? I haven't learned to ride yet."

"If I go by myself, I typically ride in on a Saturday, get my shopping done, spend the night, go to church on Sunday, do a little visiting, then head back home before noon. But with you girls not being able to ride, we'll be on the road a lot longer. I've got an old wagon I use to haul supplies that we would have had to make use of, but since Spencer hasn't bothered to send anyone out to fetch his carriage, we might as well use that this trip. But plans have changed a bit."

"Oh?"

"Stuart is spreading the word already. He's picked this Saturday for his barbecue.

I expect most the town will show up for it. So we'll be heading for the Kinkaid spread first, then stop off in town Sunday on the way back. We'll still have to leave at the crack of dawn Saturday morning, and probably won't arrive until late afternoon. But Stuart's parties typically last well into the night."

"I know it's a bother. And I will learn to ride before any more trips like this. In fact" — she grinned — "that's why I'm here."

Kathleen frowned. "Chad's not around to teach you right now. He rode over to see his father. Probably be gone a couple days. Actually, I don't expect him to return before we leave for the barbecue. But since I'm back for the day, why don't we tackle this ourselves?"

Marian nodded, relieved. She'd been ready to teach herself, but the prospect had been daunting.

Aside from giving her instructions on handling a horse and riding, Kathleen was quiet, even somewhat distracted. Marian wasn't surprised. Kathleen had a lot on her mind, and most of it probably had to do with Chad and Amanda.

During the lesson, Marian debated with herself whether to try to tell her aunt the truth. Kathleen would probably believe her, but then again, maybe she wouldn't. She'd told her a lot of outlandish things already about Amanda. Her latest stunt might just be a bit too much to swallow on top of everything else. And besides, with Chad convinced he'd made love to Amanda, he'd object, probably flatly refuse, if Kathleen tried to insist he marry Marian instead. Not that she'd want a man who was forced to marry her — not that she wanted Chad anymore at all.

She still thought she should make the effort though, not to do Chad any favors, but because he *was* getting the raw deal, and it was ultimately her fault. She could have stopped what had happened that day in the stable, but she didn't. And he might be pleased that he was getting Amanda at the moment, but he wouldn't be once they were married and she started insisting he take her home to Haverhill.

It'd be the right thing to do, whether anyone believed her or not. She just needed to make Kathleen understand that she wouldn't marry Chad, that it wouldn't be fair to him, when he'd thought he'd made love to someone else. The mistake was hers, she'd live with the consequences.

God, what an embarrassing subject to have to discuss with her aunt. At least there was no immediate hurry. She could take a few days to consider how best to approach it. Maybe after the barbecue. And maybe she'd get lucky and Amanda would find someone at the party who would suit her better than Chad and she'd have to do some confessing of her own.

Having been just as distracted as Kathleen with unwanted thoughts, Marian was quite surprised to find herself sitting on the mare, reins in hand, and her aunt telling her, "Okay, time for the test. Let's go for a ride."

# Chapter 36

The pounding on his door woke Chad. The shadows in the hotel room indicated the sun had recently set, but it wasn't quite night. He rolled out of the bed fully dressed. He'd been in no condition to think about getting comfortable when he'd crawled into it.

The pounding hadn't stopped, even though he'd mumbled, "I'm coming."

He had a feeling he knew who was on the other side, almost recognized the knock, which is why he yanked the door open angrily. He was right. "Hell, can I do nothing in this town without you hearing about it?"

"Not much." His father chuckled as he sauntered into the room.

Chad closed the door behind him and ran a hand over his face, trying to shake off his grogginess. That was a mistake. Pain shot right through his temples, reminding him why he'd come to town.

"You don't look so good," Stuart remarked as he got comfortable in the only chair.

"Had a bit too much to drink."

"I heard. I'm waiting to hear the rest. And

why aren't you staying at our place? I don't keep that house staffed here in town just for looks."

"I needed a good view of the street, and the hotel offers it."

"For what? Something else I don't know about, besides why you're here?"

"You gonna let me wake up some before badgering me to death?"

"I suppose." Stuart sighed.

Chad moved to the window. It was dusk outside, barely any gray left in the sky. A light was on in the stable down the street where Spencer lodged his horse. The horse hadn't left the stable that day.

He'd really hoped, after his talk with Spencer, that he wouldn't have to let his father know what a damn fool he was. But he should have known someone would send word to Stuart that he was in town and trying to drink himself into a stupor. And Spencer didn't head out to the Twisting Barb as he'd thought he would. He could have decided to wait until the barbecue and woo Amanda there. Or he could have decided he didn't want her now, after what Chad had told him. That was a distinct possibility.

With Stuart here and already full of questions, there was no point in beating about the bush. Chad stated bluntly, "I'm getting married."

"The nag?" Stuart guessed and sighed his displeasure. "So you came to town to celebrate? That's what the drinking was about?"

Chad shook his head with a grimace. "Not even close. I'm not exactly happy about this."

"You aren't?" Stuart said in confusion, then grinned in relief, assuming, "Ah, so you came to your senses before it's too late? Just beg off then. She might understand, and if she don't, too bad. It ain't as if she won't have most every man in the county sniffing after —"

"I can't beg off, Pa. As it stands right now, I have to marry her."

Stuart sat up, his expression gone to pure annoyance. "*Have* to? What'd you do?"

"Got real stupid."

"I already figured that, but how come you think so? Thought you were interested in her."

"I was — when I still thought the things I *didn't* like about her were just related to the trip out here. But she didn't change when she settled in, she got worse. She's a conniving, manipulative bitch."

"And a nag."

"That, too."

"So what happened to make you see the light?" Stuart asked.

"She decided to use me to get her inheritance. Since she was already sure Red would approve of me, I presented the quickest means to her goal."

Stuart growled, "If you tell me she asked you to marry her and you jumped on it, I just might take a strap to you for being that dumb."

Chad snorted. "No. I wish she could have been that straightforward, but I did mention conniving, didn't I? She tricked me into making love to her, then made sure to let Red know about it."

"I was afraid of that." Stuart sighed again, then added, "You can stop being so hard on yourself, boy. Getting seduced by a gal that pretty could have happened to the best of us, I suppose."

"You still haven't heard the clincher."

"There's more?"

Chad nodded. "You probably didn't notice — it took me a while to pick up on it myself — but they're twins, those sisters."

"No."

"Yes. And it was Marian I thought I was making love to. Amanda did herself up to look just like her, pretended to be her. And she pulled it off perfectly. I never guessed, really thought it was Marian — right up until dinner last night when Amanda came down to tell Red about it."

Stuart shot to his feet angrily. "Now that stinks. Red wouldn't hold you accountable if she heard the whole of it. Just get back there and tell —"

"Amanda was a virgin, Pa."

"Son of a bitch!"

"My thoughts exactly. But I have a glimmer of hope now. If I'm lucky, *real* lucky, Spencer is going to get me out of this."

"Now why didn't you say that to begin with? You and him friends again?"

"Hell no."

"Fighting over the same women again then?" Stuart guessed next.

"There's no fight," Chad said. "He's dumb enough to want her. I don't."

Stuart frowned. "But how's that going to help? The damage is done."

"Yes, but he knows about it and *still* wants her," Chad replied. "He showed up this morning in O'Mally's, wouldn't leave me alone till I told him why I was here. If I'd been a bit more sober, I probably would have kept it to myself. With luck, I'll be glad I didn't."

"But ain't Red insisting the girl marry

you?" Stuart pointed out.

"Red is no more happy about this than I am. If Spencer can convince Amanda to marry him instead, I think Red will give her blessing on it. She knows I was tricked."

"Damn, that's a relief." Stuart finally grinned. "Thought I was going to have to order lumber for you, to build your own house."

Chad rolled his eyes and reminded his father, "I did say *if* he can convince her. There's no guarantee, Pa. Amanda could as easily tell Spencer to get lost. She's got a guaranteed husband lined up, after all. And she went to a lot of trouble to snag me."

"Yeah, but you're hopeful," Stuart returned. "That's good enough for me."

"Only because Spencer's good at seducing, and telling a woman exactly what she wants to hear, whether it's true or not."

Stuart chuckled. "Sounds like those two were made for each other."

"I couldn't agree more."

Stuart stood up to leave, though that wasn't his intention. "Mind if I get some dinner sent up?" he said.

"Mind if I don't join you for it?" Chad replied. "In fact, why don't you let me get back to sleep."

"You can't still be tired," Stuart protested. "You slept all day."

"Not all day. I stood at that window most of the morning, waiting for Spencer to make up his mind what he was going to do. He never did ride out."

Stuart was back to frowning. "You think he's conceding to you?"

"When you put it that way, I'd have to say no. He never concedes. So maybe he is just going to wait until your barbecue, where he'll have easier access to Amanda without Red's constant supervision."

Stuart's expression softened. "And maybe I'll help by keeping Red busy myself."

# Chapter 37

It was a hectic few days, getting ready for the big barbecue. Amanda tried to pretend boredom. After all, it was a "country" barbecue. But Marian could tell she was excited about it, though not half as much as Marian was. She'd gone to a few balls at home with her sister, but hiding behind her spectacles, she hadn't enjoyed them. This Texas party, however, was like a "coming out" ball for her.

There was no time to get new gowns made for it, not that ball gowns would have been appropriate. And Marian hadn't been serious about borrowing some of Amanda's clothes, which she considered much too frilly for her taste. But with Red's help in supplying some lace, Ella Mae worked wonders with one of Marian's old beige gowns, removing the high neck and sleeves and adding white lace to the hem and the new low-cut bodice. Amanda's gown was fancier, but Marian's was prettier because of its simplicity.

Red had sent one of her hands to the sheriff with the miniature painting of the train robber just as soon as Marian finished it. They could have delivered it themselves on Sunday when they would be passing through town, but Red didn't think they should wait even for a few days to pass something that important along to the sheriff. They hadn't heard yet if the painting was going to do any good in apprehending the outlaw, but the sheriff was likely to be at the barbecue as well, so they could ask him then.

Most of Red's household was up long before dawn Saturday morning, so they could have time to dress and eat a quick breakfast before leaving. They managed to arrive at the Kinkaid ranch a little after noontime. Most of the townsfolk who were coming were already there, some having ridden over the night before so as not to miss anything.

The girls had been warned that Stuart's ranch was big, but they were still surprised at just how big it was. The main ranch house dominated the scene. Like a mansion in proportion if not design, it spread wide and tall among all the other buildings around it. The actual barbecue was taking place behind it.

Tables had been improvised from long planks of wood. There was a stage and dance area where musicians were already playing, although no one was dancing yet. Whole carcasses of meat were being roasted nearby, slowly turning on spits and being basted with sauces. A bevy of servants were making trips from the house to the tables, bringing out more and more food that got quickly covered with checkered cloths until it was time to eat. The aromas were wonderful.

Bronco riding was taking place down by one of the stables, where most of the guests were currently gathered. Shouts, bets, laughter, and goading filled the air, and everyone seemed to be having a fine time except maybe the cowboy trying to stay on the back of the bucking horse. It looked dangerous. The cowboy didn't stay on very long.

Marian decided to avoid that area. It was a bit too raucous for her tastes. There would be horse racing as well, she was told, and maybe a shooting contest and roping competition, plenty of opportunities for the cowboys to test their skills in fun, rather than work.

Kathleen introduced the girls around. Amanda began enjoying herself, but then she always shone at social gatherings, and it didn't take her long to become the "belle of the barbecue," so to speak. Marian didn't begrudge her sister that. She might have come out of her shell at last, but she would never have Amanda's self-confidence. She was surprising a lot of people, though, who had seen her arrive in town a week ago looking nothing like she did now. But twins were always a novelty.

The host showed up and after complimenting Kathleen enough to make her blush — their aunt did look exceptionally fetching in an embroidered blouse and skirt with two tiers of ruffles — he took over the introductions.

Spencer arrived, looking as dashing as ever in his black coat and string tie. It didn't take him long to find Amanda or to monopolize the conversation with her. Marian wondered if Amanda would tell him she was going to marry Chad. Probably not, since she would enjoy flirting with him.

Marian thought it was ironic that she had always figured her "unveiling" would change everything for her, yet it seemed to have changed nothing. She was pretty now, yes. But still that didn't seem to be drawing people to her or making this social event any more fun than others she'd attended.

Amanda pulled her aside, said impatiently, "Don't slouch. You have a nice figure, show it off. And stop looking down like you're trying to see over the rims of those silly spectacles. You aren't wearing them anymore."

Amanda? Trying to help her present herself better? But before Marian went into shock, Amanda added, "How am I supposed to compete if you're still trying to hide yourself?"

"I'm not hiding."

"Of course you are," Amanda replied. "It's ingrained, you've done it so long. Open up, Mari. Let the real Marian out."

Amanda flounced off after that, leaving Marian in shock. That had been sisterly advice, she just wasn't sure how to take it. She tried to guess at Amanda's ulterior motive, but other than the "compete" comment, she couldn't find one. And "competing" didn't wash. Amanda was going to be the center of attention no matter what. Her vivacity, her abundant self-confidence from years of social successes naturally drew people to her.

Marian soon wandered off by herself. Distracted by her disappointment, she found herself down by the stable without realizing it. A collective cheer by the crowd still gathered there brought her back to herself, in time to see Chad being bounced around on the back of a bucking horse.

She sucked in her breath. He was holding on with only one hand. His other arm was extended out to the side, possibly to assist with balance. The wild horse was doing its darnedest to unseat him, kicking up its hind legs, nearly jumping into the air, vicious in its determination.

Marian squeezed her eyes shut. She couldn't bear to watch Chad fall, but knew he would. The horse was too wild and too angry. She listened to the crowd to tell her when it happened. They seemed greatly annoyed when it did, as if they'd expected Chad to succeed.

"He lost his concentration."

"Probably her fault, he was looking at her."

"Rotten timing."

Marian looked around to see who they were talking about, but the dozen or so men standing near her were all staring at her. She started blushing and turned to leave.

"Well, if it ain't the tree-toting Eastern gal. How do, ma'am?"

Marian groaned inwardly. It was the mountainman, Leroy. She hadn't expected ever to see him again. And he was mistaking her for Amanda — well, actually he wasn't, but she didn't want him to know that.

She gave him a smile. "Have we met? I'm

Marian Laton. Perhaps you were referring to my twin sister?"

He raised a dubious brow. It looked rather funny, such a big man trying to look skeptical. "Twin, huh?"

"Leave her be, Leroy," Chad said, coming up beside them, still brushing the dust from his pants from the fall he'd taken.

She was relieved to see he was only dusty and didn't have any blood or hoof marks imprinted on him anywhere. And Leroy didn't seem to take offense — much.

"You give too many orders, boy, when you don' run this place yet."

"If my pa didn't warn you to stay away from his guests, he should have."

Leroy chuckled. "As it happens, he did. But I heard you were gonna try your hand at breaking the bronco I brought in. Was hoping the horse might settle our debt."

"If you want a piece of me, Leroy, just say so."

"I'm still thinking on it."

"They say bathing stimulates thinking. Why don't you try it?" Chad suggested. "Pa set up a bunch of tubs in the south barn for the men."

"I know. Wandered in there by mistake, and the little fella tending the tubs took one look at me and grabbed his shotgun. Said he wasn't gonna lug water for all them tubs again, that it would take all of them to get me clean. Told me to go find a creek."

"No offense, Leroy, but we'd all appreciate it if you did."

Leroy grinned. "This is an acquired o-door. Took me years to perfect it. Snuck up on that bronco within a hand's reach 'cause he didn't smell a human. When I give up hunting, I'll bathe."

Chad rolled his eyes. "In the meantime, you'll forgive us if we avoid your perfected odor?"

Leroy shrugged. "Most folks do."

Chad took Marian's arm to lead her back up to the food tables. She'd been holding her breath for most of that conversation, and not just because of Leroy's horrid odor. The way Chad had provoked that huge mountain of a man, as if he had no fear of him, set her nerves on edge.

"If you didn't want to watch, why'd you come down?" he asked out of the blue.

"Excuse me?"

"You had your eyes squeezed shut. Worried I was going to take a fall?"

"Of course not," she denied primly. "I merely had dust in my eyes. And I didn't go there to watch you. I was just wandering, lost in thought."

"Anything interesting?"

"What?"

"In your thoughts?"

Was he insulting her? Suggesting her thoughts were usually dull? Probably. Or maybe he thought she was Amanda. Of course! Otherwise, he would have remarked on her changed appearance. And his question could have been an attempt at flirtation with his bride-to-be. He undoubtedly expected Amanda to tell him that *he* had been in her thoughts.

"I heard the preacher isn't coming," she said. "That his wife isn't feeling well, and he didn't want to leave her alone in town."

Chad sighed in disappointment. Because she'd passed up the opportunity to flirt with him? Or because he was in a hurry to set the date for his wedding?

She should straighten him out, but she was too angry that he was mistaking her for Amanda — yet again. And it infuriated her that she'd been afraid for him, not once, but twice in the span of a few minutes. She had to stop caring what happened to him. Whether he married Amanda or not, he was still lost to her.

# Chapter 38

Chad leaned against a tree trunk, his hat tipped low, sipping a warm whiskey. One couple had approached, plates of food in hand, intending to sit under the tree to eat, but had sought shade elsewhere when they saw him there. He wasn't in a sociable mood, and it probably showed.

Confusion was giving him a headache. He watched the twins, sure he knew who was who, yet he'd made such a colossal mistake in the stable that day, he wondered if he could ever be absolutely sure. Amanda, flamboyant, flitting about, animated, with Spencer following her around like a lost puppy. Marian, quietly conversing with some of the town ladies, demure, laughing softly, smiling with genuine humor.

He had no doubt today who was who. Spencer certainly didn't have any doubt. He'd zeroed in on Amanda as soon as he'd arrived and hadn't let her out of his sight since. Chad couldn't tell if Spencer was having any luck wooing her, wasn't even sure if that was still his intent. But he sure was amusing her, and she obviously enjoyed flirting with him.

Amanda was staying well clear of Chad. Smart girl. She knew she deserved a good throttling because of the trick she'd pulled on him. She just didn't know him well enough to know he'd never hurt a woman. But he'd have no hesitation at all in telling her what he thought of her and her damn convoluted scheme to drag him to the altar.

"I thought you were pulling my leg the other day, when you said the Laton sisters are twins," Lonny remarked as he came up to join Chad beneath the tree. "I mean, I know twins are supposed to look the same, but those two were like night and day — until now. How the hell do you tell them apart?"

"Marian's wearing beige today."

"Yes, I know. I told her how pretty she looked, and she blushed up a storm. But what if they were wearing the same dress?"

"Then you'd notice the mannerisms. Marian is shy. Amanda is anything but."

"And if they're both being quiet and shy-like?" Lonny ventured.

"Then you're flat out of luck."

Lonny looked at him askance, since he'd almost growled his reply. But considering where his own thoughts had been, he didn't need it rammed home that if one of the twins wanted to pretend to be the other, how easily she could pull it off.

Lonny frowned thoughtfully before he said, "There must be another way. Surely their parents had no trouble telling them apart."

Chad shrugged and finished off the whiskey he'd been nursing. "Probably not, but then parents get the benefit of living with them from the day they're born. The rest of us get stuck with guessing — right or wrong."

"You don't sound too happy about that."

"Would you be? If the woman you thought you made love to turned out to be the wrong woman?"

Lonny blinked then crowed, "I told you it was Amanda that day!"

"Shut up, Lonny," Chad snarled, and walked away.

He headed straight for Marian. He wasn't sure what he was going to say to her, but this confusion in his mind was driving him nuts. He still felt, deep down, that it had been her that day in the stable. It had just felt so right, making love to her. Yet when all facts — including Amanda — said otherwise, he knew he was wrong, and he just couldn't bear it that he was.

He didn't reach her before she got whisked away to the dance floor by one of the men from town. There were several other couples twirling about the stage, including his father, who was dancing with Red. Spencer was also up there with Amanda, using the dance as an excuse to hold her in his arms.

Chad watched the twins for a while and managed to calm down. You could tell them apart. You just had to observe them when they didn't know you were watching, to see all the little things that made them so different from each other.

Not that it was going to help him out of the mess he'd landed in. Only Spencer could do that. But even if Spencer succeeded in getting Amanda to marry him, Chad still didn't stand a chance with Marian now. You didn't make love to one sister, then ask the other one to marry you.

Lonny approached him again, hesitantly this time. "I owe you an apology."

"Accepted," Chad said absently.

"Don't you want to know why?"

"I know why, so keep your foot out of your mouth and say no more."

"Thanks," Lonny sighed. Then, "You going to have to marry the wrong woman?"

"Probably."

"Then shouldn't you warn Spencer to back off?"

"Hell, no. I may have been stupid and blind not to realize I was getting bamboozled, but Spencer's the only hope I have right now of being saved from a marriage I don't want. He knows what happened and still wants Amanda. I'm wishing him all the luck he can muster."

"Well, hell, if you wanted someone else to win her over, why didn't you say so. I would have been happy to do you that favor."

Chad rolled his eyes. "The old saying that I wouldn't wish her on my worst enemy doesn't apply — I'm wishing just that. What I wouldn't do is wish her on a friend. She's one woman you don't want to tangle with, kid. And you're going to have your hands full. I'm not going back to Red's."

"Because of this mess?"

"No, because you're capable now of taking over."

Lonny's shoulders squared a little with pride. "I won't let you down, or Red."

"I know you won't."

The current dance ended. Lonny moved off to find a partner for the next one. Chad continued to just watch from the sidelines. Marian seemed to be enjoying herself, had men lined up waiting to dance with her, a few impatiently cutting in before each dance ended. He wasn't going to intrude, didn't want to put a damper on her fun with his current lousy mood, but he should have left the area, because he finally got annoyed enough to do some cutting in himself.

She was expecting the quick change in partners by then, which was to his advantage. It didn't give her a chance to turn him down for a dance. But he sensed the change in her immediately, he just wasn't sure what it was. Tension, annoyance, or maybe just plain dislike.

"Relax, I'm not going to step on your toes," he told her.

"Shouldn't you be dancing with Amanda?"

"She's already partnered."

"So was I."

"Yes, but you were dancing with a man known to get carried away on the dance floor, swinging his partners about, tossing them up in the air. Women who know him tend to hide if they see him coming. You couldn't have known." He said it with a straight face.

She narrowed her eyes at him. "You're joking, right? Or do I actually owe you some thanks?"

He smiled at her. She humphed, but only because she didn't get a direct answer. He even caught the slight lifting of her lips, indicating a grin was lurking there.

"Don't bust a gut laughing," he said, still straight-faced.

She laughed, and the change in her was immediate, the stiffness gone, a sparkle in her eyes. God, she was beautiful when she let her guard down. And the dance floor was crowded enough by then that no one would notice if he held her a little closer than he should. Which was a mistake. Smelling her, touching her, his desire rose so quickly, he was nearly overcome with the urge to kiss her. But the music ended, and her shyness returned.

She stepped away from him. "Thank you, that was pleasant."

He didn't trust himself to say anything at the moment. He didn't have to. She moved off the stage, unaware just how close he'd come to making a spectacle of them both.

# Chapter 39

The four men lingered behind the stable after the bronco riding ended. They hadn't watched it, but the crowd there had made enough noise that no one had heard them ride in and tie their horses behind the stable.

Two of them were throwing dice on the ground as an excuse for being there, in case someone came by. Another was keeping watch around the side of the building. And the fourth man was leaning back against the wall, nursing a hangover. He'd indulged too much the night before, and had even missed the explanation of why they were there.

"You're damn lucky my cousin Billy took that job cleaning up in the sheriff's office, hoping to get information you'd find useful," Arnie Wilson said as he tossed the dice. It was his farm they used as a hideout in the area. "Think he'd do just about anything to join up with us."

"He's too young," John Bilks replied as he stared up the hill at the crowd. " 'Sides, four is a nice even number for splitting, five ain't."

"Yeah, but he risked a lot, stealing that

painting right off the sheriff's desk," Arnie reminded them.

"So he did us a good turn," John said. "I thanked him, didn't I?"

"This is crazy, our coming here," Snake Donally complained as he took his turn at tossing the dice. "Too many people, and half of them would probably recognize you, John."

John shrugged. "They never did prove I stole that money, and they don't know what I been up to since."

"Thanks to my cousin," Arnie grumbled.

"I doubt that painting was good enough that anyone would have recognized you from it," Snake added. "Billy said it was small."

"Billy should have brought it to me so I'd know for sure, instead of destroying it."

"He figured it would be better to make sure no one else saw it," Arnie defended his cousin.

"He recognized me from it."

" 'Course he would. He knows you good, and knows we pulled that train job."

"But the cowboy who brought it to the sheriff didn't have a name to go with it," Snake said. "So what are we even doing here?"

"Because Billy stuck around while the

sheriff was looking for the 'misplaced' painting, and when he finally gave up looking for it, heard him say he'd have to get the Laton gal, Marian, to paint him another," Arnie said.

"How 'bout answering Snake's question," Dakota Jack said, his eyes squeezed shut, not that it was helping his headache much. He was their fast gun — when he wasn't drinking. "I've only asked three times myself. What the hell are we doing here at the Kinkaid spread?"

"If you'd get them cobwebs out of your head, you'd have figured out by now that John means to grab the painter."

"Should just wait till she goes home," Snake suggested. "Way too many people here."

"Which is why no one will notice," John said. "At her home, with only a few people around her, they'd notice she's missing sooner. Here, they'll just figure she's around somewhere."

"That don't tell me what you're grabbing her for."

"To kill her, of course."

Dakota Jack straightened up, opened his eyes. "Like hell you are."

"Have to," John insisted. "She painted me from memory good enough to make wanted posters. I'm not giving her a chance to do up another. They catch me, won't be long before they get the rest of you."

Dakota Jack said no more, but only because his head was throbbing again. Snake wanted to know, "How you gonna get her down here, anyway?"

"You are. You're looking clean enough today to join the party. The cowboys will think you're from town. The townsfolk will think you're one of the cowboys. And you've never passed through Trenton for anyone to know better. Just make sure you bring the right gal. According to Billy, she's got a twin. Bring the wrong one, and I'll shoot you instead."

Marian wasn't sure what to think as she headed toward the stable again. It looked deserted at the moment. The horse racing wouldn't start for another hour or so she'd been told. And most of the guests were eating or dancing. But a young man had stopped by to tell her that Mr. Kinkaid would like her to come to the stable for a few minutes. He mentioned something about a litter of puppies. Then he quickly slipped back into the crowd before she could question him.

She'd looked around for Chad and his

father before she headed down the hill, but hadn't seen either of them. Not that she thought she was meeting Chad. She would have stayed put if she did. But it would have been nice to know for sure.

Stuart was probably going to offer her a puppy. She'd never had a pet. Her father hadn't wanted animals in their home. There had been a tomcat that had hung out behind their house for a few years that she had considered hers. She'd missed it a lot when it stopped coming around.

The thought of her very own pet was rather nice. She didn't think Kathleen would object. In fact, Stuart had probably cleared it with her aunt first. She just hoped he was going to give Amanda a puppy, too. She didn't want something else for her sister to get jealous over.

The stable was empty — of people. Both doors, front and back, were wide-open, and every stall had a horse in it. She couldn't imagine where a dog would have taken root to have a litter. Surely not in one of the stalls where it might get trampled.

"Mr. Kinkaid?"

"Back here."

She didn't recognize the voice. It was muffled because it had come from behind the stable. She headed that way, stepped back into the sunlight, and gasped as a gun was stuck in her face. It was immediately knocked away by someone else, but she had no time to feel relief because a hand covered her mouth and a thick arm circled her neck to hold her still.

"What'd you do that for?" John Bilks snarled.

Marian recognized him as soon as she got a look at his eyes. The train robbers, all four of them. Were they here to rob the guests? Had she and Stuart been unfortunate enough to run into them first? Stuart could be lying hurt, even dead, behind her. The arm around her neck wasn't giving her much leeway to look around.

"You shoot her here, you'll get this whole place down on our heads," John was told.

She recognized that one, too. He was the one who'd told her she was wanted in the stable. Fear washed over her then, nearly buckling her knees. They were there for her! Because of the painting. It had to be.

"I know that," John replied testily. "I was just making sure she didn't scream."

"I don't know," another said lazily. "If I was a woman and got a gun shoved in my face, I'd still scream."

"How you gonna kill her then, if you ain't gonna shoot her?" the one holding her asked.

"I told you, no woman-shooting," still another voice said ominously. "I'd as soon shoot you."

John started to answer that, then changed his mind. He was obviously a bit leery of the last speaker, to Marian's immense relief.

"I'm inclined to agree, now that I've seen her," the one with the lazy voice remarked.

"No one said she was this pretty," the one holding her put in. "Maybe you can just cut off her hand, so she can't paint no more."

"Face it, John, you can't turn outlaw, then expect to remain a face in the crowd thereafter, not with such distinctive eyes like you got. She might have been able to paint you, but everyone you've robbed can identify you. So what's the point?"

John was obviously getting frustrated by the opposition to his plans. "The wanted posters, that's the point," he growled. "Right now there's no face on them. I plan to keep it that way."

"Get her on a horse and let's get the hell out of here. You can discuss what you're going to do with her later."

"Someone's coming."

"I'll take care of them. Just get out of here."

"Scream, and I'll have to break your neck," the man holding her whispered in her ear as he dragged her to a horse. "Won't make me happy, won't make you happy, will only make John happy."

She didn't scream when her mouth was released long enough to get her up on a horse in front of the one that had been holding her. She debated it though, frantically. He could have been bluffing just to keep her quiet. And she was facing the prospect of death or a missing hand, and Lord knew what else, if she didn't make some kind of effort to avoid being abducted by them. Which finally decided her.

She opened her mouth to scream her head off, but she'd debated too long. The hand was back over her mouth, and they were galloping away, within moments far enough away that nobody was going to hear her screams.

# Chapter 40

Chad sputtered awake, coughing, and couldn't see for a moment. When he moved pain shot through the back of his head, bringing back the memory of an explosion of pain that had knocked him out. He realized water had been thrown on him to wake him when he saw Leroy standing next to him with an empty bucket in his hand.

"That the way you settle up your debts?" Chad growled. "By sneaking up on a man and —"

"I found you here, I didn't lay you here," Leroy spit out, looking slightly offended.

"Sorry," Chad mumbled as he sat up and rubbed the back of his head.

" 'Sides," Leroy added. "I was only joshing with you earlier. You could have left me out there to rot that day, but you didn't. I reckon that squared us."

"You happen to see who broke their gun over my head?"

"No, but I'd stop jabbering if I were you and saddle up. There's fresh tracks from four mounts, with one horse toting double."

"Then they'll be slowed down."

"Not really," Leroy said as he picked something out of his teeth. "I seen your lady friend walk this way not long 'fore you did, and she ain't here now. She can't weigh more'n a speck of dust."

Chad turned pale, shot to his feet, swallowed the groan as he ran for his horse in the front of the stable. He grabbed the first saddle he found. It wasn't his.

"Want some company?" Leroy called after him.

"If you can be ready by the time I let my pa know that Marian's been abducted. You see which way they went?"

"They haven't tried to cover their tracks — yet. Since they dealt right handily with you, they probably figure they'll be a couple hours ahead of anyone who might follow."

Chad grimaced at how easily he'd been taken by surprise. "Do they? How long was I out?"

"I'd say close to an hour. Figured you and the gal was having some fun, so I didn't want to intrude too soon. But I just got plain nosey when y'all took too long to make another appearance."

Chad wished Leroy had gotten nosey sooner. Hell, he wished he had, then he might have caught up with Marian before she reached the stable. He couldn't begin to guess why she had been taken. If it had been just one man, then it wouldn't have nefarious implications, but four? Buffaloing him meant they didn't want anyone to know about it.

"You have an extra gun?" Chad asked. "Mine are up at the house, and I don't want to waste any more time here than I have to."

"You kidding me?" Leroy chuckled, and opened his bearskin coat wide.

They rode hard, but so did the men they were chasing, so they weren't gaining any ground catching up to them. Chad developed a sick feeling in the pit of his belly as the day wore on. The more time it took to rescue Marian, the more time there was for bad things to happen to her. And then darkness fell, delaying them even more.

Leroy had wanted to make camp for the night and pick up the trail in the morning, but Chad wasn't about to stop until he found Marian and knew she was all right. He knew he was acting stupid. They couldn't very well follow tracks in the dark, could even end up losing the trail completely. But they'd reached open country before dark, and he hoped that a campfire would give them away.

It didn't. A light from a window did. The trail led straight to a farm located in the middle of nowhere, miles from any town. Other than the light from the house, the whole place had an abandoned look to it. Broken barn doors, sagging porch, fields barren of crops. Whether anyone lived there on a regular basis was doubtful, but his prey were definitely there now.

They found the four horses they had tracked, in the barn, unsaddled, merely tied to a post near an old stack of hay. They'd leave their horses there while they worked their way toward the house without being seen. They didn't talk. Both men knew what to do.

And then Leroy spotted another horse and said quietly, "It's not abandoned, this place. Someone lives here."

As soon as he said it, the stack of hay started to move. Both men watched it for only a moment, figured some animal had made a bed under it, but nothing wild, since the horses nearby didn't spook. They turned away and started out of the barn. A muffled mewling sound brought Chad's eyes back to the haystack, in time to see a shape rise out of the center of it. The light in the barn was too dim to make out what it was at first, until the lighter golden hair caught his eye.

He swore under his breath. Leroy said conversationally, "Looks like they left her out here while they went to get some grub. I wonder why?"

Chad rushed to Marian, who had pushed her way out from under the hay. "Are you all right?" he hissed. "Answer me!"

She couldn't answer him yet. He was still untieing her gag. "I'm fine," she was finally able to say, "I think."

"What the hell do you mean, you think?" he demanded, starting to shake her.

"I can't feel my hands, they've been tied up so long."

Some of the tenseness went out of him. He untied her hands, then her feet. It was a wonder she'd been able to push up onto her knees to let them know she was there.

"Do you know who they are?" he asked when she was finally standing on her feet.

"The men who robbed that train I was on. They found out about the painting I did of one of them. They wanted to make sure I didn't make any more."

"But they didn't hurt you?"

"No, not yet. Bilks wanted to. I don't think the others really did. But there was talk of cutting off my hand instead." She shuddered, saying it.

He spared a moment to hug her. "You're fine now."

"I know," she said with a sigh.

"Why they leave you out here?" Leroy asked.

"The owner of the farm didn't want to disturb his wife with whatever they ended up doing to me. They decided to wait until his wife went to bed before any final decision was made, and hid me out here, warning me not to make any noise."

"I'll get you out of here — after I kill those sons of bitches," Chad said. "Wait here."

"No!" She grabbed him back, starting to tremble. "No, don't leave me alone here. Let me go with you."

"Mari, this won't take long —"

"No! Do you have any idea what it was like, listening to those men talk about killing me! If you don't stay with me, I'm leaving on my own. I am not staying here alone, not another minute!"

Leroy chuckled softly to himself. "She's got her gumption back. I can handle these outlaws myself. You go on and get her home."

"There's four of them, Leroy," Chad reminded him.

Leroy grinned. "Child's play. I'm looking forward to busting some heads. Think there might be a reward for this bunch?"

"More'n likely. The railroad usually offers a reward for anyone who's disturbed the progress of one of their trains, to discourage any future activities of that sort."

"Then leave these fellas to me. They might make up for that five hundred you cost me."

Chad rolled his eyes. "They're all yours."

# Chapter 41

After such a harrowing experience, Marian had wanted to ride straight home, no matter how long it took, not stop to sleep. Chad didn't oblige her. He got her away from the farm and the ensuing violence expected there, but then he found a lone tree to camp under for the rest of the night.

When she complained that she didn't need any rest, his rejoinder had been, "My horse does."

She hadn't considered the horse that had ridden tirelessly for half the day to find her. She was duly repentant and complained no more.

She just couldn't seem to relax. She'd rather know for certain that those men had been rendered harmless, that they wouldn't be riding after her again. Leroy might not manage to capture all of them. Four against one was — well, with Leroy, about an even fight, maybe even slightly in his favor. She probably could relax — at least about that.

But that she happened to be spending the night out on the Texas plains, alone with

Chad Kinkaid, was reason enough not to relax.

"You don't think Leroy was going to kill them all, do you?" she asked him across from the small fire he'd made.

"He probably isn't going to kill any of them," Chad replied. "That'd be too easy, break in on them sleeping, blast them all with a shotgun. Takes more skill to capture outlaws and bring them in alive, and Leroy prides himself on being skilled. 'Sides, he won't take a chance that the reward is dependent on their being alive."

She still couldn't believe that he had come to rescue her. With all the men there at the party, Chad didn't need to volunteer for the chore.

"Is anyone else looking for me?"

"No one else knows except my pa, and probably Red by now," he said.

"Ahh, so your father sent you to find me."

"No, I let him know what was happening."

"But how did you know?"

"I noticed you heading to the stable. I got curious is all, since nothing was going on down there at the time. One of them got the jump on me and knocked me out. Leroy found me a bit later, and we figured it out together. There was no time to gather a posse."

She nodded. She should have known his reason for coming wasn't entirely to do with her. He would have come no matter who had been abducted, because that's the kind of man he was.

She sat huddled in a tight ball, arms wrapped around her legs, chin resting on her knees. He'd fed her a few strips of dried beef, hardly a satisfying meal, but it had to suffice. He'd already apologized for not coming prepared, since he hadn't planned on going anywhere before he had a chance to restock his supplies. The two blankets he had wouldn't do to cover them both, unless they were going to sleep directly on the ground. An unappealing thought. And the fire was only a few twigs and wouldn't last through the night, so they would need some cover.

She'd been talking to get her mind off of shivering. It wasn't really cold, only a little chilly. But she was still wearing her sleeveless party dress, and a delayed reaction to having been abducted was probably setting in, too. She couldn't stop her teeth from chattering.

Chad finally heard the noise, and said, "Come here."

"Why?"

He gave her an impatient look. "We need

a few hours' sleep so we can get an early start. We've got one blanket to lie on, one for cover, and it's going to get colder before the sun rises."

Huddle together to exchange body heat. That's what he was suggesting. But she was afraid to get that close to him. It had been difficult enough, riding double with him on the horse. And even if her senses could handle it, it was still highly improper. He belonged to her sister — well, he would soon.

"It's nothing personal," he added. "Just good sense."

Put that way she'd be silly to object. Was he cold, too? Probably not. He was just being generous in offering her his warmth.

She moved over to his side of the little fire and lay down next to him, stiff as a board. She heard his sigh before he dragged her closer, full against his side. His arm became her pillow. One of his hands covered one of hers, which she'd hesitantly placed on his chest. Warmth seeped into it and soon into her. She actually fell asleep.

And the dreams started, nightmares, reliving her capture, the fear, watching John Bilks sharpening an axe, meeting the farmer's wife. The woman turned out to be a witch in the dream, and the leader of the gang. She wanted both of Marian's hands chopped off.

Marian sat up with a start, a gasp, and severe trembling. The gasp must have awakened Chad.

"What is it?" he asked, sitting up beside her. Then, "Never mind, I can guess."

He wrapped his arms around her and dragged her almost into his lap. He proceeded to rub her shoulders and her back, but the trembling wouldn't stop.

"I won't let anyone hurt you, Mari," he said soothingly. "I swear, you're safe now."

"I know," she replied. "It was just a dream."

"Forget it."

"I'm trying."

But she couldn't stop the shaking. Too much had happened that day and it was all catching up to her. His warmth surrounded her. That should have helped. But it wasn't cold that was making her shake. It wasn't him either. The fear she'd felt earlier had come back with the dream and it wouldn't leave now.

He continued to rub her gently, trying to soothe her, but it wasn't working. And then she heard, "Ah, hell," just before he kissed her.

That worked. There was no room for fear

in her mind when it was filled with him. She had a feeling that was his intention, just to distract her. But like that day in the stable, her passion rose with amazing speed. So did his. His kiss might have started as another form of soothing, but there was soon nothing soothing about it.

His lips parted hers, pulling her into the intimacy he offered. She had craved the taste and smell of him without realizing it, but her body knew and was thrilled beyond measure. He placed her down on the blanket, was still kissing her deeply, leaning over her now, one leg thrown over her hips. He filled his hand with her breast, uncoiling the heat deep within her. She couldn't think, didn't want to think. She held him tightly, her only fear now that he'd come to his senses and stop.

He didn't. If anything, his kiss became more intense, as if he also had a fear that she might stop him at any moment. She should. She knew that, deep down, that she really should, but every time the thought tried to surface, she pushed it away. And his hand continued to roam, over her hips, down her legs. Even with the skirt and petticoat in the way, his touch enthralled her.

But his hand found her bare skin beneath the skirt, dragged it with him as he retraced his path, and stopped at the junction of her legs. Her pulse was racing with expectancy, the coil of heat unwinding even more. And then he touched her where she thought he might, and within moments that amazing pleasure burst on her that he'd given her once before. She was incredulous. He'd only had to touch her . . .

Did he know what he'd done? She wasn't sure, but his kiss was gentle again as he smoothed her skirt back down and pulled her back toward him to sleep. Her pulse quieted. Lethargy stole over her. She slept like a baby.

# Chapter 42

Marian would swear she woke up blushing. The memory of what had happened last night was immediately in her mind. Cheeks flaming, she tried not to look at Chad, who was getting his horse ready for riding.

He must have noticed the blush, though, because after a few minutes he said, "Look, you were in shock last night. I tried to help, but I'm afraid I got a little carried away. I know you'd probably rather not talk about it, but I'm sorry, Mari."

She didn't know whether to be grateful or disappointed. But he was right, discussing what happened between them would be much too embarrassing. Carried away? She should have known that's all it had been — for him.

They rode hard to reach the ranch by midmorning, only to find out that Kathleen and Amanda hadn't returned yet. They probably thought that Chad would be bringing Marian back to Stuart's place after he found her. He left to let her aunt know that she was home, and Kathleen rode in late that afternoon — without Amanda.

Marian didn't remark on her missing sister — well, Kathleen didn't give her much chance to, she was so full of ques-/ tions, wanting to hear everything that had happened to her. And she assumed that with Spencer's having taken his carriage back to town again, Amanda was just waiting at Stuart's for Kathleen to send the wagon back for her.

But once she finished her own story, Kathleen began hers. "Your sister took advantage of the commotion caused by your disappearance to sneak off with Spencer without anyone's noticing."

"Sneak off with him? For how long?"

"She's still gone."

Marian's eyes widened. "Overnight? Where would they have gone?"

"To town to get hitched is my guess. I thought at first she might have talked him into bringing her home here, for whatever reason, but the carriage tracks point to town. I'll ride in tomorrow with some of the boys to let her know she's got my blessing."

Marian decided to join her aunt for the trip to town. She still wanted to buy some painting supplies, and she supposed it would be appropriate to congratulate her sister on her marriage. She wasn't all that surprised that Amanda had dumped Chad for Spencer. She had preferred Spencer from the start, his being the more debonair and citified of the two. She could have just said so, though, instead of eloping.

They were in for another surprise, though, when they got to town the next day. Gossip was already running rampant that Amanda had spent the night in the saloon — without benefit of marriage. Marian couldn't imagine what her sister was thinking of, but she was too sore after the ride to find out immediately and elected to rest at the hotel while Kathleen got to the bottom of what was going on.

Chad caught up to Red before she reached the saloon. He'd come to town himself just to make sure he was off the hook. After hearing that Amanda had eloped with Spencer, he wanted to verify it, so he could relax again. He'd been crushed, though, to find out they hadn't married after all. Apparently, they'd intended to but had postponed the ceremony because of an argument, and they hadn't made up yet. But Amanda had spent the night in the saloon, whether in Spencer's bed or not didn't make much difference.

Red got angry, hearing this, and went off to gather some forces. It was quite a little crowd that headed to Not Here. The sheriff did his part and cleared the lower floor of all customers and employees alike. His deputies stationed themselves out front, to keep anyone from trying to see what was happening inside — as if anyone couldn't guess. And a good number of Red's crew were on hand to gather the rest of the participants.

Chad sat back and watched the show. It was as much a surprise to him as it would soon be to Spencer that Red was going to invite Spencer to his own wedding. He'd thought she'd at least talk to him first, try to persuade him to do what was "right" for a change. But she'd obviously concluded that that would be a wasted effort — and that her shotgun would speak louder than any words.

It did. Spencer didn't need to ask why his saloon had been taken over. When he was ushered downstairs, pushed and shoved to be exact, he started laughing when he saw Red standing next to the preacher waiting on him.

"You have *got* to be kidding."

" 'Fraid not," was all Red replied.

Amanda appeared at the top of the stairs next. At least she was fully dressed for a change, though in a pink-and-black edged getup too fancy for midday, more in line with what Spencer's female employees wore day and night, semi-evening gowns. She had apparently been willing to fit right in with the atmosphere of a fancy saloon.

She didn't laugh like he did, however. When she saw Red standing next to a man with a Bible in hand, she immediately tried to head back down the hallway to Spencer's rooms. That avenue was blocked, however, with Red's cowboys shaking their heads at her. So with an indignant huff, she marched stiffly down the stairs and straight over to Red.

"I thought I told you that you have no say over what I do," Amanda said haughtily to her aunt. "I remember saying it. Others heard me say it. So just what do you think you're going to do here — aside from making a fool of yourself?"

That brought a few gasps. If anyone had been feeling sorry for Amanda by that point, they no longer did. Red didn't take the bait, though, didn't even blush. She didn't get angry again either. It might have been a hard decision to make, but having made it, she had the backbone to stick with it.

Her tone was quite placid when she answered Amanda. "I'm correcting a wrong, sweetie."

"There's been no wrong done," Amanda tried to insist, but Red wasn't finished.

"Correcting a misconception as well," she said. "When your father made me your guardian, he put the decision of whom you could marry on my shoulders. In no way conceivable did he intend for the decision to be left up to you. Now we could have accomplished this in one of two ways. You could have taken some time and reviewed your possible choices of a husband, and we would have eventually agreed on a man suitable for you, or I could have gone through all possibilities willing and able and made the decision for you. Either way, the decision was still mine in the end, and circumstances have forced me to make it without any further consideration. But at least I *have* taken your preference into account."

"You haven't!" Amanda cried. "Did you ask me? No, you didn't! Or I would have told you that *no* one around here meets my standards. So go home, Aunt Kathleen. You will accomplish nothing here."

Red still didn't get angry. Chad was feeling some inklings of disgust himself. Spencer was gritting his teeth over being included in the reference to Amanda's standards. But Red wasn't going to be goaded into backing down.

"You can say it as long as you like, as loud as you like, or until someone puts a gag in

344

your mouth," she told her niece. "You *did* state your preference when you came to town with Spencer Evans and moved right into his bed. No ifs or buts about it. Not a single person here, myself included, doubts that you made a choice. Now we'll make it legal."

"Speaking of legal, you know this won't work unless one of us agrees to it, Red," Spencer pointed out. "She obviously won't, and I sure as hell won't now. It's been amusing, but you might as well take her home with you. She's more trouble than she's worth."

"How dare you!" Amanda glared at Spencer.

"Someone have that gag? I'll be happy to do the honors," Spencer said.

Amanda blushed furiously. Spencer had obviously taken serious offense over her "no one . . . meets my standards" remark. There were a few snickers and coughs over Spencer's rejoinder, but most eyes turned back to Red for her answer to the legal issue that he'd raised.

Were it the girl's father standing there with a gun in hand, there'd be no doubts, but "guardian" was an Eastern term most of those present couldn't relate to because most of them had grown up in Texas, where things were much simpler. A gal either had her folks or other relatives to look after her or she was on her own.

Red *was* a relative, but a female one, and no one had ever heard of a female leading a shotgun wedding before. When it amounted to "say yes or die," it usually took a man to enforce such a threat. And Red wasn't even angry! If she was at least angry, then maybe . . .

"I'll be speaking for my niece, Spencer."

"I'll speak for myself, thank you," Amanda huffed.

"You already did," Red replied. "No further response is required of you."

"Well, then, thank God he isn't going to agree to this farce," Amanda said, nodding toward Spencer.

"Oh, but he will," Red returned with a firm degree of confidence as the shotgun she'd been pointing at the floor now rose toward Spencer's chest. "He'll either say his 'I do' normally, or he'll say it between screams, but he'll get around to saying it."

Spencer didn't take her seriously, even chuckled. "You aren't going to shoot me, Red, and you know it."

"Well, yes, I would," she disagreed. "I'd try not to kill you though. You have my word on that. But a few holes in your hide won't bother me too much. Let's hope this buckshot doesn't shatter any bone beyond repair."

She said it too casually. Spencer actually didn't know her well enough to determine if she was bluffing or not. That she wasn't bluffing at all was moot. It was whether or not he believed her that would determine his answer.

But in Spencer's case, there was one other determining factor. He was much too fond of his hide to want any holes in it. No matter how remote the possibility, any possibility was enough, especially when a marriage to his way of thinking could be easily ended.

But he kept them all waiting for nearly five minutes before he snarled, "Get this over with. And the lot of you can find a new saloon to frequent, because *Not Here* will have much more meaning for you after today."

# Chapter 43

It seemed to Marian that she ached from head to toe. Kathleen had warned her that she'd probably be sore after the long ride to town, but Marian had scoffed to herself. After all, she'd just ridden long distances in the last couple days with no muscles complaining about it. But it just wasn't the same, sitting sideways in someone's lap, as it was straddling a horse and trying to keep her balance on it.

She would have spent the rest of the day in that hotel room if she hadn't gotten hungry. And Ella Mae wasn't there to fetch her anything to eat. The maid had elected to stay at the ranch, since they weren't taking the wagon to town, and she'd never learned to ride a horse either.

She was also curious about what had happened today. Kathleen hadn't returned to the hotel yet to tell her, or at least, she hadn't come up to their room. Considering the hour, she was probably having dinner in the hotel and thinking Marian was going to sleep through it.

The hotel maid who had brought her

water for her bath had also taken the two dresses she'd brought along and returned them pressed. She donned one now, a dull gray color with just a sprinkling of embroidered white flowers along the sleeve and skirt edges. Her hair was a lost cause, though, without Ella Mae's assistance. The only style Marian had ever mastered without help was her tight bun, which wasn't so severe with the altered cut of her bangs. She wasn't out to impress anyone anyway; she just wanted to get something to eat.

By the time she negotiated the stairs, her movements were a little quicker, but still pretty stiff. She was hoping to find her aunt in the dining room, but if not, it wouldn't hurt her to eat alone. Her curiosity *was* getting the better of her, though, was right up there on a par with her hunger.

She was in luck on both counts, well, not really. Kathleen was in the hotel dining room, but she wasn't alone. Chad was with her. Marian hadn't counted on that and almost didn't join them. If she had to watch Chad nursing a broken heart over losing Amanda, she'd probably clobber him.

She lowered herself into the chair as gracefully as her sore muscles would allow. She avoided glancing at Chad, though she certainly felt his eyes on her.

She tried to ignore him for the moment, and asked her aunt, "Did you find her?"

"Yes."

"And?"

"They're married now," Kathleen said.

"Really? She didn't object?"

" 'Course she did. He did, too. But bullets help change a person's mind."

"You shot them!"

Kathleen chuckled over her conclusion. Chad did, too, for that matter, which brought her eyes straight to him. All she saw was his humor, which didn't add up. Shouldn't he be devastated over losing Amanda to another man? He certainly didn't look devastated, not even a little. Then again, he could just be very good at hiding his feelings.

One thing *was* obvious though. He still didn't know it had been her in the stable with him that day, rather than Amanda. That wasn't something Amanda would clear up either, whether she got a chance to or not, because she'd still want that tie to him and to be able to gloat over it just in case Marian had been lying to her about not wanting him anymore.

She'd allowed herself to be distracted from the main point. Amanda was married.

Whether by choice or not, she'd be living somewhere other than with Marian, so Marian was finally, truly free to be herself. She'd certainly thought it would be a day for rejoicing. It was, really. It was just too bad she had so many other emotions cluttering up her joy.

"I'm sorry I missed the wedding," she said, turning her attention back to Kathleen.

"You didn't miss much. It wasn't exactly a typical wedding."

"Still, I suppose I should have been there instead of pampering a few sore muscles," Marian insisted. "She is my sister, after all."

"I really doubt she would have appreciated your presence, sweetie."

That was true. She was forgetting Amanda had been forced to marry, so she would have resented Marian's witnessing the ceremony.

Fortunately, the waitress arrived to let her know what was available to eat that night, so she didn't need to make any further comments about the wedding. Unfortunately, the unhappily wedded couple arrived as well.

"Mind if we join you?" Spencer asked as he sat down next to Chad and pulled a chair over from the next table to accommodate Amanda.

"Yes, we mind," Chad answered baldly.

"Too bad," Spencer replied with a tight smile.

Chad sat back and speculated, "Shouldn't you be celebrating a wedding night? In private?"

"We did that last night, remember? Or did I miss the so-called point of the travesty that was enacted today?"

The words were really bitter, but the tone wasn't. Marian had a feeling Spencer wasn't all that displeased with his new married state. If he'd had to be forced into it, it was probably because Amanda had gotten him angry. That was certainly easy enough for her to do.

"You reap what you —"

"Spare me your corny homilies, thanks," Spencer cut Chad off. "But I've got a question for Red. Would you *really* have shot me, splattered blood all over yourself and everyone else, watched me scream, then do it all over again when I still refused to cooperate?"

"You don't run a ranch like I do and get squeamish when something needs shooting, Spencer. Yes, I would have. Now let me ask you, did you really think you could go on indefinitely, ruining decent young women, without paying up? Clare Johnson's father might not have had the gumption to bring you to account, but I did."

"I hate to remind you, Red, I really do, but your niece was already ruined."

"That's okay, we all know that. And she was all set to visit the altar before you interfered."

"Touché." He chuckled, then turned his attention on Marian. As if he hadn't noticed her until now, he said, "Well, well, the caterpillar finally broke out of her cocoon."

Marian couldn't help giving him the blush he expected. Marian really hated being the center of attention. Amanda hated it when she was, too, so her rejoinder didn't come as a complete surprise.

"She was afraid to compete with me," Amanda explained. "She knew she didn't stand a chance. But now that the field is open, she thinks she can tiptoe in my footsteps."

"You sound jealous, darlin'," Spencer surprised everyone by saying. "There's no need to be. You're still prettier."

"Beauty is in the eye of the beholder," Chad put in, then added tongue-in-cheek, "It's a good thing Spencer is half-blind."

Amanda sputtered indignantly. Red tried to hide her laugh. Spencer didn't even try, he burst out laughing. Marian just stared, not sure why Chad had come to her rescue, unless it was no more than an excuse to take a dig at Spencer, who'd stolen Amanda from him. That sounded more likely, since she'd sensed their dislike of each other from the start.

Amanda didn't appreciate being the butt of a joke though, and turned angrily to Chad. "If anyone is blind it's —"

But Spencer cut her off, told her, "Why don't you remember our little talk, darlin', and watch your tongue."

Amanda actually closed her mouth and sat back with a glower. Marian was incredulous. Spencer had managed to gain some sort of control over her sister. With threats? Or by promising her what she wanted? Either way, it was amazing to witness. Even their father had never had that kind of influence over Amanda.

But Marian couldn't have asked for better timing. She knew exactly what Amanda had been about to reveal — out of spite. Now that she was married, she'd resent seeing Marian enjoying the bevy of suitors who should have been hers, and she had the means to force a marriage on her. Of course, no one would believe it at this point, including Chad.

# Chapter 44

There was simply no way that Marian would consider riding a horse back to the Twisting Barb until all of her saddle sores went away. Neither a wagon, nor a carriage, if Spencer was so inclined to lend his again, would do either. Both were just too bumpy on dirt roads. So she wasn't ready to return the next day when Kathleen was planning to head home.

Her aunt agreed and arranged for her to stay with the preacher and his family. There was no question about staying with her newly married sister, even if Amanda hadn't been living over a saloon.

Marian had a lot of shopping to do in Trenton, as well as several appointments with a seamstress, for a complete new wardrobe. She still had enough of her travel money to pay for most of what she needed, though her aunt suggested that she wait before actually spending any of it until they heard from the lawyer. Kathleen had sent off a telegram to Albert Bridges, telling him that more funds were needed for necessities for Marian, as well as informing him of

Amanda's marriage. Marian couldn't obtain the bulk of her inheritance yet, but it was available to fund normal living expenses for her. Kathleen wasn't expected to pay for all of her needs.

She actually had fun shopping and picking out designs and pretty materials for clothes. It had been too long since she'd ordered anything other than mundane and ugly garments, and every time she'd done so, she'd felt deprived, resentful, and especially dispirited. It had all been her own doing, necessary in her mind, but certainly no fun. Finally, those days were over.

Kathleen was going to return to collect her the following weekend. The lawyer's reply, when it came in, was to be delivered to Marian first, so she would know when the funds had been transferred to the bank in Trenton. Until then, she had to be frugal, so she merely made her choices, telling the seamstress to hold off on starting anything until the money arrived to pay for it.

She managed to avoid running into Amanda that week in town. Her sister was pretty much keeping to her new home, though Marian had heard she was enjoying herself in the evenings in the saloon, acting somewhat as a hostess for the establishment. Whether Amanda and Spencer were getting along, she had no idea, and despite her curiosity, she wouldn't pay Amanda a visit to find out.

Not that Amanda would admit to any problems if she had any. If anything, she'd pretend that the marriage was all her idea and she was quite happy with it. There had been one report that made the gossip rounds, of Spencer running down the stairs with a vase thrown after him, and that he'd avoided his wife for the rest of that day. But that had been an isolated incident. For the most part, they were putting a good face on their shotgun marriage.

Albert Bridges's reply was late in arriving. Marian wasn't concerned though. He could have been out of town and not even received Kathleen's telegram yet. But by Friday there still wasn't any word, and Kathleen would arrive the next day to take Marian back to the ranch, with nothing really having been accomplished during her week in town other than the purchase of some new painting supplies and a few blouses she'd bought ready-made. Amanda was probably getting impatient as well. Until Albert acknowledged her marriage, he wouldn't be releasing her inheritance.

His letter arrived about thirty minutes before Kathleen was due on Saturday. It wasn't expected. For it to be there by then, delivered by normal post, it would have had to be sent prior to Kathleen's telegram to him. And the envelope was bulky, so it probably wasn't just a short note to find out how the girls were getting on.

Marian's curiosity was pricked, but the letter was addressed to Kathleen, so she had no right to open it. It was probably just some legal formality or forms to sign, nothing to get anxious over. She put it out of her mind and went about gathering up her belongings in the preacher's house because she'd be spending the night in the hotel again with her aunt.

Kathleen arrived within the hour that she'd been expected. With her had come most of her ranch hands for their Saturday night on the town. Chad rode in as well with some of the Kinkaid cowboys for the same reason. Marian had hoped she wouldn't see him again now that he was no longer working for her aunt. It wasn't that she couldn't tolerate his presence, she just didn't want to. And she was afraid that he might turn his attention to her, now that Amanda was unavailable. She really didn't want to have to deal with that, or with explaining why she didn't want him now. She didn't. She really didn't.

She wanted a man to call her own, yes, but she didn't want to be any man's second choice. It still hurt, that Amanda had won in the end. It still hurt, that Chad didn't even know he'd made love to her.

He'd never know now, unless Amanda bothered to fess up to her lies, which was highly doubtful. Marian certainly wasn't going to tell him at this point. She might have made an attempt to tell him the truth if he had been forced to marry Amanda, but now that that was no longer an issue, there was no reason to, and a lot of reasons not to. Mainly, she didn't want him thinking he would now be obligated to marry her instead, nor her aunt holding yet another shotgun wedding, because she certainly wouldn't agree to one.

"I heard there was no telegraphed reply," Kathleen said when she came by the preacher's house to pick Marian up. "Whole town knows by now, since Eddy yelled it at me as I was walking down the street."

Marian grinned. It probably was hard to keep personal business personal in such a friendly town, where messages got passed along with shouts, and the latest news and gossip could be found in just about every store and saloon.

"That's probably why this got delivered to me a while ago," Marian replied as she handed the letter over. "Since most of the town already knew you were riding in today."

"Yes," Kathleen agreed, and merely glanced at the letter before she stuck it in her saddlebag. "They usually do keep my mail in town if it arrives right before the weekend, then deliver it on Monday if I don't show up. You ready, sweetie? Chad has offered us the use of the Kinkaid town house for the night. He stopped there to let the staff know."

Was she ready to sleep in his house or even see him again? No. But she merely nodded and said her good-byes to the family she'd spent the week with.

She rode double with her aunt to the Kinkaid house, which was at the opposite end of town. Kathleen dropped her off at the seamstress's, though, with the advice to go ahead and get a few of her selections started, and to meet her in the general store next door when she was done.

She found Kathleen on one of the benches outside the store, reading Albert's letter. She didn't interrupt, just sat down beside her and smiled at the people who passed by tipping their hats. It really was a very friendly town, predominantly male in population, where everyone knew everyone else, so any strangers were easily identified.

Although there wasn't an extreme shortage of women, those who lived there were mostly all married already. Which might be why Marian had received four proposals of marriage during her short stay there, and nine other men had shown up at the preacher's house with one excuse or another to pass a little time with her.

It would be much easier than she'd thought to find a husband here. She just had no present desire to start looking. Which was *his* fault. All of the emotions she shouldn't currently be experiencing were his fault. And she couldn't seem to shake the anger, or the disappointment. Dammit.

When she finally glanced at her aunt again, it was to find her leaning her head back against the building with her eyes closed. She didn't really look tired, just like she didn't want to deal with whatever she'd just read.

"Is something wrong?" Marian asked hesitantly.

"Depends on how you look at it. From a Texan's point of view, not really. Folks get along fine out here without much money, and no one expects a woman to have any anyway. Men don't marry a woman here for her fortune."

Marian went very still. "There's a problem with my father's estate, isn't there?"

Kathleen sighed as she opened her eyes. She was grimacing as she glanced at Marian. "You could say that. Seems he died broke."

# Chapter 45

Marian was now the one leaning her head back with her eyes closed. There was a sick feeling in the pit of her stomach from going so quickly from being a rich heiress to a pauper. With no warning whatsoever. And there had been none. Her father had acted no different than usual, before he left on that last trip. Surely there would have been *some* sign that he had lost all his wealth.

"Sweetie, don't let this get you down. Things really are different out here. The men who'll be wanting you for a wife, will be wanting *you*, not any money you might have brought to the marriage."

"I understand that, Aunt Kathleen. I just don't understand how my father could have lost all his money. He was rich according to his will, owned many businesses, many more income properties, much more than Amanda and I ever realized, and he had a very large bank account as well."

"I know, and all of that was undoubtedly true when he made his will. He was extremely prosperous at that time. But apparently in the last couple of years he greatly overextended himself. One too many improvements on his current properties without waiting for them to pay off. Too many new purchases that he was sure he'd make a profit on when they were sold, but they didn't sell. It sounds like his intent was a period of expansion, but he just didn't spread it out over enough time. So he started selling at huge losses just to cover costs, and when his investments still didn't start paying off normally, he started borrowing as well."

"But he never told us."

"Of course he wouldn't. He still probably thought he could recover, which could be why he never updated his will to reflect so many changes. That last business trip he made was actually to borrow more money."

"Then his estate can still be salvaged?" Marian asked hopefully.

Kathleen sighed. "Unfortunately, no. There's nothing left to salvage. When he died, everything had to be sold to pay off the debtors."

Marian was still having trouble digesting this news. It was just too much of a surprise. In the weeks before he'd died her father had gone about his business as usual, with no worried looks, no frustration or anger that things weren't going well for him.

She remembered one expansion, when he'd built a new shoe store, and she and Amanda had gone to the grand opening. He'd crowed for weeks that business was booming. She didn't recall his mentioning any other improvements.

"Wouldn't Albert Bridges have had some inkling of this?" Marian asked. "Why didn't he warn us?"

"Oh, he knew," Kathleen said in disgust. "The bastard didn't have the guts to tell you before you left Haverhill. Well, he mentions not wanting to deal with Amanda's histrionics, so I suppose that's understandable. It's all here in his letter, sweetie. He was hoping you'd be well settled in with me before he had to break the news to you."

"The money he gave us for the trip?"

"Was his. A small price to pay for his cowardice. Those are his words. Go ahead and read it."

Marian did. The letter actually wasn't that long. The bulk had come from the accounting that was included, of all the properties that were sold, all the debts that were settled. Their home had been the last thing to go, auctioned off at a ridiculously low price just to satisfy the last few remaining creditors.

"I'll have to cancel that order I just placed

with the seamstress," Marian realized.

But Kathleen rolled her eyes. "Don't be silly. A few dresses aren't going to break us. And Chad has turned my own finances around, with the help he's given me. He's lined up quite a few small beef contracts in nearby counties as well, that won't require major cattle drives to fulfill. Financially, I'm pretty much back to where we were before Frank died, and the situation will be even better off soon thanks to Chad."

Marian said nothing to that, not caring to hear any more about how nice Chad Kinkaid was. She already knew how wonderful he was. Her emotions wouldn't have gotten so tied up in knots over him if he wasn't. She just didn't want to hear it.

"And it's not as if you lack spending money," Kathleen continued pragmatically. "Or even a means to make money for that matter."

"You mean get a job? Yes, I suppose I could, though then I'd have to stay in —"

"No, no." Kathleen chuckled. "I mean you can sell some of your paintings if you were so inclined. Believe it or not, this town craves such things. The few that Orvil at the general store manages to get shipped in sell pretty much before they're even unloaded. It's why he stocks painting supplies. He's hoping someone in town here will take up the hobby and create something worth selling."

"So that's why he was so pleased to show me to where he had those supplies tucked away." Marian grinned.

"No doubt. Feeling a little better now?"

Actually, she was. It wasn't as if she'd depended on her inheritance for anything in particular. It was just that she was used to coming from wealth and had never expected to be without it, she supposed. She would have to start thinking along the lines of not being able to afford everything she might need, but she could deal with that as it occurred.

"I'm adjusting," she said. "But I really doubt Amanda will."

Kathleen groaned with the reminder since she hadn't thought that far ahead herself. "No, she's placed too much significance on her inheritance," she agreed. "Though Lord knows why."

"Because she was counting on its buying her a husband who would treat her just like Papa did."

"You mean let her do whatever she pleases?"

"Yes."

"But she's already married," Kathleen

thought it prudent to point out.

"Not if she doesn't consider herself married," Marian returned. "She could already be thinking of a divorce for all we know."

"You haven't seen her since that night at dinner?" Kathleen asked.

"No, I made a point of avoiding her."

Kathleen frowned. "But Spencer would have to agree to a divorce."

"Believe me, Amanda would know how to make him think of nothing but. But that's what she *may* have been planning. Now, she'll have to reconsider. She won't like that. She won't like that she has no other options, that she'll have to make do with what she already has."

"Well, at least she's already settled, and Spencer isn't exactly poor. He's not exactly hard on the eyes either. She's better off than she thinks."

"She *won't* see it that way," Marian warned.

"I know." Kathleen groaned again. "I think I'll just have this letter delivered to her after you and I leave town tomorrow. There's no reason why we have to listen to her theatrics when she finds out about this."

# Chapter 46

Kathleen had only been joking, about having Albert Bridges's letter delivered to Amanda after she and Marian had left town. Their aunt wasn't the coward Albert had turned out to be. She sent over an invitation for the newly wedded couple to join them for dinner that night at Chad's house. Oddly, though, both declined.

Not so odd actually. Saturday night was the biggest night for business at the Not Here Saloon. And as it happened, Amanda was turning out to be the star attraction of the place, not in an entertainment capacity — well, that would depend how you looked at it. But just being her catty, sharp-tongued self, she'd been responsible for bigger than normal crowds all week. And just by doing what she was good at — insulting admirers in whom she wasn't interested.

Amazing as it seemed, apparently born-and-bred Texans found her insults amusing. It didn't matter that they knew she was a married woman now, men were still flocking to her, flirting with her, going out of their way to gain her attention, listening to her every word. And no one took offense when she cut some cowboy to the quick. The crowd would roar with laughter — even the men who were insulted took it as a compliment that she'd singled them out.

Amanda really had fit right in to this risqué night life. And by all accounts, she was having fun being the belle of a saloon. Spencer would see it as a boon for business, so he wasn't complaining.

Marian marveled when she heard all this that night at dinner. Kathleen had made the rounds that afternoon to pick up the latest gossip, so she wasn't surprised that they were eating alone that night.

"It's not the sort of life I would have wanted for one of my nieces, but in Amanda's case, it seems to be just the sort of environment she can thrive in."

"Yes, but I wonder if that's occurred to her yet, or if she's still devoting her energies to going 'home,' " Marian replied.

Chad hadn't said much yet. Even the news about the lost inheritance hadn't raised his brow. Of course, their inheritance had nothing to do with him, now that Amanda couldn't be his. Not that he'd probably been interested in it to begin with, when he was heir to the biggest cattle spread in the area.

He did seem somewhat distracted that night. Still nursing a broken heart? Possibly. He'd get no sympathy from her. He certainly wasn't showing her any for her new loss.

"I'll go over to the saloon in the morning after church, before we head out," Kathleen said.

"They'll still be sleeping," Chad remarked.

"Then they'll just have to wake up," Kathleen replied. "I really hate being the bearer of bad news, but I don't exactly have a choice here."

"Want me to handle it?" Chad suggested.

Oh, sure, he was jumping at a chance to see Amanda again, Marian thought in disgust. Kathleen even gave his suggestion some thought, but then she shook her head.

"No, it's my responsibility." And then Kathleen grinned. "I'll just allow myself barely enough time to say what needs saying before I have to leave to get home by dark. Then I can avoid most of the tantrum."

As it happened, there was no tantrum. Amanda took the news as a joke at first. Granted, she was barely awake when she heard it. When Kathleen averred that it was true, she went into shock, barely said anything else.

Marian was skeptical about her sister's being in shock, when it was typical of Amanda simply to ignore things that she didn't like. It was a greater possibility that she simply refused to believe her inheritance was gone.

Kathleen left the letter with Spencer. It would be up to him to make his wife understand the consequences of it — if he cared to bother. Like Chad, he didn't particularly see it as a disaster, so he might not bother.

He must have explained the situation to Amanda, though, because he brought her out to the Twisting Barb the very next day. And tantrum didn't come close to describing Amanda's "enlightened" reaction.

Stuart and Chad were also there. Stuart had gotten a lot more friendly with Red during the barbecue and had stopped by that afternoon to let her know he was leaving on a trip to Chicago in a few days. Actually, he'd just stopped by for dinner, since he could have sent one of his men over with the message about his trip. Although he no longer escorted his cattle to Chicago, he did go there once a year to wine and dine the buyers. Chad had merely come along for the ride, Marian assumed.

But they were all on the porch enjoying the sunset that evening when Amanda and

Spencer arrived right before dark. And Amanda was barely out of the carriage, Albert's letter twisted in her fist, before she was screeching at Kathleen, "This is a pack of lies!"

Marian couldn't help but sigh. She wondered if anyone would notice if she just slipped away, grabbed an early dinner, and retired for the night. She really didn't want to have to listen to her sister's enraged disbelief. Of course, she'd probably have to close all the windows in her room to avoid hearing it. Amanda could get that loud.

Kathleen tried to inject a note of calm. "Sit down, Amanda. We understand your disbelief. I found it incredible myself, that Mortimer could make so many bad decisions, one on top of another."

"Then you should have known better than to accept this rubbish without —"

"Proof?" Kathleen interrupted, still trying for calm. "You're holding the proof. A full accounting was included, or did you neglect to read it?"

Amanda snorted. "You mean this *forged* account? You aren't listening, Aunt Kathleen. I'm not here because I refuse to believe what this letter implies. I'm here because I know this isn't true. My God, do you think Papa never talked to me? I'm the one he shared *all* of his successes with, whether I cared to hear them or not."

"Perhaps, but did he ever share his failures?" Kathleen replied. "Or did he keep those to himself, too ashamed of them to let anyone know?"

"You still aren't listening," Amanda insisted. "His businesses were booming. They paid for themselves. There were no hidden costs to drain his wealth."

"Too many improvements can overextend anyone. He did too much in too short a time."

"No — he — didn't!" Amanda exclaimed. "That's where *your* misconception lies. If you knew him like you think you do, you'd know he was too satisfied with his profits to waste them on improving the working conditions of his employees. But of course you hadn't seen him in years, so how would you know?" Amanda ended with a sneer.

"I was making reference to the facts given," Kathleen replied stiffly.

"*I'm* giving you the facts. If his employees didn't like where they worked, they could go work somewhere else. I've heard him say *that* hundreds of times. Even Marian has heard him say that. And why not, when he had people lined up to work for him because he paid so well, not because he supplied ideal working conditions. He opened only one new shoe store in the last several years, and that was only because a new cobbler had moved in on the other side of town, and Papa wasn't about to let him steal any of his longtime customers. And even that store was thriving."

Kathleen must have finally experienced some doubt, because she turned to Marian for confirmation. Marian hated agreeing with her sister about anything, but in this case she was forced to nod.

"It's true he said that a lot," she remarked. "He did pay his employees extremely well, and because of that, he really didn't care if they complained that his stores were old and drafty. His philosophy was that people would always need new shoes, no matter where they had to go to buy them. I don't recall him improving any of his existing stores either, not that I would have noticed, since I didn't get to that part of town often."

"I did," Amanda added. "And they were just the same as always."

"There were still new property purchases that didn't turn out as he expected," Kathleen pointed out. "And he borrowed heavily to compensate."

"Why would he have borrowed money?

He had more than seven hundred thousand dollars sitting in the bank. But if you are referring to the property listed in this accounting" — Amanda raised the letter in her fist for emphasis — "I happen to know at least one of these, the Owl Roost Hotel, Papa didn't buy at all. He was going to. And Albert would have known that. He was his lawyer after all. But someone else put in a higher offer on that hotel, and Papa wasn't willing to top it. It was in a town that didn't get a lot of visitors, and while it was a good deal at the original price, it wasn't at the higher price. Papa didn't buy property to speculate —"

"She's right," Marian cut in with a gasp as the memory stirred. "I remember that incident now. Papa laughed about it at the dinner table, that someone was trying to ride on his coattails to success, but they were only cutting their own throat by overpaying instead of finding good deals. It apparently wasn't the first time an anonymous buyer went after one of the properties he was interested in. A few months later he was patting himself on the back because the foolish buyer was still at it, and Papa had started showing interest in properties he knew weren't good deals, just to help the person dig his own grave. Papa could be vindictive like that, as long as it didn't put a dent in his own pocket."

Kathleen was staring at her incredulously. She was rather incredulous herself as all the implications sank in. Amanda gave them both a triumphant look.

Of course, that wasn't enough for Amanda. She just had to say, "I told you so," too.

# Chapter 47

Everyone was full of suggestions that night at dinner — everyone who wasn't directly involved. Even Stuart got into the discussion and was heard to remark on the side to his son that he hadn't had so much fun in years.

The cattle baron was all for rounding up a posse and lynching the shyster lawyer, as he was already referring to Albert Bridges. Of course, with Albert living on the East Coast, that would be a bit far to drag a posse. And besides, though there was no doubt in any of their minds now that Albert had stolen the inheritance from the girls, it had to be proven to the authorities before anything could be done about it.

The forged accounting wouldn't do it. Albert could claim he hadn't sent it or the letter. And the properties might not even have been sold. He could be taking his time about that to get the best prices.

Obviously, he must have hoped his letter would be the end of it. He'd made sure the girls were far from home first, using the excuse that he hadn't had the guts to tell them in person. And with them both thinking they were now destitute, he probably figured they wouldn't be able to return to Haverhill to find out what he'd done. Or he could have sold everything and run off with the money. He could be out of the country already for all they knew.

And that was the bottom line. They wouldn't know, not without hiring detectives — or investigating themselves. And Amanda wasn't about to leave her inheritance in the hands of detectives.

"How soon can we leave?" Amanda asked her aunt.

"We?" Kathleen replied. "Shouldn't you be asking your husband that?"

Amanda waved a hand dismissively. "He's not going, has no interest at all in helping me."

Several pairs of eyes turned toward Spencer, but he just shrugged indifferently, and said, "I keep telling her that she doesn't *need* that money now. But she thinks it will give her the means to get rid of me."

Amanda actually blushed. Marian found that more interesting than Spencer's lack of desire to travel back East. Did Amanda just not want everyone to know that she still wanted out of her marriage? That didn't sound like something that would make Amanda blush, unless it wasn't really true.

If it was true, she wouldn't care who knew. But if it was something she'd only said to Spencer, and hadn't really meant it, she wouldn't have wanted it brought to light.

Amanda said a lot of things without really meaning them. It was one of her tools for manipulating people. There could be more than a few reasons why she'd want Spencer to think she wasn't pleased with their marriage. The obvious one being that she *wasn't* pleased with it. The less obvious one could be because he wasn't showing signs of liking it. She could also be trying to force him to make a firm declaration of his feelings. His apparent indifference toward her was probably annoying the hell out of Amanda.

Surprisingly, it was Stuart who spoke up, reminding them, "Whether she needs her inheritance or not, the shyster shouldn't be allowed to get away with the theft. That's no different than handing over your reins to a horse thief and telling him, I didn't like that horse anyway, so you're welcome to him."

"I'm in agreement with that," Kathleen put in next. "It's not so much the money involved as it is the audacity of this lawyer fellow. He pulled his deception on me, and I admit I fell for it. He was probably thinking the girls wouldn't make head nor tails of that accounting he sent, young as they are.

The entire thing was for me, to fool me into believing it. And it infuriates me that it worked so easily. I had no doubts at all."

"It ain't your fault, Red," Stuart mumbled. "It looked all legal-like, and you haven't seen your brother in years, to know any better."

"Then you'll come with us, Aunt Kathleen?" Amanda asked again.

"Oh, yes, I wouldn't miss it."

"But what about your responsibilities here?" Marian questioned, not wanting her aunt to suffer another setback on their account.

"Lonny's capable of running the ranch for me for a few months, thanks to Chad's teaching him," Kathleen replied, then she chuckled at Chad. "No, I wasn't going to ask you to take over here again till I get back."

"I can even pay for the trip," Amanda added, bringing all eyes back to her. "Well, don't look so surprised. I *will* be getting my inheritance back."

"I thought you lost all your travel money in a train robbery on the way here," Stuart remarked, then chuckled. "Stage lines don't sell tickets on promises, they want cash up front."

"I know that," Amanda huffed. "I got all

my money back when that Leroy fellow brought those train robbers in. They hadn't spent any of their loot yet. They'd just been lying low, as the sheriff put it, and Leroy brought the money in with the robbers rather than keeping it for himself."

"Leroy might be a mean old cuss, but he's honest," Stuart put in.

"He got a nice little reward for his efforts, and I got my money returned to me," Amanda continued. "All because of one of my sister's silly paintings — well, this one wasn't so silly, actually."

Every eye turned toward Marian, which accounted for the bright color rushing up her cheeks. "It was Aunt Kathleen's idea," she explained.

"And a good one." Kathleen nodded with a grin. "But then Marian has an amazing talent for painting, and just from memory. Absolutely remarkable."

The blush got worse, especially when Chad said, "Anything on hand we can see?"

"No," Marian mumbled, causing him to frown.

But Amanda had lost her audience and wanted it back. "So it's settled then?" she said to Kathleen. "You'll accompany us so I don't *need* my husband along?"

Kathleen coughed over the slur intended

for Spencer, but she replied, "Yes, I'll start packing tonight. We can head back to town in the morning with you."

Apparently, Spencer wasn't going to ignore the slur, and decided to be ornery in pointing out, "I believe you need my permission before you go anywhere, *wife*."

"Like hell — !" Amanda started to snarl.

"Now, now," Stuart cut in to prevent the rant. "There are still some things about this whole mess that bother me, with everything that's been mentioned."

"Like what?" Kathleen asked.

"This whole scheme was a really bold thing for a lawyer to do."

"Or desperate," Chad suggested.

"That's what I was thinking," Stuart said. "Makes me wonder if Bridges wasn't the anonymous buyer their pa kept running into. If he was, and he'd have the information firsthand, of which properties their pa was after, Bridges could have ended up going broke in his scheme to get rich quick. So I have to ask, was your pa's death merely convenient for him? How did he die?"

He was looking at Marian for an answer, and she was afraid she knew what he was getting at. "He fell off a train on his way home."

"Fell? Or maybe he was pushed . . ."

With Amanda blanching upon hearing that speculation, Spencer lost his indifference, and said quickly, "All right, we'll leave tomorrow, Mandy."

"Now hold on," Stuart said, having gained the response he'd prodded for. "The stage doesn't leave for another two days, unless you plan to ride your carriage out of town, so you all might as well travel with me. I keep a private train car in Kansas for my trips north. Unless you think going by ship would be quicker."

"Sea travel doesn't agree with me," Spencer replied. "As I found to my misery when my pa sent me back East. So we'll be glad to take you up on that offer."

That quickly it was decided they'd all be traveling to Haverhill together. Well, Stuart would probably go no farther than Chicago. And Chad wasn't going at all. He had no reason to, no reason at all.

Marian was already feeling his absence.

# Chapter 48

It was barely daylight when they rode out the next morning. The luggage would follow in the wagon. The sisters and their maid rode with Spencer in his carriage. Kathleen elected to ride her horse alongside it, even though the carriage did have room for her.

Marian was a bit melancholy at leaving the Twisting Barb. She wasn't sure if she'd ever see it again. Her aunt was still her guardian. She hoped to return with her after they recovered her inheritance — *if* they could recover it. But she was going back East, back to Haverhill to be exact, and who knew what might happen, now that she no longer was hiding herself behind fake spectacles nor making any attempts to push men away with contrived insults.

Stuart offered them his house in town while they awaited the stagecoach, though he didn't join them there. He rode back to his ranch that morning to do his own packing, and Chad rode with him. It would be months, if ever, before she saw Chad again. And he hadn't even said good-bye.

He spoke to Kathleen. He even spoke to

Spencer, whom he didn't like. Although she was standing there in the stable watching the luggage being piled in the wagon as he saddled up his horse, he didn't say one word to her, didn't even glance her way.

That infuriated her. It was as if he couldn't bear to look at her, now that she looked just like Amanda. No doubt, it was too much of a reminder of what he'd lost. And she couldn't deny that she'd expected him to show at least *some* interest in her, if only just to test the waters, so to speak. She'd been waiting for an opportunity to brush him off with a "no thanks, you had your chance and picked the wrong sister."

Which was being unfair. Deep down she knew that. After all, she'd tried to make herself as ugly as she could. So of course he'd pick Amanda over her. That had been the whole point of her disguise. But even after Amanda had shown him her worst side he'd still picked Amanda. *That* was what Marian couldn't forget or forgive, that men, Chad included, could be so blinded by a pretty face to the exclusion of all else.

But he wasn't going to give her a chance to rail at him for all that, to get the hurt out of the way so maybe, just maybe, she could stop experiencing so much regret. Another thing that infuriated her was that regret. She shouldn't be having any if she didn't want him anymore, should be relieved that she'd escaped from her brush with temptation unscathed.

The seamstress in Trenton worked all day and night to complete the two dresses Marian had ordered before she'd left town. Not that she'd find much use for them during the trip, when sturdier clothes were needed to deal with the sweat and dust associated with crossing the country. She wasn't looking forward to more bumpy coach rides, but her one train ride had been rather exciting and offered interesting views, so she was looking forward to more of those.

Chad showed up with Stuart the morning they were to depart, probably just to see his father off. But his presence, when she thought she wouldn't see him again, so flustered her, she found herself being as clumsy as she used to pretend being. She dropped the small bag with her few changes of traveling clothes in it, then tripped over it. When she recovered from that, she turned around and bumped into the fellow who was loading the larger trunks on top of the stagecoach, causing him to lose his hold on one. It fell to the ground, popped open, and spilled half its contents.

The trunk happened to be one of hers,

and she gasped as she saw her rolled-up canvases rolling out into the middle of the
street. She immediately ran after them, and
almost got run down by a cowboy who was
racing down the street.

It was Chad who yanked her back, with a
snarled, "Maybe you shouldn't have gotten
rid of the spectacles."

She would have been blushing if she
didn't have to stand there and watch him
pick up her canvases. She was holding her
breath instead, and praying the tied strings
holding the paintings rolled up wouldn't
break. And heaven forbid he should ask
what they were . . .

He asked, "What are these?"

She reached for them without answering
and stuffed them back in her trunk. The
fellow who had dropped the trunk was apol-
ogizing, so she spent a moment assuring
him that no harm had been done, then gathered up the rest of the scattered contents.
Chad tried to help. She slapped his hands
away, then glared at him when he persisted.
He finally chuckled and sauntered back to
his horse.

She started to breathe normally again —
until Chad returned with a bag of his own
that he tossed up to the man arranging the
luggage on top of the coach. Marian stared,

openmouthed at the conclusion she was forced to draw.

"Where do you think you're going?"

"Now that Red doesn't need me at the ranch anymore, it's back to business as usual for me," he told her.

"Are you saying going to Chicago with your father is normal for you?"

"Sure is."

"Oh."

She tried to keep the disappointment out of her tone, but she heard it anyway. He didn't. He sauntered off again to help unload the rest of their luggage from the wagon to the coach. And she castigated herself for thinking, even for a moment, that he wanted to come along to help, or, even more unlikely, that he couldn't bear to be parted from her. . . .

How vain could she get? If he couldn't bear to be parted from anyone, it was Amanda.

She supposed he *could* be hoping that Amanda would get a divorce as soon as she got her inheritance back. After all, Amanda wasn't showing signs of being happy with Spencer, and vice versa for that matter. Chad might think he still had a chance with her, and in that case, he wouldn't want to let her get too far away from him. All excellent reasons to tamp down any disappointment she'd felt.

The small stage that regularly passed through town would never have accommodated all their luggage, and it would definitely have been a tight squeeze for seven people. But apparently Stuart only traveled in comfort and once a year, a Concord Coach with its own driver came to town for his annual trip to Chicago, to take him all the way to the railroad lines up north. It was a standing arrangement he had with that company. And of course a Concord sat eight very comfortably.

Stuart also traveled with his entourage of hired guns, and this trip was no exception, though they didn't take up any of the coach seats. Two rode shotgun with the driver, and four more flanked the coach on either side as they headed out of town early that morning.

It was going to be a long trip, Marian thought miserably as she sat across from Chad in the coach. She was going to get a stiff neck, she was sure, trying to avoid looking at him — or spend most of the day with her eyes closed. She supposed she could claim she was tired, and just make sure the next time she entered the coach, she'd be on the same side of it as he was.

Just not next to him. That wouldn't do either. That would be worse, in fact.

Damn, it really was going to be an excruciatingly long journey.

# Chapter 49

Oddly enough, Amanda didn't complain about any of the traveling this time around. Of course, this trip was to *her* benefit, and that made all the difference. And everyone coming along was there to help her. At least, she'd see it that way. But the lack of complaints actually made the trip quite bearable, even pleasant, for everyone else.

Except Marian. Being forced into such close confines with Chad again wasn't pleasant at all. In fact, she spent most of the trip quite dejected, frustrated, and with a whole slew of other unwelcome emotions to annoy her. Every time she happened to look at him, he was looking at Amanda. Every conversation Amanda started, he joined in on.

Everyone else was having a fine time on their new adventure. Marian wasn't. If she were anything at all like her sister, she would have found a great deal to complain about. But she wasn't, and so she kept her unhappiness to herself. She actually kept quiet for the most part, so much so that Chad remarked on it when they found themselves briefly alone in the corridor of one of the hotels they stayed at.

"You worried that you won't be in time to recover any of your inheritance?"

"Why would I be any more worried than Amanda?"

He shrugged. "You just seem more preoccupied about it. Never known you to be so silent for so long. Barely heard a word out of you today."

When he'd laughed at one of Amanda's attempts to be funny that morning? When she hadn't been funny at all? When the only ones who would have thought so were the men who adored her? And he wondered at *her* silence?

She had stewed over Chad's response to Amanda all day, feeling more convinced than ever that Chad was still hoping to come out the winner in the end, where Amanda was concerned. Spencer hadn't thought his wife was funny either. Of course her catty remark had been at his expense, so he wouldn't.

Those two *weren't* getting along. It was patently obvious to anyone taking notes, and Chad would be taking notes. Oddly, though, Amanda was being remarkably restrained toward someone she actively disliked.

The barbs she tossed at her husband were rather tame for her, more designed to get his attention than to cut to the quick. It was almost as if she didn't really dislike him — or he held something over her to keep her from getting overly vicious.

But as for Chad's remark, and because he was standing there blocking her path as he awaited a reply, she was forced to say something, and she said it rather stiffly, "I have a lot on my mind aside from someone stealing my inheritance. Four proposals of marriage require a great deal of thought."

"What?!"

"You heard me. And I told them all I'd think about it, so I am — thinking about it."

"Who's been bothering you on this trip?"

"No one."

"Then who asked to marry you?"

"Oh, those weren't recent proposals, that was before we left Trenton."

"Who?" he persisted.

She frowned and was forced to admit, "I honestly can't remember most of their names, well, aside from that nice Dr. Willaby."

Chad snorted. "He's old enough to be your father."

Marian shrugged. "He's still very nice."

He then narrowed his eyes on her. "You pulling my leg, Mari?"

"No, I wouldn't dream of doing that," she shot back. "And besides, since none of this is any of your business anyway, you shouldn't be asking. And maybe you should keep your questions to yourself next time if the answers are going to bother you."

"I'm not bothered," he snapped.

"My mistake. You don't sound bothered at all," she snapped back, and pushed her way past him.

She didn't say another word to him that day, or the next. In fact, if she couldn't say something to him without snapping — she'd castigated herself thoroughly over that — then she'd do better to keep her mouth shut. He must have felt the same way because he went back to ignoring her.

The longest and most tedious part of the journey was over when they reached the railroad that connected to the eastern half of the country. The trip had been uneventful for the most part, no attempted robberies with such a well-armed escort, no gunfights or brawls to witness in the towns they passed through.

There had been the one morning Marian rose earlier than usual and caught her aunt leaving Stuart's hotel room. That could be considered quite eventful, she supposed, though only she knew about it. And she'd been much more embarrassed than Kathleen had been.

Her aunt had merely grinned at her, and said, "He's asked me to marry him."

"Isn't this rather sudden?"

"Not really. We — ah, sort of shared a bed the night of the barbecue. I was all worried about you, even though Chad was going out to find you. But Stuart was determined to take my mind off of it. It's pretty much why he came over that day for dinner, not just to tell me he was heading to Chicago for a spell, but to let me know when he got back that he'd be courting me proper."

"Will you marry him?"

"Oh yes. I've been in love with that man since the day I first met him, just never thought to do more'n keep it to myself. Even after Frank died, I never dreamed the day might come that he'd show some interest in me."

"Why not?" Marian asked in her aunt's defense. "You're a fine-looking woman."

"But with a small spread, while he aspires to being the cattle king of Texas. Besides, with his wealth, he could have any woman he wanted, so why would he want one who could only bring a few head of cattle to the marriage?"

Marian rolled her eyes. Trust a couple of ranchers to think in terms of cattle rather than love.

"So you were wrong."

"Actually," Kathleen replied with a chuckle, "Stuart says it's the only way he could think of to get my cook into his house."

Marian blinked, and felt her hackles rise indignantly. Kathleen burst out laughing, then put a hand to her mouth to stifle it. Considering the early hour, she didn't want to wake any of the others in their nearby rooms.

With another grin, she hooked her arm through Marian's to lead her back to her own room. "He was joking," she said in a low voice.

"You're sure?"

"Absolutely. And let's keep this to ourselves for now. Stuart wants to get married in style when we get back home. He's going to invite the whole county. Says he's going to throw the biggest shindig ever to celebrate. But in the meantime, we'd like to keep our happiness under wraps. Just ain't appropriate, with everything else still unresolved."

And Amanda would be sure to put a damper on it, since the happiness wasn't hers. But that didn't need to be said, it was understood by them both.

Marian was still amazed. She hadn't seen it coming. But then she'd been so wrapped up in her own moping, she hadn't noticed the intimate looks passing between the older couple, hadn't noticed anything at all to indicate they were having secret rendezvous. Not that they could arrange them very often, when half the hotels they stayed at didn't have enough rooms to accommodate everyone, so rarely did one of them get a room to himself or herself.

But she was very pleased for Kathleen. It did add to her own dilemma though. It meant she'd have to live on Stuart's ranch with her aunt when they got back to Texas, at least until she got married herself. But that would mean being back under the same roof as Chad, and she found that so unacceptable she didn't even want to think of it.

It did give her more incentive to find a husband before they returned to Texas, not an impossibility. She was returning to her hometown, after all, where she already knew most everyone in her social circle. And although she had alienated most of the eligible men there, she was returning a new woman — well, new in looks anyway — so she could start afresh.

There was the problem of a time constraint. They might not be in Haverhill very long, and certainly weren't going there with the intention of entertaining callers. But she could work around that if she were determined enough, and she was. Anything would be preferable to having to put up with Chad's continued presence.

# Chapter 50

Stuart's private railroad car was a marvel of elegance even for him. He'd be the first to say it was overdone. But he didn't use it often enough to bother redecorating it. While it wouldn't accommodate all of their party for sleeping purposes, the parlor area was well supplied with overstuffed chairs girded in velvet, so those who ended up sleeping in them didn't really mind. And there had only been one night that they'd had to, when the train stopped at a depot only long enough for the passengers to eat dinner, then continued on through the night.

There was a well-stocked bar, even a piano. "It came with the car," Stuart explained with a shrug. "Just never got around to getting rid of it."

Red actually knew how to play it, and entertained them a few times. Chad enjoyed that much more than playing poker with his father and his men because he couldn't concentrate long enough not to get ribbed for it. And he had no excuse to be so preoccupied, none that he was willing to share anyway.

Actually, his father seemed to be in the

same boat — of not being able to concentrate for very long. Chad had guessed why. It was pretty obvious. But he'd wait until Stuart made the announcement, that he and Red were going to get hitched, before he said, " 'Bout time."

The two made a perfect couple. Chad had thought so long before Stuart came to that realization himself. And he would have gotten a kick out of seeing his father "in love" again after all these years since his mother had died, if he weren't so aggravated over his own pathetic circumstances.

He shouldn't have come along on this trip. He'd never gone to Chicago with his father before. There was only one reason for his presence. He couldn't bear to see the woman he wanted riding off into the sunset without him. That was really stupid, because she didn't know he wanted her, and she sure as hell didn't want him. So there had been no point in going, other than to make himself miserable. And he was doing a good job of that.

It hadn't been so bad at first. Spencer and Amanda had distracted him with their odd relationship. He'd even found a lot of their bickering amusing, considering how he felt about Spencer. But it was getting harder and harder to see Marian every day and be so totally ignored.

Her behavior spoke volumes about her feelings for him. She didn't have any, though she might have previously. He'd stood a good chance with her, before Amanda had tricked him. But she'd be insulted if he turned to her now. That night under the stars, she'd been in shock, and although he hadn't intended to take advantage of that, he really had gotten carried away from wanting her so much. He should have just told her that; but she'd been so embarrassed about it afterward, he hadn't wanted to make it worse. And even if for some reason she'd welcome his suit, the incident in the stable with her sister would always stand between them. He'd be better off just to forget about her entirely.

They were at their last overnight stop before reaching Chicago, when Chad found Spencer eating alone in the hotel dining room. He'd come down late to eat himself, hoping everyone else would be done and already in their rooms. Stuart had already announced that he'd be going all the way to Haverhill with the ladies. No surprise to Chad. He'd yet to decide if he would as well.

Prolonging the agony was one way to view it, except that Marian would be returning to

Texas, probably even moving to the Kinkaid ranch if she didn't marry before Red did. Maybe he should just stay in Chicago himself, at least until Marian was out of his life.

He sat down at Spencer's table without asking permission. He and Spencer had been "getting along" if you could call not fighting getting along. And ever since the trip started, Chad had been curious what was behind Spencer's strange attitude. Half the time he seemed annoyed, and the other half he seemed to be holding back laughter.

Spencer merely glanced up when Chad sat down, then went back to cutting the meat on his plate. Chad chose not to be ignored. He'd had quite enough of that lately.

"Where's the wife?" he asked.

"A headache sent her to bed early. She seems to get a lot of them."

"I'll bet," Chad said dryly. "But as good a reason as any for you to be tarrying down here."

Spencer grinned, a secretive grin that Chad found damned annoying. But Spencer offered nothing by way of explanation, "The food's great. I decided on a second helping is all."

"Glad to hear it, since I'm starving." Chad called the waitress over and asked her to bring him what Spencer was having. Then as if they'd already been discussing it, he said "You two getting a divorce as soon as this thing with the lawyer is settled?"

Spencer almost choked at the unexpected question, but recovered with a noncommittal, "I'm beginning to like married life."

"You could have fooled the rest of us."

Spencer laughed. "Appearances can be deceiving — as we both found out."

"You wishing you'd found out sooner that the ladies are twins?"

"Hell no. Marian is too — how shall I put it — nice for my taste."

"Too nice for you, period," Chad mumbled.

Spencer sat back, took a drink of his wine, and said nonchalantly, "I sense you haven't claimed her yet. But then I always knew you were a fool."

Chad stiffened, reminding him, "I made love to her sister. That's not something a woman will overlook."

"Since when did you become an authority on women?" Spencer smirked. "You might as well run around with your head in the ground because you sure as hell aren't going to get anywhere with her by not trying."

"Look who's talking. You have a wife who claims a headache if she even looks at you."

Spencer burst out laughing. Chad gritted his teeth. His food arrived just then, or he might have sent his fist across the table.

He'd never known Spencer to be so cryptic, or to withhold what he found to be amusing. And something was sure as hell amusing him, although, for once, it didn't seem to be at Chad's expense. It was still damned annoying that Spencer was keeping it to himself.

But then Spencer surprised him. Laughter wound down, still grinning, he confessed, "I hate to disappoint you, but Amanda's 'headache' excuse isn't for me — well it is, but that's because she hopes I'll follow her right to bed. Her excuse is mainly so no one else will notice that she prefers to retire early these days — or wonder why."

Chad frowned thoughtfully. "What you're implying doesn't add up."

"That's because you're missing the main equation. How shall I put this? She loves making love."

Chad snorted. "But otherwise hates your guts?"

Spencer's grin widened. "She doesn't hate me. Far from it."

"You're just her current favorite verbal punching bag then?"

"You mean her pouting? That's all her

405

cattiness is, because I won't pamper her or give her everything she wants. Lord love her, she wouldn't be herself if she didn't pout. She is a brat, after all."

"And that doesn't bother you? Never mind. Your amusement speaks for itself."

Spencer chuckled. "She pouts over that, too. But I can't help it. I've never met such a spoiled rotten female before. I find her antics and manipulations funny as all hell."

"It would drive me up a wall."

"Well, that's you, and thank God, you and I aren't the least bit alike."

"Son of a bitch," Chad said as he realized, "you *wanted* to marry her all along, didn't you? Your protests were just for her benefit."

"Of course."

"You ever going to get around to letting her know?" Chad wondered aloud.

"Probably not." Spencer shrugged. "That would spoil her, and I'm not stupid."

"A matter of opinion," Chad said, but it was merely habit, insulting Spencer.

And Spencer ignored it. "I'm not about to make that mistake. Besides, it wouldn't make her happy. It never did. Spoiling her just made her a bitch. But she's learning — rather late, though better than never — that it's more worthwhile to earn what she wants than to have it given to her. And I'm going to enjoy every moment of teaching her."

Chad shook his head. "You amaze me, Spencer. I never would have thought you'd have that kind of patience."

"There's no patience needed. She's too predictable, my wife. She's spent her life manipulating others and never realized just how easy she is to manipulate herself."

"I almost feel sorry for her."

Spencer burst out laughing again. "For what? Getting her just deserts?"

"Something like that."

"Don't kid yourself. She's never had so much fun in her life as she's had since she met me."

# Chapter 51

On the long trip to Haverhill, there had been plenty of time to discuss a plan for confronting Albert Bridges. After going back and forth on all sorts of possibilities, they decided that the sisters would remain out of sight, until they located Albert — assuming he hadn't already taken off to other parts of the country with his ill-gotten gains. But if he was still in Haverhill, they didn't want to alert him to their presence before a confrontation could be arranged. They didn't want to give him the opportunity to run before they could get their hands on him.

Marian didn't like having to disguise herself again and stay cooped up in her hotel room. She wasn't going to get married that way. She needed to be *seen* by old acquaintances to have any hope at all of receiving any proposals before she was forced to return to Texas.

Amanda didn't care. She just wanted her inheritance back — if there was anything left of it. And if the men thought she'd have a better chance of getting it by hiding herself, she'd hide herself.

That was accomplished by the two staying in the private train car until after midnight, then pretty much sneaking into the hotel that Kathleen had checked them into earlier in the day. At least Marian had a room to herself for a change, so she could mope in peace.

Chad was still with them, too. Marian didn't ask why he'd decided to see this to the end, not because she wasn't curious, but because she refused to talk to him at all. She was too disappointed that she wasn't going to have at least a short break from his frustrating presence.

There was good and bad news by the middle of the next day. They all met in Kathleen's room for lunch and to report their findings to the girls. Spencer and Amanda had slept in late, so he had nothing to report, but Chad and his father had gone out early to locate Albert.

They were the last to arrive, and Chad told them immediately, "He's still living in town."

"Well, that's the biggest hurdle out of the way," Kathleen replied.

"Stupid of him," Stuart added. "But then he's obviously completely confident that the gals will never show up to accuse him of anything."

"It didn't look promising at first," Chad continued. "His old office has been taken over by a bookkeeper, so we thought Albert was long gone."

"But he's not?" Spencer asked.

"No," Stuart replied. "Most of the employees there didn't know who Albert was, but a new one came in before we left the building, and when he heard who we were looking for, he pointed us uptown to a new address. He used to work for Albert. Did a lot of complaining, too, that Albert didn't take him along to his new office. Had nothing but nasty things to say about his old employer because of it. He was a very bitter young man."

The plan had been that they would take Albert straight to the authorities if they got their hands on him. It was Kathleen who asked, "I take it he wasn't at his new office either?"

Stuart shook his head. "The new place is a definite improvement though. The old office was a dump, the new one as plush as a fancy — well, very rich-looking indeed."

"Decorated with *my* money, no doubt," Amanda growled in an aside to her husband.

Spencer patted her arm soothingly. "Probably."

"Where was it?" Marian asked.

"Big building next to a bank, two stories —"

Amanda gasped. "I know that building! That was one of Papa's properties."

"No need to get all indignant, Mandy," Spencer told his wife. "That's just the sort of proof we need to hang the fellow, that he's in possession of a building that should have been left to you. Sounds like we can wrap this up and go home sooner than expected."

Amanda didn't turn on him for the scolding, she actually sent him a smile. Marian was still marveling over that when Chad continued. "There'll be a short delay. Seems he's a busy man. He's gone north to finalize some land deal for one of his clients. According to his secretary, he's not expected back until Friday."

"Three more days!" Amanda moaned.

Marian was in complete agreement with her sister for once, though probably for a different reason. "I don't see the need to remain hidden, then, if Albert is out of town. There are a few people I'd like to call on —"

Chad cut her off with a flat, "No."

She raised a brow at him, and said testily, "And who put you in charge?"

He frowned at her tone, started to answer, but his father beat him to it. "He's right. There could be others here who know what the lawyer did."

"Who?"

Stuart shrugged. "A partner, an accomplice, a bribed official. Maybe even family."

"That's highly unlikely," Marian protested.

"Why?" Chad said. "He had to have bribed someone to get everything transferred to him without a hitch. And are you sure he had no family here? A wife? Parents?"

"Not sure at all," Marian mumbled.

"He mentioned a sister once, but she didn't live here in Haverhill," Amanda put in.

"Fine, I'll go back and hide in my room," Marian huffed. "But I really doubt our presence here is going to remain a secret for very long. I've already run into one hotel maid who started to ask me, 'Aren't you — ?' before I cut her off with a 'No.' As if she'd believe me. Mandy's face is well-known in this town."

Marian marched angrily out of the room, barely managing not to slam the door. She was blushing before she reached her own room down the hall. That had been too rude of her.

She was starting to behave like Amanda, and she couldn't seem to help it. She was so tired of pretending that everything was fine and normal, when she had so much turmoil ripping her up inside. Her patience was gone. Her tolerance was gone. It had been one thing to contain her emotions when she'd thought she would have some respite soon, but she was getting none.

Chad was still around, she was still seeing him daily, and she could no longer deny that all the anger she'd felt over what had happened between him and Amanda was still there, and it hadn't lessened at all.

He'd fooled her so completely. He'd kissed her the night before the incident, making her think she really had a chance with him. Then he'd made love to her, making her think he actually wanted *her*, while all along he had been sure she was Amanda. She'd been hurt then, but all that was left now was bitterness. And a lot of resentment and jealousy. She couldn't deny that anymore either. Amanda always won. She didn't even have to try, and she won.

She no sooner closed the door to her room than the tears started. She wasn't surprised. Solitude was not her friend these days. The more time she spent alone, the worse she behaved in the company of others, acting short-tempered, snappish. She barely recognized herself these days.

It might have helped if she could discuss her feelings with someone, but there was no one she could talk to. She didn't want Kathleen to know that she was the virgin Chad had deflowered, not Amanda. And besides, her aunt was too happy with her newfound love. Marian wasn't about to put a damper on that.

She could have cried on Ella Mae's shoulder. She should have. The maid was good at offering sympathy. But Marian didn't really want sympathy. Ella Mae was also good at making outlandish suggestions that were always too bold for her tastes. And for once, Marian was upset enough actually to follow them, bold or not, so she chose to not be tempted and kept what was bothering her to herself.

A mistake. She'd held it all in for too long and was turning into someone she didn't like because of it. And this solitude was not helping. Of course, she could go back down the hall to Kathleen's room and make a fool of herself again.

She shuddered at the thought and instead, dug out an old bonnet from her trunks and attached a veil to it. No one

would recognize her under it. And she
wouldn't approach anyone she knew. But
she was not staying cooped up any longer.

# Chapter 52

"Maybe you can have a little talk with her?" Stuart suggested.

Stuart and Kathleen were the only two left in her room. Spencer and Amanda had gone back to theirs, and Chad left soon after. Without actually planning it, they found themselves suddenly alone. It was still soon enough after Marian's departure that Kathleen didn't need to ask Stuart of whom he was speaking.

"I probably should. Something is definitely bothering her."

"I don't mean about that, I mean about my boy. He's got some powerful feelings for her, but she's driving him crazy. She treats him like he's invisible."

"Of course she does," Kathleen said in Marian's defense. "I would, too, if a man who'd made love to my sister suddenly started showing interest in me."

Stuart sighed. "You know that was a mistake. Dammit, Red, the boy was tricked. You know it. I know it. It's about time Marian knew it."

"I doubt it will make much difference."

"Or it could make all the difference," he insisted. "So tell her."

Kathleen shook her head. "If she hears it from anyone, it should be him. If he's got powerful feelings for her, why hasn't he told her about them?"

"Because he's thinking the same way you are, that it won't make much difference. You could at least find out if he's got any chance at all."

Kathleen rolled her eyes. "So could he. If they can't get together on their own, then they weren't meant to. I'm no matchmaker. Neither are you, for that matter. So what brought all this on?"

He mumbled, "Young folks make mistakes they end up regretting. You did. Married a man you didn't love just to get out of this town. Chad did, made love to the wrong woman. 'Course he didn't know it, and that's what really stinks about this whole thing. If that ain't enough to regret, I don't want to see him regretting a lost opportunity with the woman he does want."

"So why aren't you pestering him to do something about it already?"

"Already did," Stuart admitted in a grumble. "But you know him well enough by now to guess his answer. He told me to mind my own business."

Kathleen burst out laughing and moved over to sit on Stuart's lap. "Sound advice. And you have some business you can mind right now."

That got a smile out of him as she knew it would. They were so compatible, it seemed like they'd always been together. She pretty much knew what he was going to say before he said it. There were few surprises with Stuart. For all his gruffness, he had a big heart.

Funny thing about being happy. It made you want everyone else around you to be happy, too. So of course he'd be concerned about his son's dilemma. She was just as concerned about what was bothering Marian, but she figured it was related to where they were. Marian had a lot of unpleasant memories associated with this town. Kathleen did, too, but she'd been away long enough for it not to affect her. Not so for Marian.

What she didn't think, was that Marian's sudden bad temper had anything to do with Chad. She'd done too good a job of ignoring him. She was afraid Chad was going to be flat out of luck where she was concerned, that any feelings involved were completely one-sided. Which was too bad.

He should have told her how he felt about

her sooner. He should have at least let her know what really happened in that stable, that he'd thought it was she with him that day. But he'd let too much time go by without telling her about his feelings. Just like a man, to prevaricate too long.

Kathleen blushed with the thought. She'd done the exact same thing by not letting Stuart know about her love for him. He'd scolded her thoroughly for that. If he hadn't tried to distract her from worrying about Marian the night of the barbecue, they might never have realized that their feelings were mutual.

She hugged him, tightly, for what she might have missed out on. Her present happiness still dazed her. And she was enjoying this trip back to Haverhill immensely — because Stuart was with her.

"You getting emotional on me again, Red?" Stuart guessed, chuckling.

Kathleen leaned back, grinning at him. "It's a good thing you don't mind."

His arms gathered her closer. Their lips met, gently at first, then with a great deal of passion. Soon, they were oblivious to their surroundings, aware of nothing but each other. Making love with Stuart was like making love for the first time. Kathleen would never have guessed just how wonderful it could be — with the right man.

Marian wasn't a bit surprised to find she'd wandered toward home without paying attention. Her old home.

She stood in front of the large three-story house for the longest time, just staring at it. It wasn't vacant. New drapes adorned the front windows. Someone had redecorated, and was living in it. Albert? She could at least hope so. That would mean it hadn't been sold, and they might be able to recover it.

"Excuse me," a female voice said. And then a bit more harshly, "Excuse me, you're blocking the gate."

Marian finally heard the woman next to her and blushed, quickly stepping out of the way. "I'm sorry. I'm afraid I was lost in thought."

"An odd place to stop and think," the woman huffed, and moved the baby stroller she was pushing forward so she could open the short gate at the pathway that led up to Marian's house — her old house.

Marian frowned when it was obvious the woman and child were going to enter the house. "A moment, please," she said, quickly following her up the path to the door. "Do you know who lives here?"

"I do," the woman said impatiently.

"Oh," Marian returned in disappointment.

So much for thinking the house might be recovered. The woman wasn't a servant. She was dressed in the height of fashion. While some servants could afford fashionable clothes, they couldn't afford fashionable clothes made out of such rich materials as this woman was wearing. Besides, she was much too snippy to be a servant.

Marian turned to leave, but then thought to ask, "Do you know Albert Bridges?"

"Certainly. He's my brother."

Marian caught back the gasp before it escaped. So she *had* been right. Albert was living there and had apparently moved in his whole family — sisters, brothers-in-law, nephews, and who knew who else.

The woman was tapping her foot. The baby was starting to fuss.

"I'm sorry to have bothered you," Marian offered, and turned to leave again.

"Just a minute," the woman demanded. "What do you want with Albert?"

Marian decided a fabrication was in order, so as not to cause any suspicion. She quickly offered one.

"My husband wishes to retain Mr. Bridges's legal services. He went by his office, but was told he was presently out of town."

"And so he is. He's not due back until the end of the week."

"I'm not sure we can wait that long. The matter is rather urgent."

"Hardly my concern," Albert's sister said tersely. "Either have your husband get an appointment at Albert's office or find another lawyer. But in either case, stop bothering me. Good day."

The door was slammed shut on Marian. What a rude, unpleasant woman. She wondered if she'd always been that way, or maybe guilt over what Albert had done had turned her into a shrew.

But Marian didn't tarry any longer. She walked back to the hotel, passing through the busier areas of town, lost in thought again. She had to decide whether to confess to the others that she'd gone out, when she'd been warned not to. She'd have to if she was going to tell them what she'd found out. Or she could just say nothing.

It wasn't really pertinent, after all, that Albert was living in their old house. Only Amanda would be glad — or enraged — to hear it. And she was sure that before Friday one of the men would find out where he lived, since they would want to cover his office, his home, and the train station on the day he was due back, to make sure they didn't miss him.

And she'd already done the most that she could do to help to apprehend him. She'd painted each of the men a small portrait of Albert from memory, so they'd know who they were looking for. Albert really didn't stand a chance of eluding them — if he returned to town.

# Chapter 53

Chad knocked briskly on the door. The moment of truth was at hand, and he couldn't remember ever being quite so nervous. But, then, his future happiness was at stake.

He was going to lay his cards on the table and tell Marian everything. The delay in confronting Bridges had decided him. Three more days at loose ends with nothing to occupy him except his regrets. No thank you. So he knocked on her door. She'd either tell him to go to hell or — or make him a very happy man.

It finally broke through his nervousness that he'd been knocking for a very long time with no answer. He tried opening the door. It wasn't locked. And the room was empty. Well, what the hell?

He knew she wasn't with Red. He tried Amanda's room, but got an annoyed shout from Spencer inside, "Go away, we're sleeping!"

Yeah, right, it was obvious what those two were doing, but that meant Marian wasn't with them either. So where the hell was she?

He went downstairs to check the lobby. Mostly empty. He checked the hotel dining room. Completely empty, but then it was midafternoon, long past lunchtime and too early for dinner. Worry began to set in.

He paced about in the lobby for a while, trying to decide whether to go out and look for her in a town he didn't know at all — meaning he wasn't likely to find her — or to wait there in the lobby and catch her when she returned. She walked through the front doors before he reached a decision.

He recognized her even with the veil. There probably wasn't anything she could do to disguise herself from him anymore. But then he'd gotten into the habit, from the day she'd removed her spectacles for good to view *all* of her, not just the obvious. He'd never again be in doubt of which sister he was dealing with. Other than wearing the same faces, they weren't identical at all.

She didn't notice him approaching her until he blocked her path. "I was about to send out a posse."

"Very funny," she replied, and tried to move around him. "I haven't been gone that long."

He blocked her again. "You weren't supposed to be gone at all."

She stiffened with that reminder, and told

him, "I took precautions, or do you think I like looking at the world through black lace."

"I think you like driving me crazy with worry," he gritted out.

"How so? When I barely give you a thought?" she shot back dryly.

He growled, "Come with me," took her hand, and started dragging her out of the hotel.

"No! Stop it!"

He didn't. And it was all he could do to keep from being as snappish as she was. He didn't know why she was that way. He sure as hell knew why he would be. He said not another word. Instead he hailed a passing hack. He shoved her into the enclosed carriage the moment it pulled up to the curb. Marian sat on the seat opposite him and glared.

"Just where do you think you're taking me?" she asked in a tightly contained tone.

"Nowhere in particular, just somewhere we can talk without being interrupted."

"Well, you might want to give the driver directions. He's not going to budge without them."

He noted her smirk. She wasn't going to make this at all easy.

"This is your town, not mine," he said.

"Do you have any suggestions?"

"I'd suggest you stop trying to abduct me and let me return to my room to rest before dinner."

He ignored her dramatic interpretation of what he was doing, said, "Actually, your room sounds about perfect. Shall we?" and he opened the carriage door again.

"Oh, *now* you're asking?" she snapped, and stepped back onto the curb, then threw back, "It's perfect for me, but you aren't invited."

She marched back into the hotel without him. Chad clenched his teeth, tossed a few coins at the driver with his apology, and hurried after Marian. She was rushing up the stairs, trying to beat him to her room so she could no doubt lock the door on him. He did some rushing of his own to catch up to her and actually had to run the last few steps down the corridor to get to her door first.

He opened it. She sighed, brushed by him, removed her bonnet, and tossed it on the seat of the only chair in the room. A subtle warning that she didn't expect him to be there long enough to get comfortable.

He closed the door, decided to lock it as well. She heard the click. Her back stiffened. He crossed his arms, leaned back against the door, waited. She finally turned to look at him, but only long enough to note where he was, then glanced away again. He'd gotten used to being treated as if he weren't there, but this was one time he wouldn't allow it.

"Look at me."

She did, even raised a brow at him. He'd expected another argument, giving him a good excuse to ask why she never looked at him anymore, *really* looked at him. He would probably have found the answer interesting, but it was just as well he didn't ask. He didn't want to make her any more defensive than she already was.

"You could relax," he told her. "This won't take long — then again, it might."

"I'm perfectly relaxed," she replied, though her tone and posture belied that. Which she must have realized, because she added, "Aside from the fact that it's highly improper for you to be in here."

"Who's going to know?"

"Hardly the point," she replied in a huff, then sighed. "Very well, say what you're so determined to say, then please leave."

"I was going to wait until you settled things here in Haverhill. If you got your inheritance back, fine, you'd be relieved. If not, fine, I'd have an edge."

"What are you talking about?"

"I'm getting to it. Just letting you know why I didn't make this confession sooner."

"I'm not a priest. Why don't you —"

"Can you stop being sarcastic for one minute?" he asked her.

She closed her mouth, but was back to glaring at him. "If you're about to tell me that you have feelings for me, please don't. You made your preference clear long ago, and it wasn't me."

"Is that what you really think?"

"It's what I know," she replied. "It's what I witnessed. It's what —"

"Oh, hush up, Mari. You really don't know the half of it."

She stared at him. She started tapping her foot. She was about as receptive to hearing what he had to say as an out-of-heat cat was to a barnyard tom. He supposed he should have waited after all. *Something* had been upsetting her all week. She'd gotten more and more touchy with each passing day, a mood hardly conducive to the romantic overtures he wanted to make.

But he'd already put his foot in it. Not to tell her now would just make matters worse.

He crossed the few feet to stand in front of her. He wanted to draw her into his arms, but she was too tense. He had so much to say, but he was sure now that she didn't want to hear any of it. She'd taken a real dislike to him, obviously, and probably because of her sister. He could at least clear that up. . . .

"I was attracted to Amanda, yes. I don't deny that. I was planning to let her know about it after she got settled in with your aunt, but *only* if her attitude improved. I convinced myself the trip was responsible for her behavior, that once it was over, she'd change and become less annoying and more likable. It didn't happen. If anything, she got worse. So no, all plans for courting her ended *prior* to what happened in that stable."

"Don't bring that up, please."

He shook his head. "I have to. You need to know that it was a mistake."

"The first thing you've said that I agree with," she returned.

"No, it was a bigger mistake than you could possibly realize. I had no reason to suspect that she was pretending to be you, so who do you suppose I thought I was making love to?"

She blushed furiously, hearing that. "I know who you wanted it to be."

"Do you?" He frowned. "No, I don't think so. But then maybe you're forgetting that I kissed you twice prior to that day?"

"Once," she corrected.

"Twice," he insisted. "Don't try to deny again that it was you that night we camped by the road, you, not her, who tried to help me with Leroy. And yes, I know. At first, I thought it was your sister. I even let you convince me for a while that it was. But I don't buy it. That kiss just didn't feel right, when I was thinking it was her. But the night on the porch, that kiss felt perfect."

Her blush got worse. She turned away with it from him. He tried to draw her back, but she shrugged off his hand.

"You're confusing the issue," she stated.

"The whole damn thing *is* confusing. I'm just trying to clear it up."

She swung back around, and said accusingly, "You're making it worse! You kissed me that night on the porch just to make a comparison, not because you had any desire to kiss me. And I warned you that Amanda enjoys playing tricks of pretense like that, so you thought it was her from the start that day in the stable. You even said —" She paused, looking away again. "She told me what you said."

"What? Or more to the point, why would you believe her when you know she lies?"

"If anyone is lying, it's you," she insisted.

"Dammit, Mari, I swear I thought it was

you I was making love to. I was completely shocked that night when Amanda confessed that it was her. I wanted nothing to do with her by that point, much less marry her. She set up the trap, and I fell right into it. And I would have had to marry the wrong woman if Spencer hadn't intervened. It was *you* I wanted — and still do. I want you so much I can't think straight — which is probably why I'm making a mess of this confession."

"No, the problem is that I don't believe you. So why don't you do us both a favor and —"

He yanked her into his arms. His kiss was fraught with frustration, despair, and some anger because of it. And regret. A lot of regret, because it would probably be the last time he ever kissed her.

He'd expected a lot of things from this encounter, mostly Marian's saying it was too late. But he hadn't expected flat out disbelief. It was so frustrating! If he could convince her of the truth, he was afraid he'd then get that "it's too late," from her. So either way, he'd lose, and that infuriated him. She was too important to him to lose.

He set her back, and said harshly, "You can believe *that*. And while you're at it, figure out that I love you before it really is too late."

# Chapter 54

Chad left Marian's room, even managed not to slam the door on his way out. She opened the door behind him just to slam it shut on him. He turned back, stared at the door a moment, then smiled. If she could do something that emotional and — silly, then there was hope. At least she wasn't as indifferent to him as he'd begun to think.

The door slamming caused a few other doors in the corridor to open, though. Most of the occupants just had a quick look, saw that nothing was happening that interested them, and went back into their respective rooms. Not so with Amanda. She leaned against her doorframe, waiting for him to pass her. She was the very last person he cared to talk to about anything.

Just the sight of her raised his ire again. Amanda might be secretly enjoying her own marriage, according to Spencer, but she had left Chad's life in an emotional shambles with her selfish, one-track campaign to get her hands on her damn inheritance. And she had paid no price for it. Did she always get away unscathed by the hell she left behind her? She probably did.

He would have gone a different way to avoid her, but there was no other way to go. The room he'd just left was at the end of the corridor and his own room and the stairs were beyond Amanda's room. He could just stand there and wait for her to go away, but she looked too determined to speak to him for him to wait her out.

He decided to beat her to it, marched past her, and said, "At this precise moment, if you weren't her sister, I'd wring your neck. So don't say a —"

"So she finally told you the truth? It certainly took her long enough."

He swung around. "What truth? That she can't bear the sight of me now after what you did?"

"If you believe that, you're a fool, cowboy. She tried to convince me of the same thing. I even believed it until I opened her —"

"I have news for you, Amanda. You've lied, tricked, and manipulated once too often for anyone to believe a word you say. So save your breath, please."

"Well, I never," she huffed indignantly, her nose raised in the air. "And here I was going to do you a favor since I'm feeling so benevolent."

"Did it ever occur to you that I was making love to her, or thought I was, because I cared about her? Because I wanted to marry her. Her, not you. So the only favor you could possibly do for me is to tell me it wasn't you that day. But since that isn't possible —"

He stopped when she started to laugh. "You don't trust your own instincts much, do you, cowboy? I hate to break up a great rant, but you get your wish. It wasn't me. So I lied a little," she added with a shrug. "You got out of marrying me, so no harm was done."

He stared at her incredulously. "What the hell do you mean it wasn't you?"

She tsked at him. "Exactly that. I saw the two of you enter the stable that day, and since I was bored to tears, I went down to find out what you were up to. I overheard you making love and decided to take advantage of that knowledge. It was a gamble. If nothing else, your little secret would have been let out of the bag. But Mari was too shocked to call me a liar, and you were too dense not to know which sister you'd made love to. Like I said, you should have trusted your own instincts. If you'd called my bluff, Mari probably would have supported you, and it would have ended right there. But either way, you got out of it, so no harm was done."

"You're lying."

"Actually, for a change I'm not. Ask her. If she denies it, you'll know she's lying. She's not very good at it. Or you could just look in her trunk. She's got a couple paintings of you — one is rather revealing. I found them the day Kathleen taught her to ride. Yes, I snoop. So what? Being on that ranch was driving me mad with boredom."

She chuckled again at his expression before she stepped back into her room and closed the door on him. She'd done what she'd intended, shocked him so thoroughly that he just stood there, unable to absorb it all.

She was deliberately causing trouble again. What other reason could there be, for her? A favor? She'd probably never done anyone a favor in her life.

That he wanted to believe her was almost proof that he shouldn't, since she so often set up situations to shock or severely disappoint people. Of course it wasn't true. Marian would have told him. She wouldn't have let him go on this long, berating himself for having made such a colossal mistake.

He glanced back down the corridor. She was alone in her room. If nothing else,

436

Amanda had given him a reason to talk to Marian again. They could get angry at Amanda together. Find some common ground.

He didn't knock. Actually, he expected the door to be locked this time. It wasn't. She'd probably been too angry to think about locking it when she'd slammed it shut on him.

He found her sitting on the edge of her bed, staring at a canvas she'd unrolled. She was so deep in thought she hadn't even heard him enter and close the door again, though she did hear his footsteps as he approached. She glanced up and gasped.

But instead of telling him immediately to get out, she quickly rolled the canvas back up and shoved it on the bed behind her. She stood up, and only then started glaring at him.

"What are you doing back here?"

Without answering he nodded toward the canvas behind her, and asked, "Mind if I have a look at that?"

"I do mind."

He was standing next to her now. "I've been advised to look at it anyway, so I think I will."

"No!" she exclaimed.

Her protest wasn't going to stop him at

that point. If he had to apologize afterward, so be it, but he was going to see what she was hiding. He grabbed the canvas and turned away from her when she tried to snatch it back from him.

He unrolled it, heard her say, "Damn you, you have no right."

He was disappointed. It was a portrait of him. A damn good one, but it told him nothing. So she'd painted him. It was her hobby, something she enjoyed doing, and she was very good at it.

He turned back around, blushed a little as he handed the canvas back to her. "I'm sorry. My father would probably buy that from you. It's an amazing likeness."

"My paintings aren't for sale," she said stiffly.

He started to shrug, then remembered there were supposedly two canvases, and said, "Where's the other one?"

"What other one?"

"You painted two of me."

"I didn't," she insisted, but now she was blushing. "Who told you that?"

"Your sister just told me."

She snorted. "And you believed her?"

He frowned. "If you weren't blushing, I'd say no. But she was right, you're not very good at lying."

"I'm very good at kicking unwelcome intruders out of my room. I'm going to start screaming in one second if you aren't on your way out the door."

"Go ahead," he dared her. "Then the entire floor can find out what you're hiding."

He'd already spotted her trunks in the corner. He headed toward them. She didn't scream. She raced around him and sat down firmly on one trunk.

She pointed a finger at him. "That's far enough. You are *not* going to rifle through my personal belongings."

He shook his head at her. "Mari, do you realize how oddly you're behaving? And why? Over an exceptional talent that you want to keep to yourself?"

He didn't wait for an answer. He lifted her off the trunk, held her back with one arm while he opened it. There were two rolled canvases resting on top of the clothes she hadn't unpacked. He reached for one and howled — she'd slammed the trunk lid down on his arm.

He managed to get his arm out, and he turned toward her. But before he could say anything, she threw herself at him. And kissed him. He knew she was doing it to distract him from her trunk, and, damn, it worked.

He gathered her close, molded her body to his. She locked her arms around his neck. There was desperation in her efforts, but it was so close to passion it took him a while to note the difference. He still wasn't going to refuse what she was offering, when he'd been starving for the taste of her for too long.

He lifted her hips against the swelling in his loins. Her groan was lost in his mouth, slanting across hers. Her feet already off the floor, he started walking toward her bed, reached it, managed to get them on it without breaking the embrace, his body half-covering hers. She was clinging tightly to him still, as caught up in the kiss as he was. She wasn't in shock this time, knew what she was doing, which gave him hope. He let his desire reign unchecked, touching her, he couldn't get enough of touching her. His lips moved to her neck, kissing her there next to her ear. He reached for her skirt . . .

She immediately wiggled out from under him and shot off the bed. Now why didn't that surprise him?

"You know, darlin', you can only push a man so far," he warned as he stood up.

She was standing there panting for each breath, her lips swollen from his kisses, her blue eyes almost black they'd turned so dark. But Amanda wasn't the only twin who could have a one-track mind, and Marian's was still on what she was hiding from him.

As if he hadn't spoken, she said, "All right, I'll tell you what's in the trunk if you'll stop this nonsense. It's not something that I'm hiding from you, it's something I don't want *anyone* to see. It's a nude, the first I ever attempted, and since I didn't have a model, it's not the least bit accurate. I can easily paint from memory, but in this case I simply used my imagination. I'd always wanted to do a nude, I just never had an interesting enough subject to attempt it before, and I painted it prior to you and Amanda . . ."

She didn't finish. She didn't have to. She was blushing again, but it could just be because of the subject, rather than a lie.

Interesting she called him. She saw him as interesting — artistically. Under the circumstances, that was about as unflattering as she could get.

And he was starting to feel like an ass. So she'd painted a nude of him. Nudes were common. For all he knew, all artists painted them. And while he'd like to see it, it would prove nothing. As usual, Amanda had merely caused emotional turmoil by suggesting otherwise.

He tried to relieve her embarrassment —
as well as his own. With a grin, he asked,
"You want a model?"

"No!"

He shrugged. "Didn't think so." He
turned to leave, then paused. "My apologies, Mari. You'll think about what I said
earlier?"

"Absolutely."

Too strong a word, which meant she
wouldn't. Just as he'd feared, all his chances
to win her had died the moment she'd heard
that he had made love to her sister.

# Chapter 55

"What'd you do, press your ear to the door?"

"Of course," Amanda admitted, then complained, "My room *would* have to be across the hall from hers this time, rather than next to it."

She'd opened her door again the very moment Chad had stepped back into the corridor. He didn't try to avoid her this time. Actually, she was standing in the middle of the hall, so he couldn't.

"That does make it hard to eavesdrop, doesn't it?" he said, his tone sarcastic.

"Yes, unless voices get raised," she agreed, then raised a brow at him. "What do I have to do, lead you through this step by step?"

"You could try minding your own business, or is that too much to ask?"

"When you're making such a muck of yours?"

"*You* made a muck of mine. And you still are. If you were a man, I'd —"

"Yes, yes, I'm sure you would," she cut in impatiently. "You didn't ask her, did you? You were supposed to tell her you knew the truth. That's the only way you're going to get her to drop her defenses. You can't get rid of the hurt unless you lay it bare, and you can't get to that point unless you find it first. She'll never own up to it on her own. She's too proud for that."

"You're bored again, aren't you?" he guessed. "Three days with nothing to do until Bridges returns to town. That's what this is all about, isn't it? Just a new scheme for your entertainment because it amuses you to trifle with other people's emotions."

She sighed. "I'm trying to help you. If you'd just get over past grievances for a few minutes, you'd see that. I've given you the truth. I even told you where to find the proof of what I said. But you didn't even bother to look at the paintings, did you?"

He sighed. "The painting of a nude isn't proof of anything, Amanda."

"Of what?"

"Mari told me she painted a nude of me because she found me an interesting subject. Hardly flattering, and definitely not proof."

Amanda started to laugh. "Oh my, that's priceless. She *told* you about it instead of letting you actually see it. Good for her. Threw you off track and kept you from seeing the real painting. I didn't think she had it in her, to lie that well."

"But you do."

"Sure I do. It's an art, you know. But occasionally it isn't useful to lie, and this is one of those occasions. I told you I'm feeling benevolent, so let me tell you about the real painting. She rendered you lying in a bed of straw, in the process of removing your shirt. And looking up at her, your expression is so filled with passion, there's no doubt you're looking at a woman. She would have had to be standing over you to have that view. Did she? I only eavesdropped, so I didn't actually see you two. But the painting says it all, a perfect likeness, even shows a scar near your navel. That's not something she could have imagined, unless you don't really have a scar there. Do you?"

"You should know," he gritted out. "You were the one standing over me."

Amanda rolled her eyes. "I don't paint. I tried it once and was so embarrassed by my lack of talent, I never touched a brush again. I've always been jealous of Mari's talent. I admit it. She got all the artistic ability, leaving me none. So I had to create a talent of my own."

"To manipulate people."

"Yes, how astute of you," she said dryly. "But wake up, cowboy. That's not what I'm

445

doing here. What's preventing you from seeing the truth?"

He gritted out what she was overlooking, "For the simple reason that she would have told me. She wouldn't have let you get away with such a lie."

"But she did. Find out why, and you'll probably find the hurt you need to mend."

For the fourth time that day, Chad turned the handle on Marian's door. It was locked this time. He had no patience left to knock. He slammed his shoulder against the door. It didn't give.

But he heard from the other side, "Don't you dare!"

He slammed his shoulder against the door again. Damn door still didn't give way. But she opened it before he tried a third time and stood there with a furious glare.

"I don't believe you just did that!" she hissed.

"And I don't believe you let me think, even for a minute, that I made love to Amanda!"

She caught her breath, stared at him. He walked past her into the room, so angry at that moment that he probably shouldn't say another word.

He swung around. "You would have let

me marry her based on a lie!"

She lowered her gaze from his. "No, I wouldn't have. I would have spoken up if you'd been forced to go through with that — even though I didn't think you'd appreciate it, or that it would matter."

"How could it not matter?"

"If you didn't believe it. And at the time, I was sure you wouldn't. But I would have made the effort anyway. There was no point, though, after Amanda married Spencer."

"No point? No point! Just leave me agonizing over what I thought was the biggest mistake of my life? You were never going to tell me, were you?"

"No."

"Why the hell not?"

"You know why. I thought you were making love to me, but you weren't. You thought it was her all along."

"I told you I didn't."

"And I told you I don't believe you. I was *there!* Yes, it was me. So you can't deny you called me by her name. You were sure it was her!"

"Hell, Mari, that's what this is all about?" he said incredulously. "Yes, for the briefest moment I did get a little confused and thought it might be Amanda. Your boldness just surprised me. But only for a moment."

As she turned away from him, she saw his shoulders slump. She really didn't care. Just as on that day in the stable, she was going to say nothing.

# Chapter 56

Marian wasn't sure what to say to him, or if she could even get any words out past the lump in her throat. Was she just supposed to believe him, when all this time she'd been sure he was still pining for Amanda?

Everything he'd said sounded good. Too good. That was the problem. How could she just accept it all when she'd drawn such opposite conclusions? It would mean she'd been an utter fool. That she'd let her difficulties with her sister go too far.

But she did owe him a better explanation than she'd given. She turned back to him — and found him gone.

She caught her breath in surprise. She hadn't heard him leave. And he'd left with the wrong impression. That wouldn't do. He'd intruded in her room several times that day, she could do the same to him.

But he'd left the hotel. She began to panic, imagining what he must be thinking. She should just wait for him to return, but she couldn't. She had no idea where he might be, but she'd find him. He hadn't been gone that long.

She found him on a corner in the center of town, just standing there with his hands shoved in his pockets, as if he'd been doing the same thing she'd done earlier — wandering aimlessly in thought. It was very late in the afternoon, almost evening. Businesses were closing for the day; people were rushing home from work, making the sidewalks and streets much more crowded than usual. It was the heavy traffic that had probably stopped him where he was.

He was drawing curious stares from passersby because of his Western–style coat, boots, and the wide-brimmed hat that Easterners weren't used to seeing. At least he wasn't wearing his gun holster. That had been packed away since they'd reached Chicago.

She approached from behind him. At least she'd had the presence of mind to wear her veil again. She'd already seen three people she knew, though they hadn't recognized her.

A crowded corner wasn't exactly the ideal place to have a conversation, but no one else was standing still, so she didn't think they'd be overheard. She was jostled a few times before she got up the nerve just to say what needed to be said.

"The moment the notion took hold that

you thought I was Amanda that day, it colored my judgment on everything else."

At the sound of her voice he turned around. Realizing where they were, he took her arm and started walking, so at least no one passing would hear more than a word or two of what they were saying. "I knew you were angry. I was going to explain, but Amanda never gave me a chance to. I was shocked, more than anything else, when she claimed what she did. I knew deep down that you were the woman I'd made love to, but when you didn't correct her outlandish insinuations, I didn't know what the hell to think anymore."

She started blushing, and told him, "I suppose I didn't have enough confidence in myself to speak up immediately. I still couldn't believe that you'd prefer me over Amanda."

"But I did," he insisted.

"Let me finish. I wasn't supposed to be the sister of choice, for any man. For a long time I went through a lot of effort to make sure I wouldn't be."

"Why?"

"To prevent exactly what happened. Why do you think Amanda claimed what she did? It wasn't just about the inheritance. It was because she was jealous that you could want me instead of her. It's always been that way with her. It's why I tried to conceal the fact that we are twins. My disguise, the insults, were to make sure men would only notice her."

"So she might get jealous. That was no reason for you to change your appearance completely and live with that lie indefinitely."

"I felt it was. You see, it never failed that if a man showed even the slightest interest in me, or vice versa, she'd lure him to her instead, by any means, even making love to him if that's what it took. And after she rubbed it in my face that he was hers, she'd then cast him aside, inflicting a good deal of emotional pain in the process to punish him for having thought about me in the first place. I didn't want to see that happen to you."

"You couldn't tell me that at the time?"

"That I'd fallen in love with you? No, Amanda had to get married first before I could admit to that."

He stopped, grinned, tilted her face up to his. "You love me?"

"I didn't say that, I said — don't confuse the issue. I'm trying to explain —"

"Darlin', *nothing* else matters if you love me."

452

She should just accept that, grab her happiness, and to hell with everything else.

"Yes it does. Aside from my feelings, I still don't see how you could love me, *me,* when you didn't even know the real me. It's just this face, *her* damn face —"

"It's time for you to hush up again, Mari," he said gently and lifted her veil so he could cup her cheek. "You think I don't know you? You're the one who showed such concern for me that you nearly chewed my tail off for it when I stood down those stage robbers. You're the one who showed remarkable courage — or foolhardiness — when you thoughtlessly tried to take on a mountain man four times your size just to help me. You're kind, you're considerate, you worry about others' feelings — maybe a little too much. I admire your gumption; I admire your talent. Actually, I think you're kind of wonderful. You're the one I fell in love with, Mari, and before I ever saw your real face, before I knew you were her twin."

She stared up at him in awe. "You really mean it, don't you?"

He cupped both cheeks now. "I want you for my wife. Will you marry me?"

She threw her arms around his neck. She laughed. "Oh, yes, yes! If you hadn't asked, I probably would have."

He laughed as well and started to kiss her, but someone bumped into them with a mumbled apology. Marian was jarred enough to regain an awareness of where they were. This really hadn't been the place for such a conversation. And she thought she'd recognized that voice. She turned to look, but didn't see anyone in the crowd whom she knew — and then she did and went very still.

"What's wrong?" Chad asked.

She looked back at him, her eyes wide. But then she shook her head. "Nothing. Just my imagination seeing things."

"Bridges?"

"No, it —" She didn't finish, looked down the street again, frowning. "I know I'm being silly, but let me make sure. I'll be right back."

She hurried in the direction she'd seen the man go. Chad was close behind her, but she didn't wait for him. There was just no way in hell she could be right about who she'd seen, and it would only take a moment to prove it.

She caught up with the man, tugged on his arm to stop him. "Papa?"

He turned around, gave her an annoyed look, then continued on his way, leaving her standing there in utter shock.

# Chapter 57

Marian didn't recall much about getting back to the hotel. Chad must have found them a carriage for hire because she vaguely recalled sitting in one. She was just too dazed. So many thoughts were racing through her mind. *How could it be possible? Nothing fit. It didn't make sense!* Everything kept coming back to one glaring fact. He *knew* her, and still kept right on going.

And he'd spoiled the happiest day of her life. That was the only thing that had happened today that didn't surprise her. So typical of her father, but so utterly ironic, since for once, he didn't do it deliberately.

Chad escorted her straight to Kathleen's room. And her aunt only had to see her face to ask in alarm, "What happened?"

Chad answered, after he sat Marian down on the sofa, "She thought she saw her father."

"That isn't possible."

"I know, but the resemblance must have been close enough to —"

"It was Papa," Marian interrupted quietly, glancing up at her aunt. "He looked directly at me, not a foot away from me. It *was* Papa."

Kathleen sighed. "Well, I can't say I'm delighted to hear it. The best thing Mortimer ever did for you gals was to die. So he couldn't even do that right?"

Marian was coming out of her daze. She shot to her feet in agitation. Her aunt had been alone in her room when Chad brought her there, but it was getting close to the dinner hour when the rest of their party would be joining them. Kathleen's room was larger than the other rooms so a dining table had been set up in it.

"Mandy is going to go crazy over this news," Marian predicted.

Kathleen disagreed. "She'll probably be too happy to ask for explanations."

"I thought y'all buried him?" Chad said.

"We did, but it was a closed casket. I never thought to ask why."

"So the wrong man got buried, and your father has been missing all this time. Amnesia?" Chad guessed.

"That would certainly explain it," Kathleen agreed.

"I suppose it would," Marian added, frowning deep in thought. "Except — he would have had to only just gotten his memory back today, or within the last couple days."

"Why?"

"Because Albert's sister is living in our old house, which means Albert is, too," Marian said. "Papa probably doesn't know that yet."

"And how'd *you* find that out, when you were supposed to be lying low?" Kathleen asked.

Marian made a face. "I went for a walk. I didn't intend to go in that direction, I just wandered there aimlessly and happened upon Albert's sister coming home. But I took precautions," she added, tapping the veiled bonnet that was still on her head. Then she removed it. "No one recognized me."

Kathleen nodded, and said, "You know, there's another explanation that just occurred to me."

"What?"

"The man you saw might be your father's twin."

"He didn't have one."

"Maybe he did. They run in our family. And I wasn't around when he was born, to know one way or the other. There could have been two of them. Our mother was certainly selfish enough, and lacking in motherly love, to have given one of her babies away if she didn't want to be bothered with two."

"That's a bit far-fetched," Chad said.

"Yes, it is. But crazier things have happened," Kathleen insisted.

"Except he *knew* me," Marian reminded them.

Kathleen blinked, then said in exasperation, "That's right, you said you were standing right next to him. So what did *he* have to say about all this?"

"He didn't stay to chat, and I was too shocked to follow him again. I got his annoyed don't-bother-me-now look that he always reserved just for me."

Chad patted the seat next to him on the sofa to lure Marian back down. She obliged, and they both got a raised brow from Kathleen when his arm went around Marian's shoulder and she didn't shrug it off.

"There's more news to impart today?" Kathleen wanted to know.

"Yes," Marian said, with a slight blush and a grin. "But now isn't the best time to mention it.

Kathleen chuckled. "Congratulations anyway."

"For what?" Amanda asked as she sashayed into the room without knocking, Spencer close on her heels. Before she got an answer, she said, "Dinner isn't here yet? I'm famished."

"You ate enough for two people at lunch, and the sun hasn't even finished setting yet. What have you been doing to work up such an appetite?"

Kathleen had asked the question in all innocence, but Amanda blushed furiously, while Spencer stood there smirking. "Oh," Kathleen said, then quickly got back to answering Amanda's original question with a grin. "Mari and Chad have finally figured out that they like each other."

"Thanks to *my* help," Amanda crowed.

Kathleen and Marian both stared at her incredulously, but Chad whispered in Marian's ear, "I'll tell you about it later, but she *is* actually responsible for my persistence today."

"Amanda doing me a good turn?" Marian whispered back with a soft snort. "When cows learn how to —"

"You're procrastinating, darlin'," he cut in. "Just tell her and get it over with."

Marian blinked. He *did* know her very well. She was anticipating that her sister would throw a serious fit over this, because of all the traveling and bother she'd been put to — unnecessarily. It was yet another thing she didn't want to witness on the happiest day of her life. But there was no way of getting around it. Amanda couldn't be kept in the dark.

"Papa's alive, Mandy. I saw him today in town. There was no mistake, it was him. We've already concluded he must have lost his memory and only just now regained it."

"But what did he have to say for himself?" was all Amanda asked.

Marian frowned. Amanda's reply was way too calm under the circumstances. And then she recalled that her sister hadn't been shocked over the news of their father's death either.

"You knew!?" she accused her.

"No, I just never accepted that he was dead," Amanda said with a shrug. "It didn't feel real, if you know what I mean. And now I know why, since he wasn't dead at all. You really think he lost his memory?"

Marian was too amazed at Amanda's tepid reaction to answer immediately. "There isn't much else that can explain why we buried the wrong man."

"You didn't bury anyone," Stuart said as he entered the room.

Kathleen swung around to face him. "What's that supposed to mean?"

"The coffin was empty."

Kathleen gasped, her eyes wide with alarm. "My God, you didn't dig it up, did you?"

He snorted at her. "Didn't have to. Just

460

got back from a visit to the local police. They laughed in my face when I mentioned Mortimer Laton died a few months ago. Looks like Mortimer and his cohorts kept that funeral pretty quiet, and all traces of the burial were removed after the gals left town. The whole thing was a total sham. Mortimer Laton has been here all along, going about his business as usual."

"That isn't possible," Amanda insisted, shaking her head firmly. "Albert must have found someone who resembles him to impersonate him, to make it easier for him to get his hands on everything. But Papa's back now. It doesn't matter where he's been or why Albert thought he was dead. He'll make them pay — if he hasn't already."

# Chapter 58

It took two carriages to transport them all, since no one wanted to stay behind and miss the confrontation with Albert's sister. It was too bad Albert wouldn't be there for it. Mortimer might be, though. He'd been heading in that direction. They might arrive in time to see the woman and all her belongings being tossed out on the street. Then again, Mortimer might not even know that all his wealth had been transferred to his lawyer. It really was possible that he'd regained his memory only recently and returned to Haverhill that day.

Chad held Marian back from getting in the first carriage, then waved it on and hailed another. Rather enterprising of him, to manage to get her alone amidst all the turmoil. She didn't mind. In fact, she was pleased to have a break from discussing her father's miraculous return from the dead.

"Are you all right?" he asked her as he put his arm around her and drew her close to him.

"I'm fine now. Really." And then she grinned at him. "We may have to elope though. Papa probably won't approve of you the way Aunt Kathleen does, and approval will be back in his hands now."

He raised a brow at her. "And you find that amusing?"

"No, I don't give a damn whether he approves or not. His return means next to nothing to me. Any feelings I had for him died long before I thought he did. He was a good provider, but he wasn't a good father any way you look at it."

"I would like to marry you before we return to Texas. I suppose I could ask his permission after this all gets straightened out."

"Don't bother. Marriages can't be accomplished that quickly here anyway."

He groaned. "The thought of having to wait, even a few more days —"

He didn't finish the thought. Instead, he started kissing her. A lot of passion surfaced in that kiss with amazing speed, pointing out the frustration he'd been living with for weeks. Her response was just as passionate. Trying to deny that she loved him had been so futile. And it felt so wonderful to admit it finally, and know for sure that her love was returned.

This really was the happiest day of her life — and one of the most confusing. The confusion returned as the carriage stopped in front of her old house, which, unfortunately, wasn't very far from the hotel.

She broke the kiss, said a bit breathlessly, "A ship's captain could marry us. Actually, I think I'd really enjoy being confined with you in a small cabin on the high seas. We don't have to return on the train with the others, do we?"

He groaned at the thought of having her all to himself for weeks at sea. "No, we don't. We don't need to be here either. I'd as soon hear about this secondhand."

She chuckled. "Your impatience is showing."

"Damned right it is," he growled, but then he sighed. "All right, let's get this finished. I'm not going to get your undivided attention until this strange situation is settled. We should have brought a posse. They tend to settle things real quick."

She was laughing as she left the carriage, but sobered instantly upon seeing her sister marching up the path to the front door of their old house. Knowing her, Amanda still considered it her house, and would walk right in. Which probably wasn't a good idea, since it wasn't really theirs anymore and wouldn't be until Albert was arrested and charged with his crimes.

So she ran up the path to beat Amanda to the door and pounded on it, blocking her sister from opening it herself. It was opened almost immediately by a butler neither of them recognized.

Amanda opened her mouth to demand entrance, but got beaten to the punch again, by the butler's saying, "Come in. You're expected."

That should have been all the warning Marian needed. If she hadn't just shared such a distracting interlude with Chad on the way over, she might not have been so surprised when she and the others followed the butler to the dining room and found both her father and Albert's sister sitting there having a quiet dinner together.

"Let's keep this civil, shall we?" Mortimer said, and waved a hand toward the chairs at the long table. "Sit down. Dinner is being served."

No one moved. Amanda was displaying some long-overdue shock. Even she could see that they'd been seriously wrong in their assumptions. And for their father to be so blasé about it, as if he hadn't done anything wrong. But that was so typical of him. He didn't like confrontations. That was one of the reasons Amanda had been spoiled so badly. He simply didn't want to deal with her tantrums, so he gave her whatever she wanted instead.

"Looks like you hit it right on the nose, Stuart. A total sham," Kathleen said, shaking her head.

"Is that you, Kathy?" Mortimer asked curiously.

"Sure is, brother." Kathleen took a seat at the opposite end of the long table. "But don't worry, I don't plan on staying long."

Mortimer shrugged. "You've aged well. I wasn't quite sure."

"Of course you were," Kathleen snorted. "You're just stalling."

He flushed slightly, but the woman sitting next to him threw her napkin down on the table angrily, and said, "Get out! All of you. We don't owe you any explanations!"

That brought Amanda out of her shock long enough to screech, "Who the hell are you?"

"Albert's sister," Marian supplied.

But the woman was determined to speak for herself, "Your stepmother, though I was hoping I'd never have to say it — to you."

"You *married* her?" Amanda gasped at her father.

"Yes, it was necessary," Mortimer replied.

Not exactly a normal way to put it, which

had Marian guessing, "She was your mistress, wasn't she?"

"Mortimer!" his wife complained. "I won't stand for being insulted in my own house."

"Hardly an insult if the shoe fits, gal," Kathleen said with a smirk.

Marian realized her aunt was enjoying this, a little payback after so many years, putting her brother on the spot. She was thankful she was able to read between the lines herself. Now that she was over her initial surprise, only her curiosity remained and most of it had already been satisfied. After all, she'd seen the baby.

"If this can't be discussed in a calm manner, I will have to ask you to leave," Mortimer said to the group at large, though he was looking at Amanda when he said it. Then to his wife, he added, "That goes for you as well."

She blushed furiously, put her napkin back on her lap, and resumed eating. She might be a shrew, and rude beyond the pale, but obviously, Mortimer didn't allow her to carry on in his presence.

From their party, only Kathleen and Stuart had sat down at the table. Amanda was too agitated to sit. Marian didn't think she'd be staying long enough to bother.

Spencer and Chad were being particularly supportive in sticking close to their sides.

Kathleen sat back and said casually if still somewhat sarcastically, "So you married your mistress. Good for you. But why did you need to *die* to do it?"

He shrugged. "It was Albert's idea. I was simply going to get both daughters married off with a small dowry and be done with it. But he pointed out Amanda's temperament, and in the end I had to agree. It has been quite peaceful, having you out of the state, my dear."

Amanda was speechless for a moment, which allowed Kathleen to say, "So all this just because you figured Amanda would raise a ruckus if you married again? That's going to extremes just to avoid a tantrum or two."

Mortimer actually chuckled. "You always did have an odd way of putting things, Kathy. But no, that was only a small part of it."

"There's more?"

"Most definitely. I wasn't just starting fresh with a new wife, but a new family. I have a son now, you see."

"So *that's* why you married your mistress?"

He didn't answer directly, just said, "Regardless, I couldn't see giving the girls any of my money when I've become quite selfish in my affection for my son. They're females, after all. They will have husbands to support them. It would have been a total waste leaving them a portion of my estate when it would just have gone to their husbands — something I simply wasn't willing to allow now that I have a son."

"I understand how you managed to fool the girls," Kathleen said, "but how'd you manage to fool the whole town?"

He smiled at her. "Because hardly anyone actually knew about it."

"Impossible. A man of your prominence —"

"Let me finish," he cut in. "The news of my 'death,' the funeral, everything was planned on a very tight schedule, so the girls could be shipped off directly after the funeral, before they had a chance to talk to anyone. Their callers were turned away at the door for those few days before the funeral. No announcement was made in the newspaper, but the girls rarely read the paper to wonder about that. Only one of Amanda's beaux knew of my 'death' and we had a good tale lined up to tell him afterward, or anyone else who found out about the 'funeral,' but as it happens, he was so devastated by Amanda's rejection of him that he left town himself."

"And your servants? Did you pay them to keep silent?"

"That would have been a waste of good coin. No, the tale about my 'reappearance' worked very well for the few people who knew about the funeral. The explanation was it was merely 'assumed' that I died, but my body hadn't been recovered."

"Yes, I suppose that would keep people from wondering exactly who got buried."

"Exactly. And I pretended to have a broken leg, to account for my failure to make it back in time to prevent a funeral from taking place."

"When did you make your miraculous 'return'?"

"The day after the girls' ship sailed, of course. The whole thing was timed around that ship's departure date, to get the girls out of town before too many people found out about our little hoax. A few of my business associates were told of the 'death.' After all, the girls would have thought it strange if no one showed up for the funeral."

"I wouldn't have," Marian put in.

Her father snorted at her, but went on with his explanation. "But those who were told of the 'death' were handpicked because they weren't very astute. They readily accepted the explanation afterward, glad to have me back."

"And Amanda's endless stream of admirers?" Marian asked. "How did you explain her absence to them?"

"A planned tour of Europe before she settled down."

"That she bragged to no one about before she left?" Marian scoffed.

"She didn't want to witness their disappointment at learning that she'd be gone for a few months."

"And when she didn't return as they expected?"

He waved a hand dismissively. "Marriage, of course."

Kathleen shook her head. "Such an elaborate scheme, and all for what? You aren't dead yet, Mort. Your wealth is still yours to do with as you please. If you didn't want any uproar over making the boy your only heir, you could have just kept it to yourself."

"And have them all fighting over my money when I *am* gone? They were known as heiresses. All of Amanda's suitors here expected a piece of the pie. If something did happen to me, I didn't want anyone fighting over my estate. No, no indeed, there will be no contention. And there would have been none if the girls had just stayed in Texas where they were sent. Why *are* they back here?" he asked with distinct annoyance.

"Because your brilliant-idea man wasn't so brilliant in sending along an accounting of your estate that Amanda would recognize as a lot of bull. We *thought* Bridges had robbed the girls of their inheritance. That's the only reason we're here."

He sighed. "Yes, he can be quite stupid at times."

His wife sputtered indignantly on her brother's behalf, but still kept her mouth shut. Mortimer might have married her to get their son under his roof, but he probably didn't treat her as a real wife. It was doubtful that there was any affection between them because he'd apparently transferred all his love to the boy.

"I still don't see why you didn't just wait until the girls married and settled elsewhere. People *do* start new families late in life, Mort. It happens all the time."

"Yes, in retrospect, that might have been best. But it was preferable to have Amanda away from Haverhill. And it would have been difficult to arrange a marriage for her elsewhere, when she had no desire to leave town. Besides, she's too jealous not to have caused trouble when I married and acknowledged Andrew as my only heir."

"So what you're saying is you had to fake your death just because you spoiled your daughter so rotten that even you don't know how to deal with her?"

"Basically — yes."

He was blushing again, acknowledging his weakness. Marian understood perfectly, having lived with them both. She knew the kind of uproar Amanda could cause and knew that her father had never liked scenes of that sort. It didn't even surprise her, really, that he'd come up with a plan to get Amanda out of the picture completely. He already had a new favorite. Amanda meant next to nothing to him now; rather he considered her a liability.

Marian could care less, thankfully. But she actually felt a little sorry for her sister. Just deserts? No, his actions went beyond that. This was having the father she'd adored her whole life fake his death just to get her out of his life. And that was really the only reason he'd done it. He'd made Amanda what she was with his selfish favoritism; but he wouldn't own up to that, wouldn't consider himself at fault. The money was a minor issue. He just didn't want to be bothered with a spoiled daughter he didn't care about anymore.

It would have been much, much better if they had continued to think he was dead.

She glanced at her sister. Amanda's eyes were a little glassy with emotion. Her fists were clenched at her sides, but she hadn't blown up as everyone expected.

"You're a pathetic coward, Papa," Amanda said, surprising them all with her quiet tone. "I knew you weren't dead. It just never felt like it, so I didn't accept it. It feels like it now, though."

Having said that, Amanda turned and left the room, and the house. There was only silence in her wake for several long moments. Then Spencer walked slowly to the end of the table where Mortimer sat. The older man started to rise in alarm, because the younger man's face contained all the anger that had been missing from Amanda's. Spencer's fist sat him back down, landing squarely between his nose and mouth, doing damage to both.

"Don't worry," the Texan said in disgust. "I'm done. That was merely for my wife, since she's too much a lady to do it herself. And she doesn't need your money, old man. She'll never want for anything while I'm around."

Spencer didn't wait for a reply, didn't

want one. He did spit on the floor, though, before he followed his wife out.

Stuart stood up, stretched, held his hand out to Kathleen. "You were lucky to get away from this sickness before it infected you, darlin'. We ready to go home?"

"Hell, yes." She grinned at him and took his hand to leave. She paused at the door, though, to glance back at her brother one last time. "You know, Mort, you get out of life what you give. Ironic, isn't it, that no one gave a hoot when they thought you were dead. And you just spit on the only person who might have cared that you're still alive. Good thing she's come to her senses."

Marian and Chad were the only ones left. Mortimer hadn't bothered to glance her way even once. His wife was still eating. That was almost comic. She cared so little for him that she didn't even bother to pretend some concern over the blood he was wiping off his face.

Chad stood behind Marian, gripped her shoulders in sympathy, and said in a voice that carried down the table, "Want me to shoot him for you? I will."

She burst out laughing, not at all surprised that she could laugh under the circumstances. Her father simply had no effect on her anymore.

She turned around, grinned at Chad, and caressed his cheek. "You say the sweetest things."

He rolled his eyes at her. Her response let him know that what happened here today hadn't hurt her the way it had Amanda.

"I believe you know where the door is," Mortimer said behind them in a cold tone.

Marian merely glanced over her shoulder. She wouldn't have said anything, didn't really feel a need to confront him as the others had done, but the glare coming her way just rubbed her wrong. This man had ignored her all her life — except when he wanted to get rid of her, then she'd had his full attention.

"I'd pity you," she said in a conversational tone. "But you know, you just aren't worth it. I'd pity your new son, too, but he won't be worth it either after you get done raising him to be just like you — that's if he's even really yours or just —"

"Get out!" Mortimer cut in furiously.

"Or just another travesty concocted by a crafty lawyer who seems to prefer lies to the truth," Marian finished and, noting that Albert's sister was blushing vividly, added with a chuckle, "Oh, that's priceless. Enjoy your new *family*, Papa."

# Chapter 59

There was a ship scheduled to depart the very next day. It was recommended that the passengers board the night before, since it would be sailing with the morning tide. Stuart still had business to attend to in Chicago, so he and Kathleen were taking the train back. And as Spencer preferred trains over boats, he and Amanda were going with them. Ella Mae, who had already elected to stay with Marian, now that the sisters wouldn't be living together anymore, volunteered to accompany Marian on the sea voyage since she would need a chaperone — at least for another day.

Amanda came to say good-bye while Marian was getting her luggage ready to be transported to the ship. They would all be having dinner together before they went their separate ways. Of course, they would be meeting again in Texas in a few weeks. Still, it was the first time the sisters would be away from each other for more than a day.

At first Marian ignored Amanda. She didn't want to talk about their father, as she feared Amanda had come to do. While

Marian would just as soon forget that he existed and wanted only to concentrate on her new life and new husband-to-be, Amanda had taken a devastating blow that day. On top of that, Amanda's life wasn't settled. Spencer might think it was to go by what he'd said after Amanda had left Mortimer's house, but Amanda had yet to give that impression.

Amanda hadn't said anything yet. She was merely walking about the room, touching things absently. Marian finally stopped what she was doing and sat down on the bed with a sigh.

"You know I'm getting married tomorrow, or soon thereafter. I'm happy. I love Chad. I suspect I'm going to love being his wife. We managed to find each other despite your efforts to ruin —"

"I'm glad you got that straightened out," Amanda cut in. "I figured you would have told him the truth. I never figured you'd be so stubborn about keeping it to yourself."

Marian just stared at her. "He mentioned something about your being responsible for his persistence earlier today. Is that why?"

"Of course. It wasn't my intention to sabotage your little romance. I was just bored to pieces at the time, waiting for Spencer to show up again. You were supposed to expose the lie immediately, be a little embarrassed over it, get out of your hiding mentality, get married —"

"Wait just a minute," Marian cut in now. "If you're trying to say that it was a convoluted attempt at matchmaking on your part, remember to whom you're talking."

"Don't be silly. You'd already done the matchmaking. You *did* make love with him, after all. That spoke for itself. I was merely hurrying things along to keep them interesting."

"Because you were bored."

"Yes, and I guess I'm trying to say, well, that I'm sorry it got so messed up instead."

"All right, what do you want, Mandy?"

"Nothing."

"Bull. You don't apologize without a reason. You don't do things just to be nice, either."

"Mari, I *know* I have a lot of faults. You don't need to point them out. Being away from Father in Texas, you could say I woke up. Without him around approving of every little thing I did, I began to see that some of the things I did were just plain — horrible."

Marian was rendered speechless for a moment, then asked, "What's this really about?"

"Spencer." Amanda sighed. "He's never

going to love me the way I'd hoped — the way Chad loves you. I amuse him is all."

"Then you *want* him to love you?"

"Well, certainly. He's my husband, isn't he?"

"One you didn't want," Marian reminded her.

Amanda waved a hand. "That was merely for effect. I wasn't going to let him know just how much he means to me, when he's been mostly indifferent. I do have some pride, you know."

"You mean he's not letting you wrap him around your little finger?" Marian guessed.

"You don't have to be sarcastic about it. But no, he's not. He could care less about what I want. He doesn't make the least effort to please me."

"Do you?"

"What?"

"Make any effort to please him?"

Amanda snorted. Then she frowned and actually thought about it, finally confessing, "I suppose not. I've been too busy trying to keep him from guessing that I love him."

That sounded too familiar by half. It was exactly what Marian had done — foolishly. "I'm going to give you some sisterly advice, because I just got out of that boat myself. Be honest with him. Tell him. You might just be surprised to find out that maybe he's been doing the same thing . . . hiding his real feelings."

Amanda agreed to give it a shot and must have, because she was looking damned pleased with herself at dinner that night. Marian caught up with her as they were leaving the hotel. A coach was already waiting outside for her and Chad, but he stopped to have a few last words with his father, and Spencer was moving to join them.

Pulling her sister aside, Marian whispered, "You told him?"

"Yes."

"And found out he loves you, too?"

"No, he denied it," Amanda said, though she was grinning. "But I know he was lying, so it's okay."

Marian rolled her eyes. "I'll see you when you get home, Mandy."

Amanda chuckled, then said, "Oh, I'd like a wedding portrait, if you don't mind. Something I can throw darts at when I get annoyed with my husband."

Marian was still laughing as she joined Chad in the coach. He asked her why, but all she said was, "I think my sister is developing a sense of *real* humor."

They did get married the next day at sea, and Marian found out with a good deal of pleasure that *that* turned out to be the happiest day of her life. Nothing else could come close to the euphoria she'd experienced from the moment she'd said, "I do."

And Chad made sure the day was special in every way. For a cowboy, he was rather romantic. From the flowers he had sneaked aboard and had Ella Mae scatter about the deck during the ceremony, so Marian wouldn't see them until they'd taken their vows. From the candlelight dinner and ignoring when his wineglass rolled off the table before it was filled. From huddling with her in a blanket on deck that night to watch the full moon rising, which he swore he'd ordered just for her.

And for making love to her for most of the day. After they were married that morning, they'd retired immediately to his cabin, which they would be sharing for the rest of the trip. They didn't surface for lunch and were famished by dinner. But they'd both saved up a lot of passion for consummating their marriage. It became a joke during the day that they hadn't got it right yet, so they had to try again — and again. Another memory to savor. At one point she was sure they'd broken the bed.

They were both exhausted by the time they retired for the night. But that didn't stop Chad from pulling her close and when a few good-night kisses got prolonged, finding out they weren't so exhausted after all.

A while later Marian sighed contentedly and cuddled close. "I think we may have finally got it right." She grinned sleepily.

"You sure, darlin'?" he asked as he ran a finger down her arm, which caused a shiver on the back of her neck.

She leaned up in surprise. "You can't have any energy left. You *really* can't."

He chuckled. "No, I don't. But I'd find some, since I don't think I'll ever get enough of you." He pulled her toward him for a very gentle kiss. "I love you, Mari. I'm going to spend the rest of my life showing you just how much. When we're old and gray, and our grandchildren are gathered around us —"

"Wait a minute. How many children did we have to produce those grandchildren?"

"Oh, a half dozen or so — or maybe just three sets of twins."

She groaned. "Twins! I hope not."

"I hope so," he countered. "And they'll be raised without favoritism, with all the love and care you're capable of, because that's the way you are. You'd have it no other way."

"Okay, maybe two sets," she conceded with a grin. "And when we're old and gray?"

"You'll have no regrets, darlin'. I promise you that."

She believed him. She never dreamed she could be so happy — with a cowboy, just a cowboy, but her cowboy. At last, a man to call her own.

# About the Author

Johanna Lindsey has been hailed as one of the most popular authors of romantic fiction with over 55 million copies of her novels sold. World renowned for her novels of "first-rate romance" (*New York Daily News*), Lindsey is the author of thirty-nine previous national bestselling novels, many of which reached the number-one spot on the *New York Times* bestseller list. Lindsey lives in Hawaii with her family.

The employees of Thorndike Press hope you have enjoyed this Large Print book. All our Thorndike and Wheeler Large Print titles are designed for easy reading, and all our books are made to last. Other Thorndike Press Large Print books are available at your library, through selected bookstores, or directly from us.

For information about titles, please call:

(800) 223-1244

or visit our Web site at:

www.gale.com/thorndike
www.gale.com/wheeler

To share your comments, please write:

Publisher
Thorndike Press
295 Kennedy Memorial Drive
Waterville, ME 04901